Dear Reader,

The Black Earth saga is an incredibly touching story of family, love, sacrifice, and truth wrapped up in a cool science-fiction tale. The story of Carrick Michaels' journey to discover who he is will take him on a journey that can only lead him to one place, Home.

During Carrick's search for his truth, he comes across a man who'll define who he is and what his purpose is.

Back to Black Earth is the sequel to the highly regarded Black Earth – How We Got Here novel. This book can be read as a stand-alone story. Reading the original, however, is not necessary for your enjoyment. However, I do believe that after reading this story, you will very much want to read the original.

Your thorough enjoyment is assured by this wonderful story of love, family, truth, and the ultimate sacrifice.

I hope you fall in love with these characters and are thrilled at all of the twists and turns that this action-packed, contemporary science-fiction novel will provide.

Happy Reading,

Praise for The Black Earth Saga

I read this in one sitting!
The synopsis tells you the basics of this story. What it doesn't tell you is that the humanity between the characters and the relationships will bring you to tears.

As the title says, I read this book in one sitting and was never bored. That's unusual for me. Even the best books will quite often have parts that don't 'flow' as well as others. This causes boredom, not so with Black Earth.

The interaction between Carrick and Erik quickly formed into a beautiful friendship that spanned the 75 million miles between Earth and Black Earth. These two main characters will keep you fully involved in this lesson in alternate history.

The story answers a lot of questions that have plagued archeologists and historians for hundreds of years. It's fun to see how everything comes together. Einstein, Hitler, and Werner Von Braun we once close associates on Black Earth, as was Julius Caesar and others. The revelations you'll discover in Black Earth will leave you floored!

The ending brought tears to my eyes and made my heart swell as it describes a love story for the ages. Better than Romeo and Juliet by far. Sometimes you'll read a good book only to have the ending be disappointing or end in a cliffhanger to be continued in the next book of an expensive series. Not here! Black Earth is so satisfying from start to finish that you'll believe you have read a modern classic.

This book is fun, exciting, and charming. You could do worse, but I doubt you could find better!

-PM Steve

Highly Recommend!
Black Earth is a well-crafted tale where the author masterfully weaves history through this science fiction love story. The enchanting character, Erik, stole the heart of this reader. Erik was the wise, gentle, witty grandfather type of character who shared his stories and wisdom with his young comrade. His painstaking yet beautiful love story ultimately changed history.

-Elaine Robinson

Not a science fiction story!

As a child, I enjoyed science fiction and have always been fascinated by astronomy and our universe, but Star Wars and other stories were just not believable to me, and I sort of outgrew it. After ordering and reading this Kindle sample, I was hooked! I purchased the Kindle eBook version, but now I must have the paperback. This was a very heartwarming story that pulled me back to earth after traveling a small portion of the cosmos. The best part was that all of it is totally believable!!! There was just enough science to make it interesting but, more than that, more heart than I ever expected from this book. We all wonder, but it's so comforting to know that we can take bits and pieces of life and imagine our own afterlife. This story definitely gave me ideas, thoughts, questions, and, most importantly, hope. The author is a friend of the family that has certainly impressed me with his first novel. Thank you, Michael. What a treat!!

-Mark Rievley

Animal Farm Revisited?

Wow! As I read this book and the lessons it teaches, I was reminded of reading Animal Farm in high school. The comparisons stop there, though. I find Michel Cook's writing much more entertaining and well woven. By the time I was halfway through the prologue, I was thinking what a good movie this could be. Now, I'm hoping it will happen. It's an epic story. Best book I've read in years! I HIGHLY recommend you read this amazing book!

-Mary B.

Very Exciting, I couldn't Put It Down!

I would highly recommend Black Earth: How We Got Here to any fan of the science fiction genre. The writing style reminded me of Ray Bradbury with the modern flair of Ernest Cline. I'm planning on reading it again in the next few days to see if there was anything I missed!

-Eric M.

Excellent Read!

I could not put this book down! This was a very intriguing story. I loved all the characters and especially the relationship between Carrick and Erik. The book was beautifully written, and it definitely kept my interest from start to finish. It was well thought out and will keep you wanting to turn that next page! I am hoping there will be a sequel!

-Maribeth P.

Hooked!

From the first few pages, I was hooked! I could not put it down, and with each turn of the page, the story became more real!

His descriptive writing style had the characters jump off the page, and I could visualize each of them along with the places he took me. He has a unique way of telling a story in which instantly transported me into the world of Black Earth! It was captivating from beginning to end!

I hope that he has a follow-up in the works since I would love to see what happens to Black Earth!!

-Rhonda Koches Haydak

Newly Discovered Planet Reveals Mankind's Origins on Earth.

A gripping journey across our solar system to a newly discovered planet, revealing a rich history of a doomed civilization and the destiny of the planet's former inhabitants. A great read and well crafted, well-researched sci-fi novel that brings us along on one man's mission of both scientific and personal discovery. A heart-warming story that doesn't disappoint!

-Vern P.

Michael Cook is one damn good story-teller!

Black Earth will grab you at the get-go...but lots of books do that. What's different about this one is that it will reward you with a hundred little (and not so little) "wow" along the way. It's not a roller coaster of emotion...it's "damn the torpedoes, full speed ahead" kinda stuff. I didn't want to put it down and got to a point in the book where I couldn't. Science Fiction? Maybe...but not so technical that you need to be Albert Einstein to understand it. Sort of like a hammering drama that just happens to take place on another planet! I don't think I've cheered or cried reading a book ever but came close as the pages turned to the final chapter. It's lots of fun, and I cannot imagine anyone not enjoying it. Cannot wait to read another story... It doesn't have to be in outer space. Michael was just a great story-teller.

-William Marr

A Book Everyone Should Read!

A creative take on the question humans have had since the beginning of time. Is there life out there? Are we alone in the universe? Where did we, the human race, truly come from? This sci-fi novel is not just filled with adventure, laughter, and true love. It is also a story that delivers a powerful message that humanity desperately needs to hear.

-Amazon Customer

Acknowledgments:

Thank you for letting me share this wonderful story with you. The story of Black Earth saga came to me in a dream, but making that dream come true took many individuals that are all very important to me.

I'd like to thank my wife and children: Kristin, Aubrey Carin, Lola Kristine, Maggie Mae, and Carrick Michael, for helping me to breathe life into the characters that you're about to meet. My wonderful family members were all so supportive in my journey, and without them, this book doesn't get written.

I would also like to thank my friends on the other side of the pond who lent their out-of-this-world expertise to the telling of this story. Professor Christopher Riley and Jacqui Farnham chiseled away the rough edges and helped me refine this heart-warming story, for that, I am eternally grateful.

To my best friend and business partner, Piyush Bhula, thanks for always being there at every turn. And finally, to Jeremy Ledbetter, for always being there and for his wonderful cover design work.

Fine Print:

This book is a work of fiction and is drawn completely from my imagination. The actual historical figures characterized in this book are intended to be portrayed in a positive light. Any references to past historical events are for entertainment purposes only and not meant to be taken literally. Any actual organizations or federal entities portrayed in this book serve only to enhance the story and are not meant to defame, devalue, or besmirch those institutions in any way.

www.BlackEarthNovel.com

"A poet wanders between infinite spaces
Up and down, he knows not where
But somehow lands on empty pages
Spills his ink, and we stop to stare"

Michael Cook is a published poet, author, and accomplished business professional, and entrepreneur. Michael is also the owner of the #7 Escape Room experience in the World, Odyssey Escape Game, located in Alpharetta, GA, and Schaumburg, IL.

A resident of Suwanee, GA. Michael is a father of four children, a husband, a brother, and a friend.

Back to
Black Earth©

What truths will be revealed?

A novel by Michael Cook
© 2021

Prologue – Home

Location: Artesia, New Mexico. The Michaels' Home – Friday, September 5, 2035.

A school bus came to a stop in front of the Michaels' home, and three grade-schoolers got out and ran into their house. Lola Michaels was there to greet them, just like every other day. She was still a stay-at-home-mom and intended to remain one.

"Hey, guys! How was your day?" said Lola. Running past her were the twins as if they didn't even see her. Erik and Lilly made their way into the kitchen to get some afterschool snacks, jockeying for position along the way. Little Carrick, however, made a b-line for the stairs, as he was going to get online with his friends and play video games in his bedroom.

"Homework first, Carrick!" Lola yelled to him as he disappeared around the top of the stairs.

"Got it!" he yelled down to her.

Lola rejoined Kinzi in the kitchen, who'd been sitting at the table stuck on hold with her bank for the last twenty minutes.

"Still on hold?" mouthed Lola.

Kinzi grunted, "I hate talking to computers!"

Erik and Lilly were tearing through the pantry, it was grocery day, and they couldn't wait to see what goodies mom brought home.

"Kids, be quiet! Aunt Kinzi's on the phone."

A few minutes later, Lola made her way back over to the bottom of the stairs and yelled up to Little Carrick. "Carrick, don't forget that you and your father are going to the Mall to get new shoes. Be ready to go in thirty minutes."

"Okay!" Little Carrick yelled down from upstairs.

Kinzi was off the phone now, and Lola joined her at the table for a coffee.

"Phew, I never imagined three kids running wild in this house. I still remember when it was just Carrick and me. The house seemed so big then, now it feels like..." she paused, "well, Home, I guess." She smiled at Kinzi, who returned her smile.

"Where's Jordan, by the way?" Lola asked Kinzi.

"Chiropractor, he hasn't been the same since coming home from Zenith."

"That's an understatement!" thought Lola aloud. "None of us have, nor will we ever be."

After a few moments of reflection, Lola said, "Time has flown by so fast, Kinzi! I can't imagine what life would have been like for us if you two never moved to Artesia." Lola shook her head while taking another sip of her coffee.

"The kids are growing up so fast!" said Kinzi. "Little Carrick is as tall as the twins now."

"He's a beast!" Lola's eyes grew wide. "That kid's going to eat us out of house and home," she laughed.

Kinzi laughed along with her.

"Kinz, do you ever think of Black Earth anymore?"

Kinzi's eyes opened wide, and she took a deep breath and sighed before responding, "Lola, I think about it every day. I think about THAT day in particular."

Kinzi remembered back to that day, a day that changed everything and everyone. For everyone involved, time would be measured by what happened before September 8, 2027, and what happened after. That day, however, would be frozen in time. That day marked the beginning of the second half of their lives, and it would never compare to the first half, *NEVER!* thought Kinzi.

"We never seem to talk about it much anymore." Lola looked sad, staring into the bottom of her empty coffee cup.

Kinzi reached across the table and took Lola by the hand. "I can't speak for Jordan, but for me, the events of that day are with me every second of every day. Its memory seems to live and breathe inside of me."

"But you never talk about it." Lola wore a look of sadness, unable to understand why.

"I know. It's just that I tend to internalize everything. I always have," said Kinzi, "ever since I was a little girl. My parents thought it was weak to show emotion."

"Do you and Jordan talk about it much?"

Kinzi shook her head side to side. "Jordan rarely brings it up, but at night, I can hear him dreaming about it. Sometimes he wakes up crying but doesn't share his emotions. We save it for the anniversary. Therapy's helped him over the years, but he hasn't gone in months."

"I wish I could talk to Carrick about what happened," Lola's gaze found the bottom of her cup again.

"Lola, why don't you come to Houston with us this year? You never come. It's sad," offered Kinzi.

"Nah, that's your guy's thing. I'd feel out of place," Lola shook her head, 'no.'

"That's ridiculous!" Kinzi was always surprised by Lola's reaction. Every year they had the same conversation, and she'd always decline the invitation.

"Besides, you forgot that we're all going to Suwanee this weekend. Carrick's going to be so happy."

"Do me a favor, would you? Put a black rose on Erik's grave for me."

"You and your black roses!" Lola laughed at Kinzi.

"What?" Kinzi pushed Lola's hand and laughed.

"You and Carrick are so much alike! Black roses! Silly!" Lola laughed at her best friend.

Suddenly, a horn rang out from the driveway, startling the two. Lola started to get up out of habit when Kinzi said, "I got it," giving Lola a wink.

She walked to the foot of the stairs and yelled up, "Carrick Michael! Your father is waiting outside for you. Let's go!"

Just seconds later, Kinzi was back in the kitchen when they heard two feet hit the floor at the bottom of the stairs. Little Carrick yelled, "Bye, Mom!" a slamming of the door followed his words.

The words, "I love you too, Honey!" echoed out of the kitchen, but Carrick didn't hear them.

Chapter 1 – The Spider

Location: Beijing, China. The Ministry of State Security Building, Subfloor 3, Interrogation Room #7 – February 17, 2026 – 2:00 pm GMT +8.

In a thirteen by thirteen-foot room, with cement walls and floors, a tall metal chair stood bolted to the floor in the center of the room, beneath it a drain. A long metal table graced the wall to the left and had various surgical and dental tools laid across it on a canvas mat. The chair stood just beneath a solitary light fixture hanging in the room; its bulb sprayed with blood splatter, some old, some new. The resulting light washed the otherwise colorless walls and floor with a pinkish hue. Above the hanging light, more splatter on the ceiling and across the walls and floor.

The room was dark and dank, and the air was filled with the smell of blood, sweat, and urine. At the foot of the chair lay a man's body, hands bound behind his back, feet tied together. The white blindfold covering his mangled face was soaked with blood and tears.

Two men dressed in all black stood over the lifeless body with cocked heads, one in admiration, the other in anger and confusion.

"What should we do with him?" said a heavy breathing Chinese militant named Yun, speaking in broken English. Agent Yun was a Chinese operative from the Strategic Huyou Agency (SHA).

The Strategic Huyou Agency is an arm of the Central Military Commission for The People's Republic of China. Its focus is counterintelligence and maintaining China's spy network throughout the world.

"Get him to the Phoenix Cai brothel and make it look like a drug-fueled suicide," said the other man, whose face was veiled with shadow.

"An accident?" remarked Yun. "But look at his face? More like a car accident, no?"

"Yes, you did quite a job on him," said the man in black, now turning his angry eyes toward Agent Yun. "A car accident would be too public. Let me remind you," he paused, "we work in the shadows," now speaking in Mandarin.

Yun looked terrified as his boss now stood face to face with him out of the shadow, his breath reeking of douhua, coffee, and disdain.

"You were instructed to find out what he knew before killing him!" shouted the furious SHA militant leader, Colonel Vadik Lei, purposely expelling saliva aerosol onto the face of his subordinate.

"But..!" defended Yun, before being slapped open-handed by the now furious but almost always composed Lei.

Yun stood silent, lips red with blood, hiding his clenched teeth. He was careful to conceal his fear. If The Spider sensed fear, he would pounce.

"He thought he could outsmart me. He thought I was weak. He thought...," appealed Yun, to a man without empathy before being sharply cut-off.

"Your actions today will cause a stain on both of our reputations." Lei's face nearly touching that of Yun's. "Our beloved President will not be happy, and now I will have to deal with Minister Kenong directly. This is a loose end with political consequences. You should hope you don't suffer the same fate as this American piece of shit," scolded Lei. "Now get him out of here before two body bags are needed!"

Spitting onto the floor, then wiping his mouth and returning to attention, the obedient Yun said, "Yes, Colonel!"

Colonel Vadik Lei was a former Republic of China Army Special Forces Colonel and a former Shaolin Temple Grandmaster. Educated in the United States, Lei, code-named Zhīzhū, was a senior intelligence officer for SHA and its counter-intelligence division known as Tíqǔ, translated in English, meaning to Extract.

Vadik Lei, known only as The Spider to intelligence services around the world, was a ruthless and determined counter-intelligence officer. In his seven years since joining the Strategic Huyou Agency,

Lei had personally killed more than one-hundred and fifty of his adversaries, most in service to his country, both men and women. Some of them were simply for sport. He was trained in mixed martial arts, bladed weaponry, poison administration, and small firearms - his preferred weapon of choice, his hands.

Location: Langley, Virginia. George Bush Center for Intelligence, CIA Headquarters. Office of CIA Director James Clapper – February 20, 2026 – 9:46 am EST.

"Send him in," said Clapper, in a monotone voice hovering over the speakerphone on his desk in his third-floor office. The stoic, former U.S. Air Force Lieutenant General, Director of National Intelligence, and current CIA Director was unfazed by the urgent meeting requested just thirty minutes earlier from the CIA's Dept. of Chinese Affairs.

Standing before him moments later was a slightly winded CIA Intelligence Officer named Ronaldo Caceres.

"Sir, we have a problem!" exclaimed Caceres.

"What is it, Officer Caceres?" encouraged Clapper.

"Sir, our Ambassador to China, Dr. Carl Schoenfeld, was found by Beijing police two days ago, dead, sir."

"Manner of death?" inquired Clapper, still stoic.

"Chinese officials report that it was a suicide, sir," explained Caceres.

"Officer, there's clearly a reason you've brought this to my desk. What more is there?" a slightly agitated Clapper demanded.

"Well, sir, you need to see the photo of the body." Caceres pulled a manilla folder from beneath his arm, emptied the contents in a neat stack in front of the Director, then stood back at attention.

Clapper, almost in slow-motion, flipped through the photos and documents and calmly remarked, "Suicide, huh? Jesus Christ, his face looks like a pile of raw meat."

"They're claiming that he hung himself, and at some point, the belt broke, and he hit his face on a table. The Chinese government is claiming that there were large amounts of fentanyl and oxycontin in his system at the time of his death," explained Caceres.

"Any history of drug abuse on Ambassador Schoenfeld?" Clapper asked while suspecting that the answer was, no.

"None, sir."

"Sir, if you look at the scene,..." encouraged Caceres.

"Staged? Yes, that would be obvious to a rookie police detective," remarked Clapper. "What is this place? Where was he found?" Clapper examined the photos more closely as he squinted through his reading glasses.

Caceres hesitated for a moment.

"Spit it out, Officer," said Clapper, now looking more agitated.

"In a brothel, sir."

"A what?!" Clapper's reaction was visceral.

"A whorehouse, sir."

"I know what a brothel is, Officer Caceres!" exclaimed Clapper. "No one commits suicide in a brothel. No one kicks the shit out of themselves before hanging themself," Clapper was sickened. "This is what his family gets to bury?"

Caceres nodded in agreement.

"Very good, Officer. Keep me apprised of any new information as you get it," said Clapper. "Oh, and one more thing. Has his family been notified?"

"Yes, sir. The State Department has notified his family."

In that instant, an agent burst through the door, Clapper's secretary unable to stop him as she blurted out, "You can't go in there!"

"It's okay, Colleen," said Clapper.

"Agent Stone, you must have a good reason for barging into my office," Clapper broke from his monotone delivery. "What can Officer Caceres and I do for you?"

"Sir, we just received garbled messages recovered from our Embassy in Beijing. Apparently, the Chinese broke through our firewall and destroyed most of the data in the embassy's server," explained Stone. "We also found an interesting email that Ambassador Schoenfeld was attempting to send," Stone then paused.

"Get to the point, Agent," said an impatient Clapper.

Agent Stone handed over a file folder while simultaneously translating the gibberish.

"Sir, the Chinese have caused most of the messages to be deleted, jumbled, or have listed the words out of order, sir," said Stone, talking a little faster now.

"Go on, son," nodded Clapper. The CIA Director looked to be connecting puzzle pieces.

"Sir," hesitated Stone. "We have been able to extract words and phrases that are alarming, sir."

Clapper exhaled heavily and said. "Agent Stone, if you don't get to the point in the next five seconds, you will never work in government again." Clapper made himself abundantly clear.

"Sir, the words on those pages include, Black Earth, Salvage, and...." Stone paused before saying, "Zhīzhū."

"What in the hell does that mean?" Clapper looked perplexed.

"The Spider, sir."

Clapper's eyes went wide. "The Spider," he mouthed. He tossed the papers onto his desk, walked over to his window, and stared out at the trees that separated CIA Headquarters and the Potomac River. Removing his readers, he stared and said nothing while rubbing his face from brow to chin. The two agents looked at each other in silence, not sure what to make of Clapper's reaction.

Clapper turned to the two men seconds later and said, "You walk out of this office right now, you find me Officer Matt Solstice, former CIA Officer Jordan Spear, and three of the best field agents we have! I want everything you have on Dr. Schoenfeld, every file on every Ambassador to China, North Korea, and Japan for the last ten years. Additionally, I want every email and phone call from everyone in that embassy for the last thirty-six months."

"Yes, sir!" chorused the agents.

Now alone, Clapper sat down and thought to himself that this must be connected to China's recent rebuke of the U.N. resolution regarding the salvaging and harvesting of information and materials from Black Earth.

Just three weeks prior, the U.N. Security Council, by a vote of 14-1, China being the only dissenting country, voted that no one country on planet Earth owned salvage rights to Black Earth. Rather, the Council reaffirmed the original agreement that the contributing nations would each share in whatever scientific gains were made on Black Earth as part of their original financial contributions. They went on to say that there would be no free-for-all as the potential for war would be heightened if countries entered into a race back to Black Earth.

Clapper pushed the red button on his desk phone and said, "Colleen, come in here, please."

A moment later, his apologetic secretary walked through the door, thinking that she was in trouble.

"Director Clapper, sir, about the intrusion."

"Forget that, Colleen. I need you to do me a favor. I need you to get Mars Johnston from NASA to Washington tomorrow. Do not tell him why, just that his presence is required. Make all necessary travel arrangements and accommodations. That's Johnston with a T, Colleen. Don't forget the T."

"Yes, sir, Director Clapper, Johnston with a 'T.'" Colleen was accommodating.

The former Flight Director at Mission Control in Houston, Marcus Mars Johnston, now headed the National Aeronautics and Space Administration, taking over for James Lorenstine the previous year. Lorenstine ran for the United States senate the previous year and won, unseating Ted Cruz in November.

Location: Leesburg, Virginia. Home of Jonathan and Jocelyn Spear –
February 20, 2026 – 6:40 pm EST.

In the childhood home of Jordan Spear, the doorbell rang just as
Jordan, his parents, and Kinzi London were all sitting down to
dinner.

"I'll get it!" said Jocelyn Spear.

She answered the door. There were two men in dark suits with I.D.
badges dangling from their belts, just above their left pockets.
Without a word, Jocelyn yelled, "Jordan! There're two men here to
see you!"

A moment later, Kinzi curiously wondered who was at the door.
Hanging back, standing in the hallway, she tugged on her necklace,
trying to overhear what the men were saying.

After returning from Black Earth, both she and Jordan walked away
from their careers and began a relationship that started on the black
planet. Ever since the four-month journey back, and the nearly two
years since, the two had been inseparable.

For Kinzi, the three journeys to Black Earth and back, along with the
events that transpired there, caused her to reflect on what she
wanted most in life. After years of education and astronaut training
and the three Black Earth tours, she was completely drained. Not
knowing exactly what she needed, she knew precisely what she
wanted, a monogamous relationship with one man, Jordan Spear.

For Jordan, leaving the CIA was easy. As it turned out, he never
really wanted to follow in his father's footsteps in the CIA. During
Erik Erickson's confession, Jordan realized what he did want, a life
outside of his father's shadow. He loved his father with everything
that he had, but his shadow was long and, leaving the CIA helped
him to step out from beneath that dark umbrella and be his own
man. After returning from Black Earth, Jordan took a long break
before joining his new friends, Carrick Michaels, and Erik Erickson,
on their world tour.

"What can I do for you, gentlemen?" asked Jordan of the visitors.

Kinzi heard muffled words, and then the door closed. She quickly walked to the window and pulled back the shear, just enough to witness two men, who looked like Feds, speaking with Jordan.

Kinzi saw lots of hand gestures and heard more garbled words but couldn't make out what the three men were discussing. Whatever it was, she was sure that it would change the quiet life she now had with Jordan.

Kinzi then heard Jordan loudly say, "No way! I'm not doing it!", then saw him wave his hands violently as if to say, "FORGET IT!"

After another minute of more unintelligible dialogue, Kinzi clearly heard one of the two agents say the word 'Spider.' Jordan abruptly ended the conversation and walked back into the house. There, he summoned his father, Jonathan, to the basement of the two-story colonial house. Jordan passed Kinzi in the hallway leading to the stairs, brushing against her slightly, doing everything possible to avoid eye contact with her. He, too, knew that their lives were about to change and not for the better.

"Jordan, what is it?!" Kinzi looked frantic, grabbing at his arm as he quickly passed her by.

Jordan waved her off dismissively and said, "Nothing."

Kinzi grew even more frightened. Jordan had never once ignored her in such a manner.

Chapter 2 – The Promise

Location: Artesia, New Mexico. Home of Carrick and Lola Michaels – February 21, 2026 – 8:47 am MST – Six hundred and thirty-six days since Erik arrived on Earth.

Lola rolled over and studied the face of the only man she'd ever loved. Carrick was still asleep after a long week. He and Erik had traveled to London that week, their third such trip to the U.K. in the past year. While there, they met with Parliament, Prime Minister Martin Taylor and then gave a speech to the distinguished alumni of Lincoln University.

Lola decided to let Carrick sleep-in while she headed downstairs to get the place ready for breakfast. As usual, Erik would be joining them as he did every Saturday. She turned on the T.V. in the kitchen and flipped to channel 202, NCN News, to catch up on the week's news.

Lola was also exhausted after pulling three doubles during the week at Artesia General Hospital, where she headed the Pediatrics Department. Lola was well respected in her field and widely sought after to work at many other hospitals around the country. Artesia was home, though, and she was solely focused on her patients. Those patients included Carrick and Erik, too. The men in her life needed lots of attention and looking after due to their rigorous travel schedule and poor eating habits.

Thirty minutes later, Lola yelled from the bottom of the stairs, "Babe! You getting up anytime soon?" No reply from Carrick came back. "Let's go!" she yelled while walking back into the kitchen. Now standing at the sink, the red 'Breaking News' banner at the bottom of the television screen caught her eye.

NCN anchor Morgan Roberts filled the screen. "This just in! We've just received word from our sources at the State Department that the Ambassador to China's Beijing Embassy, Dr. Carl Schoenfeld, has died under suspicious circumstances. We are being told that officials from the Chinese Government are reporting that Ambassador Schoenfeld died of an apparent suicide. The Ambassador's body will be flown back to the United States early next week, where an autopsy will be performed to determine the actual cause of death," reported Roberts.

"In other news, China's recent rebuke of the U.N. Security Council's decision, on Black Earth salvage rights, has sparked concerns among the international community. Rumor has it that China may decide to go it alone, and travel to Black Earth without an international consensus," added Roberts. "A spokesperson for the Chinese Government stated that the U.N. Security Council has no jurisdiction over the universe and that whichever country decides to make the arduous trek to another planet has every right to do so. The spokesperson went on to say that any collected materials, technology, medical cures, IP, or otherwise, are the company's property or country that mine those items or resources."

"Professor Chris Lewicki from Michigan State University's Department of Planetary Science agrees," said Roberts. The news program then switched to a previously recorded interview with Lewicki.

"Listen," said Lewicki. "China has a point. No one has the right to intergalactic property. The 1987 paper, 'A Multilateral Solution,' written by a colleague of mine, Dr. Elaine Majovski from the University of Michigan, with regards to the recovery of shipwrecks, bears no resemblance to this argument. We're talking about the universe here, not the middle of the ocean," he argued. "Whether from the Moon, Mars, Black Earth or otherwise, no country on Earth can lay claim to something that is not from this planet." Lewicki went on to say, "It's even been rumored that one or more of the astronauts from one of the previous three missions to Black Earth may have actually brought home souvenirs."

Lola walked over to the T.V. and turned up the volume slightly.

Morgan Roberts continued. "The U.S., however, is poised to be the first country back to Black Earth since they departed there on January 26, 2024, more than two years ago. The crew will once again be comprised of an international team selected by the recently created Galactic Exploration Group. After more than a year of litigation and inter-country disputes about who would return to Black Earth, it seemed another trip would be scheduled for some time in early 2027. The U.S. is poised to provide a new type of spaceship, one that would have greater cargo capacity for returning more materials from the planet that some are now calling Zenith."

Roberts added, "The GEG was formed early last year to address salvage and exploration of the black planet, as well as the Moon and Mars. This, in large part, due to the private space-travel sector's incredible growth in just the last six years. The group's main focus will be to preserve any items returned from any celestial bodies in the future. Whether soil, rock, ancient technologies, or artifacts, the materials would serve to benefit mankind as a whole, as opposed to enriching only a segment of Earth's population."

"China, feeling snubbed, put up a legal fight after not being selected to sit on the GEG leadership council, being struck down by the U.N. Security Council," concluded Morgan Roberts.

Lola turned off the T.V. and went upstairs to see if Carrick had awakened. When entering the bedroom, she heard the shower running.

"How's it going, Babe?" she yelled over the sound of running water.

"Almost done!" shouted Carrick. "Is Erik here yet?"

"No, and he hasn't called yet either. I left the front door unlocked for him, though."

Carrick turned off the water and stepped out of the shower.

Lola looked him up and down and said, "Did you jog to London and back instead of fly? You look skinny, Babe! Did you eat okay over there?" she worried.

"Babe, I'm exhausted. I never eat well when I travel," he responded.

"You need some Red Fruit! I need your energy up! It's been weeks since we've fooled around, not that I'm counting, or anything."

"I know, I know," his eyes rolled. "This travel schedule is killing me. Erik wasn't looking too well last night either. I think he's over it already."

Carrick finished drying off and put on his Black Earth t-shirt and a pair of jeans.

"Ahem!" Lola cleared her throat and smiled flirtatiously. "No boxers today?"

Carrick innocently shrugged his shoulders and said, "It was a long flight. My boys need a break," only half-joking as he walked over to the bedside table.

Taking his phone off of silent mode, Carrick complained, "Babe, look at this! I have fifty-six emails, and eighteen missed calls just since last night! Goddammit! Everybody from everywhere wants us to speak or make an appearance. I can't do it anymore! Two years of this – feels more like ten. Before Black Earth, no one wanted my time," griped Carrick.

"I did," smiled Lola. "Some retirement, huh? I see you less now than I did before."

Now downstairs in the kitchen, the two enjoyed some coffee. "So, what did I miss in the news this week?" asked Carrick.

"Well, apparently China's making headlines again. Turns out Ambassador Carl Schoenfeld, from the Beijing Embassy, committed suicide this week," offered Lola between sips of her black coffee.

"What?! That's awful! Erik and I met him early last year when we traveled to Beijing." Carrick shook his head in disbelief. "He didn't impress me as someone who could do that. I think he has like five kids!"

Lola recoiled. "God, you actually knew him?! That's terrible!"

"Listen, don't mention it to Erik. No need for him to have that information. It'll only upset him."

"Where is he, anyway?" thought Lola aloud.

Holding his phone, Carrick said, "I'm calling him now." After a few seconds, Carrick said, "Hmmm, no answer. He's probably in the shower." Carrick looked only mildly concerned.

"I'll head over there," he said. "Be back in twenty minutes."

Carrick walked across the side yard into Erik's driveway and up onto the front porch. He knocked and rang the doorbell, but there was no answer. He then entered the passcode to the front door, 12121965. The door released, and Carrick walked in.

"Erik!" he yelled out, but there was no response. The house was eerily quiet for that time of the morning as Erik was an early riser. Carrick headed down the hallway to the bedroom on the left. There, he saw Erik still asleep in the right bed, facing the wall. Fear suddenly gripped his heart as he was acutely aware that Erik would be turning one-hundred-nineteen-years-old in June and was still adjusting to Earth's hostile atmosphere.

Additionally, the travel schedule that the two kept hadn't been kind to either of them. Erik was a trooper, though, he understood the significance of his presence on Earth and wanted to see as much of it as he could. He loved seeing all of the people, too. He felt a kindred connection to each and every one of them.

Carrick approached the bed and touched Erik's shoulder, giving him a gentle shove. "Come on, old man, it's time to get up," he encouraged, but there was no response from Erik. Slightly panicked, Carrick pushed more aggressively on Erik's shoulder. "Erik, come on! Wake up!" he said in a muffled scream.

"Mind your hand, young man," Erik said sleepily. "Unless you want to lose it."

Carrick exhaled in an audible sigh of relief, not letting Erik see the look of dread that colored his face.

"Let's go! Chop-chop!" he clapped his hands. "We're late for breakfast. Don't want to keep Lola waiting."

"What time is it?" asked Erik, now sitting up in his bed.

"10:40. Why? What's up?"

"Would you mind if I skipped breakfast this time?"

"You okay?" Carrick was worried.

"I'm a little tired from the week, but I'll be okay." Erik stood and stretched out his arms.

"Alright, go back to bed but remember, we have a date today, Home Depot, and then lunch at Monterrey."

"How could I forget, chips and queso. Fine, you win! I'll give it a try," he conceded.

While on Black Earth, Carrick longed for chips and queso. He once promised Erik that if he ever made it Home, he'd take him out to a Mexican restaurant and treat him to one of his favorite dishes.

Until now, Erik had declined, but after losing a silly bet while in London, he finally agreed to try the appetizer. Each time they went to Carrick's favorite Mexican place, Erik had always snacked on his beloved Red Fruit instead of trying any of the menu options.

On this occasion, however, Erik's stash of Red Fruit was finally depleted, so he had to be more willing to try new foods. Erik wasn't much of an eater, though, and was looking thinner than ever. Carrick's friends back at NASA tried to re-create the red concoction, and though they came close, it just didn't taste the same to Erik.

"Rest up, and I'll come back at noon to pick you up."

"No rest for me. Lilly and I have a date. At 11:00, we're doing our weekly walk around the block. Today, we're making two laps. I'll just come over at 12."

"Why so early?"

"Lilly has a birthday party this afternoon. She asked me if I wanted to go, but I declined. Don't want to scare the little ones. You know, the 'alien' from Black Earth and all?"

"Come on, Erik, you know people love you."

"You think I don't see the stares when we're out," said Erik. "I seem to do better with the adults more than I do the kids," he shrugged.

Carrick conceded with a nod and said, "Well, that little girl loves you, and she makes up for all the funny stares."

"Yes, she does," said Erik, nodding his head in agreement. "Yes, she does," he repeated.

"Okay. Well, we'll see you at noon then, don't over-do it though, you had a long week. And don't forget your oxygen this time," cautioned Carrick.

"Roger that, Carrick!" Erik jokingly saluted his grandson.

Since arriving on Earth, Erik wore an oxygen cannula whenever possible, especially when exercising. Lately, though, he would get lazy and not wear the nasal tube. Carrick would have to push his grandfather to make sure that he wore it. Erik was reluctant to wear it, though. He always said it made him look too old.

Back at home, Carrick re-joined Lola in the kitchen.

"Where's Erik?" she asked.

"He won't be joining us this morning. He and Lilly have a date. Twice around the block today."

"Don't they usually go after lunch?" Lola looked puzzled and a little concerned.

"Yep, but Lilly has a birthday party this afternoon."

"Was he awake when you went over there?"

"No, and he scared the hell out of me when he didn't answer the door. I'm starting to get a little worried about him. He didn't do so well in London. He actually stumbled at one point. It scared the hell out of me!" Carrick shook his head. "I'm thinking of canceling our trip to Brussels in two weeks."

Lola, wearing her doctor hat, asked, "What do you mean he stumbled?"

"He was probably just caught off balance for a second, but every day I seem to be reminded of his age," said Carrick.

Lola reassured Carrick, "Babe, he's just slowing down a bit. It's natural."

"I know, but he feels so obligated to accept every invitation we get. It's just not possible. It zaps me!" Carrick played with his scrambled eggs. "Can you imagine how he feels?"

"Why don't you bring him in on Monday? He's not due for his next check-up until the first, but let's not take any chances," encouraged Lola.

After breakfast, Lola rinsed her plate when she saw movement across the street from the kitchen window. She spotted Erik and Lilly hand in hand walking down the street, and a smile lit up her face.

"There they go!" she said.

"Does he have his oxygen?" asked Carrick.

"Yep!" He does hate wearing that thing around his waist, though," she laughed out loud.

"He's always been stubborn. Gotta love him." Carrick was filled with love for the old man but somehow knew that Erik's days were winding down. It was impossible for him to be genuinely happy because he knew Erik's days were numbered. He promised himself not to take one second for granted. In his broken heart, he was sure that Erik wouldn't see the end of the year.

Location: Home Depot – An hour later.

Pushing the buggy, Erik complained, "What're we here for anyway? We come here every other weekend!"

"Today, it's PVC pipe and canned air," said Carrick.

"Canned air? I have plenty at home?"

"No, no, Grandpa!" Carrick laughed. "Canned air, not oxygen."

"What's the difference?" Erik was confused.

"Never-mind," Carrick shook his head and smiled.

Later, the two men sat at their favorite booth at Monterrey when the server brought the chips and queso.

"Okay, the moment of truth," said Carrick. "You're finally going to try it instead of just watching me eat it."

"Yeah, well, I brought the knock-off Red Fruit just in case." Erik looked a little apprehensive, not sure his body was ready for such a heavy food like cheese.

"Just eat it, old man!" Carrick made fun of Erik.

Erik dipped his chip in the queso like someone dipping their foot into a pool before jumping in. He slowly raised the chip to his mouth, took a nibble, and made a sour-looking face before his eyes flew open-wide. At that moment, Erik savored the taste. In that instant, he'd regretted never trying queso in the twenty-one months since he'd arrived on Home.

"Well?" asked Carrick, anxiously awaiting the verdict.

"I mean..., It's okay, I guess. A little bland if I had to describe it," offered Erik. "I mean, I'll eat it, but only because I lost the bet."

He immediately went for another chip and then another and another. The next time the server came to the table, Erik said, "We'll need another one of these," pointing to the bowl of melted cheese. "And what's this red stuff called again? Salsa, was it?" Erik reached for the bowl of salsa that Carrick had been dipping his chips in.

Carrick just laughed, and Erik finally fessed up to loving it.

After their meal, the two sat and talked, joking about their time on Zenith, their travels around the world, little Lilly, and finally, whether or not Carrick and Lola were planning on a family.

"I mean, sure, we want to at some point, but Lola is just settling into her career, and you and me, well...we're a couple of globe-trotters. Just waiting for life to settle down a little," rationalized Carrick.

"Globe what?"

Carrick laughed off the question and just said, "Now's not the right time for children, that's all."

Erik's face turned serious. "'Settle down a little?' You mean you're waiting for me to die, don't you?"

Carrick rebuked the notion saying, "Why would you say such a thing? What would make you think that? No! No! Never!"

"Calm down, Carrick! I'm not implying that you want me dead. I'm just...I'm in the way. I'm an inconvenience...,"

Carrick cut Erik off sharply. With tears in his eyes, he said, "Never! If I could have you around forever, it wouldn't be long enough! You are not only a grandfather to me, but you're also like a father. You've always been! Since the day we first met."

Erik knew that Carrick's words were honest and from the heart but couldn't help but feeling like he was somehow holding him back from his new life and his new wife.

"Carrick, listen. I don't want to travel anymore. I'm tired, son..."

Carrick cut him off again. "You're just saying that because you feel like an imposition. You don't mean that!"

"Carrick, one has nothing to do with the other. I want to spend what few days that I have left on planet Earth watching you work in the yard, taking little Lilly for walks, and if I'm lucky," he paused, "I'll get to see my great-great-grandson or daughter."

Carrick was relieved. "Okay, fine. I was planning on canceling our upcoming trip to Brussels anyway."

Erik smiled. He'd been meaning to share his feelings with Carrick for months.

"Okay, Erik, come clean. How are you feeling? Does it hurt anywhere? You scared me this morning when you didn't show up for breakfast. When I came over to your house, things were eerily quiet. I got a little scared."

Erik smiled, "I'm not dead yet. Don't worry about that. I've got too many shows on Netflix that I have to watch first."

Carrick motioned to the waiter. "Check, please."

"Carrick, there's been something else I've been wanting to tell you."

"What is it?" prodded Carrick.

"It's Zenith..."

"What about it?"

"I don't...," Erik paused uncomfortably.

"Grandpa, what is it?"

"You can never go back there, Carrick!" Erik leaned forward, reached across the table, and placed his hand on Carrick's. "You can never go back there. Do you understand me?"

"Grandpa, I'm retired from NASA. I'm not going back to Zenith! There's nothing there for me. You're Home now! You are my home. I wouldn't leave you." Carrick was sincere but curious as to why Erik would say such a thing.

"You can't go. You can't!" Erik was flustered. His face indicated to Carrick that he somehow believed he would someday return to Zenith. He looked frightened.

"Grandpa, I'm never going back there, never. My family, my life, our life together is here on Earth. I'm never going back there," he reassured his grandfather.

"Say the words Carrick, say the words!"

"What words? What are you talking about?" Carrick was confused.

"Promise me! Promise me that you'll never go back there! Say the words, Carrick!"

"I promise! I promise! I'll never go back!" said Carrick, almost stuttering. "What in the hell is going on here? What's wrong, Grandpa?"

The waiter observed the interaction, as did several surrounding tables and booths.

"Everything okay here, guys?" said Greg, their normal server.

"Yeah-yeah-yeah, here's the card," Carrick was dismissive of the young waiter as he handed him his credit card.

"Carrick, I'm sorry. I didn't mean to make a big deal of it, but I just want to make sure you'll never go back there, that's all," explained Erik.

Chapter 3 – Operation Venom

Location: Langley, Virginia. George Bush Center for Intelligence, CIA Headquarters. First-floor conference room – February 22, 2026 – Sunday morning, 10:01 am EST.

"Ladies and Gentlemen, I'd like to thank all of you for being here on a Sunday morning. This is obviously of high importance," opened the Director of the CIA, James Clapper.

The spacious room was filled with both curiosity and anticipation. Joining Clapper around a conference table that sat twelve were several CIA Officers, they included: Officer Matt Solstice, field agents Montgomery Stevens, Cade McBride, and Virginia Worthington. Along with the four agents, the team was joined by former CIA Officer Jordan Spear, three special agents from the FBI, and a stenographer.

Clapper leaned in and interlocked his fingers on the table before him. Then, with a solemn look on his face, proceeded to explain why the team was assembled, though everyone in the group had been briefed.

Clapper was forthright. "Folks, in a few minutes, we'll be joined by NASA's Chief Administrator, Marcus 'Mars' Johnston. Some of you have already had the pleasure of making his acquaintance. Mars joins us from Houston today because of a potential risk that may or may not involve NASA. Mars has been brought up to speed....,"

At that moment, the door swung open abruptly, and in walked the gregarious Marcus 'Mars' Johnston. Heads in the room swiveled to look. "Sorry, I'm late, everyone," smiled Mars. Though he understood the gravity of the meeting, it was hard for him not to smile. "I just finished up a meeting with the head of the Space Force, Bill Rickman. Man! We've got some exciting stuff coming down the pike!"

Without acknowledging Mars, Clapper turned back to the group and continued where he'd left off. "As I was saying, today we will be putting in place a counter-intelligence operation, code-named

'Venom'. You've all been briefed on what occurred in China last week. Well, as we speak, an autopsy is being performed on the late Ambassador, Dr. Carl Schoenfeld, at Walter Reed this morning. According to Chinese officials, Dr. Schoenfeld died by his own hand, but to be clear, an autopsy is not needed to know that he was murdered. The question rather, that needs to be answered is by whom?"

"We've asked former Officer Jordan Spear here this morning because he has some insight as to who the perpetrator might be. Jordan, the room is yours."

"Thank you, Director Clapper," Spear acknowledged his former boss. "Six years ago, while undercover in London, I was assigned to infiltrate a Chinese-sponsored terror group called 'Iron Hand.' The group's goal was to assassinate the then-Speaker of the House of Commons, Sir Lindsay Bancroft. If carried out, which it was not, the assassination would've been in retaliation for the capture and imprisonment of a Chinese National named Kitan Zhao. Zhao was captured in a sting by MI6 operatives attempting to buy bogus intelligence."

"While Zhao alone wasn't critical to the Chinese counter-intelligence effort, the Chinese used diplomatic efforts to gain his release. Because he was charged as a spy, his release was not immediately granted," explained Jordan. "The Chinese feared that Zhao could collapse under interrogation or subsequent imprisonment, and spill state secrets, as he was considered mentally weak by his superiors."

"If I may," interjected Agent Virginia Worthington.

"Please, go ahead," nodded Jordan.

"If Zhao was such a small fish in China, why would the government risk war with England by assassinating the Speaker of the House of Commons?" she asked.

"Furthermore, if he was mentally weak, why would he be working in their intelligence agencies to begin with?" added Worthington.

"All fair questions," said Jordan. "Firstly, there'd be no war if the Speaker alone were killed. That's why they targeted Speaker Bancroft. Their goal was to send a message, not start World War III.

Suppose they would've hit Prime Minister Taylor or even a Royal. In that case, that may very well have started a regional conflict, or at the very least, a retaliatory strike against one of China's assets: human or infrastructure. As it were, though, the Speaker's death would somehow have been acceptable in the face of world war," explained Jordan. "They would have simply covered it up somehow: suicide, a car accident, headlong down a flight of stairs. You name it. Now we all know the pecking order in London."

"Secondly...," Jordan continued, as he was cut-off by Agent Cade McBride.

"But why risk it for a small player like Zhao," questioned aloud Agent McBride.

"That was the second part of my statement before being interrupted," said Jordan, looking directly into the eyes of McBride. "It wasn't that Zhao was important to the Chinese counter-intelligence efforts. Rather, it was who his great uncle is," offered Jordan.

"Let me guess," Agent Montgomery Stevens chimed in.

Half the room chorused with him, "Xí Shèng-Xióng."

Jordan nodded.

Shèng-Xióng was the long-time President of the People's Republic of China and had also served as the Chairman of the Central Military Commission.

"Jordan, tell the group why we're here, please," encouraged Clapper.

Former Officer Spear continued. "Everything I just told you is simply context, as a secret prisoner exchange happened the following year as cooler heads prevailed. Now, with all that being said, during the operation, I crossed paths with a man, code-named Zhīzhū. The name translates to 'The Spider.'"

Mars broke in abruptly, "Gotta tell ya, I hate spiders."

Everyone in the room turned their attention to Johnston. The group was taken aback by his failure to understand the seriousness of the matter at hand.

"They give me the heebie-jeebies! Just saying," said Mars, wide-eyed. "Just saying."

"Jordan, please continue," encouraged Clapper as he glared over at Mars.

"As I was saying," Jordan continued, "everyone in this room, except for the person taking notes, and my friend Administrator Johnston, knows exactly who The Spider is."

"How does all of this," she paused, "lead all of us here today?" asked Agent Worthington.

At that moment, Clapper took charge of the meeting and directed the senior FBI agent in the room to pass out manilla envelopes to every agent around the table.

Location: Beijing China, Macikou Area Residential District, twenty-five miles northwest of the city center. February 22, 2026 – Sunday night – 10:47pm GMT +8.

In his flat, Colonel Vadik Lei was meditating upside down while strapped to an inversion table. Lei was practicing Taoist meditation as he had since his late teens. At the end of each day, Lei would complete a rigorous workout that included ten three-minute sprints on a treadmill and a set of fifty push-ups between each of the ten sprint sets. After his work out he would shower and then meditate while inverted.

Now at the age of thirty-eight, Lei wasn't as young as he once was, but his wisdom and tenacity made him a more deadly assassin than he'd ever been before. His regimented lifestyle, coupled with weapons and mixed-martial arts training, along with the trust of his superiors, made him one of the most dangerous men in the world.

Lei would wake the following morning at 5:00 am, as he always did. His morning routine would include four sets of one hundred pull-ups and four sets of fifty sit-ups. For breakfast, he would have two pints of douhua, a type of soybean pudding, and eight ounces of black coffee.

Later in the day, Colonel Vadik Lei would be meeting with the Head of Department for The Ministry of State Security, Li Kenong. Topic du jour would be the fall-out from the failed interrogation and the murder of the American Ambassador. Lei would have to explain the inability of his subordinate to extract the necessary information from the American subject and then kill him in such a way that would make suicide more plausible.

Location: Langley, Virginia. George Bush Center for Intelligence, CIA Headquarters. First-floor conference room – February 22, 2026 – Sunday morning, 10:52 am EST.

"Folks, before we study the top-secret contents in your envelopes, we have a small matter that we need to take care of before we can proceed. Jordan, if you could, please come to the front of the room." Clapper stood and walked to the door, stepped out into the hallway, and returned only seconds later.

Clapper was followed by a middle-aged woman dressed casually in an expensive warm-up suit and carrying a black book as if heading to lunch and then off to the park for some afternoon reading.

"Ahem!" Clapper cleared his throat. "If I could have everyone's attention, please. We have a little house-cleaning to do before we can break into the classified contents of your envelopes." Clapper acted matter of fact.

"Please welcome the Honorable Judge Kerry LeCraft," Clapper announced. "Judge LeCraft is a federal judge and sits on the D.C. District Court of Appeals. The judge and I go way back, and I thank her for doing me a favor by coming in today on such short notice."

LeCraft nodded in appreciation for Clapper's kind introduction.

"To everyone in attendance, I have a special announcement to make. In the next couple of minutes, former and distinguished CIA Officer Jordan Spear will no longer be a 'former' Officer of this agency." Those in attendance perked up, now sitting erect in their chairs. The energy in the room was palpable.

After Jordan Spear returned from Black Earth, he was recognized around the world as both a legend and a hero. Within the Central Intelligence Agency ranks, he no longer had peers as his reputation preceded him. Jordan went on to give commencement speeches to college grads, hit the talk show circuit, and even made several appearances internationally with Doctors Carrick Michaels and Erik Erickson. Just two months after returning from his historic journey to Black Earth, Jordan formally retired from the C.I.A. and began a new life with his girlfriend, Dr. Kinzi London. After just shy of nineteen months of retirement, though, Jordan Spear was back.

Clapper broke a rare smile when seeing the assembled group's positive reaction. Even the stenographer couldn't mask her approval.

"After several hours of coaxing yesterday, Jordan decided that he will once again be joining the ranks of the C.I.A., and we're very thankful in advance for his future service to the agency. Judge LeCraft, please do us the honor of swearing in this young man," requested Clapper.

Jordan was both humble and nervous, but no one in the room could detect either emotion. As a former under-cover, counter-intelligence officer, he was impossible to read.

Smiling now, Judge LeCraft revealed that the book she was holding was actually a bible. "Jordan, please raise your right hand and place the other on this bible." Jordan obliged. "Now, if you would, please repeat after me," asked LeCraft.

"You know what, Judge LeCraft? I think I got this one!" Jordan winked at her and smiled confidently. "I, Jordan Christopher Spear, do solemnly swear, to support and defend the Constitution of the United States of America against all enemies, foreign and domestic. That I will bear true faith and allegiance to the same. That I take this obligation freely and without mental reservation or purpose of evasion. That I will well and faithfully discharge the duties of the office on which I am about to enter, SO HELP ME GOD." Jordan finished and turned to shake Clapper's hand.

"Welcome back, son," said Clapper. All those in attendance stood and clapped. One by one, each walked to the front of the room to shake Jordan's hand, excited to congratulate the newest member of the C.I.A. and to welcome back the legendary Officer.

"Damn!" exclaimed Solstice, "I can't believe you memorized the entire oath. That was impressive! Glad to have you back on the team! The agency is stronger right now than it was five minutes ago."

With things settled down, Judge LeCraft now gone, and everyone back in their seats, the senior-most FBI agent at the meeting began to explain to everyone what they had on The Spider.

"Folks, Special Agent John Primrose from the Bureau will take it from here," Clapper handed over the room.

"Thank you, Director Clapper," Special Agent Primrose was gracious. "The reason myself and my two colleagues are here today is to share inter-agency information with you regarding The Spider." Looking around the table, he encouraged everyone to remove the classified contents of their envelopes.

As the principles removed the contents of their envelopes, they found a picture of a dark-haired man of Chinese descent.

"The picture you're looking at is that of The Spider," said Primrose. "We have little information on him, other than the fact that roughly thirty countries around the world have reported having encountered him in some form or fashion. He is known to have killed at least two dozen of some of the most competent and highly trained combat veterans, counter-intelligence officers, and double agents from many different countries around the world. I am sad to say that two of the one-hundred and thirty-three stars on the Memorial Wall, just down the hall, are compliments of The Spider," detailed Primrose.

"Our guess, using historical run-ins with countries from across the globe, is that our 'Spider' friend is somewhere between the ages of thirty and forty, roughly 5' 6" tall, and weighs between 140 and 160lbs," Primrose informed.

Brows went up around the room, with Agent Virginia Worthington saying, "Geez, he's my size."

Solstice broke in. "I'm pretty sure I can take you, but this guy's obviously a badass."

"Don't be so sure of yourself," said Worthington, with a straight-face before smiling. "I'm a badass, too!"

Both chuckled half-heartedly.

Primrose elaborated, "Our intel suggests that he lives near Beijing when not out killing the good guys. The only other names associated with The Spider are Zhīzhū and possibly Vadik. We can't be certain about the name Vadik though, that could simply be a code name or nickname, as the name 'Vadik' is surely not Chinese. It's Slavic, meaning 'Ruler.' We do have some intel on a former Chinese Army Colonel named Vadik Lei, but cannot positively say that the two men are one and the same. I'm hoping that they're not, as the rumors on Colonel Vadik Lei are brutal, with reports of the killing and torturing of his own men."

"Jordan can perhaps offer more info on our subject and his potential origins. Take it away, Jordan."

"Thank you, Agent Primrose." Jordan eased into the conversation, reminding everyone that while in London six years ago, he crossed paths with a man named Zhīzhū.

"What were the circumstances that caused you to cross paths with him?" came the question from a secondary FBI Agent named Greg Costas.

"One evening, the group known as 'Iron Hand' was meeting at a safe house in London's East End, known as Whitechapel Market," recounted Jordan. "I was introduced to the group through a Chinese double-agent, who will remain unnamed here today. My cockney accent was pretty damn good back then, so I was brought in from Ukraine to assist. My cover was to act as a local thug, which could help connect the Chinese agents with local right-wing officials. People who likely had access to the local government officials in Westminster and Belgravia. Both locations were not far from Westminster Abbey, where Speaker Bancroft resided with his wife and three daughters."

"We were roughly an hour into the meeting when a few of the Chinese assassins started chirping about someone named Zhīzhū. Some just called him 'Z,' but a couple called him by his code name. I immediately recognized the translation as I understand a little mandarin. I started getting the feeling that the plot may have been a little more sophisticated if someone like The Spider was joining the party." Jordan looked around the room, and everyone, including the stenographer, was looking straight at him, wondering what he would reveal next.

"So, did he show up?" asked an impatient Solstice.

"Yes, he did," revealed Jordan. "And when he did, everyone in the room was on their best behavior, as if they feared the man. These men were all trained killers, and they were shaking in their shoes by his mere presence. He only stayed for five or six minutes, but the description given by Agent Primrose fits him to a tee. While slight in stature, his presence was giant," recalled Spear.

"In the short time we were together in the room, he seemed suspicious of me, making little eye contact. I returned the favor but could hear him asking who I was in mandarin. I can't say for sure if my presence spooked him, but he didn't stay for long," finished Jordan.

Clapper broke in. "Folks, we believe that The Spider was brought into London to assassinate Speaker Bancroft. We also believe that he is responsible for killing Ambassador Schoenfeld. These assumptions are partly based off of jumbled transcripts retrieved from our embassy in Beijing."

At that moment, Clapper's phone vibrated, and he excused himself, motioning that he would be back in one minute. Clapper stepped out into the hallway to return a call from Walter Reed's head pathologist, Dr. Henry Shockley.

Clapper returned moments later and informed the group of what he'd learned. "As suspected, blunt force trauma to the head of Ambassador Schoenfeld is what caused his death. It appears that the ligature marks around the Ambassador's neck were post-mortem. He also had four broken ribs, a punctured lung, and a lacerated kidney. Additionally, he was missing three of his lower molars, and all of the fingernails on his left hand were removed."

The group cringed. "Jesus Christ! Why didn't they set it up to look like a car accident? That wasn't very smart," offered Cade McBride.

Mars Johnston interjected, "Excuse me, Director Clapper, but why am I here today, sir?"

"Mars, I was just getting to that," Clapper leaned in. "Our intel suggests that the Chinese want to get to Black Earth before the next international coalition does," he paused, "and that they'll stop at nothing to get there before we do. For everyone's edification, the coalition will be riding on a NASA rocket ship."

"Sabotage?" whispered Mars, under his breath.

"What's that?" Clapper directed his question at Mars.

"You're suggesting sabotage to our new Saturn Six rocket, aren't you?" suggested Mars. "Impossible!"

"Impossible?" Clapper sat more erect now in his chair. "That's exactly what I'm suggesting, Mr. Johnston," said a stone-faced James Clapper.

"But everyone working on the project are American citizens. We would never let foreign engineers inside the deepest parts of NASA," rebutted Mars.

"While that may be true, Mars, you will have an international crew on board that ship. And, whether foreign or domestic, every human being has a price," reminded the Director.

Mars looked ill. Dread befell his face as he would now question his every decision moving forward regarding who at NASA touched the project. The new Saturn Six was thirty percent more powerful than the Saturn V rockets used during the Apollo program. And far more powerful than any of the three 'Horizon' class rockets that made the first three missions to Black Earth.

Mars knew that if something went wrong, it would've happened on his watch, as he was now the Chief Administrator at NASA, a job he earned through decades of tireless service to the Agency and his country.

For the next three hours, the group sorted through the details and worked up a division of labor between each member of the Operation Venom task force. Mars would be assigned three agents from the FBI, who would work within the confines at NASA so that he would not be distracted in his duties. They included getting the new ship, Saturn Six, and its sister ship, Neptune One, prepared for the manned-mission scheduled for December.

It was now 4:00 pm, and the meeting was wrapping up. Clapper excused the group, and one by one, they disappeared down the long hallways of the C.I.A.

Jordan, still sitting in the conference room, found himself alone. He pulled out his cellphone and called Kinzi again. No answer, just as there was no answer when he called her in the minutes before the meeting began. Jordan knew that his decision to rejoin the agency was his and not his and Kinzi's as a couple. He knew she wasn't happy about it. The night before, the two slept in separate bedrooms at his parent's house and didn't speak earlier that morning before leaving. Tensions were high between the two.

Kinzi was distant toward him. She knew that C.I.A. Officers were married to their job and would likely spend much of their time abroad. Jordan, however, knew that he would spend no time undercover, neither at home nor overseas. This was due to the world's recognition of his face and celebrity status. Jordan didn't believe that he would be put in harm's way and that his new capacity would be more consultative rather than undercover work.

Moments later, Clapper walked into the room after seeing off the meeting attendees. "Did you call your father yet?" he asked.

"No, I was just trying to call Kinzi."

Clapper's brow went up as his eyes went down. "Ah, yes, that's a tough one! No man or woman wants to know that their significant other is putting their country first. Some say they understand," he paused, "but my guess is that they'd be lying. Put it this way, if she marries you someday, Kinzi won't be able to say she didn't know what she was getting herself into."

"Yeah, we'll figure it out, I guess," Jordan muttered with little confidence.

"Just give her a little time; she'll come around," reassured Clapper.

Jordan displayed a look of discouragement.

"Jordan, look, me and the Mrs. have been married for almost sixty-one years. It's been tough for her over the years. Maybe they don't make them like her anymore, but for a woman who earned her M.D. and made three trips to another planet, I'd say Kinzi likely has what it takes. It'll all work out, son." Clapper placed an empathetic hand on Jordan's shoulder.

"I'm sure you're right, Director Clapper."

"Please, call me Jim when we're alone together. Sometimes I forget that I actually have a first name," Clapper sighed. "Until I get home anyway, and the wife calls me for dinner," he chuckled.

The two men shared a laugh and shook hands again. As Jordan went to recoil his hand, Clapper squeezed it firmly, pulled Jordan close, and said, "Son, I can't promise to keep you out of danger. You understand that, right?"

Jordan reciprocated by squeezing Clapper's hand and said, "Yes, I do, sir. Yes, I do!"

Chapter 4 – London Bridge is Falling Down

Location: Arlington, Virginia. Ronald Reagan International Airport – February 22, 2026 – 4:45 pm EST.

Kinzi London sat alone at American Airlines Gate 30, awaiting her 6:50 pm flight to Atlanta and then on to Houston, TX. Looking at her phone, Kinzi saw nine missed calls, six voicemails, and twelve text messages, all unreturned.

Sitting there, Kinzi turned off her phone and remembered back to a time when she was little, growing up in the house at 1345 Waverly Way, in the Madison Park district of Seattle, Washington. She loved growing up near the shores of Lake Washington. It was an innocent time before the expectations of her life began to pile up. For as long as she could remember, her future was not her own. As an eight-year-old, she recalled having a discussion at the kitchen table with her parents about where she would be attending college, where she would study medicine. Her parents were both highly accomplished and had high expectations for their only child. Kinzi's mother, Kate London, was a medical doctor, and former astronaut, traveling to space in 1983 on STS-8 on August 30 of that year. Her father, James, was an astrophysicist and world-renowned for his studies in the origins of space and famously authored the book, Neptune Rings in 1989.

In her moment alone, before the gate populated with travelers, Kinzi went a little further back in time, searching for a happier place. She fondly remembered the years when she was a normal little kid, the kind that played with dolls and had lots of friends. Kinzi's friends loved her last name and loved the fact that her parents were famous. Their favorite game to play with her was *London Bridge is Falling Down* because of her last name. On this day, however, Kinzi London felt herself falling down.

Since returning from Black Earth for the third and final time, Kinzi finally felt free from her parent's long shadow. Her life was about her now and not what she 'someday could become,' in her mother's words. Kinzi was accomplished and happy. It had been 637 days since she returned safely and madly in love. They were amongst her happiest days, just her and Jordan, doing as they pleased, traveling the world, not giving too much thought to what the future held. Then, when she finally did start thinking about a future with Jordan, marriage, and maybe even children, the knock on the door came, and in her mind, it changed everything. The bubble had burst, and Jordan would choose the CIA over her.

After Jordan left for CIA headquarters earlier that morning, Kinzi quietly packed her things and snuck out of Jordan's parents' house, where they had been staying for the last six months. It didn't make sense to get a place of their own because the two had lived like Nomads, always on the move, seeing the world and living off the grid for most of the year.

Am I just being selfish? she thought to herself as the gate attendant announced over the loudspeaker, "Attention passengers, American Airlines, Flight 3160 to Atlanta will be departing from Gate 30 at 6:50 pm. Boarding will begin at 6:20 pm. Thank you for flying American Airlines." She wanted to punch the girl in the face. "Thank you for flying American airlines," Kinzi whispered to herself, mocking the cutesy voice and phony smile the gate attendant wore while actually pretending to like her job.

She was only kidding herself. Kinzi had been living in a bubble for the last eighteen-plus months, a bubble she knew would eventually pop but hoped that it wouldn't. She knew she was being selfish. Kinzi would be turning thirty-seven later in the year, she knew her Black Earth honeymoon would come to an end at some point, and real-life would eclipse her fantasy world.

All Jordan had to hear was *The Spider,* and that was it. *Who is The Spider? What made him drop everything and rejoin the CIA?* Kinzi asked herself. Nothing was making sense to her, but neither was running away. She loved the man, and she felt that he loved her too. Everything else would somehow work itself out.

Kinzi extended the handle on her roller bag and headed for the Uber pick-up area. Along the way, she tossed her boarding pass into a trash can, choosing instead to walk right into an unwelcomed and uncertain future. That was hard for her to process as her future had been planned out years in advance for most of her life.

Now, in the backseat of a strange car, she whispered, "Fuck you, Mom, and Dad! From now on, I'm just gonna roll with it!" she whispered.

"I'm sorry," said the Uber driver, "were you speaking to me?"

"No-no, so sorry, I was just thinking out loud, that's all." Kinzi blushed with embarrassment.

"You wouldn't happen to be the Kinzi London from Black Earth, would you?" asked the driver.

"No-no," she smiled, "but I get that a lot," she lied while pulling her Seahawks ballcap down a little further.

Location: Leesburg, Virginia, home of Jonathan and Jocelyn Spear – February 22, 2026 – 7:27 pm EST.

The front door chimed as Kinzi entered the house. Jocelyn Spear peeked her head out from the kitchen and said, "He's upstairs in the shower."

After stashing her suitcase under the bed and removing her clothes, Kinzi snuck into the bathroom, pulled the shower curtain back, and stepped in. Jordan looked relieved and smiled; the two embraced.

"Where were you all day?"

"Just out and about. How was your meeting?"

"Kinzi, I called and texted all day. What's going on with you?"

"Sorry, my phone must've died."

The two made love in the shower and promised each other that they would stick together and never think of going it alone, whatever the future held.

Chapter 5 – Operation Black Diamond

Location: Beijing, China. The Ministry of State Security Building, Seventh Floor, Office of the Head of Department for The Ministry of State Security, Minister Li Kenong – February 23, 2026 – 9:00 am GMT +8.

"Sir! Reporting as requested, sir!"

"Please sit-down, Colonel Lei," said Li Kenong, motioning to the chair in front of his desk.

"I prefer to stand, sir."

"Sit down, Colonel Lei!" said Kenong in his native tongue.

Vadik Lei reluctantly sat at attention, hands on knees.

"Colonel Lei, I regret to inform you that your incompetent foot soldier, Field Agent Fan Yun, died this weekend."

Lei shot to the edge of his seat. "But how, sir?" Lei, normally composed, reacted with surprise and concern.

"It seems the cause of death was lack of oxygen to the brain. That happened moments after he head-butted a speeding bullet," said Kenong, with a savage smile. "He died in the same room that he over-zealously interrogated a certain American diplomat."

"But, sir!" Lei now squeezing his stomach muscles tightly and balling his fists, "Agent Yun had six children, sir!"

"And now our great country has six new fatherless children thanks to Yun's incompetence, Colonel!" Kenong, now standing, white knuckles pressed against his desktop while leaning forward. "Perhaps this is why you never had children of your own!"

Vadik Lei sat wearing a look of contempt. He could easily kill the smug Head of Department but likely wouldn't make it out of the building alive. Instead, because he made it through the weekend without meeting the same fate as Yun, he'd try his best to stomach what the Minister had to say.

Minister Kenong walked around to the front of his desk and leaned back against it, now standing just inches away from his subordinate.

"Spiders are so easily crushed beneath the shoe of simple men. But I am not a simple man, Colonel Lei. I am a genius, and like our President, I too understand that the right spider, a venomous one, can bring down even the strongest man, no matter his size."

Minister Kenong walked around to the back of his desk and looked out the window. Spinning back toward his subordinate, he asked, "Is that why they call you The Spider, Colonel? Because you can bring down big men?" Kenong was smug.

Lei just sat in his chair, his tight lips concealing his clenched teeth.

"Your President has a job for you, Colonel. A job that will extend your life for the foreseeable future." He paused and then said, "To be clear, though, if I had my way, you would've met the same fate as Field Agent Yun."

"I am listening," acknowledged Lei, without making eye contact with the man he now wanted to kill.

"Colonel Lei, your supreme President, wants you to do a service for your country. The job is a big one, and for reasons unbeknownst to me, he believes that you are the man for the job, even though you botched the simple task of extracting information from the esteemed American Ambassador. It seems he was loved by the locals here in Beijing and was widely regarded by his own State Department. Such a pity he had to die," said the insincere Minister, now laughing under his breath.

"What is it you would have me do, Minister Kenong?" Lei, now bowing his head in allegiance.

"Ah, I see you have calmed down, Spider Lei. The veins in your neck no longer protrude," said a serious-looking Kenong. "Yes, you will be very interested in what we have in store for you."

Location: Artesia, New Mexico. Home of Carrick and Lola – February 28, 2026 – 4:43 pm MST.

"Erik, we're home!" yelled Lola, entering the kitchen through the mudroom that led to the garage. No response came back.

"Erik! We're home!" yelled Carrick a little louder than Lola. Still nothing.

"Maybe he went back home," offered Lola.

"I can hear the T.V. on in the living room." Carrick looked across the kitchen and dining room to see the flickering reflection on both the dining and living room windows.

The two were a little wet and carrying bags of groceries. It was a gloomy afternoon and had been raining for days. While the average rainfall for New Mexico in the month of February was less than half an inch, El Niño was causing rainfall records to be shattered for the second year in a row. The forecast showed no let-up, so Lola and Carrick loaded up on Erik's favorites, pizza rolls, and Nestlé Crunch bars. Since coming Home, Erik was a finicky eater but had also developed some poor eating habits. Like everybody else, he had his favorite junk foods.

After getting all of the bags into the kitchen, now piled up on the counter, Carrick kicked off his wet shoes and headed down the galley-style butler's pantry. Just halfway through the ten-foot-long pantry, making his way to the huge living room, he could hear the words, "I'll be right here," coming from the television. The living room was decorated contemporarily with white carpet and gray walls. The ceilings were twelve feet high and were coffered, and ten-inch crown molding framed the room. The fireplace was made of gray cobblestone, streaked with black and brown threads, and behind it was a winding staircase making its way to the second floor. Above the mantle was a seventy-five-inch T.V. The house was still new, and the smell of fresh paint hung in the air.

Carrick spotted Erik sitting on the over-sized gray leather sectional couch. He was covered in a chenille blanket adorned by a huge NASA logo, and he was crying.

Carrick looked at Erik, then the T.V., then back to Erik and said, "Erik, come on, you're watching E.T. again?"

"He's going 'Home,' and he's taking the flowers with him," said Erik while sobbing. "Elliot loves him! It's just so sad!"

"Turn it off and come help us with the groceries," Carrick motioned with his arm.

"It's almost over. Give me a minute." Erik wiped the tears from his cheeks.

Carrick turned to walk away, and just as he entered the butler's pantry, he heard Erik say, "Did you get my queso?"

Carrick yelled back, dismissively, "Yeah, we got it!"

With a look of concern, Erik yelled, "The white cheese?"

"Yes, we got it! We got three of them for you, now let's go!"

"What about the chips?" another nervous question came from Erik.

"Got it! Let's go, Grandpa!" barked Carrick back.

Moments later, Erik walked into the kitchen to lend a hand.

"E.T. again, huh?" smiled Lola.

"Gets me every time." Erik raised his hand, covered his heart, then sighed.

Lola laughed while Carrick juggled cans of soup as he headed into the pantry.

"So, Star Wars tonight?" asked a smiling Erik.

"No, sir, we're watching Apollo 13!" Carrick was enthusiastic.

"Boring. Mars recommends Prometheus. We've been texting back and forth a lot lately."

"How's he doing?" asked Carrick.

"I guess, okay. He said he had a tough week," reported Erik.

"Yeah, he texted me last night. He told me to call him today."

"I hope everything's okay," offered Lola, looking in Carrick's direction.

Lola then turned back to Erik, "So, no walk today?"

"No. The rain." Erik looked out the window.

"Yeah, but you guys have walked in the rain before. It's fun! Didn't see any of that stuff on Zenith, did you?"

Erik nodded in agreement. "Yeah, I called Mrs. Spencer, she said Lilly was a little under the weather."

"Poor baby. I hope she's okay," offered Lola.

Carrick headed upstairs to change his shirt just as his phone rang. Looking at the screen, he saw that it was Mars.

Carrick swiped right, "Hey buddy, it's been a while! Hope you're doing okay."

"Hey Carrick, did you get my message?" asked an upbeat Mars.

"I did. I'm sorry I didn't call back right away. I was planning to call you later."

"Listen, I shouldn't be saying anything – you know, top-secret and all – but something's come up," Mars said while sounding a little concerned. "I'm sure that it's nothing."

"Mars, now wait a second! Don't be sharing classified information with me! You just got your dream job, don't blow it!" cautioned a half-smiling Carrick.

"No, of course. I just wanted to see if you guys watched Prometheus yet."

"Really? That's why you wanted me to call you?" Carrick was beyond skeptical. "That's the 'top-secret' nugget you had for me?"

"Yeah. No. That was it. I'm serious." Mars sounded unconvincing.

"Yeah-yeah. Whatever," sighed Carrick. "No, we haven't watched it yet, now spit it out! What's the real reason for the call?"

"Fine, I'll tell you then." Mars was dying to share important news. "Last Sunday, I was summoned to D.C. to meet with Clapper, a few FBI Agents, Spear, and Solstice were there, along with two others."

"Wow! What was all that about?"

"Well, I could tell you, but I'd have to kill you," Mars chuckled.

"I'll take my chances, now spit it out!" Carrick was quite curious.

"Okay, but you can't say anything, not even to Lola."

"Got it! Now get on with it!" encouraged Carrick. "But nothing classified, okay?"

"The CIA thinks China is up to no good. Clapper thinks they'll do anything to get back to Black Earth first," confessed Mars, almost whispering.

"Mars, where are you right now?" asked Carrick.

"I'm in my living room. Why?"

"Then why are you whispering?" laughed Carrick.

"You know Clapper! He could have the place bugged for all I know."

Mars had been paranoid about his calls being taped since Clapper busted him nearly four years ago. Mars had called Lola on multiple occasions to give her updates on Carrick's condition while he was on Black Earth.

"But their rocket won't be ready by December. Even if they wanted to get there before us, their CZ-2Z wouldn't be ready until late Spring at the earliest," Carrick sounded skeptical.

Along with India and Russia, the Chinese had accelerated their manned rocket technology, as had private firms like Virgin Galactic and SpaceX. The goal was for the partner countries involved in the Black Earth Salvage Agreement, nicknamed BESA by the press, to be ready to launch in succession over the next five years. NASA didn't have the financial capacity or manpower to keep building super rockets outside of their nearly completed back-up ship, the Neptune One. Other countries would have to be ready in case of disaster early on and to assist with the black planet's actual salvaging in the years following 2027.

There was no real way to stop private firms from eventually getting a manned ship to Black Earth, but it would be several years before that could happen.

As a redundancy, NASA planned to have the Neptune One rocket ready for launch by Spring of 2027, just in case there were any issues with Saturn Six after making its way to Black Earth. The worst-case scenario would be to have astronauts stranded on Black Earth. Though it would take four months to get another ship there to rescue the astronauts, the new landing modules would be twice as big and have rations to last for the four-month rescue operation. After that, the other BESA countries would journey there to rescue, salvage, or complete scientific experiments.

"Just saying," said Mars. "The FBI and CIA are on high alert. That's about all I can say."

"Mars, before you go...,"

"Yeah, go ahead," responded Mars.

"Why exactly were you at that meeting?" asked Carrick.

Mars swallowed hard. "Um, yeah, they just wanted to keep me in the loop." Once again, Mars was unconvincing. He was careful not to mention the word 'sabotage' to Carrick.

"Well, I'd say keep me posted, but I don't want to get you fired."

"Okay, take care. Oh, and Carrick..., say hello to Lola and Erik for me."

"I will. Be safe, Mars."

As Carrick was hanging up the phone, he could hear Mars say, "Enjoy Prometheus tonight...!" before he was cut-off.

Location: Beijing, China. The Ministry of State Security Building, Second Floor Secure Conference Room – March 17, 2026 – 10:07 am GMT +8.

"Gentlemen, forgive my lack of Shǒu shí. I assure you it is with good reason that I am late. Our most noble leader, President Shèng-Xióng, kept me on the phone a little longer than expected. He wanted to ensure that this meeting went well," explained Minister Kenong.

Being late in the Chinese culture is a serious offense, not taken lightly by those kept waiting. It is considered to be highly disrespectful to those in attendance.

The men in the room looked around at each other without saying anything while sizing up one another. The air was thick, and suspicions were thicker.

The room was small, too small, thought Vadik Lei. If he were to kill Minister Kenong, it would be hard to escape. Hard to maneuver around desk chairs, a conference table, file boxes, and five able-bodied men, two of them trained killers from SHA.

The Spider had been consumed by his hatred of the pompous and arrogant Kenong. Lei cracked his neck to ease the tension and to regain focus.

Colonel Vadik Lei knew that Minister Kenong's insecurities and hatred of him came from childhood. He surmised that the physically meek and weak-minded minister was likely bullied as a child by strong-minded yet ill-willed boys. He knew that the irresolute minister considered him a bully too. Kenong resented him for being a ruthless killer yet had no qualms exploiting his deadly skills to forward his nation's political and geo-global agenda. That hypocrisy is why he, too, hated Minister Kenong, the new muse of his ire. The only thing stopping him from breaking the man's neck at that moment, and each moment that followed was his position within the Ministry of State Security.

In addition to the two foes were three officials from the Ministry of State Security, and two members from the Strategic Huyou Agency, Vadik being the third member in attendance from SHA. That was seven men in total. Down one side of the table were three Ministry officials. Down the other side, the SHA assassins. At the head of the table, Minister Kenong.

"Gentlemen, let me start by saying that should any information from our meeting leak to anyone other than those who occupy this very room, in addition to our most honorable President, then we will all be killed brutally and most horrifically. We are the only living people on Earth that know of our most excellent plan. Should the jíhuá before us become public, or find itself in the hands of another nation, we will be so brutally killed that years from now, they will still be finding our bones spread throughout our great country," warned Kenong. "We are the only men that will harbor such great and wonderful plans. Plans that will make China the last and only Superpower on Earth."

The three State Security officials applauded by tapping on the table vigorously as if they had hundreds of times before. Lei and the other two SHA Agents sat motionless as if unimpressed. It took more than empty bravado to increase the heart rate of stone-cold assassins.

"Today is step one of a journey that will start in this room and end on Black Earth," said Kenong. This announcement got the attention of the SHA Agents, and they looked to be more curious now.

"Yes, I see our ruthless mercenaries blinked as I said the words Black Earth. Did I detect a subtle rise in your temperature Colonel Lei?" smirked Minister Kenong.

"You should continue with your wonderful plan, Minister, I would hate for you to lose your train of thought," encouraged Lei with an inauthentic smile, envisioning Kenong's severed head in his hands.

Kenong, with a look of disdain, continued.

"Yes, the Americans think that they will be the first to get back to Black Earth, but they would be mistaken. They will not own the precious diamonds found there! They will not own the cures for every incurable disease that plagues us as humans! They will not own the plans for propulsion systems that will make space travel faster! And finally," emphasized Kenong, "they will not own the title of world's only Superpower!" The Minister was emphatic.

Again, the three State Security officials chorused their applause, smiling as if their strings were being pulled, while the three SHA Agents were only mildly aroused.

"And just how do you stop the Great American Machine from mining the riches of Black Earth before we can get there?" asked Vadik Lei.

"The plan is simple, while they dive deep into the ocean, looking for crumbs in the sands of the dark and of the deep, and while they plan to take to the skies and stars in December of this year, we will take their heart away from them. We will take their souls. And then, when their 'iron will' rains down upon them, they will stand aside and let the inevitable course of our world's future pass them by. That course is the will of our great nation and the will of our fearless leader." Kenong stood with clenched fists, and thrust them into the air, his face red with contempt for America but filled with pride for his country.

The over-zealous Kenong took his seat and passed out envelopes with the heading Jīmì. English translation: Confidential.

"Please, gentlemen, remove the contents of your Xìnfēng," encouraged the Minister. "Now, let us begin."

The words revealed on the top of the first page were, 'Lìshǐ túshū guǎn.' English translation: The History Library.

Chapter 6 – Challenger Deep

Location: Washington D.C. NCN National Cable News Network Studios, The Situation Center with Bear Winston – March 10, 2026 – 5:01 pm EST.

"Ladies and gentlemen, in our audience here in the United States and from around the world, we are excited to have in-studio the world-famous Hal Bullard," announced Bear Winston. "Professor Bullard is the Professor of Oceanography at the University of Maine and is a former Naval Officer. Some of you, however, will recognize this man as the person who first discovered the sunken remains of the RMS Titanic back in 1985."

The camera panned to Bullard, and he blushingly nodded to the television audience.

"Professor Bullard, we understand that you have some interesting news to share with us!" Winston could not contain his excitement.

"Yes, I do. But before I get to that, let me correct for the record that I alone have discovered nothing. Behind each and every secret that's been coaxed from the ocean floor is a team of hundreds of scientists, sailors, archaeologists, technicians, and sub-mariners, whether from my team or the team of my contemporaries," said a humble Bullard.

"With that clarification, yes, I am proud to announce here today, an NCN exclusive," Bullard looked into the camera and smiled. Looking back at Winston, he professed, "My team and I have been awarded the contract, by the GEG Leadership Council, to locate the Black Earth Migrant Shuttle, located somewhere in the Mariana Trench."

"Wow, you must be excited and honored to be named the Commander of what will likely be the greatest archaeological expedition of all time." Winston was beaming with the announcement.

"That would probably be the understatement of the century. If we find ourselves floating above one of the hundreds of vessels that brought humankind to Earth from another planet, well then, that would make the discovery of the Titanic pale in comparison," said Bullard.

"So, I know the answer to this question, but our audience may not," said Winston. "Has anyone actually ever been to the deepest part of the Mariana Trench?"

"Well, as a matter of fact, yes," smiled Bullard. "Way back in 2012, the well-known writer/producer/director of The Titanic, and a very good friend of mine, James Cameron, spent about three hours in a submersible down there and came back with some incredible footage."

"Hal, tell us what special challenges will make this particular shipwreck much harder and more dangerous to find."

"Well, Bear, since we were just talking about the Titanic, let's use it as an example. The depth of the ocean of Titanic's final resting place is about 12,500 feet, or a little less than two and a half miles. The deepest part of the Mariana Trench is more than 36,200 feet, or just under seven miles deep," explained Bullard.

"Wow, that's deep!"

"To make it easier for your audience to understand, the Mariana Trench is deeper than thirteen Burj Khalifa's stacked on top of each other, or twenty-five Empire State Buildings."

"My goodness," said Bear, "that's hard to imagine."

"Bear, it's not the depth that will be the main issue, it's the pressure of the ocean at that depth. The pressure, measured in pounds per square inch, will be roughly 15,750 psi. It may not be possible to get there at all with a sub big enough to salvage anything," explained Bullard.

"In fact, the manned submersible's we will be using will be five times the size of the one James Cameron squeezed into. That makes it five thousand times more vulnerable to the pressure down there." Bullard was pragmatic.

"Why is that?" asked Bear.

"You see, the atmosphere at the bottom of that part of the ocean is roughly 1100 times denser than on the surface. However, the atmosphere inside of the submersible must be roughly the same as the surface so that a human being can survive."

"I'm following," nodded Bear.

"The dense water at the bottom of the ocean wants nothing more than to inhabit the space inside of the submersible, any submersible with air inside. The more cubic feet inside a submarine, the larger the submarine, the structure will lose integrity when the pressure becomes too great. The weaker the structure, the greater chance something will fail. If any part of the sub's exterior fails at that depth, a sudden and violent chain reaction will cause a catastrophic implosion. It would take less than a millisecond to implode," explained Bullard.

"Wow! That's pretty dramatic!" Winston's brows were raised.

"So, on a happier note, when does the expedition start?"

"We set sail on April 1. It's getting close."

"You're joking, right?" smiled Bear.

Bullard didn't make the April Fool's connection at first, but then both men chuckled a moment later.

Location: Artesia, New Mexico. Home of Carrick and Lola – March 10, 2026 – 2:21 pm MST.

Sitting on the couch, Lola, Carrick, and Erik had just watched the Winston and Bullard interview regarding the upcoming exploratory dive to find the Migration Shuttle.

"Well, that's pretty exciting," thought Lola aloud. Carrick and Erik were quiet, though.

"Maybe not so exciting," she said out loud, hoping to get a reaction from one or both of the men.

"Okay then, I'll just head to the kitchen and clean-up a little." Lola felt awkward and felt the need to leave the room.

With Lola out of the room now, the two men eventually looked over at each other, but words were hard to find. Carrick was likely thinking of his father's downed plane, while Erik was likely melancholy, thinking about the day he downed it after it dropped Lilly off in Roswell.

Carrick spoke first. "You know, it was just a matter of time."

Erik sighed. "I know. Brings it all back, though. She was on that shuttle. My mother, brother, and hundreds of my friends were on that shuttle. I felt like I was on that ship, too."

"I couldn't possibly know how you feel, but I feel for you."

"You think they'll raise it?" Erik was looking out the window when he asked Carrick.

"Raise it? No. It's too big, and it's too deep. Plus, the bacteria would have eaten away at the outer shell. No rust at that depth due to the lack of oxygen, but the bacteria would have weakened the metal significantly," surmised Carrick.

"Not that metal," said Erik.

"What do you mean?" Carrick wasn't exactly surprised.

"The metals we used on the shuttles were twice as light but ten times denser than the strongest metals found on Earth. We compared samples of various iron ore through the millennia, and nothing on Earth came close to those ores found on Zenith."

"I get it, a ship that size had to be as light as possible, or it would simply collapse under its own weight," reasoned Carrick.

"It is what it is," sighed Erik. "I'll likely be dead before they find it anyway."

"Come on, Erik. Don't say that!"

At that moment, Lola flew into view, sprinted across the living room to the front door, opened it, then ran outside into the rain without a jacket or shoes. The massive door was left wide open.

"What the...? Where in the hell is she going?" shouted Carrick.

The two men sprung from the couch and looked out the front door. They saw Lola run across the street and through the Spencer's front yard, then up their front stairs. The two could see very little through the pouring rain until the Spencer's porch light came on. Though it was the middle of the afternoon, the sky was gray, and the rain was heavy. There, in the porch light's yellow wash of rain, the two men could see Lilly's mom, Sarah, standing in the middle of the doorway.

"Something's wrong with Lilly!" Erik's heart began to hurt. He knew something was wrong earlier when she was too sick for their Saturday walk.

Both men quickly made their way across the street and walked in without knocking. Lilly's father, Doug, met them in the living room.

"Doug! What's going on?" asked Carrick. Erik looked on nervously.

"Lilly's got a high fever. It's too high, and she's shaking uncontrollably!" Doug Spencer was beside himself. "We didn't know what to do, so we called Lola."

"How long has she been sick?" asked Carrick.

"Not that long, but her appetite has been off, and we noticed she was losing a little weight."

Erik jumped in, looking panicked. "Yes, I thought the same thing!"

In the back-bedroom, Lola asked Sarah, "What else have you noticed?"

"Ah, ah," Sarah stuttered. "She's been a little restless at night. She's been waking up a little sweaty for the last two weeks."

"Doug, call 911!" Lola yelled from the bedroom.

"Lola, what is it?" cried Sarah. "What's wrong with my baby?"

"What else?" asked Lola, who was checking Lilly's pulse and listening for labored breathing. "What other symptoms does she have?"

"She's been tired and achy for days," cried Sarah.

Lilly's skin was red, and she was acting sluggish as Lola attended to her.

"I'm sorry, Mommy," Lilly touched her mom's hand. "I didn't mean to get sick. I'll get better, I promise!"

Lola lifted Lilly's shirt and rolled her over onto her belly. She observed red spots all over Lilly's lower back and a bruise on her left side.

"Did she have a fall recently?"

"No, no! We saw the bruise too, but she said she didn't fall! The rash is new." Sarah turned pale. "What is it, Lola?! What's wrong with Lilly?" she said, stricken with fear.

Doug heard Sarah crying and raced into the room. "How is she, Lola?"

"Her temperature is at 104.5°F. We need to cool her down fast! Is the ambulance on the way?" Lola remained calm and collected but feared the worst, cancer.

"Yes, yes, they're on their way!" Doug was panicked.

"Sarah, run a lukewarm bath. Quickly!" instructed Lola. "Doug, bring me juice with crushed ice in it."

"Lola, should we rub her down with alcohol?" asked Sarah.

"No, never! That will lower her temperature too fast and can lead to alcohol poisoning."

Minutes later, the sirens could be heard as they neared the house.

Location: Artesia General Hospital – Sixty minutes later.

Lola had just finished briefing the Spencers in Consultation Room 1B, just off the expansive waiting area. She then made her way over to Carrick and Erik, standing near a window opposite the consultation room. Erik was pacing in a mini-circle, and Carrick had his arms folded, looking as if he was cold.

"Lola! What is it?" Carrick spoke softly as he saw his wife approaching him and Erik.

Lola made her way over to the men and looked oddly nervous for a doctor getting ready to share a diagnosis.

Before Lola spoke, she looked at Erik, then Carrick, then back to Erik. "Erik, would you mind giving me a moment alone with Carrick, please?" It was hard for Lola to look straight into his eyes.

"I would mind that very much. Thank you." Erik spoke quietly but forcefully.

"Lola, what is it? What's wrong with Lilly?" asked a downtrodden Carrick. "Erik can stay."

"Ok," conceded Lola. "It's early, and more tests will need to be run, but all of her symptoms point to Leukemia."

Carrick's reaction was visceral. He looked as if he was going to be sick.

Erik looked confused. He first looked at Lola and then at Carrick. "What is Leukemia?"

Carrick was afraid to explain the answer when Lola spoke up.

"Erik, childhood Leukemia has a very high survival rate," Lola calmly explained.

"Survival rate?" Erik was frantic now. His face was white-washed. "You mean she could die?"

"Shhhh!" Lola tried to calm Erik's fear while trying not to upset others in the waiting area. "Erik, many forms of Leukemia can, of course, be deadly, but many types can be treated, and within five years or so, can even be cured."

Erik's face went blank. He put his head down and walked to the window, and looked out at the falling rain.

"Lola, please tell me you can save her!" whispered Carrick. "Erik has maybe a year left to live. Please tell me you can save her." Carrick was somber.

"Carrick, listen to me. We need to pray to God that Lilly has acute lymphoblastic Leukemia and not acute myelogenous. If it's the latter, her chances of survival drop considerably," Lola warned cautiously.

"How low"? Carrick was afraid of the answer.

"Sixty percent," Lola paused, "maybe more."

Carrick's exhale was long.

"Let me get back in there, Carrick. I'll be late tonight, don't wait up for me." The two hugged, and Lola was off. She re-joined the Spencer's while Carrick walked over to Erik.

"Hey," said Carrick, placing his hand on Erik's left shoulder. Erik didn't budge.

"Listen, Lola knows what she's doing. She's the head of the Pediatrics Department here. She can help."

Erik turned slowly toward Carrick. "What is Leukemia?"

"Carrick, do you remember on Zenith when I asked you if you'd ever heard of cancer?"

"I do."

"Do you remember what you told me?"

"I told you that I'd never heard of it," recalled Erik.

"Lilly has cancer, Erik. She will get the best treatment possible, and she will likely survive it, but" Carrick took a deep breath and then exhaled, "it could take years to cure her."

"Years?" Erik's eyes welled with tears. "I don't have years!"

"I'm sorry, Erik." Carrick attempted to hug him, but he shrugged him off and looked back toward the rain.

Location: The back-left bedroom of Erik's tiny house – Two hours later.

"It's my fault," said Erik.

"Don't be ridiculous!" said Carrick, sitting on the twin bed opposite of Erik's. "You can't give or catch Leukemia. You had nothing to do with her getting sick."

"I think it's because we walked in the rain three weeks ago. She didn't have her jacket on." Erik was riddled with guilt.

"Erik, that's not how it works!"

"It's my fault! She's not going to make it!" Erik just sat on the bunk, holding a stuffed bunny rabbit. It was Lilly's favorite stuffed animal when she was a toddler, but she wanted Erik to have it.

"She's only six years old! She's too young to die," mumbled Erik.

Carrick slid to the edge of his bed and assured Erik. "She's not going to die! She's strong, and Lola will make sure she gets the best care."

"We will never take another walk." A tear ran from Erik's eye as he clenched the stuffed animal tighter.

"You will," reassured Carrick. "Maybe not around our block anymore. Maybe at the hospital. You'll walk with her again," promised Carrick.

Location: Washington D.C. NCN National Cable News Network Studios, The Situation Center with Bear Winston – April 1, 2026 – 6:01 pm EST.

"Welcome to The Situation Center. I'm your host, Bear Winston. My friends, today will likely be one of the most significant days in our shared human history," Winston was sober. "Today, we continue our search for our origins here on Earth. Not since the discovery of the 4000-year-old ancient city of Troy, near the Northwest coast of Turkey in 1870, have human beings uncovered the roots of our existence like we conceivably will today."

"If you recall the history of Troy, until it was discovered by the English expatriate Frank Calvert in 1870, it was long since thought to be a mythical city," explained Winston. "Well, many people on Earth still believe that Black Earth is a myth, with many believing that it is simply a hoax or fake news. Today, however, those conspiracy theorists will likely be silenced."

"Today, explorers and marine archaeologists on the other side of the world will travel to the abyss in an attempt to discover the only known ship to have carried humans from Black Earth. The migrant shuttle used back in 1947 is purportedly sitting at the bottom of the

Mariana Trench, the deepest part of any of Earth's oceans," explained Winston. "Perhaps they'll find the Zenithian 'Troy?'"

The camera panned out to show a large graphic of the rotating planet Earth behind and to the right of Winston. The image of Earth stopped rotating and zoomed in on the South Pacific ocean, revealing Guam's small U.S. territory, the largest of the Mariana Islands chain.

"In just a few minutes, I will be joined by deep-sea explorer Hal Bullard," announced Bear Winston. "Bullard, if you recall, discovered the final resting place of the Titanic back in 1985. Bullard is also the Professor of Oceanography at the University of Maine."

Moments later, Winston was live with Bullard via satellite from Guam. "I am now joined by Professor Bullard. Professor Bullard, welcome to the show, and thank you for allowing us to speak with you before your historic trek to the bottom of Earth's deepest ocean. I know it's very early for you. I see that it's still dark there," acknowledged Winston.

"Bear, thanks for having me back on. I think we last spoke about three weeks ago, but a lot has happened since then." Bullard held a microphone and spoke loudly while trying to hold his tiny earpiece in place as the wind swirled around him.

"Tell us more about what you've been doing for the last few weeks to prepare for today's historic dive," encouraged Winston.

"Well, just three days ago, we completed our mock dives using weighted materials in place of actual humans on the submersible. We feel highly confident in the vessel." Wind whistled in the mic.

"Did you ever come up with a name for the new submarine that will carry you and four others to the bottom of the trench?" Winston's excitement and curiosity were palpable.

After the three-second time delay, a smile came over the face of Bullard. "Yes! Yes, we did, Bear! As you and I discussed privately, the team and I went back and forth with several names, but I finally won over the group with my choice," yelled Bullard.

"Well, this is Breaking News!" Winston smiled. "By all means, please tell our worldwide audience the name you settled on?" Bear encouraged Bullard.

"The name of the vessel will now and forever be known as 'Finding Zenith,'" revealed a now beaming Bullard, unable to contain himself. "It's part of the Triton family of submersibles."

"That's an awesome name! How did you come up with it?" inquired Winston.

"Sure, yeah, it was quite simple and very appropriate. As you know, Bear, Black Earth is actually called Zenith according to its former residents, Doctors Carrick Michaels, and Erik Erickson. I thought that if we were able to find the very migrant shuttle that brought Zenith's final population to Earth, then we'd be finding a piece of the actual planet itself," explained Bullard.

"I am beyond excited and nervous at what we are about to do!" Bullard sighed, brows up, then exhaled heavily.

"Wow! This will be a truly historic day!" offered Winston.

"Well, it could take days, even weeks to locate the shuttle, and that's if we're fortunate enough to do so." Bullard was careful to manage the expectations of Winston and his international audience.

"Well, we're all pulling for you. Be safe and be lucky, Professor Bullard. The world will be rooting for you and your team."

"Thank you, Bear!"

The interview ended with Bullard looking anxious and Winston excited, in anticipation of near-future updates on the progress of the search for the Zenithian Migration Shuttle.

The camera panned outward from where Bullard was standing and captured the thirty-six-foot, thirteen-ton submersible that would make history very shortly.

"Stay tuned," exclaimed Bear. "We'll be right back with another special guest who can provide more detail to what the sub-mariners will be facing as they slowly descend the nearly two hours to the bottom of the Mariana Trench. From there, it could take days to get us closer to our origins. We'll be right back!"

Location: Artesia, New Mexico. Home of Carrick and Lola Michaels – April 1, 2026 – 4:23 pm MST.

Carrick turned off the T.V. after watching the NCN broadcast with Erik, and looked anxious. Erik seemed to have something else on his mind.

"I'm going to head over to my house, I have a project I'm working on. Please call me when Lola gets home. I want to see how Lilly's doing." Erik's demeanor was inward.

"You okay?" Carrick seemed concerned.

"Yeah, just thinking about Lilly, that's all."

"What's the project you're working on?"

"Nothing. I'm just keeping a little journal. I want to update it with the day's events," said Erik, almost cryptically.

"Okay then, I'll call you when Lola gets home."

Erik walked out the door without another word and without eye contact. Carrick was sad and nervous, and wasn't sure if Erik's mood was because of Lilly, the dive to the migrant shuttle, his health, or all of it. Carrick didn't know, and he didn't know how to get the answer from Erik, who had seemed so distant and detached as of late. Carrick was worried.

Chapter 7 – The Alien

Location: The back-left bedroom of Erik's house, thirty minutes later.

Erik laid in his bunk, writing in a leather-bound journal. The journal was six by nine inches in size, and the leather was black.

Writing intently, Erik looked up from time to time, lost in thought, almost appearing to search his memory. He was looking more withered as if his time on Home was coming to an end.

There, standing at the bedroom door, was Carrick. He had shown up unannounced and was wanting to make sure that Erik was okay.

"You okay, Erik?" Carrick's voice was low so as not to alarm his grandfather.

"What the heck! Are you trying to give me a heart attack?" Erik quickly stashed the journal under his pillow, hoping to conceal from Carrick what he was doing. "How long have you been standing there?"

"Sorry, Grandpa, I didn't mean to startle you. I just got here. I wanted to make sure you were okay." Carrick saw Erik stash the little black, what appeared to be a book, under his pillow.

"Hey, listen, I wanted to talk with you before Lola got home."

"What is it?"

"Look, there's been a lot going on, and everyone is stressed. You seem to be handling everything okay, but I wanted to ask you how you were feeling. Not just your physical health, but how you're feeling emotionally, too?"

"Carrick, I'm fine..."

Carrick cut off Erik sharply. "Grandpa, please don't lie to me. This is important. I know that you're hurting."

Erik got up from the bed and walked to the window. There, he gazed into the partly cloudy sky. A full thirty seconds went by without words before he spoke.

"I miss her, Carrick." Erik's eyes were fixed on the world outside.

"Erik, she'll be fine. It will take lots of time and lots of care, but she'll pull through."

Erik turned to look at Carrick and delivered a half-smile. "I do miss that little girl, but I was actually talking about your grandmother."

Carrick was caught off guard. It had been months since Erik talked of Lilly, and while Carrick wouldn't normally find it unusual, on this occasion, however, it caused him to re-think his perception of Erik's pain.

I don't understand, Carrick thought to himself. How would this impact the way he would try to manage Erik's visible agony.

A few moments later, Erik cleared his throat. "Ahem! You okay there, son?"

"What? Yeah. I'm fine." Carrick played off his internal confusion.

"Carrick, I need some time to myself. Please give me a little privacy and just call me when Lola gets home later."

Carrick's feelings were hurt, but he would honor his grandfather's wishes.

Now alone again, Erik continued lining the pages of his journal with details of his coaxed memories. Much like The History Library, Erik was recording things he knew in case there came a day in which his memory died, a day in which he died. He knew it would be soon.

On Zenith, Erik spent his days gathering information from The History Library. Now he would spend his time sharing it, albeit on the pages of his black journal.

Back at home now, Carrick picked up his phone from the kitchen counter and saw that he had missed several calls from Lola. He also noticed he had new texts and voicemails. Before he could read the texts, the doorbell rang. Moments later, Carrick opened the front door to find Doug and Sarah Spencer standing there. While Sarah avoided eye contact with Carrick, Doug asked if Erik was with him?

Carrick responded, "No, why?"

"May we come in then?" asked Lilly's father.

Moments later, the three were all seated in the living room, and all looked very uncomfortable with the pending conversation. Carrick was sure whatever they had to say would be upsetting, in large part because he was unable to capture Sarah's gaze.

"Carrick, you know how much we love you and Lola and how much Lilly loves Erik, right?"

"What's this about?" Carrick slid up to the edge of his seat, uneasy with what would come next from the Spencers.

"We don't want Erik around Lilly anymore!" Sarah finally spoke, looking Carrick straight in the eye. Doug echoed Sarah's words by nodding in support of his wife.

"What are you talking about? Why?" Carrick was shaken and confused.

The Spencers hesitated in their response; this allowed Carrick to continue.

"My God, I'm going to be sick! You think Lilly's diagnosis is due to her being around Erik?" Dismay befell Carrick's face.

"Carrick, you have to understand..." Doug tried to explain before being cut-off by Carrick.

"You can't catch Leukemia, Doug! This is insane! That man loves your daughter. We all do. We're all like family!" Carrick couldn't grasp what was happening. Everything was going straight to hell and seemed destined to end poorly for everyone involved.

Doug was excusatory, but Sarah was firm. "You keep him away from our daughter when and if she comes home," she said in a threatening manner. "He's an alien!" she cried, then got up and stormed out the door.

"An Alien?" Carrick sat speechless, shaking his head while looking down.

"Carrick, listen. There's still so much we don't know about Black Earth. For all we know, Erik could be radioactive..."

"That's insane!" Carrick yelled and launched himself to his feet. "I'd be dead by now! I spent thirteen months there and suffered next to no radiation poisoning."

Doug shook his head. He bore a look that revealed that he actually agreed with Carrick but was simply conveying the wishes of his wife, Sarah.

"Doug, let me explain something to you," offered Carrick. "This will kill Erik. This will end him."

Doug tried to look empathetic. "We're only worried about Lilly. We can't concern ourselves with how this might impact Erik. Our little girl has cancer and needs to get better," he pleaded.

"Doug..." Carrick said before being politely cut off.

Doug Spencer stood and said, "Carrick, please respect our wishes."

Carrick nodded. "Fine. Please see yourself out."

With both of the Spencers gone, Carrick was panicked. He didn't know how he would break the news to Erik. He knew he had some time as Lilly would be hospitalized for the foreseeable future while receiving chemotherapy treatments, but at some point, he would have to break his grandfather's heart.

Carrick returned to the kitchen as his cellphone began to ring. It was Lola again.

Carrick swiped right. "They just left," he said into the phone, knowing why Lola was calling.

"Shit," Lola could be heard through Carrick's phone.

Location: The kitchen of Carrick and Lola's house - Same day, three hours later.

"Erik, nice job, you killed that spaghetti! I am so glad you got your appetite back," Carrick was impressed.

"Killed the spaghetti? I don't know what that means, but it was delicious," Erik directed his words at Lola.

"She meant you ate all of it really fast..." Carrick was cut short.

"I know what she meant, Carrick. I was just joking around with her," Erik smiled.

Carrick looked thrilled, figuratively tipping his hat at Erik. "I see you got your sense of humor back, too, huh?"

"Yeah-yeah,...what's for dessert?" Erik was now up and heading for the pantry.

"Cool your jets, Grandpa!" smiled Lola. "I picked up an Oreo pie on the way home, but it needs to defrost first. Why don't you boys head into the living room, and I'll call you when it's ready," Lola smiled.

Chapter 8 - The Chinese Eclipse

Location: Outskirts of Beijing, China. Special Operations Command Center, Sector 3, Room 223 – April 3, 2026 – 9:00 am GMT +8.

Speaking in Mandarin, Minister Kenong extended his arms, palms up, and said, "Welcome back, gentlemen!" His gesture was disingenuous, and the three assassins from the SHA organization, whom he'd last met with on March 17, knew it.

In the small meeting room, four armed bodyguards accompanied the Minister of State Security. Kenong was acutely aware that his countryman and foe, Colonel Vadik Lei, did not like him, to put it mildly. He would never place himself in a room where he would be at risk to the murderous whims of mercenaries who held great disdain for high-ranking political figures.

"Minister, I see you brought a small army to our meeting in which you are uncharacteristically on time for," said Vadik Lei, also speaking in Mandarin. Lei was purposely sarcastic as he smiled at his superior, pointing out that Kenong was late for their prior meeting.

Now speaking in English, "Yes, Spider Lei, I see you brought your charm with you again. So good to see you and your goons. Gentlemen," Kenong looked at the two men that accompanied Lei, nodded, and smiled.

"So, what surprises do you have for us today, my brave Minister?" The contempt and lack of respect were thick coming from The Spider.

"Ah, yes, the reason we are here today," continued Kenong. "Today, my countrymen, we execute step two of our master plan. When we last met, a little more than three weeks ago, we discussed the initial phases of a plan that would make China the only superpower on Earth. And today, we continue."

"I am pleased to tell you of the specific xì jié of your individual missions. While individual, the details of your missions will all result in the inevitable success of our master plan," pronounced Kenong.

"I must be transparent with you, though," Kenong was frank. "For one, and perhaps two of you," he paused and smiled, "this will be a one-way journey, I'm afraid."

The assassins turned to look at each other, showing little to no emotion.

Minister Kenong purposely switched back to speaking Mandarin, "In fact, if you fail your mission, not just one, but all of you will die at the hands of men that I will employ to kill you." Kenong laughed softly as he looked over each shoulder at the security detail behind him. He then turned back at the SHA assassins, at which point the security guards looked at each other, all unaware of what their boss's intentions were.

"Please, do tell us more, Minister," uttered Lei, now speaking in English. In his mind, he knew that he and his SHA associates could easily dispatch with Kenong and his bodyguards if things went sideways.

"It would be my pleasure," conceded Kenong. "Soldier Kai Chang, your field of expertise is in explosives. You, my friend, will begin training as a taikonaut and shall be aboard the American ship that will launch in December. *A ship that will never arrive at its destination,* thought Kenong to himself.

Kai Chang looked mildly aroused by this revelation. He slowly stood and bowed at the minister and said, "In service to my country, I shall prepare, execute, and jiao fù."

Kenong then donned his needed reading glasses and flipped through the documents in his hands. "Soldier Zhang Hui, your specialty is cyber-infiltration, along with code creation and manipulation. Your job will be to hi-jack the American satellite Interlink Communication Corridor to Black Earth. Once in, you will write code that will be invisible to the Americans. Your successful efforts will allow us to listen to and record all transmissions to and from Black Earth. It will also allow us to corrupt and jam their data and communication channels."

Kenong flipped through more papers in his hands. "It says here that you will start training in the Southern City of Guiyang in four weeks.

There, you will become an expert in the many uses of our great Five-hundred-meter Aperture Spherical Telescope, called FAST. The world thinks FAST is simply a radio telescope and astronomical observatory," the minister let out a sinister laugh, "but it can do so much more, my fellow countrymen."

The proud SHA assassin Hui stood slowly, tapped his heels together, and bowed his head. "It would be my great pleasure to prepare, execute, and jiao fù."

Spider Lei knew that the minister was saving his mission details for last in an effort to heighten his curiosity. He knew that his mission would likely be his final one, knowing that Kenong would ensure that he'd never return to ultimately fulfill his fantasy of killing the pompous Minister or any other lackey that got in his way. If his mission ended with his own death, he would make special arrangements to have the minister killed, preferably in front of his wife and children.

"Ah, Colonel Vadik Lei..." Kenong removed his reading glasses and tossed them onto the table. "You Colonel, you too, will begin taikonaut training."

The Spider's left brow rose almost imperceptibly. He stood and said, "I shall prepare, execute, and deliver."

"You, Spider Lei, will be on a Chinese Spaceship called Zhōngguó shí."

"The Chinese Eclipse," nodded Spider Lei. "Very clever, Minister. Surely that name was not your idea. For you do not appear to be either creative or clever to me."

Kenong launched a dismissive grin. "You are ever the clever one with your insubordinate jokes. You will learn one day, 'Black Spider,' as I'm sure you will ultimately become known as." Kenong chose not to acknowledge the despised Vadik Lei with eye contact.

"What will my mission be?" asked Lei.

"You will protect our contingent of scientists, computer, and medical experts," offered Kenong.

"Protection from the American counterparts to our scientific experts?" questioned Lei. Lei thought that killing innocent civilians wasn't exactly a difficult job.

"Only if your comrade, Kai Chang, fails at his assignment," Kenong wore a sly grin.

Chang and Lei looked at each other, somewhat perplexed. "Excuse me, Minister Kenong, what exactly will my job be once I get to Black Earth?"

"Soldier Chang, if the American spaceship that you're on ever makes it to Black Earth, then you will have failed in your assignment." Kenong again wore a grin. "I understand that you do not have any known family. Would I be correct in that assertion, Agent Chang?"

"Yes, sir. That is correct, sir. But why...?" Kai Chang looked a little confused.

"Perhaps you are the dumb one between the three of you, Soldier Chang. You will get all of your questions answered very soon," Kenong was dismissive.

"Sabotage," uttered The Spider. "Your job is sabotage, comrade Chang. Your job will be to bring down the American spaceship."

"Remotely?" questioned Chang, now turning to Minister Kenong with a mild look of fear.

"Again, gentlemen, your training will begin very soon. Until then, stay healthy and well. We will meet in this very office again many times in the coming days, weeks, and months." Kenong rose from his chair, indicating to his security detail that it was time to leave.

"Minister Kenong, shall I personally kill your security detail now, sir?" asked Lei with a smile.

"Why would you attempt to do that, Black Spider Lei?" mused Kenong.

"The four of them now hold all of the country's top secrets, Minister. Do you really place that much trust in these feeble-minded thugs?" Lei was again insubordinate.

"Perhaps they are related to you, Spider, as you too are feeble," Kenong smirked. "These men do not speak English, you bèn buffoon!"

The three SHA Agents remained seated until the others had left the room.

"Colonel Lei, sir. What are we to make of today's revelations, sir?" said Agent Kai Chang with a curious Agent Zhang Hui leaning in.

"Gentlemen, my guess is that each of our missions will ultimately lead to our demise, whether we find individual success or failure. We will ultimately give our lives for our country," concluded Spider Lei.

"But sir...," pleaded a confused Hui before being cut off.

"Tóngzhìmen! When we joined the Strategic Huyou Agency, we pledged our oath of allegiance and committed our very lives to further our country's strategic goals. Again, I say Comrades! If we die in an effort to fulfill the goals of The Ministry of State Security, or President Xí Shèng-Xióng himself...," Lei looked at his brothers in blood, "then we die."

Agents Hui and Chang clenched their lips, looked down, then at each other, and reluctantly chorused, "Die, we shall!"

Colonel Vadik Lei, The Spider, acknowledged his comrades and said, "Brothers, if we shall die, so then shall the Minister of State Security." Lei was resolute.

Location: Beijing China, Macikou Area Residential District. Home of The Spider – April 3, 2026, 12 hours later.

Vadik Lei stared into the mirror above his bathroom sink. It was there that his planning would begin.

No matter the outcome of his mission at hand, Vadik knew that the overly ambitious Kenong would ensure his death. No one would miss him. No one would know he was gone. Perhaps his cat would know of his absence, but then again, *cats are good at surviving and fending for themselves*, he thought, as the short-haired, black cat lay between his feet.

Lei removed a razor from behind the mirror and carefully carved the Chinese symbol for 'bao fù' into his left bicep. Translation, 'revenge.' After dousing the bloody wound with alcohol, he carefully wrapped it to prevent infection. From there, he began his nightly training regimen and meditation.

Lei would set in motion a plan for the murder of his arrogant superior, Minister Li Kenong. His own death, along with that of the Minister's, would be a righteous conclusion to the life of a less than honorable military career, one that included the senseless killing of many innocent and not so innocent men, women, and children. All but a few, in the service to his country and its ruthless leaders.

For more than twenty years, Lei had done what he was told. His obedience, loyalty, and lack of honor are the legacy he would leave behind. "But to whom?" he wondered aloud, again looking in the mirror. The cat, still at his feet? The love he never knew? The children he never had? Or, his SHA comrades, who themselves, led a similar life? Again, resolute, The Spider would carry out his mission and die alone with the conscious that he'd buried long before.

Chapter 9 – The Abyss

Location: South Pacific Ocean, 250 miles South by Southwest of Guam. The Command Center, below deck aboard the Iron Aegaeon search and recovery vessel – April 26, 2026 – 11:36 am GMT +10, Guam local time.

The Iron Aegaeon was a search and recovery vessel in operation since 2024. The highly advanced ship belonged to the Canadian-based Gweniece Offshore company. The same company that helped to locate and salvage the wreck of the SS Edmond Fitzgerald, along with dozens of other shipwrecks. The Fitzgerald was an American Oil Freighter that went down in Lake Superior in November of 1975. The ship's bell was finally recovered in July of 1995 by Gweniece dive teams, at a depth of 530 feet.

The $250 million Iron Aegaeon was more than 240 feet in length and weighed more than 9,500 tons empty. When fully equipped with fuel, water, rations, a crew of sixteen, a rescue helicopter, and two Autonomous Underwater Vehicles, the ship weighed more than 10,500 tons. It also included two hard shell-covered lifeboats. The ship had been leased to the GEG Leadership Council six months prior.

The ship had the most advanced underwater technology of any such vessel in the world. Its sonar system, including the sonar on the two submersible AUVs, cost more than $8 million and was more advanced than the sonar used in the U.S. Navy Virginia Submarine Class vessels. Its crew compartments were spacious and comfortable, and its VIP cabins had queen size beds with their own bathrooms. The galley could seat twelve people at a time, and the ship's cook was educated at the New England Culinary Institute, one of the top culinary schools in the world. No expense was spared for such a historic endeavor.

Around the Command Center, pings could be heard.

The ship's two AUVs had been mapping a small portion of the Mariana Trench for the last twenty-six days. They moved in a crisscrossing fashion and had now begun to yield results. In the previous two days, objects inconsistent with the ocean floor had been detected, but nothing larger than a small aircraft.

In the sizeable Command Center, which was an oversized sonar room, sat Sonar Technician Brad Stevens, Captain of the Ship, Hal Bullard, and co-Captain, Antonio Grangeia Carvalho. Carvalho, a Portuguese citizen living in Toronto, was the most accomplished ship Captain the Gweniece Offshore company had to offer.

In addition to borrowing Captain Carvalho from Gweniece, the GEG had also contracted scientists and oceanographers from around the world, who had previously been part of the Seabed 2030 project, which began mapping the world's oceans way back in 2017.

"What are we looking at, Brad?" Bullard leaned in close as Stevens' face was just inches from the sonar screen in the middle of the room.

"It's big, whatever it is! It can't be the shuttle, though. That thing is as big as the Louisiana Superdome,' Stevens said while keeping his eyes fixed on the screen.

"What could it be?" said Carvalho.

"It's manmade, whatever it is," offered Stevens. "Here, let me switch the feed to the main screen."

The three men pivoted and walked the five or so feet to the Command Center's main wall.

The main screen was 50" wide and was flanked by three smaller 30" screens on each side. Each monitor could be programmed to show different parts of the ship's interior and exterior, as well as monitor all underwater activity.

"Look here," said Brad. "This white outline appears to be a rectangle, and according to my quick calculations, could be a large ship, roughly the size of an aircraft carrier."

"Geez, that is big!" Bullard was now seeing what Stevens' eyes were locked onto. "Let's go ahead and mark that location to see if any World War II vessels made their way down to that general area." Bullard removed his hat and ran his fingers through his hair. "It reminds me a little of what we saw on the sonar before finding the Titanic."

"The size of this craft will help us to determine when we finally find the migrant shuttle. Its breadth will be unmistakable on the sonar," added Stevens.

After two more hours of sonar scans of the bottom of the trench, Bullard and Carvalho excused themselves from the tedious task of listening, watching, and waiting.

"Okay, Brad, you radio us if you find anything else that looks promising. We'll be in the galley above. The wives are cooking up some lunch. I'll have one of the guys bring you a plate." Bullard stretched his arms and legs then disappeared through the water-tight door with Carvalho following close behind.

In the previous twenty-six days, the team on the Iron Aegaeon had been gathering bathymetric data of the ocean floor, more than 36,000 feet below. It had mapped more than 4000 square miles to date, and while the Mariana Trench was more than 78,956 square miles, the Aegaeon was only focused on an area that was roughly 4,600 square miles in size. The longitude and latitude provided by Dr. Erik Erickson were used as a starting point, but mapping an ocean floor the depth of the Mariana Trench was far more difficult than mapping shallower waters, as it took longer to descend and ascend the depths of that part of the ocean.

Though sound travels faster in dense mediums like water, water can bend sound. The water pressure that deep can wreak havoc on the multi-beam echo sounders on the autonomous underwater vehicles.

Location: The Command Center on the Iron Aegaeon – April 26, 2026 – 11:14 pm GMT +10, Guam local time.

Brad Stevens was a little over three hours into his on-again, off-again, eight-hour shift when he'd fallen asleep at the control desk in the sonar room, known to all on board as the Command Center.

A steady ping awoke Stevens. After rubbing away the sleep from his eyes, he didn't notice anything of significance on his monitor from UAV1, yet the pinging persisted. Scratching his head for a moment, he thought to switch to the sonar feed from the UAV2. To his surprise, he saw what appeared to be a fuzzy white screen. Adjusting several settings on the control desk, Stevens was unsure why the screen was completely white.

"Okay, let's see here. Let's retract the visual sonar field on UAV2 and pan out a little," he instructed himself aloud.

Turning the dial counterclockwise 360°, nothing appeared to change on his screen. Turning it another 360°, Stevens' breath was taken away.

"Oh, my God!" His hand now covering his mouth, his eyes flew open wide. Temporarily shocked, Stevens didn't quite know what to do or say. He was staring at what looked like a giant white circle protruding out of the abyss. When it finally dawned on him what he was seeing, he immediately started laughing like a little kid. "Where's the phone?! Where's the phone?!" he said excitedly, momentarily forgetting where the ship's phone receiver was stationed.

"Get Bullard! Get Bullard!" he shouted to those on the ship's deck. "Get everybody!" he shouted into the phone. "We found it! We found it! It's huge! We found the shuttle!"

Co-Captain Carvalho was at the helm when a GVA (General Vessel Assistant) quickly handed him the phone. All he could hear was inaudible commotion until he heard the unmistakable words, "We found the shuttle!"

"We'll be right there!" yelled Carvalho. He quickly dialed the Captain's suite where Bullard and his wife were just settling in for the evening.

"Hello," answered Bullard, sitting on the left side of the bed, wearing only pajama bottoms.

"We found it, Hal! We found it!" I'm heading to the Command Center now. Get there as quickly as you can!" shouted Carvalho.

Bullard sprang from the bed, still holding the phone receiver, and shouted, "We found it, JuJu! We found it!" Bullard's wife June raced around the bed and gave her husband of forty years a big hug.

"Oh, Honey! I'm so proud of you!"

"I have to get down there!"

"Go, Honey! Go!" June cheered.

Twenty minutes later, Bullard was joined in the Command Center by several other under-water archaeologists, Stevens, and Carvalho.

Stevens tried frantically to relocate the AUV1 to the exact location of the AUV2 in an effort to get multiple images of the shuttle.

"Okay, so whatta we got, Brad?" Bullard was still in his pajama bottoms and was wearing a Black Earth t-shirt.

The group was huddled around the console, staring at the seven monitors. The large center one and two of the smaller left side monitors were a blurry white; the others were filled with random blue, red, green, and yellow lines that illustrated the contours of the ocean floor, valleys, mountains, and crevasses.

"Okay, so at 11:14, we picked up a steady pulse from AUV1...all I saw is what we're looking at on monitors 3, 5, 6, and 7. When I switched over to AUV2, I saw this." Stevens indicated to the group the white blur on monitors 1, 2, and 4.

"I'm still not sure what we're looking at, Brad," Bullard was slightly confused.

"Here. Look. This is the AUV2 scanning from 35,000 feet to this point right here." Stevens pointed to a sector of the ocean numbered 365.257. "Watch this!" he said. He then placed his right hand on the zoom dial and rotated it counter-clockwise 360°.

The image on the large screen was a perfect white circle surrounded by the black abyss. The group was shocked! Jaws were on the floor. Brad Stevens just sat back and took in the reaction of those in the room. He was glowing and enjoying the same happiness he had felt just thirty minutes earlier.

Once the group realized what they were looking at, they erupted in tears, laughter, and joy. All exchanged hugs.

"Brad, you did it! You found it, Buddy!" Bullard said as he squeezed Brad's shoulders and then hugged him.

"We did it! We all did it!" shouted an elated Stevens.

Once emotions died down, the group sat around a rectangle table against the side wall opposite the watertight door.

"Okay, let's work out the details of tomorrow's dive," Bullard was collected.

"Captain, what's the weather looking like tomorrow?" Bullard asked Captain Antonio Carvalho. Calling him 'Captain' was a show of respect.

"With all due respect Captain Bullard, you're the Captain of the ship, sir."

"Not anymore, Antonio! I just became part of the dive team!" Bullard wore a smile from ear to ear.

Carvalho was honored to be named the Captain on record for such an historic mission. A mission, that if successful, would validate claims that such a shuttle actually existed, putting an end to the speculation that a giant lie was being perpetuated onto the world regarding Black Earth and the very origins of human beings on Earth itself.

"Are you sure, Hal?" Carvalho was humbled.

"You deserve to be in the history books. I'll make history when we dive tomorrow." Bullard was filled with anticipation.

"Sorry, Hal, we won't be diving tomorrow," said Carvalho.

"No? What's the forecast looking like?" Bullard looked disappointed.

"The big front we've been watching is definitely coming our way. No one's going to want to be at sea when it hits. It shouldn't last more than a day or so, though, but we'll have to start heading back to Guam in the morning. We'll need to sit this one out on land, I'm afraid."

"And so it shall be," smiled Bullard. "And so it shall be."

"We're all gonna sleep good tonight, that's for sure!" Brad Stevens was still glowing.

Location: Apra Harbor, Guam. Naval Base Guam – Monday, April 27, 2026 – 4:27 pm GMT +10, Guam local time.

The rain pelted the metal roof of base camp headquarters for the 'Finding Zenith' mission crew. The team had been back on land for several hours now, and after showers and a hearty meal, the heads of each mission department were in attendance. The leadership team included dive team Captain Frank Folgers, Hal Bullard, Ship's Captain Antonio Carvalho, Audio/Video Specialist Helena Sequeira, and Sonar Chief Bradley Stevens.

The group sat around the table and discussed a strategy and division of responsibility for each man and woman on the ship. "Nothing can go wrong, people," said Bullard. "The world will be watching. Maybe even little green guys from other planets, too," he joked.

Later that evening – 11:32 pm, Guam local time – 8:32 am, Washington, D.C. Time.

Bullard appeared on the NCN morning news program hosted by Jake Johnson.

"Welcome to the program Captain Bullard," said Johnson. "I understand that you've got some exciting news to share with our viewers."

"Yes, I do, Jake."

Bullard, wearing a navy-blue jumpsuit, with patches down each arm, and his name embroidered on his right chest, could now be seen by millions of curious viewers worldwide.

"To bring our viewers up to speed, we reported last night that you and your team may have discovered the now-famous downed migration shuttle from Black Earth. Are you ready to confirm that news for us today?" Johnson was eager to be the journalist to first air confirmation of the historic find.

"Well, I can't confirm anything more than what appeared on our sonar screens late last night."

"And that is?" prodded Johnson.

"Well, all I can say is that I've never seen anything that looks to be man-made, as big as what we found last night sitting on the bottom of any ocean, and as you know, I've seen lots of downed vessels in my time," smiled Bullard.

"I want to remind our audience that it was you and your team that famously located the Titanic back in 1985," clarified Johnson.

"Yes, and while that would have normally been my crowning achievement, I may have outdone myself this time." Bullard continued to wear his humble smile.

"Can you describe for the viewers at home what you detected some 36,000 feet below the ocean surface?"

"I can!" nodded Bullard. "It was a rather large blip on the sonar. An object that was circular in shape and monstrous in size," he offered.

"Could you give us some perspective?" asked Johnson.

"Jake, if we found the actual shuttle, then it would be the size of a football stadium!"

"Wow! That's big!" reacted Johnson.

"The shuttle is said to have been big enough to house more than thirty-thousand passengers for up to two months. From what we know from Dr. Erik Erickson, the shuttle is 250 feet tall, with a diameter of 680 feet and a circumference of 2,136 feet. It's said to have an interior space of 125 million cubic feet, with five different levels. With each level having a total floor area of 1,345,000 square feet."

"The dimensions you just shared will be hard for our viewers to wrap their heads around...," said Johnson.

"As I mentioned before, Jake, it's the size of a domed football stadium."

"Well, listen, you have a big day scheduled for tomorrow, and it's getting late where you are. Go make some history and report back to us when you do." Jake Johnson smiled earnestly and thanked Bullard for his time.

"Oh, Jake, there is one more piece of news to share," Bullard quickly interjected before Johnson ended the interview.

"What's that?" smiled Johnson, happy to give Bullard more airtime.

"Well, as you know, I was officially the Captain on the mission for this historic find," Bullard was again humble, "but I've surrendered those duties over to the ship's co-Captain Antonio Carvalho. He's now the Captain of the ship."

"Does this mean you'll be directing affairs from the more hospitable confines of Naval Base Guam?"

"No. In fact, I'll be taking on a different role for this mission," revealed Bullard.

"Oh, and what's that?" Johnson wore a look of curiosity.

"I'll be supervising the dive team."

"Isn't that a demotion," Johnson said in jest.

"I'm going down there, Jake!" Bullard looked anxious as he hadn't planned on revealing that bit of information to the public at the start of the interview.

Johnson looked a little surprised. His research leading up to the interview revealed that Hal Bullard hadn't actually joined any of his dive teams in underwater activities in the last twenty years.

"Wow! That's amazing, considering it's been several years since you squeezed into a submersible," remarked Johnson.

"It's true! I'll be eighty-four this summer. I just want to see it with my own eyes up close."

"Well, be careful, my friend! God speed and Vaya con Dios!" Johnson wished Bullard well and told him to 'Go with God' in Spanish.

"Will do, Jake!"

Location: Naval Base Guam. Basecamp barracks for the Iron Aegaeon team. Thirty minutes later.

"What in the hell are you thinking?!" Bullard's wife, June, screamed at him as he walked through the door of their private quarters.

Bullard had finished his interview on NCN just minutes before and revealed to the world what he had yet to tell his wife. Bullard would make the dangerous journey to the bottom of the Mariana Trench.

"Honey, I'm sorry I didn't tell you earlier." NCN was still on the television playing in the background.

"You're not going down there!" she shouted.

"June, it's my final mission this time, I promise."

"You always say that! That's not the point. You're eighty-three years-old and think that you're still forty. It's too dangerous! You said it yourself."

"I know, I know, but I was just trying to talk myself out of it. The submersible is safe. There've been no issues in all of the trials."

Crying now, June pleaded, "Something bad's going to happen. I can feel it in my heart."

Hal Bullard grabbed his wife and held her in his arms. "Don't be silly. I'll just make the first descent and let the guys take it from there."

June cried, "I won't be there! I won't be on that ship!"

"June. Honey. This is bigger than anything I've ever done. It dwarfs the Titanic! This will be my legacy. This is it!" Bullard pleaded with his wife. "Please come tomorrow, please."

Location: Artesia, New Mexico. Home of Carrick and Lola – April 27, 2026– 8:47 am MST.

Sitting around the kitchen table were Carrick, Erik, and Lola. The three were having breakfast and had just turned on the morning news. The television was tuned into NCN, and the 'Breaking News' banner at the bottom of the T.V. read, 'Zenithian Migration Shuttle' Found.' Lola and Carrick went silent and slowly turned their heads to look at Erik. Erik just stared at the television, expressionless.

"I guess that's it, Grandpa. They found it." Carrick was also a little melancholy, thinking that they might run across his father's plane wreckage.

"I guess so." Erik was stoic. "You know, I think I'm going to skip breakfast. I need to walk."

"Erik, are you sure?" asked a concerned Lola.

Carrick nodded at Lola outside of Erik's view. He tried to convey to her that they should just let him go.

After the door shut, Lola asked, "What do we do? Did you see his face?"

"There's nothing we can do. It was inevitable. It had to happen. Other than Erik, that shuttle is the only connection between Zenith and Earth. Most of the world likely doesn't believe Erik's from Black Earth anyway. This will silence all the doubters,...finally."

"Carrick, the world loves Erik." Lola was confused by Carrick's words.

"They do, but they look at him like he's a circus act instead of the human being that he is."

The two saw Erik pass by the kitchen window.

"When we wake up tomorrow, the world will be a different place. They're going to dive and find it tonight," assumed Carrick.

Back outside, Erik stopped in front of Lilly's house. He knew she wasn't in there, but he pretended she was. He wanted nothing more than to see his little friend. It had been more than six weeks since Erik last saw Little Lilly, and his heart was broken. Little Lilly was his constant reminder of the only woman he'd ever loved, Lillian Koss.

Erik continued on his walk. He had only two goals left on Earth before he joined his Lilly in the cemetery in Suwanee, GA., see Little Lilly again, and finish his journal.

Chapter 10 – Vaya con Dios

Location: Apra Harbor, Guam. Naval Base Guam – Tuesday, April 28, 2026 – 7:01 am GMT +10, Guam local time.

The sunshine and calm winds were good omens for the Iron Aegaeon crew, considering the violent storm that had passed through the day prior. The ship was readied for the second phase of its mission, to dive to the bottom of the Mariana Trench in the *Finding Zenith* submersible.

The thirty-six-foot submersible had only been tested with five humans on board and at a depth of thirty thousand feet. However, it had been tested at more than thirty-six thousand feet with weighted bags of sand in place of humans. The sandbags matched the weight of the original four men and one woman that would make the dive to the migration shuttle when finally found.

The Finding Zenith submersible was so large that it would have to be towed from Apra Harbor to the Iron Aegaeon's dive site. It would be connected to the rear of the ship using a massive davit and umbilical cable.

The thirty-six-foot submersible had been flown to Guam two months earlier via a Lockheed-built C-5 Galaxy, the world's largest cargo plane. The C-5, nicknamed 'Motherload,' was built to transport multiple tanks and helicopters and was bigger than a 747-jumbo jet.

A small group had assembled on the deck of the Iron Aegaeon; they included world-renowned scientists of Microbiology, Geology, Archaeology, and Planetary Science. They were all gathered to hear Hal Bullard speak one last time before the historic dive took place.

"Hey guys and girls, come on over here. This is for you too," Bullard waved over the deckhands, divers, and launch technicians who were working on the aft deck, preparing the submersible for its release.

"Listen, I'm no poet," he said to the twenty or so gathered. "I'm not a particularly good public speaker either, but I have something to say today, and by God, I'm going to say it. Though only five of us will travel to the deepest and darkest part of Earth's ocean today, inside of that vessel," he pointed to the *Finding Zenith* submersible, "will be each and every one of you. Progress is a big thing and cannot be moved by just one. It must rather be moved by the great many who are willing to move it. You know, more than a dozen years ago, I was at the release of James Cameron's Deepsea Challenge 3D documentary when my good friend and journalist, Charlie Rose, said, 'Science is the forward march of civilization.' Today, WE are the forward march of our PAST civilizations, and God willing, we will attempt to merge the two, right here, right now!" The group broke into applause.

"Thank you for your hard work and dedication to this project. Humankind will reap the rewards of what we find here today, my friends." Bullard was now more stoic.

As the legendary underwater archaeologist was shaking hands with some of the group, he spotted his wife. June Bullard appeared in the distance coming from the basecamp barracks. After seeing her, Hal Bullard disembarked to meet her.

After clearing the gangplank, Bullard jogged the thirty yards or so to meet his wife and excitedly asked, "You changed your mind?"

"Sort of," confessed June, "but this isn't about me, though," she paused. "It's not even about you," she took a deep breath before continuing. "This is about all of us, every human being on Earth! This is our history, and finding that shuttle is what the world needs right now."

Bullard smiled and gave his wife a long hug.

"Hal, they picked the right person for the job. But after this, we're going home to Maine."

"You got it, Honey! Now let's go find that shuttle!" Hal Bullard was beaming.

Location: The Philippine Sea, 250 miles South by Southwest of Guam. Latitude 11.3733° N, Longitude 142.5917° E. April 28, 2026 – 12:13 pm GMT +10, Guam local time.

The Command Center was abuzz. At the master console, monitoring the sonar, was Brad Stevens along with another sonar technician. Down the left side of the Command Center was another wall filled with twenty monitors. This was the audio/video station that monitored every camera onboard the Aegaeon, along with the two remote AUVs and the *Finding Zenith* submersible vessel, one hundred and two cameras in total. Helena Sequeira sat between two A/V specialists.

On the center and largest monitor on her console was a live image of the *Finding Zenith* submersible. More like a submarine due to its size, thirty-six feet long, with the beam measuring fifteen feet across. A layperson could see that the crew compartment was situated on the top third of the vessel from the outside, with the bottom two-thirds of the craft taken up by ballast tanks.

The vessel was painted bright orange, with three vertical sets of wavy black and white lines encircling the entire vessel. The colors were a salute to the animated movie *Finding Nemo*, with the name serving partly as the inspiration for naming the *Finding Zenith* craft.

It would be another two and a half hours before the FZ submersible, co-piloted by Hal Bullard, and four other sub-mariners would make it to the final resting place of the migrant shuttle. The team was busy working through all logistical functions to ensure a smooth descent.

Outside the ship, the Descent Prep Team was inside the sub testing all equipment on board the FZ before Bullard, and his team boarded and began their preparations. The descent team was a group of three technicians that would survey and monitor every control setting onboard the thirty-six-foot marvel of engineering. In each of its twelve tests, the FZ submersible passed with flying colors.

"Check!" said Jon Koenig, Descent Team lead. "Camera systems are looking good."

"We're looking good on ballast pressure tanks," barked Keith Collins.

"Testing! Testing! 1-2-3! You read us, Helena?" radioed Koenig.

"Roger that, Jon! We read you just fine here in the Command Center."

In a starboard hallway just below deck, Hal Bullard, in a blue jumpsuit with orange markings, was observed speaking to his wife. "I love you, June. All in, we should resurface in about eight hours from right now. Three hours down, ninety minutes there, then three hours back up. We push off in about thirty minutes." The two embraced.

"I love you, Honey. Please be careful down there. Send back some good pictures." June's smile was a nervous one. "Get a selfie with you and Frank, too."

"Of course," Hal nodded with reassurance. "You know," he paused and sighed, "I wish I could touch the shuttle once we find it. They'll never raise it, and I won't be here when they salvage it. Oh well, just to see it with my own eyes will have to be enough."

Twenty minutes later, Bullard was joined by Frank Folgers, two crewmen, and one crewwoman on the deck of the Iron Aegaeon. There, they shook hands with Captain Carvalho and several other maritime archeologists and historians. A photographer from the Associated Press recorded the moment. Bullard's picture would soon grace nearly every notable magazine cover in the world. After making the historical find, Bullard would be interviewed remotely by Time magazine, NCN News, and nine other major news outlets throughout Europe and Asia.

Minutes later, the team maneuvered themselves into the vessel, one at a time. Inside were five leather chairs that ran single file from front to back. The row of seats had a one-foot clearance on each side so that the team could move about pre-descent. However, by design, as the vessel descended and structure compression began, the twelve-inch clearance on both sides of the chairs would disappear as the ship would contract inward. This would have a profound psychological effect on any layperson or anyone with claustrophobia, but the team was trained and understood the vessel's mechanics. Though Hal Bullard wasn't originally scheduled to be on the dive team, he had spent more than forty hours in a simulator to ensure that he understood what the crew would experience, both physically and psychologically.

Once seated in comfortable leather chairs and headsets donned, a series of checks, double, and triple-checks were conducted by the dive team, along with those back in the Command Center. Pressure sensor controls would be the most important measuring device on board. If the vessel couldn't monitor and react to pressure deficiencies, then instant implosion would occur. Oxygen was the least of the team's concerns. If all oxygen redundancies failed, the team would still have three full hours of breathable air in the cabin, which would be enough to get them back to the surface.

The vessel was built to withstand more than 16,000 lbs. of pressure. At its deepest, the ship would contract three feet in length and nearly two feet in width. This would help the vessel absorb the overwhelming pressure it would face at the bottom of Earth's deepest ocean.

Outside, the davit team, in charge of releasing the vessel from the umbilical dock of the ship, was finishing the final steps when the words rang out, "We have separation!" Every headset on the ship heard the words.

June Bullard was within earshot and, after hearing those words, invoked the Trinity and crossed herself. Touching her forehead, then sternum, then her left and right chest, she looked to the heavens and said, "In the name of the father...you bring him back to me this one last time."

Moments later, headsets around the *Iron Aegaeon* heard the words, "Here we go!" Bullard then anxiously said, "Take it away, Frank!"

Comms were set up so that every technician in the Command Center, along with each of the five sub-mariners on board, could communicate with each other at all times.

"Roger that! Dustin, we have a clean separation and are floating freely," confirmed Folgers.

Dustin Kim was responsible for manning the vessel's vital statistics back in the Command Center. The right-side wall of the Command Center had monitors that tracked and recorded everything the 'FZ' submersible was experiencing. From pressure sensors, more than two-hundred-fifty of them in and outside the sub, oxygen saturation levels, temperature, and fifty other vitals of the craft.

The crew positioning in the sub would have Hal Bullard in the bow, or front of the sub, followed by Frank Folgers, the sub's navigator, who would sit directly behind him. Continuing in single file behind Folgers was the camera operator Buck Lansing, followed by the mission's Physician, John Hagerty, who would measure the team's vitals. Lastly, Ballast Tech, Denise Shaw, was positioned in seat five, back up against the vessel's aft compartment.

There'd be no bathroom breaks on the seven-plus hour mission, so each team member wore a diaper, similar to those worn by astronauts during spaceflight.

Folgers and Hagerty were also with Bullard on the sub-maritime mission that discovered the Galapagos Rift's thermal vents. The three men were all on faculty at the University of Maine as well.

Just ten minutes into the descent, the *Finding Zenith* craft was already at a depth of 2000 feet and was now consumed by the ocean's darkness. At this depth, an interior cabin pressure warning light came on in the darkened crew compartment. Just seconds after lighting up, it went back off again.

The interior was completely dark, with only the green glow of instrument panel lights illuminating the inside of the sub. Everyone was acutely aware of the flashing light but hid any concerns they had from the others.

"Dustin, did you see that?" asked Folgers, communicating to Kim back in the Command Center.

"Negative, Frank. Everything on our end looks normal. What are you seeing down there?" Kim did a cursory scan of his console.

"A pressure sensor reading the left aft porthole popped on for a second and then went off."

Kim quickly ordered the manual stopping of the vessel's descent until the anomaly could be addressed.

"Okay, guys, let's slow it down until we resolve the issue," Kim said into his comms. "Nothing to be worried about. Stand by,"

"Denise, do you see anything happening with the back-left porthole?" Folgers asked.

Shaw turned on a small flashlight and inspected the window but could see nothing out of the ordinary. At that depth in the descent, no vessel contraction had occurred yet.

"Check all display readings, too?" asked Kim, from the Iron Aegaeon's Command Center high above.

Denise Shaw inspected sixteen different gauges that measured pressure and pressure resistance. She also had another twelve dial gauges that measured ballast intake, outtake, and vessel buoyancy. All control readings, some digital, some dial, looked normal to her.

"Everything I'm looking at is normal," she reported back.

"I got nothing either," said Kim.

"Roger that!" copied Folgers.

After five more minutes of diagnostics, Kim reported to the team, "We're clear! Everything's a go."

"Roger that!" copied Frank Folgers. "Manual descent resumed."

The craft had a large window in the front of the ship that was twenty-six inches in diameter and eight inches thick. Down each side of the thirty-six-foot craft were three smaller portholes that were fifteen inches in diameter and five inches thick. Each of the windows was recessed twelve inches into the vessel's exterior shell and could contract inward, up to two inches, when the exterior met its pressure resistance capacity of 17,000 PSI. Above the windows were monitors and control switches, almost resembling an airplane cockpit.

Folgers, occupying the second seat from the front of the sub, also had a window at his feet for navigational purposes. Outside the window was a vertical five-foot tunnel that led to the bottom of the craft pre-compression. After compression, the tunnel would be only four feet in length.

During the descent, the team on the craft and in the Command Center could hear the eerie sounds of compression as the vessel descended to the bottom of the ocean. While the sub's normal compression would yield some noise, these were unsettling but expected sounds, particularly due to the darkness and the mystery of what might be lurking just outside of their portholes. In an effort to conserve power, the craft's exterior spotlights would remain off until it reached a depth of thirty-five thousand feet.

"All ballast tanks are now full, Captain," calmly whispered Denise Shaw in the aft seat.

At a record descent speed of 200 feet per minute, now at the ninety-minute mark, the Finding Zenith submersible was at a depth of more than 18,000 feet. The fear of all on board was masked by darkness and the fact that they were seated in single file and could not see each other's faces. Temperatures outside the craft were now just above the freezing mark, but the team was comfortable in the climate-controlled cabin.

Bullard was deep in thought about the history that was about to be made. He knew before accepting the opportunity to try and locate the migrant shuttle that his legacy was already secured, as he and his team had found the long-lost Titanic back in 1985. That was more than forty years ago, though. Were his insecurity and the need to stay relevant driving his desire? Or, was it his need always to find one more lost treasure? Either way, Bullard was both terrified of the descent and elated at what would await the team. He thought again of his legacy and how the world would remember the aging explorer.

"Okay, surface team, do you read?" radioed Folgers.

"We read you loud and clear," responded Dustin Kim.

At that moment, June Bullard quietly slipped into the Command Center and was quickly absorbed by the fourteen others in the tightly packed room.

"We're showing a depth of 35,000 feet. What are you guys showing on your screens?" asked Folgers.

The twelve-inch clearance on either side of the crew chairs had evaporated down to just two at that point, and for the most part, gone unnoticed by the team. The stress was real but was comfortably managed by all five on board.

Kim, looking over all of his data, said, "That's a Roger. We show 35,100 feet. Go ahead and slow your descent to fifty feet per minute. We don't want you guys running into anything manmade down there," joked Kim.

"Roger that, we're going to hit the exterior lights now." Folgers, along with everyone else on board, was happy with the announcement.

With a soft click, partly muffled by the depth of the ocean, Folgers hit the exterior light controls, but nothing happened. Nearly all screens in the Command Center had been switched to the submersible's outer cameras, with several smaller ones still focused on the interior cabin and its crew.

June Bullard could barely make out her husband's face as most of the cabin's control panel lights were situated behind him.

After no lights came on, Folgers clicked the switch back and forth three to four times. Nothing happened.

Bullard chimed in for the first time, as he was essentially a passenger until they found the shuttle. "What are you seeing, Frank?"

"Our readings show that the lights are on, but we got nothing," said Folgers. "Dustin, what are you seeing up there?"

"Same here, Frank, we show the lights are on," confirmed Kim.

June Bullard was only mildly concerned because the people around her didn't seem to show any fear. She thought that maybe it was normal.

After several excruciating minutes of darkness and uncertainty, the exterior lights finally came on. For a moment, the crew was relieved until they heard a wrenching sound coming from the sub. The team went from nervous to relieved, back to nervous again, in just seconds. The designed interior cabin compression, which had gone unnoticed until that point, was now noticed by all. The twelve-inch clearance on each side of the cabin chairs was now gone. Each crew member could be seen looking down to their left and right, observing the ever-shrinking cabin. Some even recoiled their elbows, much like you would if seated in the middle row on a tightly packed airliner.

"Um, what was that sound down there, guys?" nervously asked Kim.

"Calm down, everybody," whispered Bullard. "That's simply the sound of the abyss wanting to come in."

Bullard's light-hearted attempt to calm the team didn't work. The sound of deep breaths and heavy exhales came from seat three on the craft.

"You okay up there?" Asked physician John Haggerty of Buck Lansing.

"I'm good!" Lansing was unconvincing.

"Dustin, not sure of the sound, but our craft integrity readings are all normal. You guys getting anything back there?" Folgers asked the team behind him while trying his darndest to look over his left shoulder.

"My readings are all normal," said Buck Lansing.

"Denise? You got anything?" Folgers asked of the vessel's Ballast Tech.

Pausing an extra moment to look over her ballast integrity data, she responded with, "No, everything looks good."

"My pulse is normal," joked Haggerty, the sub's medical doctor.

Then it happened again. The wrenching sound lasted a little longer this time, 10-12 seconds. To the crew, it felt like minutes.

The team, on the surface, heard it too. Out of an abundance of precaution Dustin Kim yelled out, "Okay, that's it! We're bringing you guys back up."

Simultaneous to that announcement, Hal Bullard muttered, "Hold it right there, guys, I see something! Twelve o'clock, dead ahead, you guys seeing this up there?"

"Holy shit! They're right in front of it! They're there!" Helena Sequeira said while pointing to her middle screen.

"Frank, move us forward fifty feet and get all lights pointing to twelve o'clock," instructed Bullard.

"Oh, my God!" Brad Stevens had just switched his monitors to the sonar view. Both AUV1 and AUV2 showed that the Finding Zenith sub was standing face to face with the enormous shuttle.

All other screens now showed ocean life swirling around between the sub and the huge object. Sea bacteria and soot were being kicked up from the smooth surface of the migration shuttle.

Dustin Kim was the only one not wide-eyed with his hand to his mouth. He knew they needed to surface and fast.

After the initial shock, everyone in the Command Center burst into cheer. The submersible team heard the cheers, and all struggled to see what was happening out the sub's front window. Frank Folgers could see what Hal Bullard was looking at, though. Dirty metal filled their view.

"Ah, guys?" said Kim. No one seemed to hear his words.

They'd found it. They'd found one of the very vehicles that had transported thousands upon thousands of Earth's human ancestors from planet Zenith.

June stood weeping tears of pride for her husband. His final accomplishment transcended time and space and would bring closure to the millions of skeptics around the world. She was at peace.

On the submersible, a hand crept over Bullard's right shoulder and squeezed. Bullard's hand met with Folgers,' and Frank said, "You did it, Hal! You did it!"

Hal was again humble. "We did it, Frank." All in the Command Center heard the poignant moment between the two close friends.

While everyone in the room was celebrating in cheers and with hugs, Dustin Kim noticed anomalies on his vast console.

Dozens of lights began flashing when Dustin Kim moaned, "Guys! We have a problem!"

At that instant, everyone in the Command Center heard a single snap, and all camera feeds coming from the sub, which filled more than twenty monitors, went white with fuzz.

Everyone in the Command Center was aghast. The words, "What happened?" in a panicked tone were chorused throughout the room.

"We lost the video feed!" Helena Sequeira anxiously began diagnostics, instructing her two technicians to do the same.

"Frank, do you read me?" shouted Dustin Kim into his comms. "Frank? Hal? Do you copy?" Kim was now frantic.

Brad Stevens could be heard sobbing. His face collapsed into his folded arms across his console. He witnessed what had happened from the view of the AUV's sonar feed. The blimp-like shape of the *Finding Zenith* vessel went flat, and a large air bubble exploded from the craft and shot upward. The vessel imploded under the immense pressure of the deep abyss.

Everyone turned in Stevens' direction.

"They're gone," he cried. "They're all gone!"

June Bullard couldn't comprehend what was happening. She just stared at the faces around the room, looking for an explanation. Everyone had their heads down, and most were sobbing. Unable to make sense of it, she pleaded, "What happened? What happened?"

It was only then that the occupants of the room even recognized that she was there. No one knew what to say, and the room quickly cleared, leaving just Dustin Kim, Brad Stevens, Helena Sequeira, and June.

June still didn't understand what was happening. A look of shock and denial consumed her face. Brad Stevens walked over to her and clutched both of her shoulders, and said, "They're gone, June. They're all gone. I'm so sorry." Both were now crying.

June collapsed into his arms and fell apart. The two ended up in a pool of sorrow on the floor of the Command Center. At that moment, Kim and Sequeira, who were also crying, exited the room.

Brad Stevens just held onto June Bullard, letting her release all of her agony.

Outside of the ship minutes later, the crew milling around the aft deck were all unaware of the tragedy when they suddenly witnessed a large air pocket explode onto the surface of the ocean.

Location: Washington, D.C., NCN Studios. *The Late Show with Rhett Marlow.* April 28, 2026 – 1:19 am.

Through his earpiece, Rhett could hear his producer break the news of the tragedy in Guam.

"Oh, my goodness," said a somber Marlow as he talked over a guest who was in the middle of speaking. "Sally, hold on a minute," he instructed his guest, holding up his index finger to the camera. "We're just receiving some breaking news, and it's bad."

Rhett composed himself, needing an extra moment to break the shocking news to the world.

"Ladies and gentlemen, we have tragic news coming out of Guam this early morning, April 28," reported Marlow. "Hal Bullard, Professor of Oceanography at the University of Maine, and the famed underwater explorer who discovered the Titanic in 1985 has died. He, along with four other crew members from the *Finding Zenith* submersible vessel, perished at sea less than an hour ago."

The television screen was now split with Rhett Marlow on the left and a still shot of the famed Hal Bullard on the right. The picture was a recent picture of a smiling Bullard, and below his image read: Halvert R. Bullard – 1942-2026.

Marlow continued, "After locating what was thought to be the highly controversial Zenithian Migration Shuttle, that crashed there in 1947, Bullard and his team were three-plus hours into their dive when disaster struck." Marlow wore a look of dread. "We cannot confirm the cause of the accident, but early reports suggest that the vessel housing the four men and one woman crew succumbed to the nearly 16,000 pounds per square inch of pressure in a part of the ocean known as the Mariana Trench. The accident occurred some 250 miles South by Southwest of Guam."

"We're learning that the NTSB was already on Guam as part of the historical exploratory dive and will likely begin their investigation immediately."

Marlow, receiving more information in his earpiece, acknowledged his producer out loud. "Got it!"

"Okay, folks, we have more to report on the four other souls lost in this terrible tragedy. We can now confirm that the other four crew members that perished along with Bullard are as follows: The Vessel's navigator, Frank Folgers, 57, of Old Town, Maine. Onboard Physician, John Haggerty, 77, of Bangor, Maine. Video technician, Buck Lansing, 49, of Houston, Texas. And finally, Ballast Technician, Denise Shaw, of Philadelphia, Pennsylvania, she was just 39 years old."

Rhett Marlow went on to memorialize Bullard.

"After a storied career, Halvert Robert Bullard is survived by his wife of sixty years, June Marjorie Bullard, four children, thirteen grandchildren, and three great-grandchildren."

Marlow took a long pause, exhaled, and said in a somber tone, "Hal Bullard. Dead. He was 83 years old. We'll be back with more in just a minute. Please stay tuned."

Chapter 11 – It's a Lie!

Location: Around the World – April 28, 2026.

Viewership on Facebook, Twitter, conspiracy blogs, and right-wing media outlets exploded with the news coming out of Guam. The phrase, 'It's a Lie,' was once again the battle cry of conspiracy theorists, doubters, and right-wing crazies, around the world. Hundreds of news publications used the three-word headline to sell newspapers and tabloid magazines. It had been more than five years since the phrase first made headlines, becoming a popular hashtag in January of 2021, soon after the discovery of Black Earth was first reported on to the world.

To hardcore conspiracy theorists and even borderline skeptics, the tragedy that unfolded in the South Pacific ocean was more proof that both Black Earth and Dr. Erik Erickson were a hoax. Some thought they were perpetuated by big government in an effort to fuel further spending and to brainwash the public.

The rest of the world was in shock, as they had anxiously awaited images of the very migration shuttle that might have brought some of their ancestors to Earth.

The world also mourned the beloved ocean archaeologist, Hal Bullard, the man who discovered the Titanic more than forty years prior.

Location: Beijing, China. The Ministry of State Security Building, Seventh Floor, Office of Minister Li Kenong – April 28, 2026 – 5:49 pm GMT +8.

Laughter could be heard erupting from the office of Li Kenong. Kenong was seeing the news report feed breaking through on his desktop computer. He laughed at his perceived incompetence of the American's ability to navigate the South Pacific's depths successfully.

"They are out of their league!" he laughed again. "We will use this fortuitous event to our advantage!" he celebrated.

Location: Washington, D.C., CIA Headquarters, Office of Director James Clapper – April 28, 2026 – 8:19 am EST.

Staring again out of his window toward the Potomac River, Director James Clapper contemplated the alleged accident in the Philippine Sea and the likelihood that it was somehow connected to China.

Moments later, now sitting at his desk, Clapper's phone buzzed. "Sir, Agent..." announced his secretary Colleen before being cut off.

"Send him in." Clapper had been expecting Jordan Spear.

The door opened, and in walked Spear wearing blue slacks, a white collared shirt, and no tie.

"No tie again this morning, huh?" Clapper spoke in a dismissive yet fatherly tone.

"Sorry, sir, I left it at my folk's house. I'm still trying to get back in the saddle. My wardrobe needs a little updating." Jordan shook his head apologetically.

"Well, we can dispense with the formalities for now, as it would appear our China problem just got bigger." Clapper looked annoyed by the events that were still unfolding in Guam.

"Yes, it's shocking," said Jordan. "I was listening to NCN on the way in. China is definitely behind it." Jordan looked pissed and appeared to take it personally.

"Listen, son, I understand your personal connection to Black Earth and subsequently to the migration shuttle, but this is business," cautioned Clapper. "Don't get caught up in emotion, or you're going to end up dead."

"Never personal, sir," Jordan lied to his boss.

"Okay then, we have some items to clear off the docket before we meet with Solstice, Stevens, and McBride, later today. Also, the head of the NTSB, Darnell Scott, will be joining us downstairs in the Truman Room."

"My guess is you brought me in a little early for a reason?" Jordan smiled.

"You're just like your father, Jordan. I like that about you." Clapper returned his smile. "Have a seat, son," Clapper motioned to the sizeable conference table on the opposite side of the expansive, third-floor corner office.

Both men now seated, Clapper opened his laptop and reviewed some items before speaking.

"Jordan, you're going to Guam. You leave tonight at midnight. He doesn't know it yet, but Mr. Scott will be accompanying you on that flight."

"Got it, sir," Jordan nodded in affirmation.

"I understand you once flew on Air Force Two with Mars Johnston. Is that correct?"

"Yes, sir. It was a great honor, sir."

"Well, this time, you'll be flying on Air Force 1 with the President of the United States."

"Sir?" Jordan looked perplexed.

"Jordan, this wasn't just a national tragedy, it was an international calamity. The President will be giving a speech and posthumously awarding The Presidential Medal of Freedom to Bullard. He'll be handing it directly to his wife, right there in Guam. Hal Bullard was more than just an American hero," Clapper paused. "He was also an international treasure."

"So, what's the plan?" Jordan grabbed a nearby legal pad and pen.

"You're going to get to the bottom of this accident, dare I call it one. I firmly believe that the Chinese are behind this tragedy, and that garners the attention of the CIA."

Jordan ground his teeth together before nodding in agreement.

"You will speak to everyone associated with the expedition, including June Bullard, the wife. No one is allowed to leave that island. You will review every piece of audio and video evidence. You will deliver to me transcripts of every conversation had on that ship, submersible, and base camp housing facility at Naval Base Guam. No stone unturned. Do you understand?"

"Yes, sir!"

"The NTSB will work collaboratively with you, but our investigation will be separate from theirs. Depending on the result of their investigation, their actual findings may or may not ever become public, as we don't want to show our hand to the Chinese," explained Clapper.

"And if it wasn't them, sir? Then what?" asked Jordan.

"Then, so be it. To be clear, though. China wants to ensure that the next American rocket ship to Black Earth never makes it there. I'll be turning over the bulk of that operation to Matt Solstice in your stead. That will become official when we all meet downstairs at four o'clock today."

After several more minutes of discussion, the two got up and were ready to leave when Clapper walked to his desk, opened his middle-left drawer, and removed something for Jordan.

As Jordan was walking out the door, Clapper yelled to him, "Officer Spear!"

"Yes, sir?" Spear turned to look just in time to see something flying through the air. Reacting instantly, he caught it in his left hand.

"Make sure you're wearing that tie for our meeting at 4:00 pm." Clapper raised his brow. "No more dress code violations, son. You work for the CIA."

Jordan looked at the outdated necktie in his hand and begrudgingly said, "Of course, sir."

Location: Artesia, New Mexico. The kitchen of Carrick and Lola's House – April 28, 2026 – 6:27 am MST.

Lola turned on the TV before leaving for her shift at Artesia General, then placed it on mute so she wouldn't wake Carrick. After getting a pot of coffee on, she glanced over at the 'Breaking News' ticker at the bottom of the T.V. screen. She saw the words, 'Tragedy in Guam: Five Dead,' then ran up the stairs in a panic.

Now in the master bedroom, she softly yelled, "Carrick! Carrick! Wake up! The shuttle!" She was now on Carrick's side of the bed, tugging on his leg. Carrick woke up to a pale-faced Lola.

"What's wrong? Is Erik okay?" he shouted.

"The shuttle!" Without another word, she grabbed the remote control from the nightstand and immediately turned on the fifty-inch television above the fireplace on the wall opposite the bed. "Look!" Lola was filled with emotion because she had no idea how the tragedy would impact the two men in her life.

Images of distraught people hugging and milling around a shipyard filled the screen; the ticker remained the same as moments earlier. 'Tragedy in Guam: Five Dead.'

"My God, what happened?" Carrick was dazed and confused.

"It says they're dead!" Lola was also confused as well as anxious.

Carrick rubbed his eyes and immediately grabbed his phone and powered it on. The sound of a journalist interviewing men in orange jumpsuits could be heard coming from the television. Jordan noticed several texts, missed calls, and voicemails.

Carrick opened the phone app while Lola stood at the foot of the bed, hand to her mouth, trembling while staring at the TV. Carrick noticed missed calls from Jordan, Mars, and six other friends.

Carrick clicked on the voicemail from Jordan and put it on 'Speaker' mode. He knew it had to be about the accident.

After pushing 'Play,' Jordan's voice came over the phone.

"Carrick, it's Jordan. It's 7:47 am here in the East. You're probably still asleep with the time difference, but I wanted to share some bad news with you. Apparently, the submersible that was to lay eyes on the migrant shuttle imploded once finally reaching it. Hal Bullard and the other four on board are all dead. No word on the cause yet, but I'll keep you posted when I get more information." Jordan's voice sounded sad.

"I know how I feel about it, but that will obviously pale in comparison to how you and Erik will be affected. Okay, take care, and we'll talk soon." The message ended with Carrick and Lola just staring at each other, not knowing what to say next.

"Let's see what Mars has to say," Carrick clicked on the earlier voicemail.

"Carrick, it's Mars. Listen, there's been a terrible accident in Guam. Hal Bullard and four other crew members died earlier this morning. Apparently, they had just made visual contact with the shuttle when there was a catastrophic structural failure of the submersible they were in. Give me a call when you get up. I'll get with my sources in Washington and see if I can learn more. Oh, and Carrick, I'm sorry. I know this will be especially hard on you and Erik. Talk to you later." The message from Mars was filled with empathy.

A few more awkward seconds of silence, and then Carrick spoke. "My God, what will Erik think of this? I know he acted like he wanted it to go undiscovered, but I think he was secretly hoping to see images of it after all of these years."

Location: Washington, D.C. The Truman Room – April 28, 2026 – 4:02 pm, later that day.

"Sorry I'm late, gentlemen." Clapper walked briskly through the door and sat his briefcase on the floor to the left of his chair, looked at Jordan, and said, "This is for you."

Jordan wore a look of acknowledgment and tilted his head.

"I see you're not wearing the tie I gave you."

"No, sir. I gave it to Colleen."

Clapper shrugged, "Where'd you get that one?"

"The gift shop, sir," Jordan's smile was modest.

"Well, okay then." Clapper shrugged with indifference.

In the large meeting room, now sat CIA Director James Clapper, who was joined by CIA Officers, Jordan Spear to his left, Matt Solstice to his right, and Cade McBride to the right of Solstice.

"Darnell Scott, head of the NTSB, will be joining us here shortly," Clapper informed the group.

The room was long and narrow, with a conference table taking up most of the square footage. The walls were adorned with framed pictures of the twenty-four former CIA Directors. A more prominent portrait hung at the head of the room, depicting President Harry S. Truman, who founded the Agency in 1947.

"Gentlemen, thank you for being here today," said Clapper. "You all know why we're here this morning. Early reports indicate that the *Finding Zenith* submersible's implosion, operated by Hal Bullard and his team of four others, was an accident. Jordan can tell you more."

"Guys, listen, while it looks like an accident, we must assume it has everything to do with the Chinese. Operation Venom now includes me going to Guam to get to the bottom of things. I leave tonight," Jordan spoke in a monotone voice.

Clapper broke in with heads turning back toward him. "Matt, you will now head up operations here in Langley. Jordan's expected to be gone for three to four weeks," Clapper's face showed no emotion. "We're counting on you to take a leadership role. I'll be assigning you two more agents."

"Of course, sir." Solstice was eager as he welcomed the opportunity.

Cade McBride jumped in. "Sir, what do we know about the accident so far?"

Clapper's gaze went toward Spear as he deferred to Jordan.

"So far, everyone who witnessed the accident from a control room on the Iron Aegaeon have reported that there was some type of warning signals before the sub was crushed, but nothing that explains a complete and utter failure of the structure," offered Jordan.

"My God, the pressure at that depth is so extreme," said McBride. "they'll be no bodies to recover. I'm a former Navy SEAL, and nothing or no one had a chance once the first domino fell."

"Well, Jordan is going to retrace the steps of those dominos and find out if it was the Chinese that pushed the first one over." Clapper exhaled through his nose and tapped the fingers on his right hand on the table, eyes down.

Location: Artesia, New Mexico. Erik's House – April 28, 2026 – Six Hours earlier.

Erik answered the door. "You don't have to knock, Carrick," Erik welcomed his grandson.

"Hey Grandpa," said Carrick, avoiding eye contact as he walked through the door. "Can I sit down?"

"What do you mean, 'Can I sit down?' Of course, you can." Erik noticed that Carrick seemed a little off. "Carrick, what is it?" Erik looked concerned. "Is it Lilly?" he said with a vacant look on his face.

"No, it's not Lilly. It's about the shuttle, Grandpa."

"They found it, didn't they?" Erik looked toward the window as he sat down next to Carrick.

"They did, but there was an accident," Carrick spoke softly.

"An accident? What happened?"

Carrick looked to his right and made eye contact with his grandfather. "The submersible imploded. Just seconds after seeing it with their own eyes, the sub was crushed. It'll take days to surface the wreckage. They've called a halt to all further activities until they know more."

"Damn it! They weren't going to get into it anyway. They'll never pierce the skin of that shuttle. They don't have the tools here on Earth to do it. Those men died for nothing." Erik showed frustration.

"And woman," said Carrick.

"What's that?" Erik looked confused.

"There was a woman on board the submersible, too."

"Hmm, I see," acknowledged Erik. "So, what now?"

"I spoke with Jordan a few minutes ago. He's heading there tonight."

Erik furrowed his brow. "Why is the CIA getting involved?" He seemed suspicious.

"They just want to make sure nothing nefarious is going on." Carrick tried to reason but also felt it reeked of something more sinister. He knew that governments from around the world would do anything to get ahold of the technology that would still be viable from the shuttle."

The two pondered for a moment when Carrick changed the subject. "You hungry?" asked Carrick.

"Nah, I just had some of that knock-off Red Fruit. It's growing on me a little." Erik had a look on his face that didn't match his assertion. He still wasn't quite sure he liked the Earth-made version of his favorite from Zenith.

"Well, get dressed. We're going to Home Depot, and then I need you in the backyard today," said Carrick.

"Sure, why not? I've got nothing else to do," he sighed.

As Carrick was opening the front door to leave, Erik got his attention. "Hey Carrick, have you heard from the Spencers?" Erik hoped that he had.

"No, sorry, Erik. Lola's her primary at the hospital and says she's responding well to her treatments. She might actually be coming home next week sometime."

Erik's spirits were buoyed a little. Maybe he could at least see her getting out of the car when she arrived home. He desperately missed his little friend.

Location: Washington, D.C. The Truman Room – April 28, 2026 – 4:40 pm.

There was a knock at the door before it opened.

"Hello Gentlemen," offered a middle-aged, distinguished-looking African American man. He was wearing slacks, a white dress shirt, and a brown flight jacket. The jacket had NTSB markings on the sleeves and the name Darnell Scott embroidered on the right chest of the jacket.

"Ahh, welcome, Director Scott, please come in." Clapper stood to shake hands with the National Transportation Safety Board Director. "Thank you for coming in today."

"Folks, this is Darnell Scott from the NTSB. His attendance here today will help us get the ball rolling in Guam."

After brief introductions with the other three CIA Agents, Darnell Scott took a seat.

"Thank you for having me, Director Clapper," Scott said while removing a notepad from his leather computer bag and taking a seat, "but I'm not exactly sure why I'm here."

"Well, let me get right to it then," said a stone-faced Clapper. "You'll be going to Guam tonight," said Clapper.

"Tonight?" Director Scott looked surprised. "I'm pretty sure I'll be attending a function at our offices in Ashburn tonight. I'm sorry my schedule doesn't match yours." Scott looked somewhat offended.

"Yes, well, that's been canceled, I'm afraid," Clapper smiled politely.

"I'm confused, Director Clapper. Perhaps you can help me out?" Darnell Scott suddenly felt a little uncomfortable as he searched for answers in the eyes of the silent agents around the table. None came.

"Director Scott, I understand that you already have several folks on the ground at Naval Base Guam and a few more on the way," said Clapper, pushing his glasses a little higher onto his nose.

"That's correct," acknowledged Scott.

"Well, you will join Officer Jordan Spear over here....," he looked in Jordan's direction, Jordan nodded at Scott, "along with the President of the United States of America, on Air Force One at midnight tonight." Clapper removed his glasses and looked at Scott to see if the reluctant NTSB Head still had questions.

Scott blushed a little. "It would be my honor, Director Clapper." The look on Scott's face didn't quite agree with his sentiment.

"I thought so," said Clapper.

"Perhaps you can fill in the blanks for me?" Scott wasn't entirely sure why the CIA would involve itself in the independent investigation by the NTSB.

"Director Scott, I'll direct you to Officer Jordan Spear." Clapper looked in Spear's direction. "Now, if you'll excuse me, gentlemen, I have a meeting with POTUS." Clapper stood and carefully tucked his chair neatly under the table. Scott looked mildly offended that the Director was leaving the meeting while he still had many questions.

After the door closed, Scott looked at Spear while the group directed their gaze toward the NTSB Director.

"Director Scott," Spear looked almost apologetic, "please excuse the mystery surrounding this meeting. I wasn't aware that you hadn't been briefed prior to coming here today."

"No, I wasn't," said Scott, repositioning himself in his chair. To all in attendance, the Director of the NTSB looked extremely uncomfortable.

"What I am about to tell you is classified, and you will not be able to discuss it with anyone in your agency." Jordan began his presentation.

"Director Scott," said Jordan, as he removed a manilla envelope from the briefcase that Clapper had left behind. "The contents of this envelope will help explain to you what's going on."

"You have my attention, Officer Spear." Darnell Scott related better to Jordan than he did to the matter-of-fact CIA Director.

"May I call you Darnell?"

"Only if I can call you Jordan."

"Of course, it would be a long flight if we weren't on a first-name basis," Jordan smiled.

"It's going to be a long flight either way," sighed Scott, as his brow furrowed in a look of resignation.

"Well, luckily, we'll have a four-hour pitstop in Honolulu." Jordan tried to ease Darnell's look of anxiety.

"Well, that's something, I guess," Scott frowned.

For the next two hours, the four men discussed the parallel investigation details that the CIA would conduct alongside the NTSB. Jordan explained that they had reason to believe a foreign agency could be involved and that the accident might be something other than what it looked like on the surface. Spear explained that the two agencies would share their findings before the NTSB went public with their own.

Scott reminded Spear that the NTSB was an independent agency and not obligated to go along with the CIA's wishes.

"Director Scott," Spear's voice went low, "may I remind you that the NTSB falls under the jurisdiction of the Federal Government." Jordan was matter of fact. "Additionally, this may be a matter of national security, and the NTSB will absolutely comply with both the wishes of POTUS, and the CIA."

Scott conceded and quickly got on board.

Chapter 12 – The Rabbit Hole

Location: Outskirts of Beijing, China. Special Operations Command Center, Sector 3, Room 225 – April 29, 2026 – 8:59 am GMT +8.

"Welcome, gentlemen! Welcome!" Minister Li Kenong was all smiles.

The conference room they were in was even smaller than the one used for the previous meeting between the Strategic Huyou Agency militants and the Ministry of State Security. A small round table that sat four was all that adorned the dank, windowless, otherwise empty room. In the back left corner, a fluorescent light flickered on its way to burning out.

In attendance, were three SHA Militants: Colonel Vadik Lie, Kai Chang, and Zhang Hui; they were joined by Minister Li Kenong.

"Our meeting rooms seem to be getting smaller, Minister Kenong. Perhaps this means our Ministry is not getting the governmental funds it used to. Perhaps you should employ your wonderful negotiation skills and request more," Vadik Lei smirked.

"Colonel Lei, the reason we are here is that the Ministry of State Security has nothing to do with what we will discuss here today." Kenong's exterior turned serious at that moment. "You would be wise never to connect those dots again. This is why we meet in less than lavish Banshì Chù."

"Very well, sir," Lei nodded again, looked at his associates, and they too, tipped their heads toward the Minister.

"That's better, gentlemen. Obedient, just like dogs." Kenong was disgusted by the trained killers his government forced him to work with.

"A most fortunate event has taken place in Guam, by now I'm sure you buffoons have heard, as I understand none of you know how to read," Kenong said with a sinister laugh.

The three bodyguards that accompanied Kenong in the previous meeting with the SHA militants were curiously absent, thought

Spider Lei. *Perhaps today is the day that I kill the infertile peasant,* the Spider thought to himself.

"Wènzi Lei, excuse me, 'Spider' Lei," wisecracked Kenong. "Are you sizing me up now that I am alone with the likes of you and your goons?"

Lei smiled. "Mosquitos take only blood, Minister. SHA Militants take the soul."

"Very well, then. You can be most assured that my highly trained bodyguards are just outside the door," smirked Kenong.

"Yes, we saw them when we arrived. I do believe one of them actually served under my command in the Army." Lei bowed his head to the Minister, feigning respect for his boss.

Kenong's expression revealed his sudden concern.

"Yes, well then, down to business, my fellow countrymen. The foolish Americans will likely suspect us of the disaster in Guam and go down the...; what do they call it in the States? The Tǔ bō shǔ Hole?"

"It's not a 'Groundhog,' Minister. It's called a Rabbit Hole," Vadik Lei reeked of petulance. He took pleasure in correcting the person he considered to be an idiot.

"Yes, of course," nodded Kenong.

Kenong pulled a small stack of file folders from his attaché case. Three of the folders were graced with the names of the three SHA militants at the table.

"Today, countrymen, we will review step three in our plan," revealed Kenong. "After today, we will not see each other again for many months. The hard part of your journey starts today, but it will end in glory for you all. Your names will become that of legend when the story is written of our final ascension to the top of all humanity, both here on Earth and in the universe!" Kenong was triumphant.

"Gentlemen, the sudden implosion of the submersible that went looking for the Black Earth Migrant Shuttle was not our handy work, as you might have thought. In fact, our sources tell us it was an actual accident that caused the small submarine to flatten itself like a Bīngzi." Kenong smiled, "Oh, I do love those American pancakes, especially when there are Americans inside of them," he laughed at his own joke.

"I'm guessing you're happy because the Americans will believe that we were behind the accident and be distracted away from the matters that we are here to discuss today?" offered Kai Chang.

"Indeed, my not so bù chènzhí de comrade," again smiled Kenong.

"Minister Kenong, may I suggest to you that calling anyone of the three of us 'incompetent' will not advance your cause. Perhaps you will decide at some point today to tell us why we are here," suggested The Spider.

"Yes, of course, Colonel. Let's begin."

After more than three hours from the beginning of the briefing, Minister Kenong asked each of the SHA Agents to summarize their marching orders.

"Gentlemen, as you can see, our mission is very detailed and masterful. Neither of you will walk out of this room today with any of the materials that lay before you, nor will you take any of your hand-written notes with you. You are only permitted to take your memory of what was discussed here today." Kenong was steady in his speech. "Who shall be first to share what they know?"

Without hesitation, Vadik Lei rose from his chair and began to speak. "Minister Kenong, brothers of SHA," he acknowledged the group with a respectful nod, "let me start by saying that it is with great pride for both my country and my very own legacy that I enter into this most honorable mission."

Kenong did not detect sincerity in the words of Vadik Lei; he was instead skeptical.

"I am to begin taikonaut training on June 1, with my fellow SHA associate Kai Chang. Together, we will complete taikonaut training and pose as seasoned taikonauts from the Chinese National Space Agency. After training, I will begin advanced explosives training in the area of Micro-Nuclear Bomb assembly and detonation. When ready, I shall board the Chinese spaceship, named The Chinese Eclipse, in the Spring of 2027."

"Once on Black Earth, I shall plant explosives around The Triad's exterior perimeter, here, and here," Lei pointed to images of The Triad on the table, "this will include The Southwest and Southeast Sectors, as well as The History Library in The Northwest Sector."

"Additionally, I shall kill anyone on the crew traveling there who might change their mind or deviate from the plan. Everyone except for the pilot, of course. I shall also protect the crew should the Americans get to Black Earth prior to our departure."

Now looking straight into the eyes of Li Kenong, The Spider said, "As in all missions for a SHA Militant, I shall give my life in honor and service to my country."

Kenong responded, "It's unlikely that the Americans will be able to respond so quickly, so you may not have to die this time, Spider Lei. Such a pity," Kenong wore a faux look of disappointment. "No matter, we must be ready for anything."

Vadik Lei again dismissed the words of the arrogant Minister.

Before sitting down, Lei asked the Minister a question. "Why employ a SHA militant at all?" asked Lei. "Why not just employ someone who can point a gun and shoot?"

Kenong laughed obnoxiously. "You, Spider, of the three of you here today, you are the simpleton. You know nothing. You possess only the primal urge to kill and the ability to do it well. This is perhaps the reason they named you after an insect. Silly man." Kenong waved at him dismissively. "Guns are not the problem, my furry little friend. Gunpowder, however, becomes volatile when exposed to high radiation levels, whether inside a spaceship or on a planetary surface, which we know little about. Also, if you were to be overpowered, the gun could fall into the wrong hands, rendering your lethal hands useless. You will kill with only your hands, knives, stars, or sticks. Whichever primitive tool that you prefer, but there will be nothing on board that ship that could possibly bring it down."

"Understood, Minister!" Lei said with a stare that shot out of the back of Kenong's head. Spider Lei was very close to ending the life of the slight man child that sat before him. He reluctantly tapped his heels together, bowed his head, and then took his seat while tightly clenching his teeth together.

The Minister took great pleasure in seeing the petty insect bow to him. Li Kenong looked at the other two hired murderers as if to say, "Who's next?"

Kai Chang stood, tapped his heels together, and bowed to the Minister of State Security. "I shall go next, your excellent Minister." Those words, like with Vadik Lei, left a bitter taste in Chang's mouth.

"Very well, Soldier Chang, but before you proceed..." the Minister removed some of the contents from his briefcase and tossed them onto the table. "...take a look at these images," he encouraged the group.

The men looked at images of a man taken from different perspectives, vantage points, places, dates, and locations. The images revealed a man who looked exactly like their SHA associate, Kai Chang. "You will notice that Kai Chang is the perfect Duo bèi gang for a great Chinese hero, the legendary CNSA taikonaut, Zhai Junlong."

The SHA militants were amazed at the man's remarkable resemblance in the photo and the SHA associate standing next to them.

Kenong had the sound of celebration in his voice, "It's as if you are twins with Junlong. This is why you were chosen, Kai Chang."

"Yes, it does seem that he is my doppelganger," Kai Chang was impressed. "Now, Minister, shall I recite my mission objectives?"

"Very well, Kai Chang, please begin," encouraged Kenong.

"On June 1, I too shall begin taikonaut training with my SHA associate, Colonel Vadik Lei. Upon completion, I shall fly to America on September 18 and begin my NASA training with the International Crew on September 21. But, prior to June 1, I will begin my education on the life and career of Zhai Junlong. I will become an expert on the man and fool the Americans into believing that I am him. Before going to America, my training will include one hundred hours in a simulator model of the NASA spaceship. I will be trained to plant a small explosive device on my body."

Kenong interjected, "We will have a man planted in NASA who will sign off on your spacesuit and the small explosive device hidden within. In fact, that man is at NASA right now and has been there since shortly after the return of the first craft to travel to Black Earth."

Looking straight into the eyes of Li Kenong, Kai Chang said, "As in all missions for a SHA Militant, I shall give my life in honor and service to my country on December 16, 2026." Chang stood up, tapped his feet, and bowed to the Minister.

"Well-done, Soldier Chang." Kenong broke into half-hearted applause.

Finally, the remaining SHA militant stood at attention before the Minister and began to speak.

"My Job, Minister Kenong, will be to conduct a cyber infiltration of the American satellite system called the Interlink Communication Corridor," pronounced Zhang Hui. "

Kenong flipped through the plans as Hui was speaking. "How is it that you will accomplish this?" he asked the SHA militant.

"My expertise is cyber code manipulation. I will use my skill set to write code that will be invisible to the Americans and highjack their weak Communication Corridor. When I am finished, we will be able to monitor and record all American transmissions." Hui was confident in his demeanor. "We will also be able to corrupt their data and delay transmissions to and from Black Earth."

"And where will you train, Soldier Hui?" Kenong looked at the papers in his hand.

"I will train in the Southern City of Guiyang beginning May 4..."

"Yes...Yes. And then?" Kenong appeared to be drooling.

"I will begin training and, within four months, become an expert on our FAST Aperture Spherical Telescope. I will set-up operations that work both independently and in conjunction with our FAST telescope. The code I write will cyber-bully the code that NASA uses and cause their team to panic. They will know not where the trouble lies. I will leave cyber trails that will lead the Americans directly to Russian intelligence in Moscow. The American scum will be baffled for years to come." Hui looked proud of his capabilities. "Additionally, I will produce a data mining farm that will be able to retrieve every transmission the Corridor has ever sent or received."

"Lastly," Zhang Hui too looked straight into the eyes of Li Kenong and said, "As in all missions for a SHA Militant, I shall give my life in honor and service to my country."

"Excellent, excellent, Soldier Hui. Excellent!" Kenong again stood and applauded.

Chapter 13 – A Wrench in the Works

Location: Guam. Naval Base Guam, USO – Sunday, May 24, 2026 –
9:01 am GMT +10, Guam local time.

Jordan Spear and Darnell Scott sat down at a table that seated four.
The USO club/restaurant was still pretty empty. The place was filled
with empty, four-chaired, shiny black tables. Leather recliners were
facing 40-inch televisions, positioned on tables against the long wall
opposite the fresh fruit cantina. The walls were covered with military
memorabilia and plaques. Beautiful flower arrangements adorned
the tables; some tables had white Melastoma malabathricum
Gafaos, while other tables had beautiful red Lumnitzera littoreas,
both flowers native to Guam.

A pool table sat empty next to a string of computer stations that
lined the back of the bar area; several sailors were observed online,
talking to their loved ones.

"That's a lot of Navy and Air Force ballcaps lining the ceiling," said
Jordan Spear, as the waitress sat him and the NTSB Chief.

The two men had just ordered breakfast. Jordan was having a six
egg, bacon, and cheese omelet, diet Pepsi, and toast, while Scott
had ordered dry toast, coffee, and orange juice.

"That's not a very big breakfast, Darnell," Jordan had a 'what gives?'
look on his face.

"I don't like to eat too much before I step onto a flight," Scott was
reserved.

"What time do you fly?"

"I fly at noon. That should give us enough time to cover my
findings."

"No, thank you," Jordan waved off the waitress, who was ready to
pour coffee into his overturned cup.

"That's me," said Darnell, turning his cup over to allow the young Chamorro woman to pour his coffee. "Thank you," Darnell nodded to the young lady.

"Ah, Ma'am, I'm with the CIA," said Jordan, flashing his credentials, "And he's with the NTSB," pointing to Scott. "We're going to need some privacy when this place starts filling up. Please make sure that those two tables remain empty, will you?" Jordan pointed to the two tables that would separate him and his associate from the breakfast crowd that would be arriving at any time.

The young, demure, native Guamanian nodded in approval to the men. Neither of which were sure she understood exactly what they were asking.

"So, I'm guessing your findings are the same as mine." The two men chorused, "Accident."

"Yeah, there's not one thing that would suggest foul play. There's a lot, however, that would suggest a negligent accident," offered the NTSB Head.

"I'd love to see what you've got in that folder there," Jordan eyeballed the brown file folder sitting on the empty place-setting to the left of Darnell Scott.

"Listen, my findings are not meant to match yours, but if we did our jobs right over the last three-plus weeks, they likely will." Darnell reached for the file folder.

"I've interviewed more than seventy people associated with the dive, and all seem credible, truthful, and incredibly remorseful," said Jordan.

"I've interviewed those same folks, and I agree with that assessment," Scott concurred.

"So, what do you have for me?" asked Jordan, again eyeballing the folder.

Scott pulled a small stack of 8x10 glossy images from the folder.

"Exhibit 1," said Scott, handing one of the pictures over to Jordan.

"A wrench?" Jordan looked puzzled.

"A mangled one," said Scott.

"We found it on the seafloor just below where the craft imploded. You see that name there?" Scott pointed to the brand name near the top of the wrench.

"DeWalt," said Jordan, recognizing the popular tool brand that could be found around the world but primarily in the United States. "What about it?"

"It's an American company, not a Black Earth one," Scott's left brow went up.

"Okay, what are you telling me here?" Jordan was slightly confused.

"That tool had no business being at the bottom of the ocean, just beneath the scene of the accident," offered Scott.

"Maybe it fell off the back of the Iron Aegaeon?" Jordan tried to offer up a logical explanation for the discovery.

"That might be the case if it wasn't mangled like that."

"What do you think caused the damage?" Jordan said in jest as he knew where the conversation was going.

"That wrench is part of a thirty-piece set of very large wrenches that belong to the Gweniece Offshore company. It belonged on that ship, Jordan, not at the bottom of the ocean."

"Okay, what else about the condition of this wrench makes you sure it was responsible for the accident?" asked Spear.

"Do you see these striations right here?" Scott pointed to five thick lines grooved into the neck of the wrench.

"Yes, and...?" Jordan's look indicated that he was begging for more.

The NTSB Director leaned in. "The striations were put there when this wrench became wedged between the vessel's structure and the retractable portion of the outer shell."

"So, a worker left it there, and as the ship descended, it stayed in place until when?" asked Jordan.

"Until the pressure of the deep activated the UAV's retractable outer shell. The wrench became wedged in place and caused additional pressure on the exterior, actually denting the metal shell inward, causing it to lose its integrity," revealed Darnell Scott, nearly leaning across the table to share his findings.

"Exhibit 2," Scott pulled a picture of a man standing on the aft deck of the Iron Aegaeon. "This man's name is John Pierre Walter," Scott tapped on the man's head in the image, "he's French Canadian, born in Quebec, and has been with the Gweniece Offshore Company since 2005. He's worked on the Iron Aegaeon since it came off the assembly line back in 2024. He was working on the left aft umbilical detachment cord just before the sub separated from the Aegaeon. We have video evidence to support that the wrench in question was in his hand in the moments before separation, but there's no evidence that he had it in his hand when he climbed back onto the ship."

"Have you done a background check on this guy?"

"An extensive one," nodded Scott. "His family moved to an area north of Toronto when he was five years old. He's lived in Lake Simcoe, Ontario, Canada, ever since. He's forty-six years old, married, and has three adult children, one of whom works on the Iron Aegaeon with him. The only travel he's ever done is with the Gweniece Offshore company," Scott was reading from a file. "He's clean. We even talked to his neighbors for Christ's sake."

"Jesus! So, the false alarms on the sub and in the Command Center weren't actually false alarms after all?" asked Jordan.

"It appears not. This image here is the back-left ballast intake portion of the sub," Scott pointed to another of the glossy images from the folder. "The first alarm that went off indicated that the back left, or aft porthole had a problem," offered Scott.

"Did it?" Jordan looked curious as he picked up the picture for a closer look.

"No, but the wire housing to that particular sensor, which would report a problem with that window, ran back along with the retractable interior shell. When the indentation occurred, it likely put pressure on the wire housing, tripping that warning light."

"Yeah, but then the light went off," Jordan challenged Scott.

"It did, yes. We're guessing that the housing repositioned itself as the water pressure compressed the sub."

"Guessing?" Jordan's brow went up.

"Jordan, there's rarely an eyewitness to a crime, or in this case, an accident. We have to compile evidence and come to the most logical conclusion. The warning lights that lit up the panel that Dustin Kim was manning indicated that, just before the implosion, the pressure sensor lights from the aft left of the vessel went on first. From there, it was dominos. Once the first warning light came on, it spelled the end to the five lives on board." Scott's face was filled with sympathy.

"Geez! They should have resurfaced the sub immediately." Jordan looked a little angry.

"That seemed to be Dustin Kim's feeling at the time. He should have put his foot down more firmly. He'll have to live with that forever," said Scott.

"Yeah! John Pierre Walter too! Imagine what that poor bastard will be thinking about every night in his bed just before he falls asleep? He'll be haunted by this forever." Jordan shrugged as both eyebrows shot to the top of his forehead, followed by a sigh.

"The whole team got caught up with getting a glimpse of the migration shuttle," said Scott. "No one more than Hal Bullard himself. Once he spotted the shuttle, his words sealed the fate of all on board."

"What was it he said again?" Spear asked Scott to remind him of the fateful utterance.

Scott, looking at the report in his hand, recited Bullard's words. "'Hold it right there, guys, I see something! Twelve o'clock, dead ahead, you guys seeing this up there?'" Scott looked exhausted. "Then he instructed them to move closer. His final words being, 'We did it, Frank.' That was it, the last words to be heard on that sub."

"Wow!" Jordan sat back in his chair. Some forty-five minutes had passed. Looking around, he could see patrons filling the USO club. The plates on the table had cold toast, and a cold six-egg omelet sat untouched on Jordan's. Both men had lost their appetite. They'd barely even noticed when the food was placed on the table.

Location: Somewhere between Guam and Japan. Asiana Airlines Flight 2463, from Guam to Tokyo – Tuesday, May 26, 2026 – 6:00 am, Guam local time.

Jordan Spear was fast asleep in his reclined first-class seat. He was exhausted and relieved. He was relieved that it wasn't the Chinese behind the events 36,000 feet below the Philippine Sea and the fact that he was headed home. He knew that the Chinese were up to no good and that this event was a three-week distraction from 'Operation Venom.' He was happy to continue his investigation in D.C., home with Kinzi and the comforts of the Central Intelligence Agency. Jordan knew he would again someday soon take to the skies in search of the bad guys, but for now, at least, he was headed home.

Location: Langley, Virginia. George Bush Center for Intelligence, CIA Headquarters. Office of CIA Director James Clapper – Memorial Day, May 25, 2026 – 3:05 pm EST.

While the offices were closed to much of the staff, key personnel were working, and Clapper was one of them. "The CIA never sleeps," was a phrase that James Clapper often used throughout his career. It rang true on this rainy Monday holiday. The CIA Director was sitting at his desk, gazing at the rain falling outside, when a secure email came through. The subject line caught his attention. GUAM – ACCIDENT, it said.

Clapper opened the email and read through Jordan Spear's findings. Reading the details, he too sympathized with all involved in the tragedy. He, like Jordan, felt relieved that the Chinese were not involved. However, the fact that it was an accident didn't cause the CIA Director to take his eye off the ball regarding the Chinese. The email that preceded Jordan's was from Matt Solstice and had the subject line: 'Operation Venom – New Findings to Report.'

James Clapper looked forward to Jordan Spear being back at CIA Headquarters, heading up Operation Venom. The two had a father/son connection, and he enjoyed collaborating with him. He thought that the younger Spear was a lot like his father, Jonathan, a man that Clapper once worked with decades ago when they were both field agents in the CIA after their time in the Navy.

He hoped that the younger Spear would stay with the agency this time, knowing in his heart that his leadership was needed to motivate the younger generation of field agents.

Chapter 14 – The Serpent Rears its Head

Location: Langley, Virginia. CIA Headquarters. Office of CIA Director James Clapper – Tuesday, May 26, 2026 – 8:59 am EST.

Clapper had convened a meeting, and in attendance were, Matt Solstice, Cade McBride, and Virginia Worthington. The three sat at the over-sized conference table, waiting for Clapper to finish his call.

"Very well then, get some rest on the last leg of your flight home, and we'll see you tomorrow. Come in at noon and report straight to my office." Clapper's conversation could be overheard by the agents sitting around the table, some ten feet away. "Oh, and Jordan, nice work on the Guam report. Travel safe, son."

"Sorry for the delay, folks, that was Jordan Spear. He's in San Francisco now and will get into Reagan later today," said Clapper as he rose from his desk and made his way over to where the others were sitting. "He'll join us for a briefing tomorrow."

After Clapper settled into his chair, Matt Solstice passed out briefing folders to each of the other three at the table.

"Before we get started, I want to personally thank Officer Solstice for taking charge of Operation Venom for the last three and a half weeks," Clapper was sincere. "Matt, you've been invaluable to me, and I do appreciate that. Now, with that being said, Officer Spear will resume the position of operation lead starting tomorrow."

"Thank you, Director Clapper. It was my honor to take the lead. I will be sure to bring Officer Spear up to speed before our meeting tomorrow." Solstice was humbled by Clapper's trust.

"So, what do we know, Matt?" Clapper put on his reading glasses and positioned them low on his nose.

"A lot, actually, sir. Our informant at the Ministry of State Security has really come through," offered Solstice.

"Matt, this audience is far too big to say his or her name out loud, but have we identified who exactly is leaking the information to us?" asked Clapper.

Solstice rummaged through his documents. "No, sir. There's no way of knowing because everything is coming through via a text-only back-channel set up by the Chinese. It would have to be someone high-ranking. I would guess."

"Or the assistant or secretary of someone high-ranking," offered Worthington.

"So, what then do we actually know from our source?" asked Clapper.

"Sir, can I make a recommendation?" asked Solstice.

"By all means, Matt. Go ahead." Clapper was becoming more and more accommodating as the trust in his agents grew.

"Sir, I have code-named our informant, The Serpent. I thought this was fitting and in line with the operation handle Venom."

"Brilliant, now before I ship you off to the FBI, tell us what you know!" The group couldn't tell if Clapper was joking or not, as his demeanor rarely ever changed.

"Of course, sir." Solstice was red-faced while Worthington and McBride fought back subdued smiles.

"Okay, so as we speak, the Chinese are working on training two of their agents as astronauts, and at the moment, we don't know what agency they're with."

"Jesus Christ!" erupted Clapper. "They'll attempt to get one of them aboard our rocket!"

"There's a lot more here, sir."

"Continue, Matt."

"Upon completion of their training, the two agents will seek to board separate spaceships, one NASA and one CNSA, scheduled less than six months apart. The first agent, we'll call him Agent X, will try to..." Solstice was cut off by Worthington.

"Sabotage," she said.

"As we suspected," sighed Clapper, now breathing heavily through his nose.

"Yes, sabotage," confirmed Solstice. "But wait, there's more, sir," he said. "If the Chinese are successful in bringing down our rocket, they plan to launch their own and...." Solstice was cut off again, this time by Clapper.

"Matt, hold it right there." Clapper motioned with his left hand and pushed the red button on the phone in the center of the table with his other hand and said, "Colleen, get Mars Johnston from NASA back up here from Houston by tomorrow morning."

"Yes, Director Clapper," Colleen could be heard saying.

"Oh, and Colleen...don't forget the 'T.'"

"Yes, Director Clapper, Johnston with a 'T.' Will that be all, sir?"

"Yes, Colleen. Thank you." Clapper released the red button.

"Matt," Clapper settled back into his chair, "you, me, Johnston, and Spear, will meet in this office tomorrow at noon!" Clapper's blood pressure was heightened.

"Is that Johnston with a 'T', sir?" joked Solstice.

Clapper went quiet. He looked at Solstice with a look of disdain and said, "Officer Solstice...does all of this seem like a laughing matter to you, son?"

Solstice lowered his head in shame while the other agents again fought hard to hide their smiles. "No, sir, it doesn't."

Clapper smirked along with the others and said, "Now, as I was about to say. I'll be damned if they think they're gonna bring down one of our rockets," his tone changed back to serious.

"Sir, there's more," revealed Solstice.

"Of course, there is. There's always more. Please continue," Clapper gestured with his right hand.

"Sir, they are looking to steal whatever information The History Library has to offer. Passenger lists of historical figures, medical cures, propulsion systems, you name it. And they plan to destroy it after they've pillaged it."

"Destroy it? How? Do we know?" asked Cade McBride.

"No, we don't have that information yet," said Solstice. "But I have another piece of information that will reveal our earliest suspicions from February 20. The other agent in question, we'll call him Agent Y, is referred to as 'The Spider.'" Solstice exhaled fully and sat back in his chair in anticipation of the group's response.

"This just keeps getting better!" Clapper thought that the information was too good to be true. "How can we trust that the information coming from The Serpent is good intel?"

"We can't, sir," Solstice was frank.

"Bullshit!" Clapper leaned forward in his chair. "If this person's on our payroll, then they need to give us more than general details and nicknames."

The three agents at the table recessed back into their chairs.

"That's just it, sir. The Serpent is not being compensated. Not with cash or minimal intel from us. Not yet."

"What in the hell are you talking about?" Clapper looked dumbfounded. "You mean to tell me that this person is spilling state secrets out of the goodness of their heart? I'm starting not to trust this information. You've heard the saying, 'if it sounds too good to be true'?"

"It is," remarked Virginia Worthington.

"Okay, Agents Worthington and McBride," Clapper stood. "I want to know who we have inside the Chinese government. Let's work backward and rule out our double agents one at a time. Matt, try to get a timeline of when all the pieces of intel came through, and we'll try to zero in on who this Serpent person really is." Clapper assigned each a task before excusing them.

"Sir, one last thing," Solstice said.

"Yes, what is it, Matt?" Clapper sat back down in his chair.

"The Serpent says there's more to come and that the cost for the information will be agreed upon before any American's have to die." Solstice lowered his gaze.

Clapper pursed his lips. "So, The Serpent is feeding us just enough intel so that we know that they're legit. Then, only after we know they're for real, the little snake gets to name his price, essentially?"

"Yes, it looks that way, sir," Solstice nodded in agreement.

"Well then, Matt, it would seem the code name Serpent fits perfectly. We'll get that snake in the end!"

"The Spider, too!" Solstice quickly added.

Clapper rose from his chair, then turned and made his way over to his desk. The three agents looked at each other, shrugged, gathered their belongings, and headed for the door.

As they exited, Clapper called out to Matt Solstice. "Matt, don't forget, tomorrow at noon."

'Yes, sir!"

"That's tomorrow, with a T," Clapper launched a smile.

"Yes, sir!" Solstice laughed with relief.

Location: Artesia, New Mexico. The backyard of Carrick's house – May 26, 2026 – 12:47 pm MST.

Carrick was trenching, laying one-inch PVC pipes for a 'do it yourself' sprinkler system while Erik sat nearby, looking on.

"What are you doing, old man?" Carrick shut down his power tool, removed his hat, and wiped his brow.

"Just writing in my journal," Erik said without looking up.

"What are you writing in that thing anyway? Your life's not that exciting since our world tour came to an end." Carrick put his hat back on.

"Just stuff, that's all." Erik lowered his sunglasses and sat up in his folding chair. "When are you going to be done?"

"Right now. I quit." Carrick looked exhausted. "I think I'm going to bring in some guys to finish this. I thought it would be fun, but it's not anymore. This is hard work!"

"Wow! I didn't see that coming. So that's it, then? What am I going to do with my days now? I've been watching you break your back for months."

"I don't know. Maybe we can go for walks like you and Lilly used to." Carrick instantly regretted bringing up Lilly's name, he knew that Erik would get sad.

"By the way, any word from Doug or Sarah?" asked Erik. "I really miss her, Carrick. Life just isn't the same anymore. Me and that little girl are buddies. She's so smart!" Erik looked resigned.

Carrick knew that Lilly was one of the only things that kept Erik going. He'd be 119 years-old in June, and for the first time, he looked every bit of his age. Planet Earth and his new diet had not been good for his health. His heart had been broken for seventy-nine years since his Lilly left him, and now it'd been seventy-eight days since March 10, the last time Erik saw little Lilly. His heart was broken, and he was literally dying before Carrick's and Lola's eyes.

"No, I'm sorry, Erik. I haven't heard anything except for what Lola's been telling both of us. I'll call them for you!" Carrick spoke in an upbeat manner in an attempt to give Erik a little hope.

"I mean, what did I do to deserve this? She's been home since the fourth, and they basically snuck her into the house under the cover of darkness." Erik looked dejected. "I just don't understand."

"We'll figure it out, Grandpa. We will. I promise you'll see her soon." Carrick was lying. He had no idea when the Spencers would relent and let Erik see her again, if ever. He was out of ideas and knew that Erik was running out of time.

Location: Langley, Virginia. CIA Headquarters. Office of CIA Director James Clapper – Wednesday, May 27, 2026 – 11:59 am EST.

Clapper's desk phone buzzed. "Send him in, Colleen." Clapper knew his secretary was calling to announce the arrival of Jordan Spear, and he was noticeably excited. Sitting at the conference table across the large room were Mars Johnston, Matt Solstice, and FBI Special Agent John Primrose. As James Clapper got up from his desk, the three noticed that he had a skip in his step as he made his way to the center of the room to greet Jordan.

The office door swung open modestly, and in walked Jordan Spear. Jordan looked a little ragged from his journey home. A flight that took him across the International Date Line, in the middle of the Pacific Ocean. While his eyes sagged, his personality did not. Jordan Spear was a magnetic force to be reckoned with; even on his worst day, he could easily own both the good and the bad guys.

Clapper, so not to show his excitement to the others, mundanely shook Jordan's hand and said, "Welcome home, son. I'm sure you must be exhausted," his voice was monotone.

Smiling big, Jordan said, "It's good to be home, Director Clapper."

The three men sitting at the conference table all stood in a show of respect to meet Spear.

As Clapper and Jordan turned toward the men, Clapper whispered, "Nice tie, son."

"It's my dad's," Jordan whispered behind his hand.

Mars stepped forward enthusiastically. "Jordan, today must be bad news because we only seem to get together when the world's on fire," joked Mars Johnston.

"I know, right?" laughed Spear.

"Air Force One, huh?" Mars was playfully jealous.

"It was awesome!" Jordan wore a huge smile as his eyes went wide.

"Gentlemen," said Spear, now turning to Matt Solstice and John Primrose, extending his hand to shake theirs.

"Good to see you, man!" said Solstice.

"Officer Spear," formally nodded the FBI's Primrose, extending his hand.

After all of the greetings subsided, the five men eased into their chairs and got down to business.

"Gentlemen, thank you all for being here. We have a great deal of information to share with you regarding Operation Venom and the possible impact that it may or may not have on NASA. That's the reason Mars and John are both here today." Clapper was stoic.

"Let's first start with an update on the tragedy in Guam. Jordan just got back in last night and will brief you now." Clapper motioned to Spear.

"Thank you, Director," Spear nodded with respect. "So, it wasn't the Chinese as we suspected from the outset, which is why I made the trip to Guam in the first place."

"I heard it's beautiful there. I've never been," said a smiling Mars, first looking at Jordan and then Clapper.

Clapper gave him a dismissive look.

"Oh, sorry. Please continue, Jordan." Mars was apologetic.

"Sure, Mars," Jordan smiled. "It is beautiful there. I just wish I could've made the trip under different circumstances, though."

Clapper exhaled through his nose, encouraging an end to the small talk. "Please continue, son."

"Of course," said Jordan. "It was definitely an accident. As I stated in my report to Director Clapper, both the NTSB findings and the official CIA report read nearly word for word."

"A sub technician on the aft deck of the Aegaeon was using a wrench when detaching the umbilical cord from the submersible. The wrench was left sitting on the AUV as it went underwater."

"A wrench brought the whole thing down, huh?" Primrose shook his head. "My God, that's terrible."

"This was no ordinary wrench. It was eighteen inches long and weighed about eight pounds. The wrench wedged itself between the retractable outer layer of the sub and the fixed shell of the interior housing compartment. When the pressure of the sea caused the sub to compress, the wrench was squeezed like a vice, causing it to dent the skin on the sub, but not puncture it."

"So, what happened then?" Solstice was on the edge of his seat.

"Sure," Jordan nodded. "The dent put pressure on a wire harness that was just inside of the dented metal skin, which triggered an alarm. After a few seconds, the alarm went off, which caused everyone to believe that it was simply a false alarm. Basically, the vessel lost its integrity. You can imagine that with 15,000 psi of water trying to get in...," Jordan paused for a moment and reflected on the lives lost, "they didn't stand a chance."

"Did they recover the bodies?" asked Matt.

"It wasn't pretty when they pulled that submersible from the ocean. It looked like a pancake. Even I had to look away. It was rough." Jordan looked bereaved. "Not much left to bury, I'm afraid."

Jordan finished, and the group took a moment to process the circumstances of the fatal accident.

"That's tough," Clapper was glum. "I actually knew Hal Bullard."

After a few respectful moments of silence, Clapper spoke again. "Alright, moving on. So, Matt here is going to brief you on some new information regarding Operation Venom. Listen, Mars, John, this is big news, and our efforts at NASA will have to be stepped up." Clapper looked stern.

"Thank you, Director." Matt Solstice passed out manilla file folders to all. "In your hands is a brief of what I'm about to cover with you. Of course, the information is top secret and can only be shared with those with the proper security clearance," cautioned Solstice.

Clapper interjected, "Mars, earlier today, your security clearance was upgraded from Baseline Personnel Security Standard, or BPSS, to Counter-Terrorist Check, or CTC. We trust that you'll keep this information to yourself and not feel the need to share it with anyone who doesn't have clearance. I have personally vouched for you."

More than three years earlier, Clapper recalled a time when he chastised Johnston for sharing confidential information with Carrick Michaels' then-girlfriend, Lola Cook.

"Of course, Director Clapper," said Mars. "Your trust is my honor. Loose lips sink ships." Mars smiled gregariously while the others at the table, by their facial expressions, conveyed that the phrase he uttered wasn't quite appropriate due to the Guam tragedy's findings just minutes before.

Jordan gently kicked Mars under the table to remind him that less is more in this setting. He and Mars then made subtle eye contact, and Mars instantly realized his poor judgment.

"Thank you again, Director." Mars nodded in Clapper's direction.

"Continuing," Solstice sifted through the brief, "I'll share highlights for now, and then we can enter into a Q&A and deep-dive from there."

Mars looked at Matt and gave him the stink eye for saying the phrase 'deep dive.' Mars thought it was too soon after his ill-timed utterance just moments before. Matt studied Johnston's face and had no idea why Mars wore the look he did.

"Where was I?" asked Solstice figuratively. "Oh, yes, the CIA has obtained information that would indicate that the next NASA rocket to launch may be the likely target of saboteurs."

"Officer Solstice, is this intel different than what we covered during our last meeting?" asked John Primrose.

"Yes, the intel we gathered before our last meeting only hinted at the notion of sabotage. The information we now possess comes from a source from within the Chinese government."

Primrose mouthed the word, "Wow!"

"Director Clapper...," Mars spoke up, "Matt, are you telling us that you believe that China is actively seeking to bring down our Saturn Six rocket?"

Clapper looked at Solstice as if to say, "I got this one."

"Mars, you'll forgive me for taking the potential human cost out of this equation for a moment...,"

Mars nodded as if to say, "Okay."

Clapper continued, "...but how soon can you have the Saturn Six's sister ship ready to go after the scheduled December launch?"

"The Neptune One? My God, what are you saying?" Mars looked horrified.

"I'm saying that if China is successful in their goals, then they'll launch their own ship just days, weeks, or months after the Saturn Six falls from the sky. If they do, and if they get to Black Earth before we do, they will rape, pillage, and plunder the resources and secrets of that planet. That simply cannot happen."

"So again, I ask you, how long before the Neptune One would be ready for launch?" Clapper was adamant.

Mars sank back into his chair and pondered.

"The plan was to have Neptune One ready four months after the December lift-off, just in case anything went wrong once the Saturn Six landed on the surface of Black Earth."

"That's too long! If China launches, we will have only days to lift-off," warned Clapper.

"Well, China is simply nowhere near ready to launch its Shenzhou 2 rocket. They still need a year," Mars claimed.

"Mars, China is up to no good, and have likely been planning this for years. Whatever you think you know about their space program is only what they want you to know." Jordan was trying to provide a wake-up call to his friend.

"Mars," Clapper leaned in, "think about what would happen if China raided The History Library and found the plans for propulsion systems that are millennia ahead of ours? What if they found the cure for every disease known to man? What if they uncovered migrant shuttle manifests and used them to blackmail modern-day descendants?"

"They'd become the only superpower on Earth!" Clapper said with a stone-cold look on his face. "I don't want to live in that world, do you?" His question was pointed.

At that moment, Mars understood.

Primrose broke in, "Director...," he nodded, "Officer Spear and Officer Solstice, how do you suppose they will try to bring down that rocket, a surface to air missile? Booby trap? Thoughts?"

"There are a multitude of ways...?" said Jordan before being cut off by Mars.

"From the inside," said Mars, staring into blank space. "They'll try to bring it down with no evidence to suggest it was purposeful." Mars was now fully engaged and finally understood his value to the conversation.

Clapper and Jordan could see the determined look in his eyes.

"Go on, Mars. Tell us what you think." With a look, Clapper encouraged the group to stay silent and to let Mars finish his thought.

"They'll try to get a rogue crew member on board that ship. It'll be near impossible, though, because there will only be ten astronauts on board," said Mars.

Clapper added, "But hundreds are working on it. They may already have someone on the inside."

"Matt, how long do you believe China has been planning this?" Mars was on a roll.

"We believe since the return of the Sagittarian Recovery 2, maybe before."

"What are you thinking, Mars?" Primrose slid to the edge of his seat.

"We have brought on no less than fifty additional personnel in the last two years. Several of which are recent grads that studied abroad."

"You think there's a chance some could be compromised?" asked Clapper.

"I didn't think so the last time we met, but now," he paused, "I believe anything is possible?" Mars wore a look of revelation.

"Mars, our list of those who might engage in espionage, and sabotage, is far greater than just any new NASA employees," suggested Clapper.

Mars wasn't convinced. "I have worked with those people for years, some decades. I don't know."

"Mars, imagine this," said Jordan, "you have an engineer who's been with you for twenty years. In the last year, he's discovered that his wife or child has cancer. His salary doesn't come close to paying the bills when all of a sudden, a Chinese operative approaches him with a bag full of money. Or, imagine that you have a systems engineer who got involved with the wrong man and is being blackmailed by him, now imagine that man is a foreign national."

Clapper added, "Mars, people who have been honorable for their entire lives have become dishonorable in a single day. Love, money, sex, greed, revenge; they all play a part in what can turn someone from good to bad."

"My God, we have a software engineer whose wife has terminal cancer. We have a project manager that's going through a rough divorce. We have a design engineer that's been asking for a pay raise for months. I get it," Mars looked exasperated.

"John," Clapper said, "I'll need a list of everyone who could do harm to the Saturn Six."

The eyes of Primrose went big. "That'll take a while."

"Hundreds," said Mars. "There are hundreds of people involved."

"From the political side of things...," Clapper knew there'd be fallout from the White House and the State Department, "there can be no Chinese astronauts on that crew."

"Taikonauts," Mars said under his breath.

"What's that?" asked Clapper.

"They're called Taikonauts. The Chinese counterparts to American Astronauts are called Taikonauts.

"Well, now they're called Uninvited Guests," Clapper was firm.

Everyone in the room agreed. The plan was simple going forward, everyone with clearance to work on the Saturn Six project would need to be re-issued their credentials. All work would stop. The delay would cost weeks, maybe months. The Saturn Six would not keep its December launch date.

Chapter 15 – Black Roses

Location: Suwanee, GA., Level Creek Cemetery – June 11, 2026

"On Earth, we usually visit someone's grave on the anniversary of their death," said Carrick, as the two men stood looking over Lilly's grave.

"On Zenith, we chose to celebrate their life, not their death," Erik countered.

"That makes a lot of sense," thought Carrick aloud.

"Is that one for me?" Erik looked at the empty headstone to the left of Lilly's grave.

"Yes, I bought plots for you and me. You'll be left of Lilly, and I'll be right of my father."

"What about Lola?" asked Erik.

"No, we agreed, this gravesite is just for the Ericksons."

"I see mine, but where's your headstone?"

"Lola's afraid to pick it out. She thinks it's a bad omen to buy the headstone while I'm still so young."

"What's an omen?" asked Erik.

"Have you learned nothing in your two-plus years on Earth?" laughed Carrick. "It doesn't matter. I don't believe in that stuff anyway."

"What do you believe in, Carrick? What do you think happens when people die?"

"I don't know. I just think they're gone. Although, I do believe that people don't die until they're eventually forgotten. As long as they're remembered, they live on," said Carrick philosophically.

"Interesting. I guess I feel the same," Erik shrugged. "I mean, Lilly was dead for more than thirty years before I got to Earth, but I felt like she was with me every single day since she'd left Zenith. You might be on to something, son."

After a moment, Erik said, "Do you think people will remember me?"

"Oh yeah!" Carrick's brows went up, shaking his head in the affirmative. "100%...you'll never be forgotten."

Carrick added, "I'll tell you something else, too...,"

"What's that?" asked Erik.

"Cremate me!" Carrick was adamant. "I don't want to be put in a box and shoved into the dirt. I'm okay with an empty grave, though. It was good enough for my dad. It'll do just fine for me." Carrick was clear with his wishes.

"Me too," said Erik. "everyone on Zenith was cremated. You can put my ashes in the dirt, though, right next to Lilly."

"Anyway, it won't be long for me now." Erik was resigned to the fact that his time was drawing near.

"Ouch! I sure hope not, Grandpa. I would miss you so much."

"Just don't forget about me, and I'll be around." Erik looked at Carrick reassuringly and smiled.

The two men made their way back to the car. As they walked, Erik put his arm around Carrick's shoulder in a fatherly gesture. Carrick looked at the hand on his right shoulder and then looked back to his left. "This doesn't mean we're going to share a shower later, does it?" They both laughed out loud, remembering a time on Zenith when they first discovered the unquestionable bond between the two.

Two hours later, while waiting for their flight home from the Atlanta airport, Carrick answered a call from Lola. It was great news.

"Hey, Babe, we're at the airport now." Carrick listened to an excited Lola. "Oh, okay, here he is. It's for you, Grandpa." Carrick handed the phone over to Erik.

"Hi, Lola!" Erik smiled into the phone. "Ok, ok, slow down, I can't understand you. What do you mean? Oh, my goodness! That's amazing!" Erik began to tear up. "When? Okay. Is she alright?"

Carrick saw tears welling in his grandfather's eyes. He was nervous and excited at the same time, having no idea what news Lola shared but knew that it had to be good.

"Okay, we'll call you when we land. Thank you so much! And tell the Spencers I said thank you, too."

"What is it?! What is it?" Carrick was dying to know.

"The Spencers...," Erik couldn't quite get the words out.

"What?! What is it, dammit?"

"They've agreed to let me see Lilly! I can't believe it!"

Carrick had an 'I told you so' look on his face. "I told you they'd come around. That little girl loves you! Everybody loves you!"

"That's an early birthday gift for you!" Carrick said.

"Darn, I was hoping you didn't remember," said Erik.

"One-hundred and nineteen tomorrow, that's a big day!" smiled Carrick.

Erik wasn't worried about his 119th birthday, but rather seeing his best little friend, Lilly.

"I just don't know how we're going to fit 119 candles on that cake. We almost burnt down the house last year."

"Ha-ha," smirked Erik.

"So, when do you get to see her?"

"They said it would be a few weeks. She's headed to the Cleveland Clinic for a series of radiation treatments. They said they thought it would give her something to look forward to when she got back home."

"That's amazing!" Carrick said aloud.

"I wish I didn't have to wait, but now I have something to look forward to. I hope I can make it until then." Erik looked off into the distance.

Carrick's heart froze, not sure of what he'd just heard. Was Erik forecasting his own death? Did he actually just say that he wasn't sure if he'd make it another few weeks? Carrick was too scared to ask for clarification.

Location: Artesia, New Mexico. The front porch of Carrick's house – July 5, 2026 – Mid-day.

"Great! We're sitting outside on the porch. We'll see you in a few!" Carrick ended a call with Lola. "They'll be here in five minutes. They're just getting off the highway."

Lola had offered to drop off and pick up the Spencers from the airport so that they didn't have to deal with Uber.

"What am I going to say to her? It's been months. I'm so nervous." Erik hid his tears and fears under his ball cap.

"Just hug her and tell her how much you missed her. Tell her you love her. She probably needs to hear that. It's been a long time, and that little girl has gone through hell."

"One-hundred and seventeen days," Erik said with angst. He was happy he'd see her when she got home, but he felt cheated out of all of that time without her.

"Wow! That's a long time! Geez!" Carrick didn't realize that it'd been that long or that Erik was actually counting the days. "Oh well, it ends today, Grandpa. Lilly's coming home!"

Another minute had passed by when they saw Lola's silver Honda Pilot turn the corner. The moment had arrived, and Erik was a ball of nerves.

Lola turned into the Spencer's driveway as Erik and Carrick made their way down the driveway. Before they got to the street, Little Lilly got out of the car and ran toward the two men.

"Erik!" she yelled, running across the street without looking.

Everyone held their collective breath for a second until they saw no cars coming.

Erik couldn't breathe. He had no words, only tears. Little Lilly ran to him and launched herself into his arms.

"I missed you so much, Lilly!" Erik was now sobbing.

"I missed you too, Erik!" Lilly was crying too. "I'll never stop seeing you again!" she promised, through her tears.

Carrick couldn't stop his flood of emotion. He looked across the street and saw the Spencers crying, too. Their tears could not mask their look of guilt.

Lola ran over and hugged Carrick. No words were spoken.

Lilly pulled away from Erik to see his face. She looked closer and then grabbed his hat and pulled it away. "What happened to your hair? You're bald!" she laughed and cried at the same time.

"I wanted to look just like you," he cried. "You're so beautiful!"

"I love it!" said Lilly. "We're twins!" She rubbed Erik's shaved head and hugged him again. She was so happy to have her friend back.

Erik held Lilly tightly and kissed her forehead. Sarah Spencer couldn't contain her guilt or tears, and ran into her house crying.

While hugging Lilly, Erik looked up at Lola and Carrick without words. He then turned to look across the street at the Spencers and looked toward Lilly's father. "Can we please go for a walk around the block?" he cried. "Just one lap, I promise?"

Doug Spencer said, "Of course! Go!" his hand now covering his mouth as he choked back the tears.

Erik stood and extended his hand, "You ready, Lilly?"

"I was born ready!" said Lilly, laughing through her tears.

The two walked off, and Lola and Carrick looked over at Doug and mouthed the words, "Thank you." Lola placed her hand on her heart in a display of gratitude.

Doug Spencer made his way to the front porch. Sarah had come back out to meet him there. The two just hugged and cried it out. They were overcome by the regret of somehow thinking that Erik might be responsible for Lilly's diagnosis.

Each of the next two Saturdays, Erik and Lilly took their weekly walks, twice around the block. Erik was in rare form and was as happy as he'd been in many, many months.

When he wasn't writing in his journal, he was hanging out with Lola and Carrick. They had all watched Prometheus, Star Wars, Close Encounters of the Third Kind, Apollo 13, and ET twice in the previous two weeks. Erik was in heaven, but Lola and Carrick were exhausted from watching all of the old movies.

Location: Carrick's house – Saturday morning, July 25, 2026.

Carrick slept in and was awaken by Lola. "Carrick, Lilly's downstairs. She said she rang Erik's doorbell, but there was no answer. She said they were supposed to take an early walk today."

"Did you call him?" Carrick was sleepy-eyed.

"Yes, no answer. I hope he's okay," worried Lola.

"He's fine. He's been sleeping later and later lately. I'm glad. He needs the rest." Carrick dialed his number and awaited Erik's answer. "Nope, no answer." He hit the end call button and tossed the phone onto the bed. "I'll go over there and check on him. Go tell Lilly to go back home and that he'll come and get her when he's ready."

"Got it," said Lola, while looking a little nervous.

Carrick threw on some pants and the dirty t-shirt that he'd worn the day before. He headed to Erik's house. Standing at the door, he dispensed with the doorbell and entered the code 12121965, the same code that opened the Temperature Regulation Chamber on The Triad's main entrance of The Northwest Sector.

When walking into the living room, he noticed that the place looked spotless. Nothing was out of place. Erik was a creature of habit, and one of those habits was keeping things in order, particularly if he was leaving to go somewhere.

"Erik, you dressed? I'm coming back!" yelled Carrick.

The door was closed to the back-left bedroom where Erik chose to sleep. He didn't like the bigger bedroom, with just the one bed. He chose to sleep in the room with the empty bed across from his, as it reminded him of Barrack 5 in The Triad. It reminded him of the seventy-five years alone in The Triad without his Lilly; it reminded him of the thirteen months he shared his barracks with Carrick.

"Knock-knock," Carrick said as he pushed the door open. The room was dark, and the shades were drawn. There, Carrick could see Erik was fast asleep. Next to him on the bed was the book that Carrick gave him his first day home to Lilly's old house. 'Where Once We Stood' was Erik's favorite book. Carrick used to laugh that it was Erik's only book.

"Come on, Grandpa! Your little friend wants to go for her walk." There was no response as Carrick opened the shades.

Carrick was leery of kicking Erik's bed to wake him as he'd always threatened Carrick playfully when he did.

"Come on, Erik, wake up!" Carrick was now nervous, paralyzed by fear as he was back in February when Erik slept in late and didn't wake when Carrick yelled for him.

"Grandpa?" Carrick touched his shoulder. "Grandpa?" No response came from Erik.

Lying on the twin bed, Erik had his back to Carrick, facing the wall. Carrick tugged on Erik's shoulder and pulled him toward him. Erik's eyes were closed, but his mouth hung wide open. There was no sound of breathing. Erik was gone. Carrick pulled the old man to his chest, wailing through his tears.

"Erik! Wake up! Grandpa!" he yelled while hugging his grandfather. "Wake up!"

Lola was curious about what was taking Carrick so long. She thought the worst and decided to walk over to check on the two men in her life. Walking through the yard, she looked across the street and saw little Lilly sitting on her front porch. Lilly waved at Lola. She looked sad while waiting for her friend to come out.

As Lola approached the front door, she could see that it was open, and her heart sank. As she crossed the threshold, she heard the heart-wrenching tears coming from the man she loved. She gasped, hand to her mouth, then walked backwards out of the house and ran to Lilly across the street.

Back in the bedroom, Carrick cried. "I will miss you, Erik! I will miss you. You were everything to me. I will never forget you! You will never be gone. You will live on in my heart, forever!"

Carrick squeezed the lifeless body that no longer contained the spirit of the man he loved more than anything else. The man who gave him a father, a grandfather, and a best friend. The man who connected every missing dot in his life.

As Carrick laid his grandfather back down, placing his head gently on the pillow, then adjusting the blankets back up to his neck, the black journal that Erik had been consumed with for months fell to the floor. After landing, it opened itself to a page full of words.

Wiping his tears, Carrick picked up the journal and was confused by the words he saw. 'Black Diamond Reactor' was the heading on the page. Carrick quickly closed the journal and placed it under the pillow of the adjoining bed across from Erik's, a bed he'd slept in many nights while he and Lola's house was being built. Lola would sleep in the bigger bedroom with the queen-sized bed. She knew the boys needed their time together for their late-night talks, like those they had on Black Earth back in 2022.

After Carrick ensured that Erik was comfortable, he walked out of the bedroom. Looking back, he cried again. Standing there for another moment, he just stared, unable to turn away. He stared at the man that willed him to Black Earth. From seventy-five million miles away, Erik's pull was undeniable. Erik was the reason Carrick became an astronaut. Erik was the reason Carrick was selected to be the first human to set foot on the surface of Black Earth. He was the reason Carrick was chosen to inspect The Triad. Erik was the reason for everything in Carrick's life, and now he was gone. A hole that could never be filled now cratered Carrick's broken heart.

Carrick walked down the platinum hallway with the faux diamond light fixtures, but this time, they no longer shined. He passed by the kitchen and saw an empty can of the knock-off Red Fruit. He was going to miss his grandfather, but most of all, he was going to miss his friend.

Carrick emerged from the front door and spotted Lola and Lilly across the street. Standing behind them on the front porch was Doug and Sarah Spencer.

They looked closely at Carrick's face, and they could see him slowly shaking his head from side to side and then down. Lola burst into tears and ran to her husband. The Spencers embraced and began to cry. Little Lily stood up from the top stair and said, "What's going on?! Where's Erik?!".

Her mother reached down and hugged her daughter and just cried.

"Mommy, what's wrong? Why are you crying? Where's Erik?" Little Lilly looked across the street and saw Carrick and Lola on Erik's front porch. They had collapsed into each other's arms, heartbroken.

Looking across the street again, Lola could see the Spencers walking back inside, towing Little Lily, who was resisting their tug.

Location: Washington D.C., NCN Studios. Sunday morning news show, 'State of Affairs with Jake Johnson' – Saturday, July 26, 2026.

The upbeat music introduced Johnson to the viewers, but as the camera panned in, he looked downtrodden.

"We have sad news to report to the world this morning. Black Earth Erik has died." The screen split to live images around the world where mourners gathered to celebrate the life of Dr. Erik Erickson and to mourn his death. Church services were scheduled at thousands of churches around the world. People wore their Black Earth t-shirts and flew flags that bore the word, ZENITH, in white letters over a black sphere.

"Dr. Erik Erickson was, and is revered, by billions around the world," expressed Johnson. "So many have been touched, not only by the story of Dr. Erickson's life on Zenith but also by his charm, wit, sincerity, and his truth. Erik Erickson believed that one truth was more powerful than a million lies. On many occasions, he famously said that, and I'll quote, 'The truth never lies. The truth never changes. No matter how much time goes by, no matter how much the world, things, or people around us change, the truth never does. The truth unifies the righteous and fractures the corrupt.' Erik Erickson would repeat that speech on every stop in his travels around the world. His powerful message will never die, will never get old, and will never be untrue."

Johnson continued, "While there are people that still believe that Erik Erickson was not a real person and that Black Earth is not a real place, I say this to you, I have personally met the man and met the astronauts who traveled to the black planet: have you?" Johnson was passionate.

"We now bring in the Chief Administrator of NASA, Dr. Marcus 'Mars' Johnston. Mars joins us via satellite from Houston this morning. Welcome, Mars."

"Thanks for having me, Jake! Happy to be here." Johnston's smile filled the screen.

"Chief Administrator Johnston, please tell us what you know of Dr. Erickson, as you were the Flight Director at NASA for all three missions to Black Earth."

"First of all, please call me Mars," he said. "I'd be happy to share my thoughts on Dr. Erickson."

Mars adjusted his earpiece and then continued. "I first met Dr. Erickson upon his arrival to Earth back in the Spring of 2024 and spoke extensively with him at that time. Since then, we have also had the opportunity to talk to each other while at several of the same speaking engagements."

"What can you tell us about the man?" Jake probed.

"Wow, so much to say! Dr. Erickson was charming and personable. He was quiet and usually didn't speak unless spoken to. Unless, of course, he was giving a speech about Black Earth or climate change," offered Mars. "You see, Dr. Erickson was alone on that planet for seventy-five years with no one to talk to. For a man with so much information to share, he would tell whoever was listening, even though he was uncomfortable in the spotlight. He never wanted the attention; he only wanted his truths to garner people's time and curiosity." Mars was reflective.

"Sounds like a remarkable man."

"He was! So kind!" Mars nodded.

"What can you tell us about his death? I understand you are somewhat close with former astronaut, Dr. Carrick Michaels."

"Yes, I am. All I can say is that Erik died peacefully in his sleep while at home in Artesia, New Mexico."

"Mars, we're just getting word that Dr. Erik Erickson will lie in state at the Pentagon in Washington, D.C. before being buried in Suwanee, GA. Will you attend the service?"

"I wouldn't miss the chance to say goodbye to such a universal hero." Mars was humbled.

"Why the Pentagon?" asked Jake.

Mars was happy to answer that question. "Sure, well, many of your viewers may not know, but the structure that Dr. Erickson lived in on Black Earth resembled the actual Pentagon. It's fitting that he be remembered for his actual home on Zenith."

"Yes, I understand world leaders will be paying their respects there in the coming days," added Jake Johnson.

"And finally, Chief Administrator Johnston, what do you say to those around the world who question the existence of Black Earth and the hero that the world just lost?" Jake Johnson wanted to put the conspiracy questions to rest.

"Take a walk in my shoes," said Johnston. "I was there every step of the way for all three missions to Black Earth and back. I met and got to know the man. If you don't believe the truth of Black Earth, and my friend Erik Erickson, then you don't need to be speaking on the subject." Mars spoke with passion. "The hell with the nay-sayers!"

"Dr. Mars Johnston, thank you for your time."

Johnson turned toward the camera and said, "Dr. Erik Erickson, dead. He was 119 years old."

"Stay tuned. We'll be right back," Johnson told his international audience.

In the weeks and months following the death of Dr. Erik Erickson, the world mourned. World leaders from every country ordered flags to fly at half-staff. Though he was the world's most famous atheist, the faithful were calling for sainthood. In London, Queen Elizabeth II posthumously granted him honorary Knighthood. There was a spike in newborn baby boys named Erickson, just as there was when Erik first came to Earth two years prior.

In his brief two-plus years on Earth, millions had flocked to see the man from Black Earth. Erik Erickson spoke to the United Nations assembly and to Pope Francis, with more than 60,000 faithful in attendance in St. Peter's Square. Erik and his grandson traveled to more than sixty cities in thirteen countries. Erik's story of the fall of the once-great planet Zenith was a universal tale that influenced climate change policies worldwide. He also spoke of world war, racism, and segregation; and how it brought down a once utopian society. Erik's mantra was always about the survival of all species, not just humans. His most retweeted quote was, "All living things deserve to live."

Location: Suwanee, GA., Level Creek Cemetery – Sunday, August 9, 2026

Carrick, Lola, Mars Johnston, Jordan Spear, and Kinzi London had flown in directly from Washington, D.C., and met the Spencers at the Level Creek Cemetery in Suwanee, GA. Some of the group stood back and watched as Lilly Spencer placed a white rose on Erik's grave. Standing next to her were Carrick and Lola. Each hugged her before she walked away to join her parents and the others.

Lola hugged Carrick and said, "I'll give you a moment to say goodbye."

"I might need more than a moment," Carrick joked through teary eyes.

Lola laughed and said, "Take all the time you need, honey."

"Thank you," said Carrick.

Carrick laid thirteen black roses on Erik's grave. His ashes were buried just feet from his eternal bride Lillian Koss Michaels. There was one rose for every month the he and Erik had shared on Black Earth. *Thirteen lucky months,* thought Carrick.

"Thank you, Erik Erickson. Thank you for saving me. I was a man without a course, a man without a past, and a man without a destiny. That all changed on March 23, 2022. Yes, I have been counting and cherishing the days since we first met." Carrick chuckled while wiping his runny nose. "That was the day, Grandpa, the day that I stopped looking back and started looking forward. I haven't looked back once since then." Carrick spoke out loud to his grandfather's grave.

"Well, I hope you don't mind if I look back every once in a while now, to remember our time together on this Earth and the other one up there." Carrick looked skyward and then back down. "I promise you that I will return to this spot every year on your birthday to celebrate your life and not your death. I will celebrate your life every day from this day forward. I love you, Grandpa. I will see you on June 12 next year. I love you. Goodbye for now. I will see you every night in my dreams and every day in my memories. I will see you every time I look up at the night sky."

Carrick walked away and met up with Lola. They shared a long hug, and Lola said, "I'm gonna miss that old guy."

Carrick looked back at his father's, Lilly's, and Erik's graves and said, "Erik's finally Home. He's finally with his Lilly again, and with his son."

When Carrick, Lola, and the Spencers all returned home to Artesia, the airport seemed busier than usual, with many people dressed in all black, which seemed unusual. Several travelers noticed Carrick hiding under his ball cap and ran up to him, asking for an autograph.

Less than an hour later, as they turned down their block, they noticed cars and people lining the street; there were hundreds of people holding candles and flowers. As they passed Erik's house, getting ready to turn into their driveway, they saw hundreds of bouquets and flower arrangements, crosses, and pictures of Erik, all neatly placed on his front lawn. The vigil appeared to have been going on for days.

"They did love Erik, didn't they?" Lola was in tears.

"They 'DO' love Erik. His memory will never die." Carrick was so proud of his grandfather.

Chapter 16 – FAST

Location: China, Southern Suburb of the City of Guiyang. Remote Safehouse, Huaxi District – September 5, 2026 – 6:00 am.

In a tiny, abandoned house, absent of electricity, sat two men. There was only one table and two chairs inside the dank, dark, dilapidated structure that had not been lived in for many years. Gray walls revealed remnants of brownish blood splatter from long ago. On the floor were dozens of cigarette butts, a syringe in the corner, and an old, used condom lay beneath a broken window. Kids and drug addicts likely frequented the dilapidated house.

Outside, still dark, a car sat empty with the engine idling, two men stood nearby smoking xiāngyāns. Another car was parked unattended just feet away. The area was industrial yet quiet and felt like the ideal place for a murder.

The orange glow from each puff of the cigarettes reminded SHA Agent Zhang Hui that even though he was alone inside of the dark house with Minister Li Kenong, the hated Minister was still protected. He could see Kenong's bodyguards through a small window in the front of the house. Like his SHA associate Vadik Lei, he would enjoy killing his boss. He'd likely not get far, though, from the heavily armed men waiting outside. While he did not fear the men or dying, he'd rationalized that the Minister's life was not worth that of his own. Perhaps he could quietly snap the Minister's neck and simply sneak out the back, he thought. No, he was more than a thousand miles from home and couldn't chance it. Zhang Hui would die for his country, but not for a coward like Kenong.

"So, Soldier Zhang Hui, please tell me of your progress with the FAST telescope. My hope is that you are well on your way to high-jacking the Interlink Communications Corridor."

"Minister Kenong, the news is all good. Breaking through the American NGFW firewall of the corridor proved far easier than expected," explained Hui.

"Please spare me the details, Soldier Hui. I want to know only of our capabilities after your four months of cyber infiltration." Kenong was dismissive and bored.

"Of course, Minister," said Zhang Hui, "we now have the ability to listen and record all transmissions from the Interlink Network."

"Fascinating, tell me more."

"We created a mirror of their version of SMLI filter packets and then.....," Hui said before being sharply cut off.

"Soldier Dumb-Dumb! You must not understand me," shouted Kenong, who was sharp in his tone. "I said, spare me the details. Instead, I would like you to tell me what we will be doing going forward."

The two henchmen outside were mildly alarmed. One raised his back end off of the idling car, tossed his cigarette, and began walking toward the house. The other grabbed his arm with a wave of the finger, and a "Shhhh" sign from his mouth, discouraged him from interfering. The goon nodded his head in affirmation.

Back in the house, Hui responded, "We will intercept all transmissions for our use, we will send messages of our own that will be undetectable to the Americans, and we can delay, jam, or delete their transmissions completely, your excellent Minister." Zhang Hui was itching to kill his boss's boss.

"When can we start?" asked Kenong.

"We already have, sir. We have three days of data that can be translated by our cyber team now."

"Excellent! Excellent!" said Kenong, waving clasped hands. "Here are your orders going forward. First, you will jam their system for one minute and gauge how long it takes them to notice. You will then do it for one hour, and then two, and then three. I want to know if and when they detect us sneaking around in their cloud."

"This has already been done, Minister. It was part of our testing...," Hui was again cut off.

"Who gave the orders to do this?" Kenong seemed to feign his anger.

"I did, Minister," said Hui. "It was part of the trial process. It was required to see if our efforts were successful."

"Only I will determine who or what succeeds or fails!" Kenong again seemed to fake his anger.

"Minister, you must trust that you hired the right man for the job. I know what I am doing. I code more efficiently than I kill." Hui had closed the distance between him and Kenong as he spoke.

"Of course, Soldier Hui, of course." Kenong launched a nervous smile. He knew that his life would be at risk if he continued to belittle the SHA killer.

"What are my dìngdāns going forward, your excellent Minister?"

"You shall report back to the FAST Observatory and await your orders, Killer Hui."

Minister Li Kenong opened the door and walked out, and only after he felt like he was at a safe distance from Zhang Hui he said, "You know, your fellow SHA associates are dead as a result of my orders, don't you?"

Zhang Hui looked surprised.

"Yes, they disobeyed me, and now they are both dead. I hope you can follow orders Soldier Hui and not lose sight of our goal."

"Yes, sir!" Hui stood at attention, tapped his heels, and reluctantly bowed in compliance.

Kenong laughed and quickly closed the door, leaving a seething killer behind. As he got closer to his bodyguards, he released a deep breath, relieved that he was still alive.

Once in the car, the Minister shouted an order to one of his two men, "Get me the hell out of here before that goon kills us all!" After several minutes of driving, Kenong said, "Get me, Colonel Vadik Lei, on the phone."

The Minister lied to Hui to encourage loyalty. His style of motivating men, while effective, was also extremely dangerous. Each time he poked the snake, there was a chance of being bitten.

Location: China, suburbs of Beijing. China Astronaut Research and Training Center – September 7, 2026 – 11:00 am, Beijing local time.

In a small office building, at the C.A.R.T. Center, Minister Lei Kenong met with Colonel Vadik Lei and SHA associate Kai Chang.

"I have received comprehensive progress reports on your training thus far. It seems that the two of you are near the top of your class. Very good gentlemen. Not bad for a couple of gorillas," Kenong laughed at his own words.

"What can we do for you, Minister Kenong?" The taste of pure disdain coated the tongue of The Spider.

"I am here to regretfully inform you that just two days ago, I watched as your SHA associate, Zhang Hui, was murdered before my eyes." Kenong smiled.

"Minister, please. I know that you are lying, so what is the purpose of your visit here today?" said Lei.

"Ah, what gave it away, my little Spider? Did he contact you crying after I told him that the two of you were dead?"

"No, you said that you were here to 'regretfully' inform us that Hui was dead. You of all people would not be regretful about having one of us killed, nor would we regret killing you if ordered to do so." Lei was straight-faced.

"Is that a threat, Colonel Deathwish?" asked Kenong, no longer smug.

"No, your excellent Minister, SHA militants do not make threats. We only carry out orders."

"Okay, gentlemen, let's discuss why I am here today," Kenong was now more businesslike. "The purpose of my visit is to share a change in our master plan. Our plant at NASA in Houston has fallen under Shěnchá by the CIA. I'm afraid he will be unable to overcome that scrutiny. We have made plans to pull him from the States immediately."

"What does that change, Minister?" asked Kai Chang.

"The American Saturn Six will still be blown out of the sky, but not by a bomb sewn into your suit, you imbecile!"

Chang overlooked the insult and was relieved that the plan as written had changed.

"How then will we bring the craft down?" asked Chang.

"Our chemical explosives department is working on a new bomb that will be placed onto a mini-drone. That drone will be operated by you remotely from a boat in the Atlantic ocean, just off of Florida's coast. You will fly the drone to Cape Canaveral and, without being detected, you will place the bomb on the third stage of the rocket so that it will not explode until it nearly reaches orbit." Kenong looked almost celebratory in his detail.

"But Minister Kenong," countered Chang, "they will have cameras watching every square meter of the rocket. How will a drone with an explosives package go undetected?"

"Silly man, Kai Chang!" Kenong was dismissive. "We are the Chinese. We have many different ways to go undetected. We are working on a drone that yields no heat signature. It will be invisible to infrared and not visible to the naked eye while being monitored by any camera. It will make no sound either. They will only notice the bomb on video playback as they conduct their investigation."

"But...," Chang paused in confusion, "the distance, sir? A drone of that size, while being silent, would need a battery. Can it travel that far?" asked Chang.

"Indeed!" said Kenong. "Our teams will be using the new TESLA B2C battery. It will allow the drone to travel roughly 125 miles before it ditches itself into the ocean."

"And the G-Forces, sir?" asked a persistent Chang.

"What of them?" Kenong was becoming perturbed with his subordinate.

"How will the bomb remain attached to the rocket as it exceeds speeds of more than 40,000 kilometers per hour, sir?" questioned Chang.

"Again, those are concerns for our engineers. You do not need that information to fulfill your duty, Soldier Kai Chang. Am I clear?"

"Yes, sir! Very good, Minister!" Chang bowed in respect. "It seems that there would be no need for me to complete astronaut training then. Is my assumption correct, your excellent Minister?" Kai Chang perked up with the revelation that he would likely not be on a spaceship that would explode during liftoff.

"Ah, very perceptive, you idiot!" Kenong raised his voice. "Of course, you will not be completing your training here. You will come with me today. You will begin drone operations training at once."

"Very well, Minister!" Kai Chang rose to his feet, tapped his heels, and bowed to Kenong.

Vadik Lei, however, remained seated and observed the insincere respect given to a dead man. Lei was sure he would personally kill Kenong one day.

Location: New York City. NCN Studios, 'Real Talk with Jonathan Cooper' – September 15, 2026 – 8:00 pm EST.

The banner at the bottom of the screen read, 'Breaking News.'

"Good evening, everyone! We have breaking news tonight. NASA has just announced the crew for the December launch of their Saturn Six series rocket. The name of the spaceship has also been released. The 'Silver Comet' will carry ten astronauts from six different countries, four women and six men. Stay tuned. We'll be back to talk about those lucky men and women that got the call and will be part of history. Not since early October 2023 has a rocket been launched to Black Earth. We'll be right back!"

Moments later, Cooper's big smile filled television screens around the world. "Welcome back, everyone! With me now is NASA's Chief Administrator, Dr. Marcus Johnston." Cooper was thrilled to have the legendary NASA Chief on his show for the first time. "May I call you Mars?" he asked.

"Please do," responded the gregarious Johnston.

"So, Mars, we understand the name, 'Silver Comet', has been officially painted on the side of the massive rocket. Why 'Silver Comet'? Who came up with the name?" Cooper was curious.

"You know, we had a bucket full of awesome ideas for the name, and then the executive team at NASA took a vote, and it won out."

"The name itself makes it sound really fast!" thought Cooper aloud.

"Well, we also decided to paint it silver instead of the traditional white. That had a lot to do with it," explained Johnston. "It's also really fast!" Mars smiled proudly.

"How fast?" Cooper tried to get Johnston to reveal the speed.

"Fast! That's all I can say." Mars was chomping at the bit to reveal the progress his engineers had made with the new Saturn and Neptune series rockets, but he resisted.

The head of NASA stopped short of revealing that the Saturn Six series rocket would travel at a top speed of 30,000 mph, instead of the 25,000 mph achieved by the previous three rockets that went to Black Earth. While the world knew the rocket would be faster, exactly how fast was classified as top-secret. The US did not want foreign adversaries to possess that information.

The increase in speed would shed more than two full weeks off of the trip to Black Earth each way. Instead of the 120 days, or so, that it took to make the one-way journey; it would now only take 104 days to get there.

"Fascinating," said Cooper. "Listen, before we get to the names of the crew, I'd like first to speak about NASA's most famous astronaut of all time...."

"Dr. Carrick Michaels is a true American hero!" Mars blurted out before Jonathan Cooper could finish his thought.

"No, I was thinking of the other famous 'Universal Hero'...."

Again, interrupting Cooper, Johnston said, "Oh, so sorry! You're referring to everyone's favorite astronaut, Dr. Erik Erickson." Mars blushed in embarrassment.

"That's the one!" said Cooper, now smiling. "It was such a sad day when we heard of his passing. The world is still mourning." Cooper's smile disappeared.

"He was a great man, and I feel very fortunate to have been able to call him a friend." Mars looked humbled.

"That's right. You were part of the world tour. I felt slighted that you guys did a show with Bear Winston but not me," joked Cooper.

"Well, there were a lot of talk shows that wanted us to come, but we couldn't do them all. I was only on the tour for four weeks. Dr. Carrick Michaels, also my friend," Mars looked at the camera directly, making sure that the international audience knew of his relationship with Carrick Michaels, "did most of the touring. They were the two the world wanted to meet and hear from. Not me." Mars wore his trademark grin.

"Yes, both will be remembered forever, in life, and in death. The world will always know their names," offered Cooper.

"You know, I did a segment at the Pentagon while Dr. Erickson lay in state. I saw you there but didn't get a chance to speak with you. Your eulogy was beautiful. You nearly had me in tears," admitted Cooper.

"Talk about tears!" Mars' eyes went wide. "When Carrick, Jordan Spear, and Kinzi London each spoke...whew! There wasn't a dry eye in the room."

Cooper agreed. "Particularly when Carrick spoke of his grandfather. The fact that the whole time, thirteen months, that they were on Black Earth together, they had no idea they were actually related."

"I know, the story is amazing and will transcend time. All time!" said, Mars.

"Okay, we need to take a commercial break, but when we get back...the big reveal! Mars will announce to the world who the ten brave men and women are, and from which countries they hail, that will be next to travel to Black Earth. Stay tuned."

After the commercial break, the camera captured the two men chatting but then panned in on a close-up of the silver-haired Jonathan Cooper.

"Welcome back, everyone! And now time for the exciting news. Who will be next to travel to Black Earth after more than three years?" Cooper built the anticipation for his audience.

Mars Johnston pulled the list of men and women from his breast pocket. "Jonathan, before I name the lucky men and women who were selected, I just want to say that dozens were not only considered but were also deserving of the opportunity. Frankly, we could only select ten."

"Thank you for that, Mars." Cooper was eager for his audience to hear the names first on this exclusive broadcast.

"Okay, here we go!" Mars studied the list. "By country, they are as follows: from the United States, we have geologist, Dr. Casey Anderson; chemist, Dr. Abigale Behrendt; biologist, Dr. Candice Lyons; physicist, Dr. Simone Washington; and aviator, Jack White."

"Continuing on," said Mars. "From the United Kingdom, we have biologist, Dr. Sebastian Colt; from South Korea, physicist, Jin Ho Mae; from Japan, meteorologist, Chiemi 'Cindy' Nakamura. Hailing from Australia, we have aviator, Martin Kelly; and finally, from India, medical doctor, Rajendra Phalke."

"There you have it! This is an impressive list of space travelers. Each has spent at least six months on the International Space Station," Mars finished.

"Wow! That's quite a list!" said Cooper.

"The list of understudies is just as impressive," added Johnston.

"Well, Mars, thank you so much for coming in tonight. We look forward to the launch coming at the end of the year. Is there a date yet"? Cooper wondered aloud.

"It keeps changing, but I'll make sure you're the first to know," Mars smiled.

Location: Dawodang Depression, Guizhou Province, Southern China – September 21, 2026 – 9:00 am, Local time.

The five-hundred-meter-wide, Aperture Spherical radio Telescope, called FAST, is primarily used to detect, and study distant pulsars and exoplanets. It does so by utilizing gravitational wave detection and is the second-largest telescope in the world. The giant parabolic dish also looks for signals that could be from extraterrestrial intelligence. Since September 9, 2026, it had also served in a more nefarious manner, collecting, and storing data hi-jacked from the Interlink Communications Corridor.

SHA Agent Zhang Hui, and two other undercover agents from the Ministry of State Security, studied data around the clock and monitored and recorded all communications to and from Earth to Black Earth. Since there had been no human activity on the black planet for more than two years, only atmospheric conditions and infrared images from the American satellite Walker Trace had been retrieved and archived.

In a small but sophisticated communication shed, built specifically for Operation Black Diamond, Zhang Hui sat with Dewei Wan.

The building was twenty feet by twenty feet, and only three men had access to it, Zhang Hui, Dewei Wan, and another communications expert, Dong Wei. Wan and Wei worked twelve-hour shifts, and Hui worked two eight-hour shifts daily but was on-call 24/7.

The building was cramped; barely large enough for two men to sit at its computers and large console. The console was packed with hundreds of dials, switches, and gauges that were collecting and monitoring sound data. The information was displayed on fourteen monitors while also recording and storing everything to be sent to Beijing through its direct communication channel.

Of the more than sixty employees working at FAST, including scientists, astronomers, data technicians, engineers, and maintenance workers, no one was privy to Operation Black

Diamond. Everyone on staff was told that the building was an electrical closet, explaining why dozens of cables ran between the main campus building and the shed. All were forbidden to inquire about the operations happening there or even discussing it amongst themselves. The regimented and dutiful employees just went about their business of studying the universe and searching for distant pulsars.

As the two men were making small talk, a series of pings were heard. This was the first such detection of the pinging sound. The equipment used to analyze the radio waves indicated that the sounds originated from Earth and were directed toward Black Earth. After sixty more minutes of tracing the pings, it was confirmed to the men that the sound was coming from longitude 29.7604° N and 95.3698° W.

"That's Houston, Texas!" shouted Wan.

"As expected," says Zhang Hui, "they are testing the frequency prior to launch."

"This means they will not launch on time," surmised Wan. "Testing should have started weeks ago if they are to launch on time."

"That is correct," Hui looked puzzled. "They are delayed for some reason. They may not launch until the end of January if my assumptions are correct. I must notify Minister Kenong."

"The news is not bad, though. This gives us more time to refine our interpretations of the data," thought Dewei Wan aloud.

"You are mistaken, Dewei," Hui was firm. "There is something wrong. The Americans sense something is not right. If they suspect something is amiss, they may try to disguise their transmissions through the Interlink Corridor."

"We must get to work immediately to mask our signal further." Zhang Hui thought aloud.

Chapter 17 – The Journal

Location: Artesia, New Mexico. The Michaels Home – September 26, 2026

Sitting at the kitchen table, Carrick just stared at the steam rising out of his coffee cup. Lola tried to look busy cleaning the breakfast mess but was just waiting to say what needed to be said.

Moments later, Lola finally spoke up. "Carrick, you haven't said a word since you came downstairs. You need to talk to me."

"Ugh," Carrick groaned.

"Babe, it's been two months since he died, and every Saturday it's the same, you just mill around the house and barely say a word."

Carrick finally spoke, "He died on Saturday. Every Saturday reminds me of that day. I don't know how to move on. I'm lost." Carrick just sat and stirred his black coffee over and over.

"I have an idea." Lola had been waiting to share something with Carrick for weeks but didn't feel that he was ready yet.

"I'm listening," Carrick played with his eggs, not making eye contact with his wife.

"It's time, Babe," Lola was resolute.

"Time for what?"

"We're going over there..." Lola was quickly cut off.

"No way!" Carrick lashed out. "No, Lola! I'm not ready for that yet."

"Carrick, you said that Erik told you to remember his life and not his death. You said that."

"You need to make peace with him being gone. You can do that by starting to enjoy the memories that you have of him."

"And how exactly do I do that?" Carrick was frustrated.

"By being thankful for the time that the two of you had together."

"I'm just not ready yet." Carrick was in denial. He knew it was time, he just didn't have the courage.

"Will you go with me?" Carrick looked at Lola with a profound sadness in his eyes.

"Of course. Get a shower and get dressed. We're going to remember Erik today. The living years," she said reassuringly.

An hour later, Lola and Carrick stood at the front door of Erik's house. Carrick was hesitant.

"I'll enter the code," offered Lola. "What was it again, 1212?"

"12121965," Carrick said, trembling.

"Come on! Let's go remember Erik!" Lola was encouraging.

As the two entered the tiny home, they saw the living room exactly how Erik had left it; it was spotless. They took small steps, walking through the tiny room. Carrick was afraid to enter the hallway that led to the kitchen, bathroom, and two back bedrooms.

He smiled though when he saw the pictures above the fireplace. There were pictures of he and Erik in London, Brazil, Copenhagen, and countless other places.

"Look at this guy!" Carrick laughed a little, handing a framed picture to Lola.

"He's chatting with Pope Francis like they were old friends."

"Hilarious!" thought Lola aloud. "Pope Francis, having a good old time with the most celebrated atheist in the universe."

She turned to find Carrick, but he wasn't there. She didn't yell out for him but rather peeked down the hallway. She saw Carrick touching the faux diamond light fixtures. Without looking back, Carrick walked into the kitchen, Lola following closely behind. The house was small and old, but Carrick had everything remodeled; the place looked brand new inside.

The kitchen cabinets were gray, the counters and backsplash were black granite, and all of the appliances were stainless steel.

Carrick opened a couple of the cabinets and laughed through his tears. "Look at this," he wiped his tears away.

Lola peeked into the cabinet and laughed with Carrick.

"They're all cups, no plates," Carrick said. "He loved his Red Fruit!"

"That's funny!" said Lola. "He only ate real food at our house."

"It is real food, Lola!" Carrick defended the powdery drink.

"I know." Lola rolled her eyes.

"Lola, that's all we had on Zenith! That stuff is amazing."

Lola could see Carrick lost in thought for a moment. "Everything okay?" she put her hand on his shoulder.

"I wonder..." Carrick shook his head.

"What is it?" Lola looked concerned.

"His diet. I wonder if the crap we fed him for the last two years contributed to his death." Carrick wore his guilt like a soldier wearing a red badge of courage.

"That's ridiculous!" Lola shut Carrick down. "He was 119 years old, Carrick. It was his time."

"You saved him from Zenith and brought him home to be with you and his Lilly. Then he met little Lilly, and saw the world he always wanted to see with his own eyes. He was happy, Carrick. He died in Lilly's old home. You saved him, Babe. You saved him." Lola pulled Carrick close. "He's Home, Carrick. Erik is Home."

The two hugged for a moment, and as Carrick pulled away, Lola was holding a picture in her hand. She held it up and pointed it toward him.

"What's this?" Carrick looked puzzled. It was a sonogram she was holding. He knew what it was but was stunned for a moment.

"Twins," Lola teared up. She was happy to share the news but also feared the worst.

"Oh, my God! You're pregnant!" Carrick was thrilled and pulled Lola back in for a longer hug. "This is amazing! How far along?"

"Six weeks!"

"How long have you...?" Carrick was cut off.

"I found out last week," Lola smiled. "Twins, Carrick! Twins!" she said, now crying happy tears.

"Okay, we have to celebrate! Let's get out of here and go someplace special." Carrick was sincerely happy but also thought this was a good reason to avoid the back-left bedroom.

"No-no," Lola shook her head. "You have to do it, Carrick. You must." Lola was encouraging.

"You're right. You're right. He is home. He got to die on Earth instead of that black menace. If we were just a couple of years later to Zenith, he might have died there. Imagine if Phillip Blakely never spotted Zenith back in 2019. My God. He would've died alone, and I would never have known my father's father."

"C'mon." Lola motioned to the hall. "One more room to visit."

Carrick was reluctant but followed his wife.

"Go ahead." Lola tilted her head to the back-left bedroom door. "Do it!"

Carrick put his head down and opened the door. As he crossed the threshold to the room where his grandfather and best friend died two months prior, he could smell his scent.

"My God, I can still smell him." Carrick looked amazed. "I never noticed before until now."

"I think it's so funny that the two of you shared this room after he came Home." Lola smiled. "It was like six months wasn't it?"

"About that, yeah."

Carrick and Lola sat on the left bed and stared for a moment at Erik's disheveled bed. It hadn't been touched since the day Carrick found him.

"Can I make it?" Lola thought Erik's bed should be made to look nice, the way Erik did every morning.

"I think Erik would appreciate that."

As Lola shook out Erik's blankets, Carrick laid his head down on the pillow on the adjacent bed and remembered he and Erik's late-night talks there and while on Black Earth.

"You know, these beds are actually pretty comfortable." Carrick laid on his side, facing Lola, and slid his left hand under the pillow like he always did. There, he felt something and pulled it out.

Holding it in his hand, Lola looked over and said, "What's that?"

Carrick was melancholy. "It's Erik's journal. I forgot about it. I put it here the day he died."

"Wow. Have you looked inside? He always seemed to be writing in that thing after the Spencers didn't let him see little Lilly anymore."

"Yeah, he bought it only after Lilly's diagnosis." Carrick held the journal with care but was afraid to open it.

"You know, we need to pack up all of his stuff at some point," Lola mistakenly thought out loud.

"Not until I'm dead and gone!" Carrick's tone turned serious. "This place is hallowed ground. It stays as is, do you understand me?"

A lump quickly formed in Lola's throat. "Yes, yes, of course. Sorry, Babe, I wasn't thinking." She instantly realized that it was way too soon to talk about packing up Erik's memories into tiny boxes.

Two days later, while Lola was at work, Carrick sat in the living room holding Erik's journal. He was hesitant to open it. He remembered back to that morning when it hit the floor and opened to a page; on the header were the words, 'Black Diamond Reactor.' Staring at the journal, his curiosity took over.

Would it be an invasion of privacy? Carrick thought to himself.

Erik was dead after all; maybe he wanted Carrick to find it. What if he read something that would change the way he saw his grandfather?

"Damn it! Here goes!" said Carrick, after mustering the courage.

He opened it to the first page and on it read the words:

"Carrick, if you're reading this journal, it means that I'm gone, but hopefully not forgotten. I remember what you said when we visited Lilly's grave back in July. You said that 'people aren't actually dead until they're eventually forgotten.' Well, I hope people don't forget me. I know that you never will. I'm sorry that you were the one to find me lying here in my bed. I figured that when I went, it would be right here where I am now, in my bed."

"I want you to tell everyone I said goodbye and that I died a very happy man. Please tell Lola that, like you, I was so lucky to have her in my life. Let her know that I loved her very much. Also, give Mars a call and tell him I enjoyed our time on the road and that he made me laugh until it hurt. Also, let him know that I didn't really like *Prometheus* that much."

"Then there's my buddy Jordan, tell him not to forget about our first conversation in The History Library. The truth can hurt. Sometimes, the truth can heal, but mostly, it's just the truth. The truth is what everyone needs to hear, whether good or bad, it will always bring people together. Celebrate life, but most of all, celebrate the truth. Tell him I said so, ok?"

Carrick let a tear go at that moment, thinking how much he missed Erik's honest humor.

"If I may, I'd like to talk about Kinzi London for a second. That woman always meant a lot to me. After seventy-five years alone on Zenith, you two were the first people I saw. It was such a breath of fresh air to see the two of you standing there before me. I thought I was dreaming. Please let her know that I still bleed red and that she'll always hold a special place in my heart, and that as I pass through into oblivion, wherever that might be, I'll always remember her fainting when she saw 'Roswell 1947' on your computer armband. That girl fell like a bag of rocks. Please tell her how much she meant to me."

Carrick laughed out loud, wiped his tears away, and continued reading.

"Carrick, please tell Lilly I said, 'Happy Birthday.' I hope I make it to September 23, but I don't think that I will. She really wants a motorized scooter, check with her parents first and then buy her one and tell her that it's from me; would you? I also need a special favor from you. If you're willing, I would appreciate it if you would take little Lilly for a walk every Saturday, when you can. I would like it very much if you could talk to her about me. As she gets older, she might forget about me, that would make me very sad. Gone, but not forgotten, I hope."

"Another thing, I left my will in my safe in the closet. You probably know the combination; if you don't, it'll come to you."

"My will leaves most of my money to the Spencers. They're good people, and I know they meant well. I want to ensure Lilly gets the best things that life has to offer. Please ensure that all of her medical bills are paid for and that her college education is taken care of. After she graduates, please ensure that she gets the car of her dreams and a small financial sum each year of her life. Not one that would change who she is as a person, but rather one that will afford her to manage any hardships that might befall her."

"I also want to leave this house to her. It would be great if her parents didn't have to bear the notion of her moving away from them someday. Even if she did, she would have this house to come back to. Please tell her how much I loved her. She was my second favorite Lilly of all-time. The thought of her maybe living here one day would be kind of poetic as my Lilly lived here, and now perhaps my Little Lilly will, too. Let her know that she made it so easy for me to leave my real home on Zenith and come back to your Home."

Carrick had to put down the journal for a moment and collect himself. His grandfather's words felt as if they were coming from the actual man. It was like Erik was sitting right next to him on the couch.

"Okay, before we talk about us, I need another favor. I need you to go to my house and into my bedroom. I'll wait a moment until you get there."

Carrick was startled by the request. He looked around the room, feeling as if he wasn't alone. He collected himself and made his way to Erik's house. Now in the back-left bedroom, he opened the journal to the page he had left off on.

"Now that you're situated, I want you to lie in my bed and look across to yours. From the vantage point in which you now see, I, as a human being, learned more than I did studying in The History Library for seventy-five years. The talks we had, the words we shared, the tears we shed, and the laughs out loud. The conversations we had made me more complete than I had been in the first 115 years of my life. I learned not only about you, but I learned about me. I learned my truth from looking into your eyes, by absorbing your words, and by understanding the greatness that true love could produce. Lilly and I made your father, your mother and father then made you. You are me, and I will always be you. The endless nights in Barrack 5, I'll never forget them. I would almost race to the end of our days just to hear you tell a story that was way too long. In truth, I was glad you talked too much. Just hearing the sound of your voice was all I really needed. I didn't really need to come Home; I could've died right then and there."

"Anyway, look who's talking too much now? Like you, I could go on, but I won't."

"As you flip through the pages that follow, you will realize one truth. For the sake of Lilly's health, and for the sake of all humankind, I am letting you break your promise to me."

Carrick closed the journal. "What promise?" Carrick said aloud as he racked his brain. Was there a promise he made to Erik that he might one day want to break? One that he might have to break?

After pondering his thoughts for another moment, he gasped. "I promised him that I would never go back to Zenith." He said as he sat up in the bed. He opened up the journal to where he had left off and then slowly turned the page.

"Carrick, time for part two of this story." The words read. "If you're continuing to read this journal, you might find it a little confusing. Well, let me end the confusion. If there comes a day when and if you feel compelled to return to Zenith, you can break your promise, and I'll be okay with it."

"After Little Lilly was diagnosed with cancer, I remembered back to a time on Zenith, during one of our late-night chats, when you asked me if I'd ever heard the term cancer. I told you then that I never had. I now know why I had never heard of it. It's because Zenithians must have eradicated it thousands of years before me. I never went back that far in The History Library. After I got to Earth and traveled your world, I quickly realized how much Earth and Earth humans were like Zenith and Zenithians. Of course, cancer existed at one point. Of course, we found the cure. Diabetes, heart, and liver disease, the common cold. The cures for all of these ailments are there; they're all in The History Library."

Carrick felt a sudden obligation to get back to Black Earth, but he would never go. He was retired, and now Lola was pregnant. The diamond he brought back to Earth from Zenith meant he would never experience financial hardship, the only thing he would need to ensure happiness...... "My health," he said out loud. "Oh, my God! All the money in the world can't buy my loved ones or me their health." Carrick now hesitated to turn the page.

Overcoming his fear, he did just that.

"Carrick, I'm not saying I expect you to be the one to get back to Zenith and find these things that will enable humans to live on for millennia. I'm saying that the truths you need can be found in The History Library."

"In the pages that follow, I have left you a road map on how to funnel electricity to the needed places in each of the three sectors that comprise The Triad. Read on only when you need the information, or pass it along to someone else, your choice."

"One last thing, before we finish our little conversation. After you brought me Home, I wanted to walk in my Lilly's shoes for a moment once she'd arrived. I know that the Liaisons would have given her a history book to learn of her new world. Well, I did some reading of my own. Read on once you find a comfortable chair; what I'm about to say may or may not surprise you."

Carrick remained seated and turned the page.

"Carrick, did you know that your country's Declaration of Independence was signed by a total of seven men that were migrants from Zenith?"

Carrick was shocked as he read the list of names. On the page were the following names: Benjamin Harrison, John Hancock, Thomas Jefferson, John Adams, Samuel Adams, Benjamin Franklin, and Button Gwinnett.

Carrick read on, "Oh, and a few more of your Presidents, too. All of the names will appear on past shuttle manifests if you can find them. Likely thousands more. I take such great pride in how Zenithians came to Home and made a difference."

"In closing Carrick, I'd like to say that of all the people that I ever knew, on Earth or on Zenith, including my Lilly, I loved you more than all of them. You are me, and I am you. That is our truth, and that truth can never be denied. I love you, son. I will never forget you, and please never forget me. Goodbye, until our paths cross again. All of my love, Erik."

Chapter 18 – The Pearl

Location: Outskirts of Beijing, China. Counterintelligence and Espionage Training Facility, Room 218 – December 5, 2026.

"It's official!" celebrated Minister Li Kenong. "The Americans have announced that they are postponing their rocket launch until early next year."

Kenong sat in a room with SHA Militants, Kai Chang, and Colonel Vadik Lei, The Spider.

"This means CNSA will have more time to prepare our mega-rocket, The Chinese Eclipse. We want to launch as soon as we can after the destruction of the American Saturn Six rocket!" Kenong could not contain his joy.

"Very good Minister, time will prove us ready," said Kai Chang.

"Spider Lei, you seem unenthused. What, does the cat have The Spider's tongue?" Kenong smirked.

"I don't get too excited about anything. You lose focus when you wastefully expend energy." Vadik Lei seemed wise and composed.

"Right, right, Little Spider! You're the smart one, aren't you?" Kenong paused. "So, you think." Lei's demeanor always threatened Kenong. He knew the SHA killer was calculating, and that unnerved the Minister of State Security.

"Kai Chang, report to us on your training." Kenong was eager to hear of any progress.

"Oh, wise one, my excellent Minister," Chang feigned sincerity. "There is great progress to report."

"Go on!" Kenong nodded in anticipation, almost drooling.

"Our scientific team in our explosives division have developed a bomb that will explode from one side, much like a claymore mine does."

"Yes, yes. Tell me more." Again, Kenong's attention deficit disorder kicked in.

Vadik Lei looked on and thought that the Minister would look good with missing hands and feet. He could also not wait to cut out his tongue so that he would never have to hear his disgusting voice ever again. He knew the Minister's days were numbered; that thought brought him great joy. A joy that was masked to the world, for now.

Chang continued. "Once the bomb explodes, it will explode inward, toward the rocket's fuel tank, causing a massive explosion, that from the ground, will simply look like the rocket failed."

"Most excellent!" Kenong rubbed his hands together.

"The package will be known as, 'The Pearl,' your excellent Minister," revealed Chang.

"The Pearl, yes, I like that." Kenong nodded excessively with approval.

"Your honorable Minister, there is more." Chang wasn't finished.

"Of course, tell me more, you buffoon."

Kai paused to process the insult before continuing. "Our engineers working on the drone have made a great break-through. They have developed a cloaking skin that will be comprised of a thin sheet of Teflon. The Teflon will be studded with highly reflective, hexagonal ceramic tiles. The material will actually absorb light preventing the casting of a shadow. The only problem we will have now will be once the device is planted on the rocket, how will the device remain attached as the rocket approaches speeds of Mach 13?"

"This is good news, my little vegetable." Kenong could not help but to insult Chang again and again. "Keep me apprised of how it will stay affixed to the skin of the rocket."

Kai Chang looked over to Vadik Lei. The two men laughed as they spoke in Spanish, with Lei saying, "No puedo esperar para matara este tonto!" Translation: I can't wait to kill this fool.

Kai Chang laughed out loud and said, "Sì, què placer me daría verlo muertro en un charco de su propia orina." Translation: Yes, what pleasure I would take seeing him dead in a puddle of his own piss.

Kenong laughed along with the two SHA militants, unaware of what they said. "What did you say?" Kenong knew it was a joke about him.

"Your Excellent Minister, I was just saying how excellent you were, in one of the eight languages that I speak." Vadik Lei shot a grin to the Minister.

Kenong did not believe his subordinate but decided not to pursue the comment further.

"Tell me, Minister Kenong, how many languages do you speak?" Lei jabbed at his boss.

Location: Washington, D.C. CIA Headquarters – December 7, 2026 – 9:10 am EST.

In the office of CIA Director James Clapper sat the Director, Jordan Spear, Cade McBride, Matt Solstice, Montgomery Stevens, and Virginia Worthington. The team was gathered around the large conference table with coffee cups adorning the tabletop.

"As always, thank you for being here today, everyone,"

Clapper, as always, was mundane and stoic. "Our goals for today are simple, find out what the Chinese are up to and to make sure they don't bring down our Saturn Six Rocket. Jordan, please give us your update." Clapper began the meeting.

"Thank you, Director Clapper. Okay, here's what we know as of an hour ago." Jordan was reading from a laptop.

"Our source in Beijing continues to be silent. It's been four weeks since our last contact."

Clapper interjected, "Prior to radio silence, did he demand intel or payment in return for the information that he's been passing to us yet?"

"No, Director, nothing," responded Jordan.

"That can't be a good thing." Virginia Worthington spoke up.

"Tell us what you're thinking, Virginia," encouraged Clapper.

"Well, to date, he's given us information that could possibly head off a world war, and information, that if it didn't prevent a war, at the very least is helping the U.S. avoid a disaster far greater than the 1986 Challenger explosion...."

McBride interjected, "Maybe it's the 'World War' part that's motivating our friend."

"Hmm," Clapper somewhat agreed with a nod.

"That does make sense," said Jordan. "However, the information provided, if it's good intel, is worth a great deal."

"Why, then, has he gone silent?" mused McBride.

"He's dead!" offered Solstice, nodding his head. "It would make sense. He got caught sharing state secrets, and they got rid of him."

"Well then, if he's dead," Worthington paused, "that critical intel will likely stop coming. That's a big problem!"

Clapper broke in. Tapping his pen and grumbling, he said, "Folks, while the 'dead' part makes sense, you NEVER go with that assumption. The moment you do, you stop asking the question, why."

The five agents all nodded their heads in agreement.

"So, back to the question of why. Why does this person give us intel that could be reciprocated with valuable counter-intel, that could make him either rich or make him a hero to his bosses?" Jordan wondered aloud.

Clapper shrugged again. "He wants to come here!" He laid his pen down. "He wants to give us one more warning of something big, and then he'll make his offer. We get him, and probably his family, out of China and make him a rich American."

"That means we need to be on the look-out for another piece of major information. It'll be then that he'll throw out the quid pro quo," Jordan surmised to the group.

The group was startled by the speakerphone at the center of the table as it began to buzz.

Clapper pressed the red button and said, "What is it, Colleen?"

"Sir, Agent Cole Slater is here and says that it's urgent."

"Send him in." Clapper raised his brow, "This should be interesting!"

Clapper stood to greet his guest as the door opened. "Agent Slater, as you can see, we're in a meeting here."

"Hey, guys!" Slater acknowledged the group sitting at the table. "Sorry, Director Clapper, but you're going to want to hear this." Slater was holding onto a thick manilla folder.

"Only if it pertains to 'Operation Venom,'" Clapper was stern.

"It does, sir," Slater was eager to share the info.

"By all means, have a seat then!" Clapper motioned to the empty chair next to Worthington.

Pushing the red button on the phone, Clapper said, "Colleen, get Zoe's Kitchen in here for lunch. Make sure I get two steak-kabobs and a salad. Get a whole bunch of other stuff, but make sure I get two kabobs. Oh, and there are seven of us now."

"Yes, sir," came the words through the phone.

"Oh, and make sure you get yourself something too!" Clapper was always thinking of his longtime secretary, who'd been with him since his days as the Director of National Intelligence.

"Thank you, sir!" Colleen sounded appreciative.

"Okay, Cole, whatta ya got for us?" Clapper was eager, but his expression would never reveal it.

"Sir, we heard from our contact, 'The Serpent', just minutes ago."

The agents at the table were amazed. They thought to themselves, did Clapper know something before Slater walked through the door?

"Continue, please," said Clapper.

"He's ready to make a deal, sir," Slater revealed.

"CIA Officer Slater, for the love of God, will you get to the point?" Clapper displayed apathy.

"Yes, sir!" Slater showed more urgency, now quickly opening the large envelope in his hand.

Slater placed the contents on the table and each of the agents took a moment to review the documents and images.

Clapper showed rare emotion on his face and said, "My God!". He then tossed some papers on the table along with his readers and added, "This would have indeed caused world war three."

The information dumbfounded the group. Those in attendance shook their heads in disbelief.

"Okay, Cole, let me get this straight," Jordan shook his head to clear his thoughts. "You're telling me that the Chinese will attempt to plant an invisible bomb on the third stage of the Saturn Six rocket and then detonate it after stages one and two fell away?"

"Yes, Jordan, that's what the intel is showing," responded Slater.

Solstice added, "It says here they intend to plant it the night before the launch, using a drone that will take off from a fishing boat in the Atlantic, just off the east coast of Florida. It suggests the drone will be undetectable because of its ceramic skin."

Worthington read deeper into the packet. "Holy crap! Director, you were right! It says here that our source wants to defect." Her facial expression displayed her amazement at Clapper's prognostication. "Wow! I don't know what to say!" she added.

Jordan jumped in, "How in the hell do we approach this scenario?" He looked to Clapper.

"Simple, lady and gentlemen," Clapper gave the nod to Virginia Worthington. "We'll let them plant the bomb."

Gasps could be heard.

"But sir!" McBride, Slater, and Worthington chorused.

"Hang on, guys." Jordan shut down the gallery to let the Director continue.

Clapper nodded in small appreciation to Jordan. "We'll let the Chinese plant the bomb. Of course, we'll remove it before lift-off, delaying it another week, or so." Clapper sighed.

"But why take the chance, sir? Letting the Chinese anywhere near that spaceship doesn't sound like a good idea to me," said McBride.

"For a couple of reasons, Cade." Clapper leaned forward with both elbows now on the table and made his case. "One, we need to see how they do it. The technology could be very useful to us in the future. Two, we need to make sure that The Serpent is passing along real intel, and not some bogus stuff trying to get a FREE ticket into the U.S."

"The other thing to remember is," Clapper paused, "the minute the rocket doesn't explode, The Serpent will be at risk and want to get out of China as soon as possible. The Chinese will know they have a leak. If nothing else, he'll become vulnerable and might show his cards to his own people. The notion of retiring and living a good life in the States could all go away fast the moment we delay the launch and find that bomb."

"Or, he'll find a scapegoat," offered Jordan.

"What about the S.O.B. fishing out in the Atlantic, looking to reel in the big one?" Cade McBride asked.

"Jordan and Matt over here will be there to scoop him up in one of our Coast Guard Cutters." Clapper let out a rare laugh. "I'd love to see the look on that guy's face when a 210-foot Legend Class Cutter pulls up next to him."

Jordan and Matt Solstice looked pumped at the notion of snatching a Chinese spy out of a boat, in the middle of the Atlantic, at night.

"Jordan, Cole, everyone." Clapper addressed the group. "We need to get as much information out of The Serpent before someone cuts off the head of the snake."

"Make sure we have an offer in place to entice him further."

"Sir, he mentioned in his request that he thought Ohio was beautiful."

Clapper shrugged. "Perhaps this Chinese snake was educated in the States. Virginia...."

"Yes, sir?"

"Follow that angle, would you?"

"Yes, sir!" Worthington was excited.

Location: Beijing China, Macikou Area Residential District, twenty-five miles northwest of city center. February 21, 2027 – Saturday night – 11:01 pm GMT +8.

Spider Lei stared at himself in the mirror while completing his final set of pull-ups. With Astronaut training complete, he had more time to contemplate his future. He finished his set and walked to the tiny mirror above the sink in the small bathroom just off the kitchen.

Wiping his brow, he spoke in Mandarin, "Guāngróng de sǐwáng, guāngróng de sǐwáng." Translation: An honorable death, for an honorable death.

The Spider was persistent; this would be his final mission. When it was complete, Minister Li Kenong would die, and he would disappear into the night, never to be seen or heard from again. If he didn't live to see the mission's completion, then neither would his nemesis, Li Kenong.

Chapter 19 – Saturn Six

By the end of the third manned mission to Black Earth, NASA knew it needed a bigger rocket. The USA's next rocket would need to carry a bigger payload, not only a greater human cargo, but more scientific equipment and even a mobile lab for use on the surface. The New Horizon series, previously used to get astronauts to Black Earth, had become obsolete after just three manned and one unmanned mission.

NASA engineers had been working on a rocket so big that it had to be named after its forefather, the Saturn 5 rocket, retired in 1973. The new rocket was called Saturn Six, and the production of its twin, Neptune One, was happening concurrently. The Neptune One would serve initially as a redundancy to the Saturn Six rocket. Should anything go wrong during launch or after dropping its cargo off on Black Earth, Neptune One would be at the ready. Neptune One would also serve as the following mission's spaceship, tentatively scheduled to launch in late 2028.

The new rockets would each cost ninety-billion dollars. They would stand at a height of 370 feet and have a diameter of 39 feet across, exceeding the Saturn 5 rocket's 363-foot height and 33-foot diameter.

By 2024, NASA, like SpaceX, had mastered reusing its first and second stage portions of their rockets. As each of the first and second stages of the rocket burned off its Boost Fuel, they would fall back to Earth and then, at an altitude of 30,000 feet, would flip over and sprout fins resembling giant tennis rackets, each roughly the size of a pick-up truck. Then, at 20,000 feet, the rocket thrusters would burn in an effort to slow their descent. Onboard computers would account for unpredictable environmental occurrences like wind and air pressure. Then, tiny nitrogen gas thrusters would guide and stabilize the booster as it fell, in a controlled fashion, to a barge waiting in the Atlantic Ocean. The barge would be the size of an oil tanker. With each stage successfully retrieved, NASA would save roughly twenty-million dollars per stage, making the rocket's second and third launches far less expensive.

Additionally, crew safety had advanced, as well. Should a cataclysmic event occur during lift-off, such as an explosion of either rocket stages one or two, the crew compartment would jettison skyward, launching itself clear of the destruction below. It would then fall safely back to Earth as parachutes deployed. The world could not bear another disaster like that of the Space Shuttle Challenger in 1986. The Challenger, carrying seven astronauts, broke apart just seventy-three seconds into flight. The launch was televised around the world, and the international community was in shock by the event.

The Saturn Six's power would exceed the previously planned SLS rocket, which was designed as part of NASA's Artemis mission to send humans back to the moon.

Location: Artesia, New Mexico. Artesia General Hospital – March 24, 2027, 11:50 am MST.

The sound of crying babies could be heard coming from delivery room 123. Lola and Carrick had just welcomed twins. Lillian Koss Michaels came into the world at 11:43 am, followed by Erickson Michael Michaels at 11:45 am. Lola held baby Lilly while Carrick took extra care of baby Erik; the two were as proud as they could possibly be. Naming the children after Carrick's grandparents was the easiest decision they'd ever made. The tiny Michaels twins would carry on the greatest family legacy ever known to humans on Earth.

The day was bitter-sweet however, little Lilly Spencer suffered a relapse just three days before and needed to be hospitalized for more Leukemia treatments. Though Lola was her primary doctor while being treated at AGH, she would not attend to her medical needs for several weeks after giving birth.

Later that afternoon, after Lola was transferred to the room where she'd spend the next twenty-four hours recovering, there was a knock at the door; it was Doug and Sarah Spencer.

"Hi, guys!" Doug and Sarah looked happy to see Lola and Carrick after the birth. "Congratulations! We are so happy for you two!"

"How's Lilly, Sarah?" Lola asked while holding a sleeping baby Erik.

"She's feeling a little better. They have to run more tests, so we're in a 'wait and see' mode for now." Sarah was optimistic.

"The timing of everything really sucks! We feel terrible." Carrick felt guilty that his good fortune came when their dearest friends were going through hell.

"It's okay, man!" said Doug. "Today is all about you guys! This is amazing! Twins!" he was all smiles.

"So, you went with little Erik and little Lilly?" Sarah's smile went from ear to ear. "And now there's two Little Lillys."

"We did!" Lola smiled then released a sigh; she was both exhausted and proud. "We should be able to tell them apart, for at least a few years, anyway."

"What a tribute to the old man, huh?" said Doug.

"We miss him so much. If only he were here to see this." Carrick still hadn't fully gotten over Erik's passing. The feeling of being incomplete, the feeling he had when searching his way through the universe prior to meeting Erik, was back. The hole in his heart was bigger than ever, but he'd hoped the twins would help make him feel complete again.

"Well, listen, we have to get back to Lilly soon, she wants McDonald's. I hope they'll let us smuggle some up to her," Sarah joked.

"You tell them that Dr. Lola Michaels said it was okay." Lola returned Sarah's laugh.

Moments later, with the babies in their bassinettes, Carrick sat on the edge of Lola's bed.

"You did it, Babe! You really did it!" Carrick was so proud of his Lola.

"WE did it, Babe," Lola whispered. "We did it."

Later on, after a nap, Lola needed to share something with Carrick.

"Honey, I wanted to pass something by you."

"What is it?" asked Carrick.

"I was thinking that after I'm no longer caring for Lilly Spencer, that I might take some time away. You know, for the babies." Lola was worried about how Carrick might feel about her desire to be a stay-at-home Mom.

"That would make me so happy!" Carrick beamed. "Our babies deserve to have a full-time Mommy."

Lola was so relieved. The two were in Heaven.

Location: Titusville, FL., Cape Canaveral Air Force Station Space Launch Complex 41 – March 27, 2027 – 10:07 am EST – T-Minus Twenty-four hours until launch.

The international crew conducted a final walk-through of launch day activities. Engineers worked in the spacious crew cabin, testing to ensure all systems functioned properly; everything was a go.

After a four-month delay, NASA and the crew were chomping at the bit to get back into space. Delays were caused by the FBI and CIA's multiple investigations and unseasonal storm activity in the Atlantic. Hurricane season carried on into January.

More than a dozen staff, engineers, scientists, and astronaut understudies were removed from the Saturn Six project during the multiple investigations. While no arrests were made, the U.S. spy and counter-intelligence agencies erred on the side of caution. If anyone under scrutiny cast a shadow of a doubt, they were removed from the project.

NASA, the CIA, and the FBI ensured that everyone associated with the mission was squeaky clean and beyond reproach. In a move that many outsiders considered equivalent to the Japanese internment camps during the World War II era, no Chinese Taikonauts would occupy a seat on the spaceship, as they had in the two of the previous three trips to Black Earth. Nor would anyone with Chinese ties be allowed to work on the Saturn Six project. The public relations blow-back would be minuscule compared to the nightmare scenario of a ninety-billion dollar rocket, carrying a payload of ten humans, and scientific equipment, such as rovers, and a mobile laboratory, exploding upon lift-off.

Location: Titusville, FL., Cape Canaveral Air Force Station. Office of Marcus Johnston – March 27, 2027 – 8:14 pm – T-Minus less than twelve hours until launch.

Mars was sitting at his desk in his Florida office, reviewing some last-minute details before the launch. Suddenly, the door burst open, and in walked James Clapper, Jordan Spear, and Matt Solstice.

Mars was startled. "What the hell is going on here?!" He jumped from his seat. "Director Clapper? Jordan?"

"Mars," nodded Clapper.

"What's happening?" Mars felt like a school kid being stared down by the principal. He was sure he had mistakenly passed classified information to someone by accident. "I can explain, sir!" He jumped to his own defense without knowing what exactly he needed to defend.

"Relax, Administrator Johnson."

"Ah, that's Johnston, with a 'T,' sir."

"I know Mars, have a seat, would you?" A placid look on Clapper's face replaced an eyeroll. The CIA Director was simply displaying humor in the face of dire circumstances and Mars didn't get it.

Mars fell back into his seat, completely confused by the unfolding events.

"Jordan," said Clapper, "tell him why we're here."

"Mars, the Silver Comet isn't going to launch tomorrow."

"What are you talking about? We launch in less than twelve hours." Mars had no idea what was happening. "You guys need to tell me what's going on here! I have two hundred people getting ready to send THAT into space," Mars pointed out his window.

Sitting just two miles away was the biggest and most powerful spaceship ever built. The Silver Comet was lit up like a Christmas tree as dozens of spotlights washed over the rocket.

"Mars, on December 7 of last year, we received intelligence that a bomb would be planted on the third stage of that rocket," Jordan, like Mars, pointed out the same window.

"What?! December 7! And you're just telling me now?!" Mars was both shocked and offended.

"Calm down, Mars," encouraged Clapper.

Mars swallowed hard.

"We needed to keep everything on schedule so that the Chinese weren't tipped off to the fact that we knew of their plan," explained Jordan.

"Mars, for the next twelve hours, everything must go exactly as planned. Every person, the crew, engineers, everyone must do exactly what they were going to do, just as if that spaceship were going to launch tomorrow at 10:00 am," Jordan was adamant.

Clapper spoke, "Mars, if you tell one person, your ex-wife, your kid, an administrator, a friend, anyone, you will be tried for treason. Do I make myself clear?" Clapper's face was hushed.

"I don't understand!" Mars was still confused.

Clapper sat down in front of Mars' desk and said, "The Chinese are watching. They cannot know that we were tipped off until after we cancel the launch."

"Mars, as we speak, we have eyes on a small vessel about ninety miles off the coast of Cape Canaveral. On what appears to be a simple fishing boat is a Chinese counter-intelligence officer. His job is to bring down that rocket." Jordan again pointed out the window.

"Jesus Christ!" Mars was flustered. "So, you guys burst in here, completely unexpected, and tell me there's a bomb on board my ship!" Mars shook his head and paced the floor. "You could've called!" Mars' eyes went wide as the wrinkles on his forehead gathered.

"We couldn't call. We didn't know who'd be listening," explained Matt Solstice. "For all we know, the whole place is being surveilled by the Chinese."

"Mars, Matt's right. Either way, here we are, and now we have work to do," offered Jordan.

"Mars, is there a place we can go that's secure and not monitored by NASA?" Clapper paused, "Or the CIA?"

"What?! You guys have this place bugged?!" Mars was overcome by fear, thinking that his personal conversations might be on record somewhere.

After a few moments of wrapping his head around the circumstances, Mars said, "Follow me!" He then led the way to a large, secure conference room just down the second-floor hall.

As Mars led the three men, he felt like a junior CIA Officer, a man of international intrigue: like his friend Jordan Spear.

Now sitting down in Conference Room A, Clapper spoke. "Gentlemen, here's what's going to happen. Tomorrow morning, the ten Astronauts will board the rocket, followed by the Close-out team. The hatch will be sealed, and count-down will begin as the whole thing is televised to the world. At T-minus eight seconds, the word abort will be shouted by the Flight Director, Vance McDonald. No explanation will be given to the world until the following day."

Mars put his foot down. "I'm not having my people, including the astronauts, board that ship if there's a bomb attached to it."

"You will," Clapper paused for dramatic effect. "Or, you know? The whole treason thing?" he grumbled.

"Mars, tonight we have to allow the Chinese agent to place the bomb as we're certain that his people will be watching him," Jordan explained. "They'll likely view the same feed coming from the drone that he'll be seeing."

"Once the bomb is placed, and he closes down his feed, Matt here, and I," Jordan looked in Matt's direction, "will pounce on him with the help of the U.S. Coast Guard."

"Okay, I got it! I'll agree to it under one condition," Mars seemed eager. "I'll be on that Cutter!"

The three men rolled their eyes with Jordan, saying, "Come on, Mars, that's ridiculous!"

Clapper interjected, "Mars, listen, how about I let you watch the takedown take place from our Command Outpost just down the road?" The CIA Director was attempting to pacify Mars.

Mars looked bummed and didn't respond.

"And....how about this?" Clapper sweetened the deal for Mars. "How about I get you an official CIA jacket to wear, too?"

Mars perked up. "It's got to be the exact jacket that the three of you are wearing right now!"

"Deal!" said Clapper with a smile. The two men shook on it.

"And I get to keep it?!" Mars made a wishful demand.

"Fine." Clapper conceded while shooting Mars a rare smile.

As the men filed out of the room, Mars grabbed Clapper by the arm, holding him back for a moment. "Director Clapper, if there is even a remote chance any of my people could possibly be put in harm's way, I will not let them board that ship."

Clapper looked down at Mars' hand on his arm and said, "Mars, I can promise you that your people will not get hurt tomorrow. Now, if you'd kindly remove your hand from my arm..." Clapper gave Mars a look.

"Oh, yes, of course. Sorry, Director." Though a former Marine, Mars was intimidated by the former Air Force Officer. He did have great respect and admiration for him, as well. He was confident in Clapper's promise.

Location: Port St. John, Southern Suburb of Titusville, Florida. Gymnasium of the Challenger 7 Elementary Middle School.

The CIA used the inconspicuous location as a remote Command Post for Operation Take Down. Inside the Gym, more than twenty agents from the CIA and more than a dozen FBI personnel, including Special Agent John Primrose, were on scene.

Standing outside of the school, near a little league football field, were Clapper, Mars Johnston, Matt Solstice, and Jordan Spear.

"Okay, Gentlemen...," Clapper spoke loudly as the roar of the Coast Guard Sikorsky MH 60-T helicopter was deafening. The seventeen-million dollar, twin-engine, Jayhawk stood by to transport Spear and Solstice to the USCGC Vigilant, standing by in Port Canaveral, Florida.

"...Jordan, you know the drill, kill only if you have to. This guy is highly trained and might know who The Serpent is. Let's take him alive unless he has a death wish." Clapper understood the value of the asset and hoped things went smoothly, with no bloodshed.

"Yes, sir!" Jordan yelled, "We got this!" Jordan didn't want bloodshed either.

"Keep an eye on our boy!" Clapper winked at Matt Solstice.

"10-4, sir!" Mars could hear Solstice shout over the loud twin engines' sound and the flapping of his new CIA jacket.

Mars was excited to be a part of the mission to capture the bad guy. The *son of a bitch*, he thought, who was trained to bring a fiery end to what would be his greatest achievement, the launching of the new Saturn Six series rocket, The Silver Comet.

As Spear and Solstice disappeared into the body of the 14,000 lbs. orange and white beast, Clapper placed his hand on Mars' shoulder and spoke loudly into his ear, "Come on Mars, let's go watch these kids do what they do best...?"

"Catch the bad guys?" Mars yelled back, thinking that's what Clapper was going to say.

"That's right, Mars!" responded Clapper. "Catch the bad guys!" The two men smiled and jogged off.

Chapter 20 – Operation Take Down

Location: the Atlantic Ocean, aboard the USCGC Vigilant. Thirty miles due East of Cape Canaveral - March 27, 2027 – 10:59 pm – T-Minus eleven hours until launch.

Standing on the ship's aft deck, just feet away from the helipad, Jordan Spear and Matt Solstice shook hands with the ship's Captain, Roger Ferrell, as the Jayhawk MH 60-T disappeared into the jet-black western sky. Accompanying the CIA Officers were five Navy SEALs, led by Master Chief Alphonso Stryker. The Cutter also had a crew of forty men and women that included the Captain.

"Gentlemen, follow me. We'll get you below deck to the ship's Ready Room. You'll wait there until mission brief, which will happen in short order."

Captain Ferrell led the way. Behind him, Spear and Solstice followed closely, outfitted with Kevlar vests and .40 caliber sidearms. The SEALs were armed with Sig Sauer P228s sidearms and silenced HK MP5 9mm sub-machine guns, with red dot laser scopes and muzzle blast suppressors. The SEAL team would also be equipped with underwater headgear with night-vision goggles and comms headsets. They would be able to speak to one another, and those listening back on the Vigilant and at basecamp, while submerged.

Fifteen minutes later, the seven men were now situated in the ship's Comms Center and were briefed by CIA Operations Specialist Cameron Ridgeway.

"Officers Spear, Solstice," Ridgeway acknowledged his CIA brothers. He then looked at the five SEALs and said, "Sure am happy you Navy boys came along for the ride!"

The five SEALs remained silent and just nodded.

"Okay, gentlemen, here's what we're looking at." Ridgeway reviewed the fishing vessel's layout by pointing to several screens on the Comms Center's starboard wall.

Location: St. David's Island, Bermuda – Four days earlier – Mid-day.

Kai Chang and his female accomplice, SHA Agent Jenny Lee, deplaned at the Bermuda International Airport.

"Business, or pleasure, sir?" asked a middle-aged, male Customs Agent.

"Lèqù," answered Chang with a smile.

"English, please."

Chang looked at the man and just smiled.

"Do you speak English, Mr. Wong?"

"Oh, English? Oh, ...tiny little," responded Kai Chang, posing as tourist Liang Wong, and pretending to know little English.

"I see you are a Chinese citizen flying in from Morocco, is that correct?"

Chang nodded excessively and smiled. "Yes, Chinese, Morocco, yes."

"Hmm," The Customs Agent became only mildly suspicious.

"Excuse me," Chang's female accomplice stepped forward. "My husband doesn't speak very good English. Perhaps I can translate?"

"Ms. Wong? Is it?" the Customs Agent was pleasant.

"Mrs.," she responded.

"Of course, Mrs. Wong." The Customs Agent nodded with respect. "Can you please tell me the nature of your visit to Bermuda?" The agent repeatedly looked down at the couple's passports and then back up again, as if to examine their faces more closely.

"We are on a long-planned vacation. A second honeymoon, sort of," said Jenny Lee, posing as tourist, Mrs. Annchi Wong.

"Where will you be staying while in Bermuda, Mrs. Wong?"

"We are renting a cottage at the Lemon and Ginger Village."

"May I see both of your departing flight itineraries as well as your reservation receipt for the cottage?"

"Fēijī piào." Speaking in Mandarin, Jenny Lee directed Kai Chang to produce his airline ticket, as she produced the other requested documents.

Chang produced the returning flight ticket, and Lee handed them to the agent.

After looking them over, the agent said, "Please follow me." He took the couple to a holding area where several armed Customs Agents were standing by.

The two Chinese counter-intelligence agents kept their composure and stuck to the plan.

Moments later, after contacting the Lemon and Ginger management office, the Customs Agent returned.

"Thank you for your patience, Mr. and Mrs. Wong." The Customs agent returned with another agent in tow. The second agent could speak Mandarin fluently.

"At this time, we only have one more question for you. But we'll need to ask you separately. Mrs. Wong, please come with me, Mr. Wong, please stay here."

"Liú zài zhè'er," Jenny Lee instructed Kai Chang in Mandarin, keeping up the charade of husband and wife.

The agent pulled Mrs. Wong to the side and asked her, "Can you please tell me the date you were married on, and in what city it was?"

Just ten feet away, the other Customs Agent asked Mr. Wong the exact same question.

"We were married in Tianjin, China, on July 18, 2012."

"Thank you, Mrs. Wong. Please remain here for just another moment."

The Customs Agent then walked over to the agent, questioning Mr. Wong.

"What answer did he provide you with?" asked one agent of the other, as Kai Chang stood posing as Mr. Liang Wong.

"He told me that they were married 18 July 2012, in the city of Tianjin, China."

"Very good!" said one agent to the other.

"Mrs. Wong, please." The first agent waved her over to where he and her professed husband were standing.

"Again, thank you for your patience. Please enjoy your stay while in Bermuda." He then handed them back their passports and airline tickets, and the two smiled and nodded.

"Sir, can you tell us the way to baggage claim?" Jenny Lee remained in character. The agent pointed to a nearby sign, and the two walked off.

"Tài jin," said Lee.

"That was not close at all. We stick to the plan, and we will be successful," Kai Chang said.

"I won't be sleeping with you tonight, Chang," his female accomplice said.

"I am a professional Mrs. Wong, as are you," said Chang, "you will stay in character and sleep with me tonight, and then I am off, never to be seen again." Chang smiled flirtatiously.

"Always the dramatic one," said Lee, rolling her eyes as the two approached the baggage claim area.

SHA Agent, Jenny Lee, had been on several missions with Kai Chang previous to this one, and they had had sexual relations on and off for the past five years. Their superiors had once scolded the two for being romantically connected.

The following day Kai Chang met with a Chinese/Bermudian double agent and a reservation desk clerk at the Paradise Fishing Charters company. The two men would use aliases and fake I.D.s when making the reservation. Both would also be disguised.

"We will need a twenty-six-foot fishing boat beginning tomorrow. The vessel will need two sleeping cabins, refrigerated storage, and a captain to man the boat. We plan on being out for three days and will need plenty of bait and tackle," said the local Bermudian agent."

The Chinese agents would only need the boat for two days; the third day would be their day to escape the island before the boat company would miss the rental return.

"What will you be fishing for while out?" asked the clerk.

"Swordfish!" Kai Chang spoke up.

"Very good!" said the clerk.

After completing the boat reservation, the two men rendezvoused back at the condo with Jenny Lee.

"After we reach the spot, one hundred miles off of Port Canaveral, we will subdue and isolate the Captain, only keeping him alive until we are successful," Chang said. "Later, we'll tie him to the anchor and send him to the bottom of the ocean after the bomb is planted."

The Bermudian agent nodded in affirmation.

"I will remain on the island and keep up appearances," said Jenny Lee. "I will shop and dine and have receipts for all of our time while in Bermuda," she said while reviewing each step of her actions. "I will even make sure that it sounds like two passionate lovers are rekindling their marriage. Nighttime will not be quiet around here. The neighbors will think we're animals." Lee would ensure that the two could be placed in their cottage at night.

Kai Chang shot a smile at Lee and said, "Once we're one hundred miles from Florida, we will set up our equipment and bring down that rocket." Chang was confident.

Location: the Atlantic Ocean, aboard the USCGC Vigilant. Seventy miles due East of Cape Canaveral - March 28, 2027 – 12:57 am – T-Minus eight hours until launch.

After two hours of briefing, Spear, Solstice, and the five SEALs were ready to go. The plan was to come within two nautical miles of the fishing boat and then stand down. The five SEALs would then enter a motorized raft and maneuver to within two hundred yards; they'd then swim the remaining distance. Once the SEAL team was wading beneath the vessel, the Vigilant would close distance and be ready to support the SEALs just moments after the team boarded the vessel.

A U.S. drone had been circling the chartered boat at an altitude of 15,000 feet. The drone was silent and undetectable, so the two operatives on board suspected nothing. The drone would serve in two capacities; one, to monitor and record the takedown; and two, to hack the Chinese drone feed.

"It looks like we won't have too big of a firefight on our hands," said CIA Operations Specialist Cameron Ridgeway, "infrared only shows three subjects on the boat."

"Two bad guys and likely the boat's Captain," offered Spear.

"British officials tell us that the boat was chartered, so yes, they would have a navigator on board to get them to where they were going."

Back on the island of Bermuda, Jenny Lee, posing as Mrs. Annchi Wong, was under surveillance by British officials. The Brits were brought in days earlier to assist with Operation Takedown.

"I'm certain the Captain of that boat will soon be at the bottom of the Atlantic," surmised Spear. "They'll kill him after they plant the package. They'll need to keep him alive until then in case the boat company tries to contact the vessel."

"Good call!" said Ridgeway. "So, we have two armed tangos on that boat, gentlemen." Ridgeway nodded to the SEALs.

"I'd say those odds are in our favor," said SEAL Team Eight leader Master Chief Alphonso Stryker. "We got this, boys! Stay focused!"

"Hooyah!" the remaining SEALs chanted.

Listening in, Clapper said, "Boys, let's try to keep that boat captain alive. I'm sure he's got a family back in Bermuda."

One hour later.

"We have movement on the deck, fellas," alerted Ridgeway. "You guys seeing this back at base camp?"

"Roger that!" said James Clapper. "Mars, you might want to get over here." Clapper looked around and witnessed Mars sleeping on a cot in the far corner of the gymnasium.

"Boys, I'm handing comms over to Operations Specialist Marc Jenner here at base camp. You boys get this done!" said Clapper.

Jenner came on the comms, "Cam, we're opening the hacked comms on that boat now."

Roger that!" said Cameron Ridgeway, on the USCGC Vigilant, now less than thirty miles from the fishing vessel.

"Okay, we're going split-screen," said Jenner. "On the left is the infrared of the boat and its subjects. The right side will display what the Chinese drone can see. Let's all assume that Beijing has a feed of the comms. They'll want to take joy in their plan and make sure their agent comes through."

"Oh, Shit! Did you guys see that?" said a tech monitoring the infrared images of the boat.

Everyone monitoring the boat saw three infrared images turn into just two. This came after all three subjects were huddled near the back of the boat.

"Did they just kill the captain and throw him overboard?" asked Jenner while displaying some angst.

"I don't know if he's dead or not, but they didn't throw him overboard," offered Ridgeway from the Comms Center on the Vigilant. "It appears the subject disappeared into a rear storage compartment on the vessel."

"It's the refrigerated cargo hold where they stow their catch," said Spear. "I'm familiar with the set-up on a boat that size as I rented a similar one a year ago, while on vacation."

The screen monitoring the drone feed came to life, and everyone involved briefly got a glimpse of Kai Chang and the Bermudian operative. When the drone feed booted up, it captured both men on the bow of the vessel.

"Okay, boys, take note of the ship's bow layout," said SEAL team leader Stryker. "It ain't much, but every little bit helps."

Jenner came on the comms. "Let's get facial recognition on both of those subjects."

"Roger that!" said an unknown agent at Challenger 7 basecamp.

Back on the Vigilant, Stryker said, "Officer Spear, it's your takedown, but since we're better equipped, I'd recommend you let us board that vessel at least three minutes before you do. It likely won't take us more than sixty seconds to do our job, but give us a little extra time just in case we run into a snag."

Ridgeway and Solstice agreed without words. The two exchanged a look of subtle relief. This is what SEAL Team Eight was built for, they thought.

"Roger that, Master Chief," Jordan nodded in affirmation. "But if bullets fly, we won't hesitate to get in there."

"I'm worried about friendly fire," added Stryker.

"Fair enough!" Jordan agreed that they would stand down on the Vigilant until the subjects were either detained or killed.

"Remember, let's try to keep everyone breathing, boys." Jenner's voice came over the comms from base camp and echoed Clapper's from earlier.

"Roger that!" copied Ridgeway.

"Okay, the bird has wings!" said Jenner over the comms. "We're gonna have to rely on the camera feed only as the drone won't be radiating a heat signature or making any noise."

"Guys, listen, we'll be going to a third screen when the drone is two miles out." Jenner stood near Clapper and fifteen other agents in the elementary school gym. "The screen will be a scrolling feed from all the cameras locked onto the Saturn Six Rocket. Let's see if we can pick it up on approach. We'll see if this thing is truly invisible or not."

Mars Johnston walked over to where Clapper was standing and said, "What's going on? What did I miss?" while rubbing his eyes.

"No fireworks yet, Mars."

"Director Clapper, considering that a bomb is about to be attached to the biggest rocket ever built, your 'fireworks' metaphor doesn't exactly put me at ease." Mars looked appalled.

"Very well, Marcus, I'll refrain from 'exploding' terms." Clapper was expressionless.

Mars wore a look that told Clapper that he was uncomfortable with the 'exploding' term, too.

It was 3:14 am EST when the drone's camera captured a white tower in the distance. It was unmistakable; the drone had eyes on the Saturn Six rocket. The Vigilant was now within striking distance of the fishing vessel, just two miles away.

"Oh, Shit!" said Mars, who looked drenched in fear.

"Easy, Mars," offered Clapper, trying to reel in Mars' anxiety level. The two men stood back about fifteen feet from the control boards and monitors. "Our boys know what they're doing."

"There's a lot of fuel on that craft," Mars reminded Clapper. "I hope the Chinese don't decide to blow it up while it's still on the ground." Mars was terrified at the notion.

"Our intel is good," said Clapper. "The Chinese want a spectacle that is televised to the world. They want us to be humiliated."

"Okay folks, the drone is about a mile out," said Jenner, as he, Clapper, Mars, the others at base camp, and those on the Vigilant would all be spectators for the next several minutes. "Let's sit back and watch the Chinese work."

The drone now slowed as it approached the tower. It circled the rocket several times as if to determine if it could be detected.

"Are we getting anything on the tower cameras?" Jenner asked one of his technicians.

"I don't see anything, sir!" The video tech, along with everyone else, was amazed.

Ridgeway said, "I'll be damned! Our cameras aren't picking it up."

Back at Challenger 7 basecamp, Mars Johnston was red-faced. "How could NASA surveillance not see the drone in its airspace?" he wondered to himself.

Clapper looked over and knew exactly what Mars was thinking. Covering his comms, he said, "Mars, don't worry about it. This is why we do counter-intelligence. No system is full proof." He paused for a moment and added, "The Chinese just proved that."

Location: Outskirts of Beijing, current time.

"The Americans do not detect the drone!" yelled a triumphant Li Kenong. "Kai Chang is doing his country proud, hairy Spider, Vadik Lei." Kenong needled the SHA militant.

In a secure facility sat State Security, Minister Li Kenong and Vadik Lei; with them were a dozen counter-intelligence officials and technicians.

"Minister Kenong, the job is not yet done, sir," cautioned another high-ranking member of the Chinese Counter-Intelligence program.

"We will be victorious, and rain fire on the Americans in just a few hours. The whole world will see their inept failure!" Kenong's words rang out.

Spider Lei secretly hoped the Americans detected the drone. Anything that would embarrass his boss would bring him great joy. He could not wait until the Minister of State Security was dead.

Location: The Vigilant. Two miles from the fishing vessel – 3:47 am EST.

"Look at that thing!" said Jenner. "I've never seen anything like it."

The Vigilant and base camp teams marveled as the drone lowered the explosive device out from its belly. The mechanical arm sprang an elbow and then extended the device onto the skin of the rocket.

"Our intelligence said it would be attached to the third stage boys. That looks like the third stage to me," Clapper said into his comms.

Mars, not wearing comms, said, "Those sons of bitches! They're placing it right under the American Flag. Mother fuckers!"

Back on the Vigilant, Jordan Spear was thinking the same thing. He now regretted that he would not be the first one to board that vessel.

"SEAL Team Eight, do you copy?" radioed Ridgeway. "What's your twenty?"

"We are directly beneath the vessel. Over," said Master Chief Stryker.

"Can they see or hear you?"

"Negative," responded Stryker.

"Listen, we've got a tango on the deck of the ship. He's walking around looking over the side," warned Ridgeway. "He may have been out for a smoke and heard you guys."

"No chance!" said Spear. "He wouldn't be out for a stroll at the moment they're about to connect the bomb."

"Fuck! They know we're there!" Jordan blurted out. "It's a fishing vessel. They have sonar capabilities to detect fish. Our cover is blown!"

"God-dammit!" said Clapper. "How in the hell did we not account for that!"

"What's going on?" asked a concerned Mars.

"They made our SEALs." Clapper was pissed but didn't show it. "No fireworks yet," he said, forgetting that the term upset Mars.

Back on the Vigilant, Ridgeway said, "SEAL Team Leader, you have clearance to take out the tango walking around on the deck. Proceed with caution. The other SEALS should spread out and do their best impression of a dolphin pod."

"Roger that." Stryker was as calm as a professional golfer standing over a two-foot putt when holding a ten-stroke lead. "Let me know when the tango is on the bow. I'll board in the aft."

"Copy that," said Ridgeway.

While the SEALS were getting ready to board the vessel, the rest of the teams on the Vigilant and back at basecamp continued to watch in horror and amazement as the undetectable drone planted the device on the Saturn Six's third stage.

"Mars, based off of the tile sizes on the rocket, how big would you say that bomb is?" Specialist Jenner asked of Johnston.

Mars perked up. "The riveted tiles are two foot by two foot."

"That makes the bomb about a foot in diameter. It's small." Jenner was thinking out loud for all to hear.

"Whatever it's packing must be deadly!" he added.

"At the speed that rocket would be traveling," said Mars, "it wouldn't take a big hole to bring it all down. Hell, a hand grenade would do the job," said the former United States Marine.

"Well, our techs will get inside that package and find out exactly what's in there," stated Clapper confidently.

All teams focused their attention on the aft deck of the fishing boat. A heat signature, appearing as hazy white, could now be detected on the back of the vessel. It was SEAL Team leader Alphonso Stryker boarding the boat. The other SEALS positioned themselves equal distances apart just below the waterline, around the base of the boat. The Bermudian agent appeared to be less interested in what was happening in the water now, thinking that the boat's radar was simply picking up large ocean life, like swordfish or dolphins.

"Oh shit! Look at that!" said Jenner.

Everyone watching could see Stryker sneaking up on the tango and didn't see the other Chinese agent or the boat's Captain.

Onboard the boat, Stryker, who left his breathing apparatus in the water, pulled an 8" knife from its holster. He crept around the starboard side of the boat after first examining the wheelhouse. Ducking to avoid one of the two lifeboats onboard, Stryker could now see the tango. The orange glow of his cigarette made him easy to identify. He crept slowly behind the Bermudian agent and was about to pounce.

The teams witnessed Stryker sneak up right behind the tango.

"Come on, son. Come on," whispered Clapper.

Mars held his hand to his mouth.

Without a sound, Stryker wrapped his left arm around the left side of the subject and gripped his forehead, pulling it upward. He slit the Bermudian counter-intelligence agent's throat with his right hand, then slowly and quietly sat him down on the boat's deck.

It took Stryker less than a second to execute the bad guy once he made contact. The teams on the Vigilant and back at basecamp witnessed the white heat signature from the blood spray. They also detected a white pool running from Stryker's motionless victim as he lay on the deck.

Stryker's action was both lethal and stealthy, making it impossible for Kai Chang, who was finishing attaching the bomb below, to know what happened above deck.

All eyes were back on the drone feed. The drone appeared to be successful and was now moving away from the launch tower. It appeared to be admiring its work, but what it was actually doing was making sure the package could not be detected.

"I'll be damned!" said CIA technician Wally Reeves. "You can't see it! It's invisible!"

The others all squinted to see if they could make out an outline or a silhouette on the skin of the rocket; they could not.

"That dumbass placed it right under the American Flag on the third stage," Clapper spoke up. "Mars, how many American flags grace the third stage of that rocket?"

Mars half-smiled, "Just the one, Director Clapper."

"Well, we now know exactly where to look tomorrow, don't we, fellas?" Clapper smiled.

The drone then drifted out into the darkness of the Atlantic, with the comms feed turning into white fuzz minutes later. When the battery died, it would ditch in the ocean miles out to sea.

"I'm guessing it ditched itself," said Clapper. "I want a mark on exactly where that thing fell out of the sky. Perhaps it's retrievable."

"Roger that!" said Reeves.

Back on the Vigilant. "Go-Go-Go!" yelled Ridgeway into his comms.

From their feed, both groups could see the remaining four SEALS board the boat.

The SEALS could now hear the Chinese agent below deck getting ready to come topside. In the distance, only the darkness witnessed the menacing silhouette of the 210 foot Vigilant, creeping silently across the black water, slowly stalking its prey. Jordan Spear and Matt Solstice stood near the bow and were prepared to board the fishing boat.

The infrared witnessed the SEAL team leader, Master Chief Stryker, subdue the Chinese agent Kai Chang without killing him. From the wheelhouse, just six feet above the aft stairwell to the vessel's bowels, Stryker pounced, taking an unarmed Chang by surprise. Though an expert in mixed martial arts, Chang was no match for the heavily equipped and highly trained Stryker and his four counterparts, who were just feet away.

"Holy shit!" uttered Mars Johnston. "That was amazing!"

Johnston was proud to be an American and was excited to be wearing a CIA jacket. He was honored to be part of Operation Takedown. However, he was still incredibly nervous regarding the fate of the 'Silver Comet.'

"It never gets old," smiled Clapper. "It's when they put up a fight that I get a little nervous."

Moments later, on the fishing boat's aft deck, Jordan Spear stood face to face with Kai Chang. "Wǒmen zhuā dào nǐle," said Jordan Spear in Mandarin, while smiling. The SHA Agent said nothing when a man he recognized as Captain America said, 'Gotcha!' in Mandarin.

After the SEALs took Kai Chang aboard the Vigilant, Spear called Solstice to the aft deck. "This is the refrigerated hold." Spear pointed to a four-foot by four-foot hatch that stood raised six inches from the deck surface. "Let's hope this poor son of a bitch is still alive."

Pulling upward on the unlocked hatch, the smell of chum and live bait invaded the nostrils of the two CIA Officers, causing them to recoil. As their flashlights flooded the fish-blood covered cargo bay, they could see the Captain. With a gag in his mouth and a lacerated forehead, he looked up at the two in terror while squinting. He was crying but happy to be alive. He took relief in seeing the letters 'CIA' written across the center of the men's Kevlar vests.

Back at basecamp and aboard the Vigilant, spirits were high. "Good guys one, bad guys zero. All of our men are safe," said Clapper, "and the Captain's going home to his family, too."

Mars wasn't so happy. "There's still a bomb attached to my rocket, and I want it off!" he said.

"Our work is not done yet, Mars. We still have to act like we're launching in just over four hours," said Clapper.

It was nearly dawn as the two men exited the elementary school. "Go get an hour's worth of sleep, and I'll meet you in your office at 7:30 am," said Clapper.

Mars was wide-eyed. "I won't be getting any sleep!" NASA's Chief Administrator was exhausted.

Chapter 21 – The Interrogation

Location: Aboard the USCGC Vigilant. 6:20 am EST.

In a large holding cell, handcuffed to a bolted chair, sat SHA Militant Kai Chang. Opposite of Chang, CIA Interrogation Specialist Jordan Spear.

"So, here we are," said Spear. "What do you have to say for yourself?"

"Méiyǒu yīngyǔ!" said Kai Chang, with a look of disdain.

"No English, huh?" smiled Spear. "Wǒ zhīdào nǐ huì yīngyǔ," Spear smiled again, catching his captive off guard. "Not only do you know English, but you know five other languages, too. Isn't that right, Kai Chang?"

"Seven, actually," Chang smiled.

"That's impressive!" Jordan thought anyone who could speak seven languages should be in a more credible line of work as opposed to being a hired assassin.

"So, the famous Captain America speaks Mandarin, huh?" Chang spit on the table, smiled, and released a sinister laugh.

"Is that what they call me back at the Strategic Huyou Agency?" asked Jordan.

Chang was silent; he just looked off into the dead space behind Jordan.

"Mrs. Wong, aka Jenny Lee, sends her regards. Oh, and your Bermudian friend from the fishing boat? Yeah, ...he's dead." Jordan made it clear that the U.S. was one step ahead of the Chinese.

"So, Super-Hero, what now?" Chang was defiant.

"We just sit here and talk until one of us gets hungry or thirsty. If it's me, then I get up and have a sandwich. If it's you, I just sit here and watch you look hungry."

Spear then pulled out a piece of gum, unwrapped it, and started chewing. "Mmm, good. It so mouth-watering," Jordan liked how the interrogation was unfolding.

Again, Chang spit on the table in front of Spear.

Smiling, Jordan said, "My guess is that before too long, you'll run out of spit."

Chang just groaned, as if to say, "So what!"

Silence ensued for several minutes before Chang spoke again. "We met once."

"Did we?" Jordan feigned surprise.

"In England. Maybe seven years ago...London," Chang seemed to be warming up to Spear.

"I thought you looked familiar when I saw you on the fishing boat. It was dark, though, so I wasn't sure," said Chang.

Jordan Spear had somewhat of an admiration for Chang as well. After all, they had a lot in common, and now they also shared a past.

"Oh yes," said Spear, with a look of spurious enlightenment. "I nearly met The Spider that night, too. "He seemed to leave rather quickly when he saw me standing there. He looked intimidated by me. I think."

Kai Chang just smiled at Spear. He knew that he could kill the CIA Officer in just seconds; he also knew that Vadik Lei could easily kill him, too. Spear would be no match for The Spider. He knew it, and from Jordan's words, he knew that the CIA Officer sitting in front of him knew it, too.

From an adjacent room, Solstice, Ridgeway, and SEAL Team leader Stryker observed the interrogation through a closed-circuit monitor.

"He's smooth," said Stryker.

"Yeah, the ladies think so, too," offered Solstice.

Ridgeway just chuckled.

Chang addressed Spear's assumption. "Yes, The Spider was there in London, but he didn't want to be. He has a disdain for Governmental officials and does not like doing their dirty work. He likes killing, though, that's why he does what he does."

"So, he didn't think highly of Kitan Zhao, the nephew of your President, Xí Shèng-Xióng?"

Chang was impressed with Spear's tenacity and astuteness. He offered up only information that he determined Spear already possessed and would not fall into the trap the CIA Officer was setting. 'Win his trust, and he'll confess all,' Chang surmised but was too seasoned for that.

"Listen, I know that you can probably kill me with one hand tied behind your back, and while blind-folded," Jordan tried to look sincere, not believing his lie, though. "But...," Jordan paused, "your hands being cuffed behind your back....probably not that comfortable, I'm guessing."

Ridgeway sat up in his seat. "Jordan? Don't do it, man!"

Solstice and Stryker smiled at Jordan's actions. Stryker said, "I'm not going to have to go in there and break up a fight, am I?" He looked quite amused at the unfolding events.

Kai Chang said to himself, "Is this fool really going to uncuff me? I can kill him in under fifteen seconds."

Solstice looked over at Stryker and Ridgeway and said, "Chang would have a fighting chance. A wild haymaker could catch him on the chin, maybe," Matt looked skeptical. "He could get lucky, I guess. If I were a betting man, though, my guess is that Chang would be dead before we could even get in there."

Jordan stood and presided over his captive. At 225lbs and a height of 6' 4", he was nearly a foot taller than Chang and had roughly 50lbs. on him, too. The square footage was plentiful in the holding cell, but the ceilings were low; this made Jordan appear to be even taller to the SHA Agent.

Spear walked around the table and removed the cuffs from Chang's hands, freeing him from the metal chair. Jordan was not over-confident, though; he knew the cuffs could be used as a weapon and was careful to pocket them quickly. The SHA militant had already observed that the table and chairs were all bolted down to the floor. He had also surveyed the room for other potential weapons; there were none. Lastly, he reasoned that there were at least a hundred men on the ship, many of them armed; he'd never get out alive. For the moment, Chang was content on not making a move, as his survival was priority one. Their duel would have to happen using words, and not weapons.

Jordan sat back down and tossed the gum to Chang. He'd noticed earlier that Chang looked at the pack of gum on the table with interest.

Chang picked up the gum and withdrew a piece from the pack, then opened it up without words. For just a moment, he thought to himself, *how might this wrapper be used as a weapon?* He concluded that it couldn't. He then laid the stick of gum flat across his tongue and savored the taste. "Mmm, Juicy Fruit."

"Not everything about America is bad. Wouldn't you agree?" asked Jordan in an effort to disarm his adversary.

"Perhaps," said Chang. "I like the women, too." Chang also admired his CIA nemesis. He thought that under different circumstances that perhaps they could be friends.

"Listen, Kai, may I call you Kai?

"May I call you Jordan?"

"I liked Captain America better, but yeah, Jordan's fine."

"Kai would be fine then," Chang was acting outwardly like he was warming up to Jordan. He admitted to himself that the CIA Officer was charismatic.

"Kai, listen, you might not be going home, ever. But...," Spear paused, "let's just say for fun that you might. We could probably work something out. You know, 'double-agent' stuff. Anything is possible, right?"

Chang laughed out loud. "You were starting to impress me as someone who was smart," he paused, "but now I'm not so sure.

There is no way! Double agent? I'm sorry, it will never happen. You could take away my freedom, but you will never take away my honor."

Chang was lying. He knew that Spear was right. He had no honor; he was a hired killer for the Chinese government. They did not care about him. He knew that Minister Li Kenong sent him on a one-way journey and knew that he'd likely die. After all, he was going to strap a bomb to his chest and blow him and the spaceship into tiny pieces.

"Kai, you have no honor. You're like me, a hired gun. The CIA doesn't care about me dead or alive, and SHA doesn't care about you. My country will use me until someone like you puts me in the ground, and then it's next man up."

"You think you know me, Jordan, you do not!" Chang was cool.

"I don't know you, Kai," Jordan paused, "But I know me, and we are the same. I AM you."

In the next room, Ridgeway said, "Damn, this guy is good."

"Yeah, apparently he got schooled on Black Earth when interrogating Black Earth Erik. He said he learned a lot from the old man," revealed Matt Solstice.

"Listen," said Jordan, "It's been a long night for both of us. I'm going to have my guys fix you a sandwich before they put you in your cell. Get some sleep, and we'll talk later today when our heads are a little clearer."

Jordan stood to shake Kai Chang's hand, but Chang declined by looking away.

As Jordan turned to walk out the door, Chang said, "Jordan, what will happen to Jenny Lee?"

Before Jordan answered the question, he immediately realized that Chang showed his hand. He now knew that one of his weaknesses was his female accomplice.

"She will be tried and convicted of espionage and sent to Guantanamo Bay in Cuba. One day she'll be used as trade bait if

China ever convicts one of ours. I doubt that you'll ever see her again."

"Hmm," Kai Chang muttered.

"Goodnight, Brother," Spear nodded before walking out the door.

Chang smirked, exhaling through his nose, and thought to himself that the foolish American just played him.

Location: Titusville, FL., Cape Canaveral Air Force Station Space Launch Complex 41. Florida Office of Marcus Johnston – March 28, 2027 – 7:30 am – T-Minus less than three hours until scheduled launch.

Mars Johnston was awakened by the opening of his office door as it banged a table on the wall just behind it. Mars had fallen asleep at his desk while awaiting James Clapper.

Through the door walked James Clapper, Operations Specialist Marc Jenner, and FBI Agent John Primrose.

Mars awoke from what he thought was a dream. It had been less than twelve hours prior that Clapper had burst through the door with Spear and Solstice, flipping his life on its head. This was *either a dream or déjà vu,* he thought to himself.

"Up and at 'em, Mars! We need to review a plan that I've drawn up!" said Clapper, trying to get Mars alert and fully awake.

James Clapper laid a legal pad with scribbled notes on Mars' desk and said, "This is what I've come up with."

Mars picked up the pad, looked over the crude notes and pencil sketches, and smirked. "This doesn't look very official!" he said while tossing the plans back onto the desk.

"Well, Mars, while you were sleeping, I was brainstorming with these two highly trained gentlemen here," Clapper looked over at Jenner and Primrose and then back to Mars. "How do my notes compare to yours?"

"Okay, okay. I get it." Mars picked up the legal pad and took a closer look.

"Mars, I'll just summarize it for you. I have ten FBI and CIA Officers on standby, volunteers. Men and women who understand the risks. They will pose as your Astronauts and make it look like they're ready to board that ship. They will take the elevator to the top of that tower," Clapper pointed out the window, "and then make an about-face, and come right back down again. The international team doesn't have to risk it."

"Why the charade? We can just say the weather is bad and delay it," offered Mars.

"You see that beautiful blue sky and sunshine out there?" Clapper again looked out the window. "Mars, news helicopters are flying around out there. Reporters are everywhere. We can't fake them all out with a bogus weather report."

"Yeah, and I have a news conference in sixty minutes, so we need to get to work," said Mars, agreeing with Clapper. "Your plan is too elaborate. I've got another idea, one where no one will be put at risk."

Location: Cape Canaveral, Florida. Air Force Station Space Launch Complex 41, Press Room – 8:47 am.

A large contingent of press credentials were issued, and more than fifty news agencies from around the world were in attendance. Mars and several other NASA officials were lined up on a stage, sitting behind four long folding tables covered in white tablecloths. In front of each official was a folded paper nameplate, adorned with each official's NASA logo, name, and title.

Mars was understandably nervous. This would be the last press conference he would give before launching the biggest rocket ever built. This was to be his crowning achievement, the first manned mission to space by NASA in more than three years, and the first of his tenure as Chief Administrator of NASA.

Mars Johnston sat there as the audience of reporters settled in while his officials took their seats. He poured a glass of water and took a nervous swig. He looked around as if to see support from the very men who helped him concoct the lie he was about to tell. The CIA, FBI, and Clapper, however, were conspicuously absent. Behind the scenes, the ten men and women scheduled to begin their journey to Black Earth were quarantined and awaiting more information. They were instructed to be radio silent and not allowed to use their phones or watch television.

Why would the CIA be here? Mars rationalized in his head. He would have to be ready should any questions come out of left field. *Moments like this one are the reason I'm here. It's why I was chosen to head NASA*, he thought to himself.

At that moment, Mars felt a calm come over himself; the feeling of dread had receded. Pulling the microphone close to his mouth, he began the live press conference that would be televised around the world.

"Ladies and gentlemen, please, let's get started." Mars looked like his normal self; easy-going and approachable. He opened with a statement. "Folks, before we take questions, I'd like to read from a prepared statement."

"A little more than two hours ago, at around 6:00 am, our technicians detected an anomaly in our read-outs at Mission Control in Houston versus what we were seeing here at Canaveral. This conflict in our data has unfortunately resulted in the delay of the 10:00 am launch of The Saturn Six Series, The Silver Comet..." Mars was instantly bombarded with questions from the press pool.

Dozens of questions were being shouted at him. He picked a random reporter to begin what was to be an uncomfortable thirty-minute Q&A session.

"Yes, Bob, go ahead." Mars recognized Bob Stevens from CBS News first.

"Administrator Johnston, sir!" Stevens recoiled his penned hand and prepared to write Johnston's response. "Can you be more specific? What problems are occurring exactly, communication, electrical, computer? Can you elaborate, sir?"

"No, we cannot go into that kind of detail, other than to say that unless all systems check, we don't launch! That's always been the protocol here at NASA. We're going to do this right." Mars was calm and confident in his delivery.

"Our schedule is based on safety, not the eyes of the world hoping to see a launch today." Mars was resolute in his lie.

Another reporter shouted, "How long will the delay be for?"

"We expect that the delay could be days, likely, but not weeks."

The goal of the announced delayed timeframe was meant to discourage the press from sticking around for hours or even days. NASA and the CIA needed secrecy and time. Time to remove the explosive device without causing suspicion or curiosity.

The pool of reporters groaned. The questions just kept coming, and Mars handled them with grace.

Back in Beijing, a small contingent of government officials, led by the Minister of State Security, Li Kenong, were furious at the news. They had hoped to see American aspirations go up in flames.

"He has failed!" Kenong shouted while throwing a bowl of rice across the room. "Kai Chang has failed his government and his people."

"Minister Kenong! Control yourself!" said an official that was senior to Kenong. "Launch delays are routine. They happen all the time, even with our program. There have been several delays this year already. You're over-reacting. We all watched as the device was successfully planted on the rocket."

"Am I over-reacting, Honorable Haoran Shieh? We will know in a matter of hours if we don't hear from our agents on the ground in Bermuda," challenged Kenong.

"We already have, you fool! Jenny Lee reported in after Chang returned," revealed Haoran Shieh.

Kenong was surprised. "Why did no one notify me of this?"

"I just did, you fool!" The official didn't like the Minister or his inability to manage his stress level.

"They are headed to the airport now and will arrive in Morocco in roughly eight hours."

Thirty minutes later, back at Cape Canaveral, Mars Johnston emerged from the Press Room looking haggard. Before the conference, his engineers, who now had a look of confusion on their faces, were told to sit there and direct all of their questions to Johnston. Before going into the gaggle, Mars told them that they'd be filled in after the press conference was over. Now, he had some explaining to do.

Fifteen minutes later, in the building's largest conference room, more than thirty NASA personnel and national security officials met. No press were allowed.

Clapper took the microphone and addressed the curious, confused, and concerned attendees.

"Folks," Clapper, as always, was stoic. "Today I am going to share some disturbing news with you. Prior to leaving this room, you will all be given a document to sign. That document will include a Non-disclosure agreement, and you will all be sworn to secrecy."

Muffled groans could be heard amongst the staff as the security officials looked at each other and, without words, asked themselves the obvious question, "How do we keep this a secret from the world?"

Clapper continued, "You are all here because you possess Level 1 security credentials. With that being said, NOTHING leaves this room!" In a rare gesture of authoritarianism, Clapper raised his voice. His tone even startled the National Security personnel in attendance. Mars was also taken aback. "The future of our space program is at stake!" he added forcefully.

"I hope I have your attention, along with your discretion going forward. If I don't, you will never work in government or for this space agency again. I hope that I'm clear."

Clapper continued. "Earlier this morning, just before 5:00 am EST., an explosive device was planted on the Saturn Six Rocket by a foreign adversary."

The room exploded into shock, audible gasps filled the air, as terror colored the faces of those who were unaware of the earlier events that'd transpired overnight.

"Folks, let's all calm down!" Mars spoke up.

Clapper continued. "The mission to Black Earth will proceed in the coming weeks, perhaps maybe even days, but not until after about a hundred people say that it is safe to do so."

"We all have a collective mission at this point. We must locate the device, and we have a good idea of exactly where it is," Clapper nodded at Mars, "and remove it safely. That ship doesn't fly until it's safe to do so," Clapper finished.

The CIA Director gave the nod to Johnston, asking him to continue the session.

"Listen, ladies and gentlemen, a select few of us will be working with the FBI and CIA to locate and remove the device. Just a heads-up though, it appears that it will be hard to detect, until at which point it's actually in our hands." Mars' words caused even more confusion for those in the room.

"I'll tell you more as we break out into smaller groups. Everyone will be required to stay here for the entire day. You are all sequestered until further notice. No one goes home," he ordered.

The group again chorused with moans and groans.

Mars concluded, "At the end of today, you'll all be bussed to the Hilton Garden Inn, just off-campus. You'll all be permitted to make a supervised call to your spouses for a change of clothes. You're already good to go as your stays have been extended for those of you here from Houston. Remember, this is a national security issue, and no calls to anyone about this is permitted. More info will be forthcoming, so stay tuned until we meet later."

"FBI Agent Primrose, right over there, will be speaking to everyone individually before you get back to your desks. Thank you, folks!" Mars was grateful to his team.

As Clapper and Johnston walked away from the meeting, Clapper said, "You did great in there and at the press conference, too."

Mars took no satisfaction in Clapper's words. "Yeah, well, that was the easy part. Now I have to tell ten Astronauts that they aren't flying today because their spaceship was almost blown up with them inside of it."

"Yeah, that's a tough one!" Clapper sighed, exhaling through his nose.

"Then," Mars looked exasperated, "I have to convince them to get back on that very spaceship in a week!" Mars was emotionally drained.

Clapper reasoned, "Well, at least everyone will sleep good tonight."

"Not me!" said Mars. "Not me," he repeated.

Location: Langley, Virginia. CIA Headquarters. The Blue Room – March 28, 2027 – 6:26 pm EST.

The Blue Room was the most sophisticated interrogation room in the world. Located on sub-floor 2 at CIA Headquarters, it is equipped with forty cameras that can be monitored from various places around the complex, including the office of CIA Director James Clapper. Because high-level counter-intelligence foreign agents, both foreign and domestic, are trained to beat polygraph examinations, the secure room was equipped with monitors and sensors that would track their breathing, body temperature, and heart-rate without them knowing it.

Agents and spies are trained to overcome the physiological changes in the body when they lie. An elevated level of breathing, heart rate, blood pressure, and perspiration rates can tell a polygraph examiner if the examinee is lying. The purpose of the Blue Room is to set the examinee at ease so that they don't know that they are actually being polygraphed at all.

The result is a more confident and relaxed examinee or suspect.

The Blue Room was actually stark white, with nothing of color in the room. The room earned its name because as detainees confessed under interrogation over the years, they would appear to become melancholy, even sad, and blue. The table and chairs were white, and the light washing the room is a soft white, meant to relax its occupants but not put them to sleep.

The room was eighteen by eighteen feet, rather large for an interrogation room, and had mirrored windows on three of the four sides. Behind the mirrors were observation rooms for those in training or those who were part of the investigation.

"Nice place," said Kai Chang. "I feel like...what do you call...a VIP," Chang spoke to Jordan Spear, who was the only other occupant in the room.

"You are a VIP, Kai," Jordan seemed sincere. "It's not every day that we have a Chinese, SHA militant, in the building, fresh off of trying to blow up an American spaceship." Jordan was attempting to lighten the mood.

"I will say, though, you're not the most famous person to ever sit in that chair, however."

"No?" questioned Chang.

"No, in fact," said Jordan, "Black Earth Erik sat in that chair and was interrogated for more than eight hours. The entire time, he didn't even ask for a drink of water or to use the restroom. That old guy wore down our agents that day." Jordan shook his head and smiled.

"Yes, I heard the old man finally died," said Chang. "That must've upset you, no?"

"Upset me? Sure, I guess." Jordan purposely downplayed his affection for Erik Erickson. "He was a good man, the very reason you and I sit here today." Jordan wasn't completely honest with Chang. He'd grown fond of Erik Erickson during the four-month journey back to Earth from Zenith. Jordan took Erik's death hard the previous summer.

"Foolish to believe any of that American conspiracy nonsense." Chang never believed that anyone was brought back from Black Earth that was native to the planet.

"Funny, I didn't take you for a conspiracy theorist," Jordan smiled. "Well, that's not why we're here now, is it?" Spear wanted to bring the conversation back to Chang, the Chinese, and the bomb.

"So, is my associate here in the building, too?" asked a curious and hopeful Chang.

"Kai, Jenny Lee has already been interviewed and confirmed everything we already knew. She confessed Kai." Jordan wore a look of empathy. "She told everything to British authorities in Bermuda. She has already been processed and taken to Guantanamo Bay."

"Never!" Chang banged on the table in anger. Spear didn't flinch.

"She would never reveal operational tactics! She is a strong woman." Chang was certain his associate would never give in.

"You see Kai, good old Jenny Lee has a weakness," smiled Jordan.

"She has no weaknesses!" Chang was defiant. "What weakness could she have?"

"You," Jordan paused, "you are her weakness."

Chang swallowed hard, as the revelation caught him off guard.

Jordan, resisting the urge to smile, knew that it was game, set, and match. The look on Chang's face revealed to Jordan that he loved Jenny Lee.

Just like on Black Earth when Erik Erickson said to him during the confession, 'The two of us have been playing a game of cards. A game in which I have been holding a hand full of truths while you, on the other hand, have been holding a hand full of lies. Who wins that game every time, Mr. Spear?' asked Erik Erickson of Jordan Spear rhetorically, recalled Jordan.

"Kai, what you don't know is that I have been in possession of all of the answers to every question that I have asked of you. Jenny Lee has contacted your bosses and told them that you have reported back and that the two of you are en route to Morocco. You are to arrive in eight hours."

"You lie, CIA fool! She did not do what you say." Chang was again in denial.

"Kai, I know that the night before you boarded that boat, the two of you made love. I know that she confessed her love for you for the very first time since you first met, more than five years ago."

Kai Chang's exterior began to show cracks. "It's not true!" he said, shaking his head side to side. His words were now reduced to a whisper.

"Kai, it's over. I don't need you anymore. I never actually needed you. Jenny gave our British counterparts in Bermuda everything we needed."

"Then why am I here?" Kai felt like there was something Spear hadn't yet told him.

"There is one thing. I have a deal for you," said Jordan.

"No deal!" Chang was again defiant.

"Kai, you might want to hear me out." Jordan stood and waved toward the mirror to his immediate left. "Bring her in, boys."

The SHA Militant looked confused. He looked around, not knowing what was about to happen.

A moment later, the door directly behind Jordan opened up. In walked CIA Officer Matt Solstice, with him, Jenny Lee.

Kai Chang choked up, "Jenny! I told them nothing! Jenny!" he was anguished.

"I know, Kai! I told them what they needed in order to protect your honor. I knew you would never say anything,..." she paused, now crying. "I told them so that you wouldn't have to. I love you, Kai Chang." Jenny then lowered her head in shame.

Kai Chang attempted to get to Lee, in an act of consolation, but Solstice and Spear quickly came between them. Other agents were looking on from outside the room all stood-by, ready to pounce.

"What is it you want, Jordan?" Chang yelled in an act of concession.

"I am going to allow the two of you to sit down at this table and speak to Officer Solstice and me. You will remain calm, or you will never see each other again. Do I make myself clear?"

Kai Chang stood at attention, faced Spear and Solstice, tapped his heels, and bowed his head. He then returned to his seat and remained quiet and listened to what Spear had to say.

"Jenny, Kai," Spear looked sincere, "I cannot promise you your freedom. But I can offer you something in exchange for your cooperation.

Jenny Lee and Kai Chang sat quietly, thankful that they were reunited, if even only for a moment.

"Do not speak until my offer is on the table, then you'll have one hour to accept or not."

The two SHA Agents bowed their heads in agreement.

"In less than two hours, the two of you will make a recorded statement in which you will both say, in part, that you are defecting and seek asylum in the United States of America. You will confess to attempting to bring down our rocket and will state that you are cooperating with CIA officials."

Chang ground his teeth. "And in return?" he looked at Spear, then to Jenny Lee, then back to Spear again.

"In return, you will both be imprisoned at a maximum-security facility in the northern part of the United States. You will be given a cell with two bunks," Jordan offered.

Chang and Lee looked at each other and attempted to process what that might mean.

The two of you will spend your days and nights together for many years to come if you choose to cooperate with our investigation. Who knows, you might even be handed back to the Chinese government in a prisoner exchange one day. If you decide against this offer, however, you will never see each other again."

Lee and Chang clutched hands under the table. They both knew what their answers would be.

Chapter 22 – The Chameleon

Location: Beijing, China. Ministry of State Security – 10:01 am, Beijing local time.

"Minister Kenong, the Honorable Haoran Shieh, is here to see you, sir." A female voice loudly broadcasted through the desktop phone in Kenong's office.

"Send him in." Kenong rose to meet his boss.

"Minister Kenong, please be seated," said Haoran Shieh, senior adviser to President Xí Shèng-Xióng.

Now seated, Shieh said, "Minister Kenong, I have troubling news for both you and your agency."

"What is it? Tell me at once, your Excellency." Kenong again stood to accept the news that he felt would not favor either he or his agency.

"Your man has failed in his efforts to complete the first of three stages of Operation Black Diamond," said Shieh.

Kenong flew into a rage. "I told you that last night! I told you!"

Haoran Shieh stood from his chair. "Minister Kenong, as I instructed you last evening, you are to control your emotions when in my presence. Additionally, you must help us understand your ineptness."

"The agents that you hand-selected to go to Bermuda have officially defected to the United States. Defection, Minister Kenong!" Shieh raised his voice slightly. "This is an embarrassment that cannot stand. It is your agency that was tasked with Operation Black Diamond, and a portion of your job has resulted in humiliation for you and your agency, and now, our great country."

Kenong's face went pale.

Shieh composed himself. "You will succeed, or you shall die an un-ceremonial death."

"I don't understand," Kenong said aloud as he looked away. "Not Kai Chang. He is a ruthless killer and is loyal to his country."

"Perhaps he did not feel that his country was loyal to him?" Shieh raised the question. "I understand that your original plan included him acting like some Japanese Kamikaze and blowing himself up? What do ideas like that do for the morale of your people? I wonder," said Shieh.

Kenong again lost his cool. "SHA Militants are not people! They are animals!" he shouted.

Shieh launched a look at the mindless Minister, one that conveyed his continued disapproval of how he carried himself in the presence of his superiors and with the way he treated those who reported to him.

Kenong quickly came to his senses and remembered who it was that he was talking to. He also realized that this failure could lead to his execution.

"Your Excellency," Kenong bowed, "please allow me to finish the operation. If you do, I will guarantee that there are no more failures."

"Very well, Minister Kenong. If you are to die, it will only come after we take Black Earth before the Americans," assured Shieh.

"But...," Kenong seemed confused, "how will we stop the Americans from getting to Black Earth before our scientists, engineers, and physicists can get there?"

"All plans have contingencies Minister Kenong. Our beautiful rocket, 'The Chinese Eclipse,' is nearly ready," Shieh spoke with pride. "Now, if you would please come with me, our glorious President would like to see you."

Location: Artesia, New Mexico. The Michaels Home – March 28, 2027 – 8:57 pm MST.

Carrick was talking on his cell phone in the kitchen when Lola walked in from the grocery store. "Hey! Thanks for calling back! I know, it's crazy. It's been decades since NASA scrubbed a launch right before lift-off."

"Yeah, I talked to Jordan earlier, and he was tight-lipped. He said he couldn't talk," said Kinzi London. "He just got back from Canaveral earlier today. Hmm," Kinzi paused. "I wonder if the two are connected."

"That would be quite a coincidence if they weren't," said Carrick. "I left Mars a voicemail, but I'm sure he's swamped right now. This was supposed to be his big day." Carrick looked at Lola, held up his index finger, and mouthed the words, "Give me a minute."

"I bet the crew's bumming right now." Kinzi's voice could be heard by Lola standing just feet away. "It was already delayed for four months."

"Well, yeah, let me know if you hear anything," said Carrick.

"Switching gears, how are the babies?" asked Kinzi. "You guys getting any sleep over there?"

"They've been great, actually, mostly sleeping right now. They say this is the honeymoon phase. They'll be getting fidgety soon, I'm sure."

Lola caught Carrick's eye and mouthed, "Have they heard anything yet?"

Carrick shook his head, indicating 'No.'

Carrick, distracted by Lola, missed the first part of Kinzi's next question regarding Lilly Spencer. "I know. It's terrible. Jordan and I are just sick about it. I'm glad Erik isn't here to see it. That little girl has been through so much. She's such a sweetie. Please tell the Spencers that we're praying for them," Kinzi offered her thoughts and prayers to little Lilly.

"I will. Oh, and Kinzi, great to hear your voice again. Listen, outside of the birth and the delay at NASA, we haven't really talked to you guys very much. We haven't seen each other since Erik's funeral. Let's all get together soon. We really want you to see the babies. Either way, let's talk soon."

"I know, I know," said Kinzi, "Jordan's been so busy with work. He's back in the saddle and loving it. Me though, I'm BORED out of my mind! Maybe I can come out to see you guys, just me. Jordan won't get any time off soon as he's working on something big."

"I'll have Lola call to compare schedules. Look for her call."

"Okay, I'll keep you posted if we hear anything about the delay at NASA. Tell Lola I'll be looking for that call."

"10-4 Kinz! Love you guys! Take care." Carrick swiped left on his phone and gave Lola a big smile.

Lola was unpacking the few items she picked up from the store and asked, "Well, has she heard anything yet?"

"Nope." Carrick grabbed a bag and started removing its contents, lending Lola a hand.

"What's that look on your face? What's going on?" Lola knew her husband and knew Kinzi said something to get him thinking.

"No," Carrick paused and pondered, "it's nothing." Carrick blew her off and stepped into the pantry.

"Listen here, Mister! I know that look. Now, what's bothering you?"

"It was something Kinzi said..." Carrick looked perplexed.

"Spit it out for the love of God!" Lola prodded Carrick.

Carrick winced and said, "She said Jordan just got back from Canaveral. And that he was working on something big."

"You connecting dots that aren't there, Babe?" Lola pulled on the front of Carrick's shirt as he passed her.

"No, it's just my gut talking to me," reasoned Carrick.

Lola looked at Carrick and knew his brain was working overtime. She knew he missed the old crew: Erik, Kinzi, Mars, and Jordan. She would definitely call Kinzi and invite her out. From what she overheard on the phone, it sounded like Kinzi needed an escape, too.

Later, in the living room, Lola joined Carrick on the couch. Plopping down close to him, she said, "You miss it, don't you?"

"Miss what?"

"Carrick, give me a break. In December, you were all fired up when they canceled the launch, and now you're in a funk about the delay." Lola was genuinely concerned with her husband. She never thought that he would unretire, just that something was missing in his life, ...again. *He always seemed to be missing something in his life until he found Erik, now Erik was gone, and he's become the same empty man again, searching for something, but what?* Lola thought to herself.

Carrick exhaled heavily. "I don't know. I'm just nervous, excited, and now this delay....something's not right." Carrick looked out of sorts. "Mars hasn't gotten back to me, and Jordan is working at 11 o'clock at night? I just don't know."

"Try Mars again tomorrow. It's too late now. He'll be straight with you," encouraged Lola.

"Lola, you saw the press conference this morning. That did not seem like Mars. He'd be the first one to turn the questions over to his Engineers. Did you see Pete? He looked like he had no idea what Mars was even talking about." Carrick referred to Pete Henderson, a senior NASA engineer he became close to during his time at NASA.

"Call Mars in the morning," again suggested Lola.

Location: Titusville, FL., NASA Engineering Department – March 29, 2027.

Standing around a stainless-steel table in the vast Engineering lab were Mars Johnston, FBI Agent John Primrose, and three NASA Engineers.

"What in the hell is this thing?" Mars was dumbfounded. "You wouldn't know it was there unless you were looking right at it."

"Yes," said Kyle Bradshaw, a thirty-one-year-old metallurgical and computer engineer, who'd been with NASA for three years, "it's unusual, and it's not metal."

"Kyle, you specialize in the manipulation of steel and different types of alloys. If it's not metal, then what is it?" asked Primrose.

"It's ceramic!" said Danny Trippedo, a two-year NASA veteran who specialized in ceramics.

"Ceramic?" Primrose questioned aloud.

"Yeah," Mars smiled, "Just like we used on the Space Shuttle."

"It's amazing!" Primrose and the others were in awe. "It seems to take on the color of its surroundings."

"Funny you say that. We nicknamed it The Chameleon!" said Bradshaw. The others nodded their head in agreement.

"Well, chameleons aren't known to explode at high altitudes," argued Primrose.

"Well, this one didn't either!" Bradshaw pushed back with an awkward smile.

"The CIA had their hands on this for a few hours earlier, and their technicians detected no explosive residue. It's certainly in there, but they assured us that it wouldn't explode."

"If you look here," using a pencil, Bradshaw pointed to a mechanism on the bottom of the device, "this screw right here," he looked at the others, "removes the bottom cover plate."

After Bradshaw removed the plate, the inner workings were revealed to those in the room.

"Where's the C-4?" Primrose challenged the engineers.

The third engineer in the room stepped forward and took the device from Bradshaw's hands, who willingly handed it over to him.

Setting the device on the table, belly up, Clifford Elliott adjusted the glasses on his face and said, "We haven't breached the explosives chamber yet, but I can assure you that it's safe to handle."

Elliott was an MIT Grad and newcomer to NASA, having been with the program for twenty-six months. His co-workers called him 'Erkel,' and it was easy to see why. The twenty-nine-year-old Clifford Elliot was short, skinny, had thick glasses, and almost always wore a bowtie. His high-pitched voice captured the attention of all when he spoke.

"How's that? asked Primrose, who looked antsy.

"You see this button right here?" pointed Elliot. Everyone nervously leaned in. "This is called a 'Fusion Coil Glider.'"

"A what?" Primrose looked puzzled.

Mars spoke up, "It's a barometer and an altimeter."

"And?" Primrose felt left out of the high-level scientific discussion.

"It measures air pressure," said Elliot. "The device was designed to explode when the rocket reached a certain altitude."

"That's some diabolical shit right there!" said Primrose. "So that's why we all feel comfortable right now?"

"No one should ever feel comfortable around a bomb. That's how accidental explosions happen." Elliot remained straight-faced and pushed his glasses back up to the top of his nose."

"Well, you guys keep plugging away and let me know when you get into the inner chamber." Mars patted Primrose on the back and motioned him to the hallway.

Outside, a spectacle was going on. On and around the launch tower were more than one-hundred men and women: Engineers, all at the top of their respective fields. Every square inch of the Silver Comet was getting scrubbed for any type of device or anomaly. If it wasn't supposed to be on the rocket, the team would find it.

Inside the halls of NASA, Canaveral, D.C., and Houston, technicians worked around the clock, running diagnostics on the onboard computers, propulsion systems, and communications systems. Before the Saturn Six series rocket could launch, it would need a clean bill of health from more than one hundred people and a half-dozen agencies.

Location: Langley, Virginia. Federal Housing Unit 859 – April 1, 2027 – Thursday morning, 9:01 am EST.

Sitting in their separate and adjacent cells, the two SHA Militants spoke about their fate. They could not be sure that the promise Jordan Spear made them would be honored. No matter their future,

America was home now. After defecting publicly, they could never show their faces in China again; they would be executed without a trial.

"I love you, Kai Chang," Jenny Lee said to Kai across the aisle, running between their cells. She did not regret her actions in Bermuda. With the promise of leniency for Kai Chang, Jenny willingly confessed her and his actions, under the conditions that he would not have to. She saved the honor of the man she loved, and she held the recognition that he never felt he deserved.

Kai Chang returned Jenny's stare and said, "I love you too, Jenny Lee." He paused for several seconds and then added, "I fear this is as close as we will be for the rest of our lives. The Americans will never keep their promise. Why would they? They owe us nothing," Chang bowed his head.

"But Kai, Jordan Spear seems like an honorable man," cried Jenny.

"Jenny Lee, you are a warrior. Let no one see you cry!" Chang was stern.

"I WAS a warrior," said Lee. "Not anymore. I am a prisoner now, and nothing more." She, too, bowed her head.

The sound of a metal latch clanking came from down the hall. The two took no solace that it might be news of their fate. As Chang said moments ago, if they were to leave this place, they would never see each other again.

Before the door closed, the imprisoned SHA Agents heard Jordan Spear say, "We will use interrogation room 219, please boot up the cameras."

Seconds later, Spear stood in front of Kai Chang's cell and looked down into his eyes. "Kai, we need to talk a little more before they move the two of you out of here."

"Jordan Spear, you said that Jenny and I would share a cell. You spoke with honor," said Chang.

"You will share a cell, if..."

"If?" Kai Chang interrupted Jordan.

"Kai, when you reach your final destination in upstate New York two weeks from now, you will share a cell IF the rocket we launch enters space safely, and nothing happens as a result of your actions. If the International crew doesn't make it to Black Earth, the fault will fall upon you, Jenny, and the Chinese Government." Jordan was forthright.

Twenty minutes later, in an interrogation room two floors below, Jordan sat waiting for Kai Chang. The door opened, and two officers escorted Chang to the chair opposite Spear.

The men were in the process of shackling their Chinese prisoner to the chair when Spear interjected. "That won't be necessary, gentlemen."

"It's protocol, sir."

"I don't care, uncuff the man," ordered Spear.

"Very well," the Federal Corrections Officer nodded. "We'll be right outside the door if you need us."

Moments later, Jordan, sitting across from Kai Chang, said, "You could take all three of us, couldn't you?" smiled Jordan.

"Those two? Yes," grinned Chang. "Perhaps not you, Captain America."

"I'm not the fighter I used to be," said Jordan. "I'm getting old." Jordan unwrenched his shoulder, spinning his bent arm in a clockwise fashion in a show of self-deprecation.

"It appears the two of us have much in common, my friend," smiled Chang.

"Kai, listen." Jordan looked both ways. "We need to talk. Is there anything else I need to know before that rocket launches?"

Chang looked puzzled. "Jordan, I was originally supposed to die on this mission. When I learned of that fate, I nearly disappeared off the grid. I didn't want to die." Chang now looked resigned. "I accepted my fate. I would die like so many others had at my hands."

Jordan sat listening as if Chang were about to walk the mile and was given a chance to confess his sins.

Chang continued, "My bosses must have somehow sensed my reservation, so they had Jenny Lee accompany me as she had on several missions in the past. They knew I would follow through on their plan if she were there to push me along and to make certain that I succeeded." Chang seemed sincere.

He continued, "Die or not, this was to be my last mission. I would've returned to China and disappeared forever," he paused, "with Jenny Lee. They would never have found us. This is my fate now, Jordan," Chang looked finished. "I will die in America. Young or old, that is no longer my decision. There is nothing else I know about that rocket ship. If you found the bomb, there is only one. I planted nothing else on that ship. I hope the Americans make it to Black Earth first. The Chinese government has intentions of owning everything Black Earth has to offer, and that would not be good for global peace. If your country gets there first, then the Chinese will abort their efforts. They do not want a war with America, either here on Earth or Black Earth."

Jordan spoke, "If there is something you're not telling me, then you and Jenny Lee will never see each other again. I need to be clear about that."

"Jordan, there is something else, although it may not be relevant."

Jordan leaned in, "I'm listening."

"My country is readying their own rocket to go to Black Earth. On that rocket will be several scientists, computer experts, and...." Kai Chang paused uncomfortably.

"And what, Kai?"

"The Spider will be on that rocket."

Spear nodded his head. "Yes, our Intel suggests that as well," revealed Jordan. "What's his real name, Kai?"

"I will not give you his real name. I will not," Chang was adamant.

"He is my SHA Brother, and I owe my life to him." Chang paused again for several seconds. "I will give my life to protect his identity. You could kill Jenny Lee or me, but I will never give you his name."

"He means that much to you, huh?"

"He is my brother," Chang bowed his head. "You don't need his identity, though. That cannot help you, anyway."

Jordan pursed his lips and pondered for a second.

"Jordan, you cannot defeat The Spider. He will kill you if given the chance. No matter your level of skill and determination, The Spider cannot be defeated," Chang sounded convincing.

"Jordan, SHA Agents have a picture of Captain America with them at all times. They have all sworn to kill the great American Heroes: Dr. Carrick Michaels and CIA Officer Jordan Spear. You should've stayed retired, my friend."

Jordan shrugged off the threat, but inside, he immediately felt vulnerable.

"It matters not, however, Jordan. The Chinese will abort their plans if The Saturn Six launches first. My government's political aspirations rest on getting to the riches of Black Earth first. Then, they will own all medical cures and technologies. They will win World War III without firing a shot. That is their goal," said Chang. "Their goal, however, was never my goal. I was a good soldier, but now I am dead to them."

"Anything else you want to tell me?" Jordan's demeanor changed; he now seemed more distant.

"The Interlink Communications Corridor..."

"I'm guessing the Chinese are trying to hack it." Jordan cut Chang off.

"Yes, but I know nothing of their progress. Nothing. I swear." Chang stood, tapped his heels, and bowed to the American CIA Officer.

Chapter 23 – God Speed

Location: Washington, D.C., The Pentagon – April 5, 2027, 9:00 am
EST.

At the direction of the President of the United States, a meeting was
called by the Director of National Intelligence, Dianna Mayfield; it
would take place at the Pentagon. The meeting goals would be to
discuss the intentions of the Chinese regarding Black Earth and the
current safety status of the Saturn Six series rocket. A date for liftoff
of the Silver Comet would be discussed as well, contingent upon
safety protocols being met.

The meeting was held in The Nine Eleven Room on the Pentagon's
outer ring on the western side. The Nine Eleven Room, named after
the tragic events, that occurred on September 11, 2001, was
completed after reconstruction to that portion of the structure. The
terrorist attacks on 9/11 decimated nearly forty percent of the
world's largest building's western side.

The large conference room, a thousand square feet, could seat as
many as twenty people around a solid oak conference table.
Around the room hung framed pictures of the workers who rebuilt
the section of the Pentagon struck by American Airlines Flight 77.
There were also tributes to those who died that day. One hundred
twenty-five people lost their lives while working in the Pentagon on
that fateful September day, along with the plane's fifty-nine victims.
A large bronze nameplate hung atop the wall at the room's head; it
read, 'We Shall Never Forget.'

Presenting at the meeting would be CIA Director James Clapper,
CIA Officer in charge of Operation Venom, Jordan Spear, and
NASA's Chief Administrator, Marcus Johnston. In addition to the
DNI and three presenters, would be the Joint Chiefs of Staff;
Secretary of State Jennifer Granholm; Secretary of Defense, Mack
Reynolds; Director of the FBI, John Calhoun; and several other high-
ranking government officials.

After the group settled in for a long meeting, Dianna Mayfield
walked to the podium at the front of the room. Behind her was a

one-hundred-inch flatscreen that had the words Operation Venom displayed across it. Each presenter would utilize the screen for the purpose of visual aids.

"Director Clapper, Joint Chiefs, Officers, Agents, Secretaries, and Administrator Johnson, welcome. Thank you all for making the trip into Washington this morning." Mayfield acknowledged and welcomed the esteemed group.

Clapper immediately looked at Mars and, with a look, encouraged him not to correct Mayfield's mispronunciation of his last name, as she had omitted the 'T.'

"Today, we're here to discuss the ever-familiar topic of the last three years, China." The mere mention of the U.S.'s ongoing geopolitical nemesis frustrated the DNI and nearly all of the room's occupants.

"In a moment, CIA Director James Clapper will brief everyone on an operation that's been ongoing since February of last year. Today, with Director Clapper is CIA Officer Jordan Spear," Mayfield acknowledged Jordan's presence even though everyone knew who he was due to his Black Earth fame. "Jordan has been in charge of the operation, and as I understand it, has some updates as to the recent delay of our Saturn Six rocket, as well as China's potential involvement."

"As I mentioned earlier, we have Marcus Johnson, as you all know, Marcus is the Chief Administrator at NASA." Mayfield again unintentionally mispronounced Mars' last name.

Clapper again looked over at Mars, who was biting his lip, when Mayfield added. "My apologies, Dr. Johnston. I see that I mispronounced your name. Twice, apparently," she blushed.

"No worries, it happens all the time, in fact...," said Mars, before Clapper got his attention.

Clapper cleared his throat and looked over at Mars.

Mars, slightly embarrassed, looked at Clapper and then back at Director Mayfield and said, "Glad to be here today."

"Director Clapper, if you'd like to get things started?" Mayfield conceded the room to the CIA Director.

Clapper made his way to the head of the room, carrying a legal pad and remote control for the slideshow presentation he was about to give.

"Ladies and Gentlemen, the information that I'm about to share with you is classified and should remain in this room unless you're speaking with POTUS himself." Clapper was stone-faced. He preferred to share information rather than share his opinion of it.

"In just a moment, CIA Officer Jordan Spear will brief you in greater detail, but I'll start with some high-level information first." Clapper started his slideshow.

Clapper clicked the button in his hand, and the screen changed to an image of the Saturn Six series rocket, the Silver Comet, sitting next to its launch tower in Cape Canaveral.

Clapper began, "On the evening of March 27, Operation 'Take-Down' commenced. After learning from an anonymous source within the Chinese government, weeks prior, that a bomb would be attached to the Silver Comet rocket," explained Clapper, "we sprang into action."

"As the DNI mentioned moments ago, the CIA has been conducting an operation called Venom. Operation Venom was initiated after the murder of our Ambassador to China, Dr. Carl Schoenfeld," Clapper was both frank and calm.

"When scrubbing all communications in and out of the Beijing Embassy, which has since been closed, our agents determined that Dr. Schoenfeld was attempting to relay a plan by the Chinese to sidestep U.N. Resolution 2978. The resolution, if you'll recall..." Clapper clicked to the next slide, "voted that no one country on planet Earth owned salvage rights to Black Earth. Rather, the Council reaffirmed the original agreement that the contributing nations, as part of their financial stake, would each share in whatever scientific gains were made on Black Earth," Clapper explained. "They went on to say; there would be no free-for-all as the potential for war would be heightened if countries entered into a race back to Black Earth. And here we are, with China looking to go on its own."

Those in attendance held back their questions and concerns momentarily.

"We have since learned that that is what their plan is. The Chinese want to pillage Black Earth and take possession of the planet's intellectual properties, including technologies and medical advancements. Not to mention some very large diamonds," Clapper shrugged and shook his head side to side. "After getting the goods on Black Earth, they plan on destroying The Triad."

"Jesus!" exclaimed Defense Secretary Mack Reynolds. "If they get what they're after, then World War III would be pointless. They'd have the markets cornered in medical science and space travel. They would instantly be centuries ahead of the rest of the world. No one would ever catch up."

The meeting attendees were now sitting upright in their chairs. All were anxious with the unfolding intel and wondered how their particular agency would be affected by the revelations.

"He's right," said the Chairman of the Joint Chiefs. "They would have the world knocking at their door for medical cures and propulsion systems."

"The vaccines, they'd sell, but they'd never give up the propulsion system technologies," added General Michael Alexander Wiley. Wiley was a U.S. Army General and was the Joint Chiefs' twentieth Chairman since it was first founded in 1942. He'd been the Chairman since 2019. "The world would have to pay top dollar to hitch a ride with the Chinese anytime it wanted to travel in space."

While all of the Joint Chiefs in attendance would prefer to avoid a war with China, they most certainly understood what a post-Black Earth salvage China would look like.

Clapper continued, "As I ask Jordan Spear to come up to the front of the room, I would like to thank the senior members of the CIA, the FBI, and NASA, for their cooperation in Operation Take Down. The multi-agency collaboration resulted in two arrests of Chinese SHA Militant agents and the successful removal of an explosive device that we're now calling, The Chameleon." Looking in the direction of

Mars Johnston, Clapper said, "Administrator Johnston can provide more details later in the meeting."

Clapper placed the clicker he was holding on the podium and motioned to Jordan to come to the front of the room.

The CIA legend had the respect of every member in the room. Even the highest-ranking members of the United States Marine Corp., Army; Navy; Air Force; and Coast Guard; were quietly in awe of the young man that in service to his country boarded a spaceship and traveled to Black Earth to depose Dr. Erik Erickson. All concurred that his actions went far and above what any other civil servant would do for their country. Both Clapper and Mars Johnston looked like proud fathers as Spear made his way to the head of the room.

Now standing behind the podium, Spear opened. "Thank you, Director Clapper, Joint Chiefs, Secretaries, Director Mayfield, Chief Administrator Johnston, and other esteemed officials."

Spear pressed the clicker in his hand and behind him, on the one-hundred-inch monitor, appeared an image of SHA Militant, Kai Chang.

"The man you see over my shoulder is a SHA militant from the Strategic Huyou Agency, which is an arm of the Central Military Commission for The People's Republic of China. Its focus is counterintelligence and maintaining China's spy network throughout the world," explained Spear.

"This man is responsible for placing The Chameleon on the Saturn Six rocket. His name is Kai Chang."

"On March 27, Kai Chang, and his SHA associate Jenny Lee, flew into Bermuda from Morocco, posing as a married couple on vacation. Shortly after their arrival, they met up with a Bermudian double agent and then rented a fishing vessel. Working with the FBI and Coast Guard, our goal was to uncover what technology the Chinese would employ so we allowed Chang to place the device on the Silver Comet successfully."

Jordan was interrupted. "Am I to understand that you could've taken down the Chinese agent before allowing him to get into the airspace around Cape Canaveral?" asked Marine Commandant David Brighthouse.

Clapper cut in, "That's correct, Commandant." All heads turned toward the CIA Director.

"We learned from our source in China that the Chinese were unleashing never before seen technology." Clapper caught his choice of words and immediately looked over to Mars and gave him a look. Mars was eager to point out Clapper's choice of words but declined after his glare.

Clapper continued, "This technology would not only make the explosive device invisible to radar and cameras, but would also make the drone carrying it undetectable."

Defense Secretary Reynolds spoke up, "And how exactly do we know our source in China is reputable?"

"I was just wondering that myself," added Secretary of State Granholm, as she leaned forward in her chair to ensure Clapper could see her.

"Our source has been right on every bit of intel provided to us. At this point, we have no reason to doubt the information coming out of Beijing." Clapper now looked mildly perturbed.

"Well, that was quite a gamble you took with a ninety-billion-dollar rocket, Director Clapper," said the Marine Commandant, criticizing the decision.

Mars, wanting to come to Clapper's defense, began to say, "I think the decision..."

Clapper immediately defended the decision, "The decision we made means that no foreign adversary will be able to do it again." Clapper was adamant.

"Ahem," Mars cleared his throat, "as I was saying, We very quickly designed and produced a massive net that will cover both the launch tower and rocket. It will be used for all future launches," Mars revealed.

"A net?" Commandant Brighthouse looked puzzled.

"That's correct. It was just completed yesterday and is being put in place as we speak. Nothing will get through the net. The rocket will be shielded from such a device." Mars' smile nearly exceeded his enthusiasm.

"Very well," said Brighthouse. Now looking more satisfied with Clapper's gamble. "Please continue, Officer Spear."

"Once the package was delivered, with the help of General Ratcliff Hogan," Spear nodded to the Chief of the Coast Guard Bureau, "and his incredibly competent men and women of the U.S. Coast Guard, we intercepted the fishing boat as it was attempting to turn back for Bermuda."

"I understand you had some Navy boys on the ship, too," proudly interjected Admiral Michael Gilliam of the U.S. Navy.

"Seal Team Eight made the takedown on board the vessel," Spear offered.

Clapper broke back in, "Our British counter-intelligence partners on the ground in Bermuda were also pivotal. They scooped up the female SHA Agent in Bermuda while she slept. No shots were fired, and only one tango was eliminated." Clapper looked back at Jordan and encouraged him to continue.

"As the Director pointed out, the two SHA Agents were taken without being harmed," Jordan looked proud of that accomplishment. "That made it possible to convince them to talk once under interrogation."

"We currently have both in custody in Langley, and they are providing us with a great deal of information."

DNI Mayfield spoke up, "What more do we know, Jordan?"

"It appears the Chinese are attempting to hack into our Interlink Communications Corridor," responded Jordan. "If they do, they'll again be one step ahead of us."

"Our intel suggests several foreign foes have been actively trying to hack into the Interlink Corridor; Russia and North Korea, to name just two," Clapper interjected without looking too worried.

Jordan Continued, "Captive Kai Chang, doesn't seem too fond of his leadership in China. We get the sense that he may continue to be a source of information if we push."

"Well, push harder, young man!" The Marine Commandant said while tapping on the table to cheer on the CIA efforts.

"Of course, sir," Jordan was respectful. What Jordan didn't offer up to the group was the fact that another SHA Militant was scheduled to be on the Chinese Rocket, The Spider.

After the group returned from lunch, Mars Johnston presented to the group. His forty-five-minute dissertation included safety measures that NASA had taken, from the giant net to sonar and listening technologies that would listen for the hum of an approaching drone. The technology would be capable of hearing a bumblebee from two-hundred yards away. Finally, NASA would employ sensors on each stage of the rocket. The sensors would be able to detect something making actual contact with the surface of the rocket.

Mars confidently announced, "To date, NASA can sign off on the future launch based on all information I just shared with you."

Mayfield again spoke up, "Director Clapper, has the CIA signed off on the launch yet?"

"No, but we're nearly there. We will need another couple of days speaking with our Chinese friends, currently locked up at our Langley facility." Clapper was always pragmatic.

"I just have one question before we finish our meeting today," said Army General John Patrick Cook. Until that moment, he had been silent for the entire meeting. "What type of explosive was found inside The Chameleon device?"

Clapper smiled at his longtime friend of thirty years. "It's a great question, John. The simple answer is that we haven't been able to breach the belly of the device yet."

Mars interjected, "Our engineers are diligently working on it now. Around the clock!" he added with vigor.

"Here is our problem," Clapper was again pragmatic. "The Chinese Eclipse is nearly ready for launch. Though their attempt to blow up our rocket failed, it bought them much needed time. If they launch before us, then they may have succeeded in their efforts without bringing down our Saturn Six rocket."

"I might add for the edification of all," Mars wanted everyone to be aware of the speed capabilities of the Saturn Six. "Both the Saturn Six and Neptune One can travel as many as five thousand miles per hour faster than our Horizon Class rockets, that made the four previous journeys to Black Earth."

"How does that help us in this case, Mars?" asked DNI Mayfield.

"It means that the Chinese Eclipse rocket can leave sixteen days before us, and both rockets would get there at the same time. Their technology won't let them travel as fast as ours does." Mars was proud of the men and women in his agency.

The meeting ended with just one more question, again from the Army's General Cook. "Director Calhoun, you, like me, have been, for the most part, quiet today. Can you endorse the lift-off of the Saturn Six rocket with what you've learned today?"

The FBI's top man stated for the record, "The FBI has been on site since the night before the launch, and we have no reservations at this moment that would result in any further delays. We have our best men and women down there at Canaveral."

"Thank you for weighing in, Director," said Cook.

Location: Washington, D.C. NCN Studios, The Situation Center with Bear Winston. April 9, 2027 – 5:00pm EST.

Winston sat at his desk on the set of the Situation Center. Swiveling in his chair to face his international audience, the camera closed in.

"Breaking News!" Winston was unusually excited. "Officials at NASA have just announced that the rescheduled launch date of the Silver Comet has been set for April 14. You'll remember that the initial launch, scheduled for March 28, was canceled just hours before lift-off. The official reason was an anomaly in communication between NASA's Florida team and Mission Control back in Houston. Our experts have more information that suggests other factors were considered. Adding to the speculation is the amount of time between the original March 28 date and the rescheduled date of April 14."

"Joining me now is NCN Contributor and the Senior Editor of the Washington Post, Davin Schulten."

The camera panned out and revealed The salt and pepper haired Schulten, who smiled to the television audience before turning to Bear.

"Davin, tell us what you've heard from your sources at NASA," encouraged Winston.

"That's just it, Bear, I'm not hearing much. Usually, my sources at this stage of launch preparation are thrilled to hear from me and want to talk off the record about the pride they're feeling and their excitement about the pending launch. Right now, it's crickets, and no one is returning my calls."

"What should the folks at home take away from that revelation?" asked Winston.

"It's a mystery, Bear," Schulten acknowledged. "But they did experience issues grave enough to postpone the launch for more than two weeks, that would indicate they had some real problems."

"Well, safety first when you're sending ten humans into space on a ninety-billion-dollar rocket," reasoned Winston. "Please let us know if you learn more."

"Will do, Bear!" smiled Schulten.

Location: Artesia, New Mexico. Home of the Michaels Family – April 9, 2027.

Lola and Carrick were folding a load of laundry in the master bedroom when Carrick's cell phone rang. Carrick pulled it from his back pocket and saw that it was Mars.

"Oh shit! It's Mars," Carrick was surprised because he hadn't heard from Mars since the twins were born, and Mars never returned his calls after the canceled launch date.

"Hey, Mars! How are you?" Lola could hear Mars return the pleasantry. "Yeah, we just saw it on NCN. You must be excited as hell."

Carrick now turned away from Lola so that he could have a little more privacy. He could tell she was as anxious as he to hear from Mars and that she would attempt to listen in on the call.

"I'm pumped! We just got the clearance from all agencies last night. I was excited to make the announcement this afternoon," said Mars.

"What do you mean 'clearance from all agencies'? What agencies Mars?" Carrick was immediately suspicious by the comment.

Mars recognized his slip-up and tried to cover it, "I meant Departments, not 'Agencies.'" Mars was lucky that he was on the phone and not face to face with Carrick. He knew that Carrick would recognize his lie.

"Okay...," Carrick paused with skepticism. "So, how's the team feeling about the announced date?"

"They're over the moon!" Mars laughed at his silly reference.

"Nice one, Mars! I bet you've been waiting to share that one."

Mars confessed, "That's like the fourth time I've used it today," he chuckled.

Carrick's tone went serious. "Mars, listen, what exactly happened to cause the delay? You never returned any of my calls."

"Um, so yeah, we had a communication issue between the Cape and Houston." Mars didn't sound convincing.

"What kind of communication issues?" Skepticism could be detected through the phone.

"Yeah, sure, you know, there was a delay, and we couldn't figure it out." Mars was now dying to get off the phone.

"So, how's Lola and the little ones?" he quickly changed the subject.

Lola continued to fold clothes, pairing little infant socks, pink and blue. She tried her best to hear what Mars was saying.

"They're great!" Carrick said proudly.

"What's that?" Carrick could hear someone calling out to Mars on the other end of the line.

"Carrick, hey, listen, let's catch up soon. I need to run now. I'll be swamped until after lift-off. Let's plan to talk then. Be patient with me if I don't return your calls until then. It's going to continue to be busy around here."

"Yeah, no worries, Mars. Thanks for getting back to me! Good luck, man! We'll talk soon," said Carrick.

Carrick could hear Mars hang up the phone before he finished saying goodbye. His feelings were only mildly hurt; he knew his good friend was busy as hell and had a great deal of work to do preparing for the launch in the coming days.

"So, what did he have to say? Is he excited?" Lola was smiling ear to ear, curious about what Mars had to say.

"I need to call Jordan!" Carrick looked determined. "When you talked to Kinzi last week, did she reveal anything to you about the aborted launch?"

"No, but how would she know anything?"

"I don't know, but Mars is hiding something, I can tell."

Without a word, Carrick left the room. Lola just watched him walk out of the bedroom and go down the hall past the nursery. At that moment, the babies started crying; Carrick didn't seem to notice.

Carrick stood looking out the window of the first guest bedroom, which looked over the backyard of his expansive home. He was impatiently waiting for Jordan to answer his phone. After five rings, it went to voicemail; Carrick was pissed. Lola was now standing quietly in the doorway of the guestroom just out of Carrick's view. She held little Erik in her arms. The two-week-old little boy was sucking on a pacifier.

Carrick was in the middle of leaving a message to his friend when the call-waiting alerted him to Jordan's incoming call.

"Jordan, hey! Thanks for calling me right back."

"How are you, man! Sorry, I've been out of touch. Been busy as hell lately." Jordan seemed a little winded.

"Yeah, Kinzi mentioned that to Lola." Carrick sounded impatient. He was on a mission for the truth. "Jordan, listen, I know something's up. I was talking to Mars, and I know something's up at the Cape. What's going on? Be straight with me."

"Carrick, am I on speaker?" Jordan wanted to make sure that what he was about to say was heard by only Carrick.

"Hold on a sec!"

Carrick turned when he heard suckling, noticed Lola, and shooed her away with a violent hand wave. He then walked over and closed the door. Lola scoffed at him and was miffed, not knowing how to interpret his actions.

"I'm good now," assured Carrick. "What the hell is happening?"

"Carrick, listen," Jordan went into the bedroom he shared with Kinzi at his parent's house in Leesburg, Virginia. "I can only tell you some high-level stuff but can't get down into the weeds with you."

"What is it?" Carrick finally felt he was getting somewhere and that his gut was right the whole time. He knew that something was amiss.

"Do you remember the news reports about Ambassador Schoenfeld dying last year?"

"Yeah, he committed suicide. I met him in Beijing, with Erik. Why?"

"It wasn't a suicide Carrick. The Chinese had him killed."

Carrick sat back onto the bed and exhaled heavily after hearing the revelation.

"We found out some stuff while investigating his murder. The Chinese are attempting to bypass the U.N. Resolution and get to Black Earth before us," Jordan confessed to his good friend.

"So how does that connect to the delay of the Saturn Six rocket? I know they had something to do with it." Carrick acted like he knew more than he did. "I know you were in Canaveral the day of the launch."

"Man, Mars just can't keep his mouth shut!" Jordan was pissed.

"Mars said nothing to me, Jordan, but you've said plenty. Let's go! Fess up!"

"Not gonna happen, Bro!" said Jordan. "All I'll say is that we had a scare, and now we're all clear. It's highly classified, and I can't say anything else."

"I get it, Brother! Thanks for trusting me." Carrick was relieved that his imagination wasn't running wild for no reason.

"You can't tell Lola anything. Do you understand me, Carrick?"

"I got it, Jordan. She'll hear nothing from me," he reassured his friend. "Jordan, listen, Mars said nothing to me. He kept his mouth shut. I was going off of a hunch. He said nothing to me about the delay of the launch."

"Gotta go, Carrick," Jordan heard Kinzi calling for him. "Kiss Lola and the babies for me. Kinzi said she might be heading out there. I encouraged her to go."

"The invitation is for both of you." Carrick desperately wanted to see his old friends again. Erik's death had left a black hole in his heart, and being able to see Jordan, Kinzi, and even Mars again would be welcomed.

"Trust me, man, you'll see Kinzi long before you'll see me! Take care, Brother!"

"All the best!" Carrick hit the end call button.

Carrick stood and stared out the window again. His eyes suddenly focused on the chair that Erik sat in the last time he worked in the yard, the previous May. It suddenly hit him that it hadn't moved in almost a year. He was a shut-in since Erik's death; he didn't get out very often anymore. He was lost again, and the births of baby Erik and baby Lilly did little to fill the black void inside of him. He was a tortured soul, and without Erik, he was once again incomplete.

Exiting the room, he ran into Lola standing in the hallway just outside the door, waiting for him to emerge.

"What was all that about?" Lola, still holding little Erik, acted pissed but was only concerned.

"Nothing, Jordan's doing fine, and it looks like Kinzi might come out after all."

"Horseshit!" Lola knew better. Carrick wasn't telling her the truth, and she knew it.

"What are you keeping from me?" she said.

Carrick just walked away.

"Where are you going? I'm talking to you!" Lola was livid.

"I'm going for a walk," he yelled as he rounded the corner into the master bath.

"A walk?!" Lola was trying to catch up to him. "It's feeding time! I need help!" A muffled, "You son of a bitch!" came flying from beneath her breath.

Carrick walked out of the bathroom, whizzed by Lola, nearly running into her and the baby. Hopping on one foot, he tried to get his left running shoe on.

Lola threw up her left arm in frustration while juggling little Erik in the other. "I don't like you right now!" she yelled from the catwalk that hovered high above the living room. Carrick bolted out the front door as Lola yelled, "Ya know, that's little Lilly crying, don't ya?!"

Moments later, Carrick found himself sitting in the very chair Erik would always sit in, watching his grandson do yard work. He could almost hear his words, "Just writing in my Journal." Carrick looked down in his hands at the journal that Erik had left him. "What does he want me to do with this? Give it to Mars for the other astronauts?

Go back to Black Earth?" He was so confused as he spoke out loud to himself.

He got up from the chair and headed to Erik's house and the back-left bedroom. There, he sat in Erik's bed and began flipping through the pages of the journal.

Location: Cape Canaveral – Wednesday, April 14, 2027 – 9:00 am EST – T-minus sixty minutes to launch.

"Did you get it yet?" Mars stopped by the Engineering Lab and asked Kyle Bradshaw if he'd accessed The Chameleon's inner chamber.

"Not yet, but I think I'm getting close. The Chinese techs put a password protected mechanism on it. Because it's likely in Chinese, I have to work around it." Bradshaw didn't even lift his head from the device when speaking to Mars.

"Well, keep me posted." Mars was as curious as anyone.

"Oh, are you gonna watch the launch?" Mars asked before walking out.

"From in here," Bradshaw motioned to his laptop with a head nod, "if that's okay? I'm getting close and don't want to stop just yet."

"Of course, Kyle, thanks for all of your hard work." Mars left the lab.

Fifty minutes later, Mars was outside of NASA's main observatory building at the Cape. He was joined by dozens of personnel who would take in the spectacle of the launch. Across the Indian River, the body of water that separated Titusville and Cape Canaveral, Mars could see thousands lining the river. Spectators wanted to see the historic launch; families, tourists, students, and professionals played hooky. Everyone wanted to be a part of the historical maiden voyage of the Saturn Six rocket.

For Mars, it was bittersweet. Normally, he'd be back at Houston's Mission Control, but for the first time in nearly two decades, he was able to watch the launch in person.

It was now sixty seconds to launch, and Mars donned his headset. The butterflies were out of control. He would hear all the chatter between Mission Control and those in Florida. The voice of Flight Director Mitchell Oswald was prominent.

"Okay, folks, here we go!" said Oswald. "Buckle your chinstraps," he joked to the ten men and women on board the Silver Comet. "This should be quite a ride."

Nervous laughter could be heard from the crew compartment.

"We're now at 10-9-8," Oswald counted down, "4-3-2-1, and we have ignition!"

Everyone on the ground and back in Houston held their collective breath. The Chinese incident was not far from people's minds. Additionally, never had there been a rocket the size of the Saturn Six liftoff before.

Far below the crew compartment, the massive thrusters spit their fuel, making an ungodly sound. The ground shook beneath the spectators, causing some actually to worry for their safety.

The rocket's power violently shook the crew compartment and caused vibrations that far exceeded what the team had experienced in simulation. The shaking caused some to open their eyes and question if it was normal.

Kyle Bradshaw was watching the launch with one eye in the lab while fiddling with The Chameleon. Biting his tongue, he said, "Come on!"

Pop! There it was. The cap popped off of the inner belly, and Bradshaw could now see the inside of the device. He was both shocked and surprised. As he observed the inner contents of the strange device more closely, he said, "What the hell!" then his face went white.

Back outside, the rocket cleared the tower and was now traveling at more than 100 mph. Mars watched nervously and said, "God Speed," as he always had while serving as the Flight Director on eleven different missions to space. "There's no turning back now," he thought aloud.

Chapter 24 – The Belly of the Beast

Back inside, Kyle Bradshaw raced from the room, screaming. Making his way outside to where Mars and others were standing, he yelled, "It's not a bomb!"

Mars had trouble understanding Bradshaw due to the roaring chorus of the engines. He took off his headphones and listened more closely.

"It's not a bomb!" Bradshaw repeated.

Mars could hear more clearly now but wasn't entirely sure of what Bradshaw's words meant. "What are you saying?"

Bradshaw screamed, "It's a computer!"

The two men's faces went white, and they looked skyward. The rocket was now at an altitude of roughly twelve miles.

Mars held the headphones up to one ear and listened to the chatter coming from Mission Control and the team just inside the building he was standing next to.

"We're looking good!" Oswald could be heard saying. "Stage one separation will occur in 3-2-1, and we have a clean separation!" said Oswald.

Mars just stared as closely as he could, frozen with fear.

"We have an anomaly...hold that...," said Oswald. "Stage three is active! Crew, what are you seeing up there?"

"We've got a premature ignition light flashing for stage three," said Aviator Jack White.

Dread befell the face of Mars Johnston. He'd heard 'stage three' and looked back at Bradshaw and mouthed the word, "Chameleon."

He looked back up to the rocket, now at an altitude of 18 miles.

In Beijing, the Serpent was smiling, the liftoff was a success, and his future life in America, with his family, was all but assured.

In Artesia, Lola and Carrick held hands and nervously smiled. This was the first lift-off of a NASA rocket since the Fall of 2023, and it was going to Zenith. Carrick found it hard to reconcile his feelings.

In Leesburg, Jordan, Kinzi, and Jordan's parents were watching from their home. Jordan was sick to his stomach while Kinzi gave him a hard time.

Back at the CIA, James Clapper, Matt Solstice, and his secretary Colleen, all watched from the television in Clapper's office. All were smiling proudly, knowing what went into keeping the rocket and its crew safe. "To hell with the Chinese," Clapper clenched his fist in triumph.

Mars looked on and, with each passing second, felt more relieved.

Then, in an instant, a massive explosion could be seen in the sky. Seconds later came the thundering clap. The world looked on as the massive rocket exploded. Onlookers were in shock. Just minutes after shedding its first stage, the massive ship was now in thousands of flaming pieces, raining down over the Atlantic.

Jonathan Cooper, broadcasting live from Titusville, in tears, said, "Ladies and gentlemen, the worst possible thing has happened. Forgive me, as I, like you, am having trouble processing what we're all seeing," he said through tears.

Watching from their home in Artesia, Carrick and Lola were devastated. Carrick immediately tied the disaster back to the Chinese, recalling the conversation he'd had with Jordan.

Watching from their living room in Leesburg, Jocelyn Spear and Kinzi London were in shock while the two Spear men exchanged glances. Jordan had previously shared some confidential information with his father about the intentions of the Chinese. It was still a gutshot for Jordan, as everyone involved in clearing the rocket for launch signed off on the rocket's safety and integrity. Jordan's mind then immediately went to Kai Chang. He now knew that he had been fooled by the SHA militant after all.

The rest of the world mourned those on board the Silver Comet.

"We have a catastrophic failure of stages two and three," said Mission Control's Mitchell Oswald, through his comms.

While panic ensued on the ground, spectators could be seen crying in each other's arms, with parents holding their confused children. At NASA's Cape observatory and Mission Control, hands covered mouths, and many had their heads down.

Mars and Oswald could be heard chanting, "Come on, baby! Come on, baby!"

Then suddenly, massive chutes could be seen deploying many miles above the Atlantic. Onlookers pointed to the sky and were immediately hopeful. The coast guard scrambled every vessel they had, as well as two massive Chinook helicopters.

NASA officials knew what most of the world did not. A safety feature that could save the crew in the event of a catastrophic failure was a crew compartment that would separate and jettison skyward in the event of engine failure. NASA would not allow another Space Shuttle Challenger disaster.

Internally, NASA personnel cheered and hugged each other through their tears. They knew that there was a chance that the crew possibly survived. It would be another twenty minutes before they'd know.

"Jack, are you there?" Oswald tried to raise communications with the crew. "Jack, do you read?"

There was no communication coming from the jettisoned compartment.

"Dammit!" Mars said to himself. "C'mon Jack, answer."

"Pray hard, people!" Oswald said into his comms. "There's still a chance."

"Rick, whatta ya got on the ship's comms?" said Oswald, asking a member of his team if readings indicated intact comms on the crew compartment.

"Not getting any readings, Skip!" Rick Wilson said to Oswald, whom everyone referred to as 'Skip' or 'Skipper.'

An agonizing twelve minutes later, static could be heard coming from the crew compartment.

"Jack, do you read? Jack, it's Oswald here, do you read?"

Through the static, a faint voice was heard. "We read you, Skipper!" said Jack White, aviator of the Silver Comet.

Cheers could be heard chorusing through the Comms. Mars lowered his head, grabbed Kyle Bradshaw, and hugged him.

"Jack, what is the condition of the crew?"

"We're pretty banged up, but I think everyone's okay?" said Jack White.

The world didn't know the fate of the crew yet and wouldn't for another hour. NASA had to ensure they knew each crew member's condition before releasing any information to the public.

Back at CIA Headquarters, Clapper, with clenched fists, ordered Solstice and his secretary out of his office. Moments later, Clapper's cell phone rang; it was Jordan Spear.

Clapper answered and said, "Jordan, get here ASAP!" He kept his cool but was simmering.

"I'm going to kill Chang! I will be there only after he's dead. Fire me! Arrest me! I don't care!" Spear said, then hung up on Clapper.

Clapper immediately called the Langley Federal Holding Facility and alerted them that Jordan Spear was on the way. They should stop him from approaching inmate 61776, Kai Chang, and inmate 61775, Jenny Lee.

"Call me the minute he arrives," Clapper was adamant.

Sixty minutes later, Jordan Spear arrived at the temporary federal prisoner housing facility and barged through the front door. Two Federal Corrections Officers met him in the lobby area and instructed him not to proceed by orders of the Director of the CIA. Another female C.O. could be seen behind glass putting in a call to Clapper's office.

"Officer Spear, we have been ordered not to let you proceed."

"Get out of my way!" said Jordan as he forced his way through the first set of double doors.

The next set of doors were locked, and any individual aggressing the door would either need to be buzzed in or need an RFID card.

Jordan ordered the men to open the door, but they refused. "Open the door, or I'll have your job!" threatened Spear.

"I can't, sir, the orders are from Director Clapper himself," said one of the officers.

Jordan immediately called Clapper from his cell. "Director Clapper, sir!" Jordan was stern, "please instruct these men to stand down and allow me to speak with Chang."

"Jordan, listen, I won't have you assaulting a federal prisoner," said Clapper. "You'll need to calm down first before proceeding."

"Director Clapper, I am calm, and I request access to prisoner Chang at once."

"I'm trusting you, Jordan. They'll be no coming back from this if you harm either one of those prisoners."

"You have my word, sir!" Jordan was only slightly convincing.

"Very well, put your phone on speaker so that I can authorize your access."

"Go ahead, Director Clapper." Spear held his phone out in front of himself after placing it in speaker mode.

"Gentlemen, this is CIA Director James Clapper." The Corrections Officers instantly recognized the Director's voice. "I am authorizing you to allow access to prisoners Chang and Lee to Officer Jordan Spear."

The C.O.s looked at each other and then back through the double doors, making eye contact with the female officer behind the one-inch thick glass in the outer lobby. The female agent, who was actually on the phone with Clapper's office, shook her head in affirmation.

"Very well, sir," the senior of the two officers responded.

"Ah, gentlemen, before Officer Spear proceeds, I want him patted down for weapons before he enters the holding cells." Clapper wasn't taking any chances. "Additionally, I want one or both of you to accompany Officer Spear. Neither prisoner is to be harmed by our Officer Spear."

"Yes, sir."

Seconds later, a buzzing sound could be heard signaling the release of the door lock. The senior officer said, "This way, sir," motioning Spear with his left arm while standing in front of the door, holding it open for Jordan.

After a pat-down revealed that Jordan had no weapons, the two Corrections Officers escorted Spear to the holding cells where Kai Chang and Jenny Lee were held. As the steel door swung open, Jordan yelled, "Kai, you lied to me!"

Jordan trudged heavily and with purpose down the narrow corridor separating the two SHA Militants. The cell block included five cells down each side, but all were empty due to the two Chinese prisoners' high-profile status.

No words returned Jordan's, and as he got closer, he saw something that didn't appear normal, some sort of fabric was knotted up on the crossbar of both of the Chinese prisoner cells. As Jordan got closer, a look of horror washed over his face.

"Get the cell doors open!" he screamed. "Open the cells!" Jordan was in a state of sheer panic.

The two officers trailing Jordan feared that he wanted to harm the prisoners. They quickly closed the distance with him and restrained him from behind. As they got close enough to the cells, they saw what Jordan saw. Both prisoners had hung themselves from the crossbar of their cell door.

Jordan observed that both Chang and Jenny Lee were naked from the waist down. Each had had one pantleg of their government-issued orange jumpsuit wrapped around their neck, with the other pantleg tied to the bar. Both appeared to be dead; their faces and lower extremities were purple, and their mouths contained a white foam in the corner of their lips.

"Open the doors!" Jordan screamed again, reaching through the cell door in an effort to perch Chang upward, relieving pressure on his neck from the ligature.

Seconds later, the doors were released, but Jordan and the officers had trouble sliding them open due to the weight of each of the bodies tied to the door's crossbar.

Once the three were able to untie the knot from the crossbar, they immediately laid the deceased prisoners onto the floor. Jenny Lee was laid out in her cell, while Kai Chang had his upper torso laid out onto the corridor. Jordan Spear immediately untied the ligature from Chang's neck, cleared the foam from his mouth, and began CPR and mouth to mouth resuscitation. The senior officer on the scene tried in vain to resuscitate Lee but, like Jordan, was unsuccessful.

Jordan was close to tears; not only did he need more information from Chang and Lee, but he also felt a strange bond between he and Chang. Kai was a man who was a trained killer and was responsible for taking down the Saturn Six Rocket, possibly killing one or more of its crew, but it didn't register. The scene Jordan walked into was horrifying, and there would be many questions that would need to be answered.

Both SHA Militants, Kai Chang, 33; and Jenny Lee, 32, were dead while in the U.S. Marshall service's custody. How? Why?

Location, Atlantic Ocean, sixteen miles off the coast of Cape Canaveral, the debris field became evident as searchers and rescuers were told to stand down until all exploded debris fell back to Earth. The crew compartment fell safely back to earth and landed in the ocean, some twenty miles northeast of Melbourne, Florida.

While the world watched in horror as the ship inexplicably exploded on live television, those inside NASA knew what likely caused the explosion. At the same time, those within the Chinese government secretly cheered their nefarious accomplishment. People within the Strategic Huyou Agency, and the Ministry of State Security, also cheered the very public American failure. Still, only a select few knew all the details of what brought down the silver goliath.

NASA's Flight Director at Mission Control, Mitchell Oswald, and NASA's Chief Administrator, Mars Johnston, were in constant contact. The crew's status was still uncertain, but both surface vessels and rescue helicopters were on the scene of the floating crew compartment.

"Mitch, what are we looking at?" Mars Johnston was on the phone with Oswald getting an update on the crew's condition.

"Jack White says that three of the crew have been unconscious since the explosion," Oswald reported to Mars, "but we've ordered all crew members to stay in their couches until the Coast Guard breaches the compartment. We don't want to risk their safety."

"Of course," concurred Mars. "Who are the three that aren't responding over the comms?"

"There's no response when we try to raise either Abigale Behrendt, Cindy Nakamura, or Rajendra Phalke," said Oswald.

"Jesus!" Mars responded, "They were all in the back row, weren't they?" he sounded horrified.

"I'm afraid so, Mars." Like Mars Johnston, Mitchell Oswald feared the worst for the three that were seated closest to the back of the crew compartment when the second and third stages exploded behind them.

"Mars, the good news is, the other seven are all responsive and in seemingly good shape considering. They just can't get themselves turned around to see what's happening behind them. When are you getting back here to Houston?" asked Mitchell.

"Not until the entire crew is safely back on land," Mars was mortified.

"Listen, Mars, these things happen. Everybody signed off on the launch. You're not solely to blame." Oswald and Mars had worked together for more than twenty years, and both were stricken with guilt. But Mars was inconsolable, and the responsibility of both the crew and the vessel was all his, and he knew it. The price to pay would be a heavy one, both professionally and personally, but Mars wasn't worried about that, not now. Mars Johnston just wanted his crew returned to shore safely; that's all. The aftermath would come later.

Location: Langley, Virginia. CIA Headquarters. Office of James Clapper – Wednesday, April 14, 2027 – 5:46 pm EST.

Jordan Spear entered the office of James Clapper and said nothing. He could see that Clapper was staring out into the nothingness of trees.

A minute later, Clapper turned and said, "What happened, Jordan?"

"It's my fault, sir. If I didn't go there, they'd still be alive. Both of them." Jordan was solemn.

Clapper walked over to Spear, looked him straight in the eye, and said, "Now you explain to me how someone hangs themselves from a metal bar four feet from the ground?" he was livid.

Jordan took half a step back and said, "It's easier just to show you, sir." He pulled a flash drive from his pocket and plugged it into the large wall-mounted television.

"Sir, what you're about to see is awful, but the contents of this flash drive contain much more than two people dying," explained Jordan. "Kai Chang died wanting to help us. He wanted to prove to me that he didn't withhold information regarding the bomb on that rocket, sir."

Clapper looked skeptical.

Jordan grabbed the television remote and pulled up the recorded feed from the cellblock where the Chinese agents died.

"Sir, if you're not up for this, I can just summarize what happened." Jordan exercised caution.

"Play the goddamn video Jordan! I am at the end of my rope with you! Now quit screwing around and get on with it!" Colleen, sitting at her desk, heard Clapper's eruption, and got up and walked away from her desk momentarily, hoping not to get caught in the crossfire.

Jordan pushed the play button and began to narrate the events as they unfolded. "After the Saturn Six exploded, one of the Corrections Officers, Sam Fricke, thought he would taunt Kai Chang and let him know that the rocket blew up. He gave him a hard time, telling him that 'it was all over' for him and 'his girlfriend.' Later, after you called the holding facility, letting them know I was en route, the same officer went back to the cell block again to taunt Chang, warning him that I was on the way and that they were ordered to stop me from physically harming either prisoner."

"Are you suggesting that Chang and Lee were fearful of your arrival?" Clapper thought that that was a stretch.

Without audio, the video showed C.O. Fricke walk into the cell block, hours between visits, and on both occasions, was seen speaking to and laughing at Chang and Lee. "Taunting them both," said Jordan.

"Have you spoken to that son of a bitch?" Clapper was pissed.

"Yes, after the events of this afternoon, I informally deposed everyone involved."

"We'll need to get them deposed on record," Clapper said.

"Of course." Jordan acknowledged Clapper.

"Okay, this part is critical," Jordan underscored what was about to be revealed on the surveillance footage. "As you can see here, Chang and Lee are pressed up against their cell doors, talking to each other after the guard left."

The footage then revealed to Spear and Clapper that the two extended their arms through the cell doors in an effort to touch hands.

"Sir, while the aisle is narrow, the two were unable to make physical contact. My guess is that this was the moment the two understood they would never be that close again. Look here," Jordan paused the footage, "If you look closely, Lee lowers her head and appears to be sobbing."

"Now what you're about to see," Jordan paused the footage, looking a little emotional, he said, "I have never seen anything like it.

I was shocked when I saw it." Jordan seemed almost nervous to un-pause the video.

"Sir, before I hit 'play,' I need to give you some background. When I first interrogated Chang on the USCGC Vigilant, he pretended not to speak English. When doing so, I responded to him in Mandarin."

Clapper looked impressed that Jordan knew Mandarin.

"It was at that moment that we started to connect. He seemed flattered that I could understand his native tongue. We discussed how many languages each of us knew, and he told me that he could speak and understand eight different languages. I was impressed, and I let him know it."

"What does all of this mean?" Clapper wanted Jordan to get to the point.

Jordan hit the 'play' button and said, "watch this."

The two men observed on the recording, Kai Chang walking away from his cell door and squaring himself to the camera in his cell. Chang looked up to the camera and began signing to the camera.

"I guess he was under the assumption that the camera was recording video but not audio, or perhaps he wasn't sure," said Jordan.

"He's communicating in sign language?" Clapper wasn't sure what he was looking at.

'Yes, sir," said Jordan. "He's signing a message."

"Well, what's he saying?" Clapper was still confused.

"It's not just what he's saying, sir, but to whom he's saying it." Jordan again seemed a little off with the events from earlier in the day.

"Officer Spear, if you tell me that he's communicating to you right now," paused Clapper, "then I'm gonna..." Clapper was dumbfounded. "So, what's he saying?"

"Right here he's saying, 'Jordan, it is important for you to know that I told you everything I knew about the bomb attached to the rocket. I told you everything I knew about the Interlink system hack, and I told you everything I knew about The Spider going to Black Earth on the Chinese Eclipse. Everything I told you is the truth'," translated Jordan.

Clapper and Jordan watched as Chang signed. "Wait a second! Are you interpreting this right now?" Clapper was astonished at the notion that Jordan knew sign language, too.

Jordan paused the recording. "Yes, sir, my first girlfriend was deaf, and I wanted to be able to speak to her through signing even though she could read lips," revealed Jordan.

Clapper thought that he knew Officer Jordan Spear very well but was surprised to know that he could also sign. "Did Chang know that you knew sign language?"

"No, sir."

"Then why is he signing to you?" Clapper was perplexed.

"Again, I don't think he was sure that his words could be heard and that the message he was sending to me would be translated," surmised Jordan.

"Astonishing," thought Clapper aloud. "Continue translating, son."

The two men continued to watch Chang sign into the camera while Jordan translated.

"Here, he is saying, 'I gave you my word, and I am a man of honor. You gave me your word that if I were truthful, and if the Saturn rocket made it safely to Black Earth, that Jenny Lee and I could be together in the same cell while imprisoned in America'."

"You promised him what?!" Clapper was surprised Jordan would make such a guarantee to the SHA assassin. "That would go against every norm ever established."

"I had to get him to talk, and I would have kept my promise to him, sir," Jordan was sincere.

"Well, it doesn't matter now, does it?" Clapper capitulated. "Continue."

Jordan continued translating, "'I now know that after the rocket came down that I will never be allowed to see Jenny again. We have decided that we choose death over dying alone in a cell thousands of miles from home. Our pride and honor,' Chang signed, 'will not allow us to do that.'"

"Pause it there, son. So, your contending that this is the moment that they decided to commit suicide?" asked Clapper.

"Yes, sir. Earlier, when we observed Jenny Lee crying, that was her moment of concession."

"Please summarize what else he says before we witness the actual suicide."

"Sir, I think it's important that you watch it so that you can witness the sincerity in his words."

"Very well. Continue," conceded Clapper.

Jordan hit play. "Here, Chang makes an astonishing gesture," said Jordan. "Right now, he is communicating the name of The Spider."

"What?! Why would he betray his SHA associate? That doesn't make any sense." Clapper didn't believe Chang would do such a thing and was skeptical that the hired assassin might be trying to set up Jordan in his final act. He was also skeptical that Chang knew nothing of the bomb that brought down the Silver Comet.

"Sir, here he is explaining why he would give up the name of his comrade. 'Jordan, in an attempt to win back your trust and to be remembered by you as an honorable man, I will answer the question that I refused to answer just days ago. The name of The Spider is Colonel Vadik Lei. Vadik is my SHA Brother, but he no longer thirsts for killing for his government like me. He too, knows that he is on a one-way mission and will likely not return home safely.' Jordan continued to interpret. "He says here that, 'Vadik Lei is a lethal killer, he is a Shaolin Temple Grandmaster that cannot be defeated in hand to hand combat. He will take with him to Black Earth Chinese stars, and his weapon of choice, his Zhàndòu bang'."

"His what?" Clapper didn't understand.

"His battle stick, sir. It's called a Krabong. It's a five-foot-long piece of bamboo and can be deadly when in the right hands."

"No guns on Black Earth, huh?" asked Clapper.

"Guns are fine, ammunition, no. The radiation could set it off. Not a good idea on a spacecraft," explained Jordan.

"I see. That makes sense." Clapper nodded.

"Here, he is telling me that The Spider has one weakness in hand to hand combat, being attacked from his left side. He's telling me that it would be wise to circle to Lei's left before striking."

"And you believe him?" Clapper again showed skepticism.

"Sir, the man unceremoniously hung himself with a prison jumpsuit."

"Watch this part, sir," Jordan encouraged Clapper.

"This is the moment, sir. Are you sure you want to watch it?"

"Play the tape, son. I've seen worse in my career."

Clapper and Jordan watched as Chang stood at attention, arms stiff and pointing down, glued to his side, tapped his heels together, and bowed his head.

"Did he just bow to you, Jordan?" Clapper continued to be astonished.

"Yes, sir, and the first time he did it was in the Blue Room on March 28, when he first confessed. I believe him, sir."

Jordan pushed the 'play' button, and the two men just watched in horror. Kai Chang walked over to his cell door and called out to Jenny Lee. Chang communicated to her that it was time. Lee could be seen bowing her head to Chang in compliance. The two each removed their pants; the Marshal service issued no undergarments. Chang then reached through the cell door and tossed his pants to Lee. Lee then tossed hers to Chang.

The two crumpled the pants in their hands in a heart-breaking gesture and raised them to their noses, and inhaled. It was as if it would be their last chance to experience the scent of the other.

The two then tied a pantleg around their neck and tightened it. They then placed their backs against the cell door, reached behind, and tied the other pant leg to the cell's crossbar. After that, they could be seen saying something, perhaps 'goodbye' to each other. From there, they appear to test the strength of the ligature and slowly began to choke themselves out. After each fell unconscious, the asphyxiation continued until they both died. Twitching of their legs could be seen at the moment they likely were dying.

"My God, I wasn't ready for that." Clapper looked sick to his stomach. "How could someone hang themself when all they had to do was stand up to live?"

"Those two were hired killers, and know how to kill, others and themselves. No different than biting down on a cyanide capsule after being captured," Jordan thought aloud.

"I guess so." Clapper just shook his head and thought that he wouldn't be able to erase that image from his mind any time soon.

After another moment of reflection, Clapper regained his composure and said, "Okay, let's run a check on Vadik Lei and see if what he told us was true." Clapper then stood and said, "Jordan, if you ever threaten to do what you did earlier, you will be out of the CIA forever, and we will be done. Do you understand me, son?"

"Yes, sir." Jordan stood and extended his hand to shake Clapper's.

Clapper reciprocated and shook his protégé's hand.

As Jordan walked to the door, Clapper stopped him.'

"Jordan," said Clapper, "They're alive, son." Clapper was reserved.

"I'm sorry, sir?" Jordan looked puzzled.

"The crew. Nine of the ten astronauts on the Saturn six survived the explosion."

Jordan looked shocked. "But how, sir?"

"The crew compartment had a jettison contingency. At the moment before the explosion, the crew compartment separated and jettisoned skyward, deployed its chutes, and fell to the Atlantic," explained Clapper.

"The Japanese Meteorologist, Cindy Nakamura, didn't make it. Abigale Behrendt, and the crew's medical doctor, Rajendra Phalke, are in critical condition but are expected to survive."

"That's a miracle, sir," Jordan lowered his head, relieved for those who survived but heartbroken for the family of Nakamura.

Jordan nodded to Clapper and continued out the door.

Chapter 25 – Aftermath

Location: The Atlantic Ocean, Twenty Miles Northeast of Melbourne, Florida – Five Hours Earlier.

The Silver Comet search area for both floating and sunken parts was more than 500 square miles. The recovery of the rocket's parts would take many weeks and even months, with some spacecraft portions never to be found. However, the search was secondary to the recovery of the rocket's crew compartment and its crew.

Location: Titusville, Florida. NASA Office of Mars Johnston. Wednesday, April 14, 2027 – 4:42 pm EST.

Mars sat in his office and looked at his cellphone. He scrolled through his missed calls, emails, and text messages. He was nearly faint with exhaustion, and his heart was sick. The successful launch of the Saturn Six was to be his moment to shine; the biggest rocket to ever travel into space would do so under his watch. Instead, he'd be remembered for one of the worst space-flight accidents of all time. As he scrolled through the messages, one, in particular, caught his eye. It was from his ex-wife, Karen. She sent her condolences from both her and her husband of two years. In the moment of his life when Mars most needed someone to lean on, he realized that he had no one. Mars had been divorced for six years, and at that moment, it felt like twenty. He had been married to his job for decades. His inability to separate his personal and professional lives led to the failure of his marriage.

Mars continued to scroll through his phone, and the more he did, the more he felt alone. There was no one there to save him, to bail him out, to offer a warm hug, or a shoulder to cry on. In a moment of deep reflection, Mars realized that he'd been alone for many years, but never more than at that moment.

Mars turned off his cell phone and was resigned to wallow in his sadness for a little while longer. At that moment, the red phone on his desk rang; it was Houston. "Mars, they got 'em! They got the crew, turn on your television!" yelled Oswald Mitchell, through the phone.

"What about Behrendt, Nakamura, and Phalke?" Mars was concerned with the three astronauts that were positioned in the back row of the crew compartment.

"They have all been non-responsive to our radio communications. We'll know more soon," offered Mitchell.

On the television, a massive Coast Guard chinook helicopter hovered above the floating crew compartment. Four divers were in the water, with two divers positioned on top of the crew compartment assisting the astronauts in getting through the escape hatch.

Mars recognized the first person to be extracted; it was the British biologist Sebastian Colt. Colt was a ten-year veteran of the European Space Agency, and at only thirty-six years old, was recognized as one of the brightest young biologists in the world. He was considered the best Biologist in any space agency in the world. Mars was a mixed martial arts fan and had followed Colt's early years when he was a rising star on the Bellator MMA Circuit. Colt left MMA for a career that would prove more beneficial to the world of science and space exploration. He was done using his fists and on to using his brain.

Colt could be seen giving the thumbs-up to the divers below as he was hoisted to safety by the winchman in the thirteen-ton chinook, hovering overhead. The ocean was littered with Coast Guard and Navy vessels, and smaller ships and boats could be seen in every direction for miles. The vessels were pulling debris from the ocean.

The underwater search efforts would include a navy submarine, dozens of U.S. Navy and Coast Guard vessels, and the Canadian based Gweniece Offshore Company.

Mars watched the events unfold and took in the spectacle of the failed mission that would, no doubt, stain his previously untarnished career and reputation.

Mars Johnston wasn't alone in his guilt and responsibility, though; the CIA, FBI, and dozens of NASA Departmental Officials and engineers signed off on the safety of the Silver Comet.

Location: Beijing, China, Ministry of State Security – April 15, 2027 – Early Morning Hours, Beijing local time.

In the office of Minister Li Kenong, Kenong was sitting at his desk contemplating his future when the phone buzzed. Sir, the Honorable Haoran Shieh is here to see you, sir." Kenong's secretary announced.

"Send him in." Kenong rose to greet his boss.

"Minister Kenong!" Haoran Shieh was glowing. "A glorious day is what today is!" said the senior adviser to President Xí Shèng-Xióng.

Kenong launched in without a formal greeting. "Please explain to me how it is that the American rocket ship exploded, your Honorable Shieh?" Kenong's joy in the Chinese sabotage effort was subdued.

"Minister Kenong, you don't seem to share in our milestone achievement." Shieh looked only somewhat surprised.

"We both know that the SHA defectors gave the Americans the information they needed to find and remove the bomb from the rocket." Kenong wanted to know how it was that the ship blew up anyway. He felt that his superiors weren't forthright with him.

"Ahh, Minister, perhaps our agents did their jobs after all?" smiled Shieh. "Or, perhaps, our computer technicians did theirs?"

"I don't understand," Kenong looked puzzled.

"You forgot our last conversation, Minister Kenong. Contingencies! When we spoke last, I told you that all plans have Contingencies." Shieh thought Kenong was a fool. "It was not a bomb that was attached to the American rocket. It was a computer."

"Computer?" Kenong's face contorted because he was furious. "What does that mean? Why was I not told of this?" he said with disdain dripping from his words.

"Minister Kenong, you are known to have a big mouth. The reason you hold your position is well-known. It was your late father that got you this prestigious title and office in the Ministry of State Security, but you cannot seem to keep your mouth shut."

Kenong's father, the Honorable Longwei Kenong, was the predecessor of Haoran Shieh, and the senior-most adviser to President Xí Shèng-Xióng.

Kenong was incensed, "How dare you insinuate that I am not trustworthy or honorable! How dare you speak of my late father!"

"Your father was an honorable and highly respected man for many decades," Shieh feigned being contrite. "I'm sorry that his son has fallen so far from the family tree," Shieh said. "And may I remind you, yet again, that you are speaking to the current righthand of our most excellent President Xí Shèng-Xióng?"

Kenong recoiled.

"Kenong, you will never be trusted completely. Your ambitions will always get in your way. You should always believe that you will receive only half of the information until after the fact. Please, don't let that upset you," Shieh reeked of insincerity.

Kenong ground his teeth and took the medicine that his boss was administering.

"Well then, now that it is after the fact, please explain to me how our engineers did it?" Kenong was more respectful now.

"It was a computer, not an explosive. The computer, once attached to the skin of the rocket, hacked into the computer of the third stage of the Saturn Six," explained Shieh. "The Americans, with their small financial budget, used reusable rocket boosters, and each of those boosters had a computer on them."

Kenong looked confused but still curious.

"You see, Kenong," Shieh went slow as he believed the man in front of him was quite dense. "Each of the reusable booster stages has a computer in them that tells the booster when to fire and how to land back on Earth. Each stage fires only after the previous stage burns out. Our geniuses in the lab programmed our computer to instruct the stage three computer to fire when the rocket's stage two booster was to fire. If two boosters fire at the same time..., well, let's just say, the results are and were catastrophic," Shieh gloated.

"So, this caused the third stage to fire into the completely fueled second stage?" Kenong reasoned aloud while bobbing his head in enlightenment.

"Yes, Minister Kenong, now you have it."

"The only downside was that their astronauts survived. The American engineers are not as inferior as we suspected. We must be careful not to underestimate them, ever!" warned Shieh.

"Yes, of course!" Kenong bowed.

"Very well, then. Please update me now on the progress of our other two SHA Militants and their assigned goals," requested Shieh.

"Certainly, Honorable Shieh," Kenong bowed in compliance and turned to sit back down at his desk.

Flipping through his notes, he shared the status of the Interlink hack of the American's communication corridor, as well as the astronaut training of Vadik Lei.

"We have pierced the veil of their computer firewalls, and they are none the wiser. We have planted information that would cause the Americans to act, and their failure to do so indicates to us that they cannot see our channel running parallel to theirs." Kenong looked boastful.

"Very good, Minister! And what of our merciless Killer, Vadik Lei?"

"He has long since completed his training and has been working side by side with the team that will travel to Black Earth in the coming days," revealed Kenong. "When do we lift-off your honorable Haoran Shieh?" Kenong displayed an eagerness about him.

"Trust me, Minister Kenong, you will be the last to know," Shieh smiled. "Stay vigilant and ensure our man Vadik Lei is at the ready!"

Kenong's smile disappeared as he again reluctantly bowed to his father's successor.

Location: Artesia, New Mexico – April 15, 2027 – 11:15 am MST

Lola and Carrick sat at the kitchen table, Carrick just waiting for a return call from either Jordan or Mars, both of whom he'd left several voicemails and text messages.

"Nothing yet, huh?" Lola asked her husband.

"Nothing," Carrick exhaled heavily. He'd spoken very little since the explosion. It was personal for him, and he couldn't wrap his head around how he might become involved. Lost again, he knew that Lola could see it but was powerless to change his mindset.

Location: Washington, D.C., NCN Studios: The Situation Center with Bear Winston – April 15, 2027 – 5:30 pm EST.

The world was glued to their televisions and smartphones; everyone was still in shock with the disaster that unfolded the day before in Florida.

The camera zoomed in on Bear Winston as he sat at his glass desk with his special guest.

"Welcome to the Situation Center, I'm Bear Winston. Joining me tonight from Houston, the state's Junior Senator from Texas, and the former Chief Administrator at NASA, James Lorenstine." Bear turned to his guest.

"Welcome, Senator Lorenstine," Winston eased into the interview.

"Thanks for having me, Bear." Lorenstine felt obligated to be there. More importantly, he'd hoped to provide insight into the tragic events from the day before and offer up his condolences for the lost Japanese astronaut, Cindy Nakamura.

"Senator Lorenstine, what can you tell us about the accident yesterday?" asked Winston. "I understand that it's still early and that the investigation is just beginning, but any information that you can provide to our audience would be helpful."

"Well, Bear, as you mentioned, it's still very early," said Lorenstine. "I'd first like to send my condolences and prayers to the family of Cindy Nakamura. Dr. Nakamura and I go way back from my days with NASA, and I can only imagine what her family must be going through right now."

Michael Cook

"Yes, what a horrific tragedy," Bear was empathetic.

"I'd also like to send my thoughts and prayers to all the astronauts that were involved in the accident, as well as their families. What they went through yesterday will be hard to cope with moving forward," said Lorenstine.

"Yes, what can you tell us about the condition of the two astronauts who are currently in critical condition?"

"I just got off the phone with the current Chief Administrator at NASA, Mars Johnston. He tells me that the two are conscious and talking. It appears that they will make a full recovery," offered Lorenstine.

"Senator, let me ask you about a rumor that is currently making the rounds on the internet, that somehow this might not have been an accident."

"Bear, I think that it's natural for people to want to believe that an accident of this magnitude wasn't an accident," Lorenstine paused. "But accidents in the spaceflight industry happen all the time, just not always of this significance . It's a dangerous business to be in, and everyone involved understands the risks."

"So, you're saying that as a United States Senator, and the former head of NASA, that you know nothing about the possible sabotage of the Saturn Six rocket."

"Whoa! Bear, let's not even entertain the notion! It would be grossly irresponsible to perpetuate such a rumor." Lorenstine was surprised that Bear Winston would sensationalize the tragedy. "I won't even consider entering into that conversation."

"There is nothing to suggest such a thing occurred," Lorenstine continued, "and the experts at NASA are less than thirty-six hours into their investigation." Lorenstine looked right into the camera and was direct. "It will be many months before anyone knows what caused that rocket to explode mid-flight. What I can say is that it looks like a catastrophic engine failure of stages two and three of the Silver Comet."

"Let me ask you one more question as a U.S. Senator. Suppose the Chinese attempted to go around the U.N.'s Resolution 2978. Would the U.S. and its international partners bypass a self-imposed moratorium on space travel before the current investigation is complete?" Winston was direct.

"Wow, that's a good question," acknowledged Lorenstine. "First of all, there has been no moratorium put in place as far as I know. Second, the Chinese have made their intentions pretty clear; they want to salvage Black Earth, breaking the original agreement made by the U.N. G-8 plus 5 group, and all of the other contributing countries from the first four missions to Black Earth."

"Black Earth and the technologies that live there can and should benefit all of humankind and not just one greedy country. The Chinese going it alone cannot be allowed to happen." Lorenstine was stern. "It simply wouldn't stand," he concluded.

"You don't believe that mere sanctions would be a suitable deterrent, do you?" asked Winston.

"No comment," said a poker-faced Lorenstine.

"Senator James Lorenstine, thank you for your valuable insight." Bear turned to the camera and said, "We'll be right back! Stay tuned!"

Location: Titusville, Florida, NASA's Florida Headquarters. The Tranquility Room – April 27, 2027 – Mid-Morning

In the largest conference room at the Florida Headquarters of NASA, a briefing was held to discuss the Silver Comet accident's initial findings. In attendance were more than a dozen government officials and engineers. The group would attempt to dissect the events that led up to the tragedy and then determine a plan to prevent it from ever happening again.

Sitting at a large conference table was NASA Chief, Mars Johnston; Flight Director, Oswald Mitchell; Chief Engineer, George Ford; Junior Engineers: Kyle Bradshaw, Danny Trippedo, and Clifford Elliott. The FBI was represented by Director John Calhoun, Special Agent in charge, John Primrose, and Special Agent Debbie Scott. From the CIA were Director James Clapper, Officers Matt Solstice, and Jordan Spear. Lastly, the NTSB was represented by its head, Darnell Scott, and his Field Chief, Daniel Schafstall.

Mars began the meeting. "Ladies and gentlemen, thank you for being here today. The reason your presence was requested today is because you're the most qualified people in the world to assist NASA and its engineers in determining the cause of this horrific accident." Even though Mars felt ragged and broken on the inside, he put on a brave face and hid his true feelings from most of the people in the room about what had transpired in the last two weeks. The people who knew him best, Clapper and Jordan Spear, could see through the very thin facade and knew he was suffering.

"Before the meeting," said Mars, "we went through informal introductions, but I'd like to call out just a few people in the room, as their presence will benefit the entire team greatly. First off, the CIA Director, James Clapper. Director Clapper and I have worked closely over the last five years, and I am grateful in advance for his contributions to this investigation."

"Next up, from the NTSB," Mars directed his sights on Scott. "I want to thank Darnell Scott for being here personally. The experience he brings will help us keep this investigation moving forward. And lastly, I'd like to acknowledge CIA Officer Jordan Spear. His insight will be keen as he is a special operator for the CIA and formerly a NASA astronaut. Jordan is the only person in this room to have lifted off in a spaceship, doing it twice, I might add. Thank you, Jordan," Mars nodded in a show of respect.

The three men called out by Mars Johnston all nodded in appreciation for the special recognition.

"Okay, before we get started, I want to give everyone here an update on the status of the astronauts who were injured in the explosion," Mars looked anguished. "American, Abigale Behrendt, is out of the hospital and resting comfortably at her home in Columbus, Ohio. Rajendra Phalke, the crew's medical doctor, is out of intensive care and resting comfortably at the University of Miami Hospital. He will likely be there for another four weeks with a broken back."

"Lastly, Cindy Nakamura's ashes were buried last week near her home in Nagano, Japan."

Those in attendance avoided eye contact with one another, either looking directly at Mars or down into their laps.

Mars was poignant. "The loss of Cindy Nakamura wasn't just to her family and friends, but to the world. She made the ultimate sacrifice that an astronaut can make. She gave her young life in the continuing effort to forward space travel. Cindy's name will forever grace the Space Mirror Memorial at the Kennedy Space Center on Merritt Island, here in Florida. If you've never been, I encourage all of you to go. The Space Mirror is a place no astronaut wants to be remembered, but be remembered, they will," he paused, "forever."

Mars shook off his emotions and opened his itinerary for the day, then cleared his throat. "We'll start the meeting by reviewing the agenda in front of you."

Those gathered around the table flipped through the pamphlet and then looked back to Mars.

Mars began, "I'll go first." He then took his seat. "To date, the US Navy, Coast Guard, and the Gweniece Offshore salvage company have recovered more than two thousand tons of debris from the Silver Comet. That is an amazing feat in just two weeks, but that's only half of what the Saturn Six rocket weighed before lift-off. The good news is that the fuel alone was more than a million pounds, so we're looking at about a third of the rocket still not recovered. The biggest issue we face is that the portion of the rocket where the initial blast came from hasn't been located yet."

NTSB Field Chief Dan Schafstall raised his hand. Mars acknowledged him with a nod. "What part of the rocket is that Mars?"

"It's called an 'Interstage Ring,' and we'll be discussing that portion of the rocket in great detail today. Great question, and thank you for asking," responded Mars.

"Before we get into the particulars of the ship's explosion and subsequent break-up, I'd like Kyle Bradshaw to come up and illustrate the lynchpin that was responsible for the disaster, a device we're calling 'The Chameleon'." Mars motioned for Bradshaw to come to the front of the room. He then pushed a button on a remote-control device behind the podium, and a massive cabinet, roughly 8' x 8', opened to reveal a one-hundred-fifty-inch monitor on the wall.

Bradshaw waited for Mars to vacate the space between the podium and the wall with the monitor.

Mars stepped to the side and Bradshaw re-positioned the podium so that no one's view of the monitor was obstructed. The introverted Bradshaw looked awkward and uncomfortable, wearing a tie to work for the first time since he interviewed with NASA more than three years ago.

Bradshaw fumbled through his notes before saying, "Thank you, Mr. Johnston, it's an honor to be here. I wish it could've been under different circumstances."

"Today, I have been asked to breakdown the composition of The Chameleon and the role it played in bringing down our rocket." Bradshaw turned to the monitor to his back and left. On the screen was a blown-up picture of the device in its camouflaged or invisible stage.

Grumbles and mumbles filled the air, with several in attendance unsure of what they were looking at. All they could make out was a blurry looking form sitting on a white lab table.

"Exactly the response I was expecting," smiled Bradshaw. "So, as you can see here," using a red laser, Bradshaw pointed to the center mass of the near-invisible device, "this is the device when it's in its clear, or invisible stage."

"What the hell are we looking at, son?" asked a confused FBI Director, John Calhoun.

Debbie Scott and Dan Schafstall looked equally confused.

Mars observed their confusion and took relief that the device's technology was so advanced that it fooled many experts from several governmental agencies. He felt that if dozens of scientists and engineers were fooled, he would somehow bear less responsibility.

"Yes, Director Calhoun! Hard to see, indeed," said Bradshaw.

Clapper broke in, "Kyle, my guess is the next slide will be the device in its actual form, correct?"

"Yes, sir."

"Before you get there, I'd like to address the group," said Clapper. "For everyone's edification, this device was planted on the side of the Saturn Six rocket, in the wee hours of the morning, on a ship with a diameter of nearly 40 feet. Additionally, it was placed near the top of a rocket which stood more than 360 feet tall."

Mars bobbed his head and looked impressed with his CIA friend, as the Director nearly got the rocket's dimensions correct.

"The reason I bring this up is that if we weren't tipped off to the device being there, we would never have known of its presence." Clapper was methodical in his delivery. "This meeting would look a lot different as we'd all believe that it was a mechanical failure. Hell, it's likely that the CIA wouldn't be at this meeting at all. Now please continue, son." Clapper motioned to Bradshaw.

Bradshaw continued after his audience leaned in with curiosity. Clicking the remote-control in his hand, the group could now see the device without its cloak on.

"That's the same device we just saw?" asked Debbie Scott, from the FBI, while looking astonished.

"Yes, Ma'am!" said Bradshaw.

"So, beneath the device, we found a switch that controls the camouflage mechanism and simply turned it off. This is the result of that. From there, we needed to penetrate the belly of the device, and this proved to be very difficult," explained Bradshaw.

"Kyle, what made it adhere to the rocket? Was it a magnet or adhesive? Bolted in? What?" asked the NTSB's, Darnell Scott.

"Very strong earth magnets," responded Kyle.

"Yeah, but nowhere near strong enough to keep that thing attached while the rocket barreled through the atmosphere, right?" Scott looked a little perplexed.

"That was our first mistake,....," answered Kyle before being quickly cut off by Mars Johnston.

"What Kyle is trying to say is that if it was possible for us to remove the device without cutting into the skin of the third stage, we should have questioned its ability to stay intact upon lift-off and ascent. That was a missed opportunity, and we'll learn from that," Mars wore a look of humility. He signaled to Kyle with a mere look that he should stick to the facts and not assign fault or blame. Mars guessed that the assignment of fault would come later in the meeting. He wasn't looking forward to that.

Bradshaw continued, "After its removal from the ship, we dissected the device, and with the help of the CIA," Bradshaw nodded to those three members at the table, "determined that there was a barometer and an altimeter, called a 'Fusion Coil Glider'..." Bradshaw was once again cut-off, this time by Jordan Spear.

Spear wanted to get Mars off of the hot seat by assigning some blame to the CIA. "The 'Fusion Coil Glider' on that device is a sophisticated decoy," explained Jordan.

"I'm sorry, I'm confused," Scott said while shaking his head and looking lost.

Jordan added, "The Chinese wanted us to think that if we found the device, that we would have successfully averted disaster. We were fooled," he paused, "all of us."

"It wasn't an explosive device!" announced Mars.

"It's a computer," revealed Bradshaw.

For the first time, the group hearing this revelation sat up in their seats, as if desperate to know more.

"Okay, here comes the clinical part of the post-mortem of what happened." Bradshaw looked excited to dig into the nuts and bolts of it all.

"Pay close attention, folks," encouraged Mars.

For the remainder of the meeting, Bradshaw would explain that the computer hiding in The Chameleon's belly, once attached to the third stage of the rocket, wirelessly hacked into the computer that controlled stage firing, stage separation, and stage descent, and return to Earth capabilities.

Bradshaw explained to the group how the process was designed to work. "Once a stage burns itself out, a separation of stages occurs. For example, after stage one exhausts its fuel, it then severs itself from the second stage. It does this by detonating mild explosives that cut the umbilical cords between stages one and two, exploding bridge wire and detachable tension straps that hold the stages together. This creates enough separation for a successful detachment. After that, the second stage thrusters and gravity do the rest. The process then repeats itself after stage two burns off all of its fuel."

"But that's not what happened," Mars chimed in.

"The Chameleon cloaked its presence," said Bradshaw, "and then commanded the third stage to simultaneously initiate its burn at the exact moment the second stage was signaled to initiate its burn."

"My god," Schafstall blurted out while shaking his head.

"Continuing," said Bradshaw. "The Chameleon successfully programmed stage three to initiate its burn prematurely, without initiating the stages to separate. This caused stage three to fire its thrusters into the rocket's second stage. The force eventually caused separation of the second and third stages, but not until enough damage was done. The rocket's shell first lost its integrity, and then within .66 milliseconds, caused the second and third stage to explode almost simultaneously," explained Bradshaw.

"So, basically, the Chinese used the fuel on the Saturn Six as their explosive, making our Saturn Six the largest bomb ever made," Mars said almost apologetically.

"And they did it with just a tiny computer," added Clapper.

"Jesus!" Darnell Scott was in disbelief. "It was a smart bomb, and those sons of bitches pulled it off!"

The group as a whole was in awe by the technical execution of the Chinese.

"The million-dollar question I have," said FBI Director, John Calhoun, now sitting erect in his chair, "is why was the rocket allowed to lift-off before knowing what the internal composition of the device was?"

"I was also wondering about that," added the NTSB's, Darnell Scott.

Several around the table concurred with a look of curiosity.

Mars began to speak when Clapper cut him off with a clearing of his throat.

"Ahem!" Clapper leaned forward and interlocked his fingers, making sure that everyone sitting at the table could see him. "The reason we launched that rocket before we knew what was in the belly of the beast is because the Chinese, within a matter of days, will launch their Chinese Eclipse rocket and fly it to Black Earth. Once there, they will pillage it for all that it's worth. They will then blow up The Triad, thus ensuring that the once-great society that lived on Zenith for millennia, before migrating to Earth, could no longer benefit any other country on Earth, making them the sole super-power for centuries to come. We had to launch first!" Clapper's tone was intended to end that line of discussion full stop.

In the end, blame was never assigned. It was agreed that the Chinese executed the perfect plan. The group would finish the day discussing ways to improve perimeter security of NASA's subsequent rocket launches.

Once the meeting recessed, Jordan Spear and James Clapper pulled Mars to the side.

"Mars, you carried yourself well today," said Clapper. "It wasn't your fault. With that, you need to get back in the saddle. Not only does NASA need you, but the entire country is counting on your administration to get us back to Black Earth, and soon. Your leadership is critical, and history will thank you for it."

Clapper's words buoyed Mars' confidence.

"Did Gene Thomas pack it in after the Challenger disaster?" asked Clapper of Mars.

Mars responded with pride, "No, he didn't. In fact, he went on to ensure that future shuttle missions were safer. Gene would also become the Director of Safety, Reliability, and Quality Assurance at the Kennedy Space Center. After that, he would become The KSC's Deputy Director. Gene Thomas was both my friend and mentor."

"I, too, knew Gene," said Clapper. Mars was surprised by the revelation.

"So, if he would've retired after the disaster, would he have ever become your mentor?" asked Clapper.

Mars pondered for a while before answering, "No, I guess not."

"Mars," Clapper placed his hand on Johnston's shoulder, "How long did Gene continue with the space program after 1986?"

"Until 1997," said Mars, not sure where Clapper was going with his line of questioning.

"And that's how many years, Mars?" asked Clapper.

"Eleven. Why?"

"So, we've got you for at least another eleven years, is that right?" Clapper was stoic, gently squeezing Mars' shoulder, then gave him a subtle smile and a wink.

Mars smiled and immediately perked up. The tragedy would help him to find new meaning in his role. "If they'll have me that long!" he said.

"Mars, now that you're officially back on board, I have a serious question for you," said Clapper.

"What is it?" asked Mars.

"Would you authorize your boys to assist my cyber technicians at the CIA in the reprogramming of The Chameleon?"

"I don't understand what you're asking me, Jim," Mars responded while looking confused.

"I want to return the favor and have that device planted on the Chinese landing craft after we land on the surface of Zenith." Clapper was dead serious.

Mars looked dumbfounded. His attention went to Jordan, then back to Clapper, who said nothing while wearing a sly grin. It was obvious to Mars that the CIA had a plan in the works that included preventing any Chinese craft from lift-off after landing on the black planet.

Mars was insulted. "You expect me to be part of bringing down a Chinese ship filled with Taikonauts?"

"No, I don't," said Clapper. "That burden, I'm afraid, will fall on my shoulders," he paused. "It's a matter of international security, Mars."

Mars looked lost, though he reluctantly agreed.

"Mars," said Clapper, "we need the Neptune One ready to go ASAP. The moment the Chinese launch their Eclipse rocket, we'll only have a matter of days."

"That's not my call," Mars looked flushed.

"Then I will have POTUS call you this evening." Clapper was again dead serious.

Mars gulped. He knew the circumstances with China were dire, and he knew that he was the right man for the job of Chief Administrator of NASA.

"Oh, and Mars, we'll need a crew to be named ASAP. Leave a seat open for our man here." Clapper looked over at Jordan Spear and smiled.

Chapter 26 – The Long Shadow

Location: Beijing China, Macikou Area Residential District, twenty-five miles northwest of city center, Vadik Lei's Flat – May 8, 2027 – Saturday night – 11:07 pm GMT +8.

Vadik Lei organized his three-room flat, sweeping the floor and tidying his bathroom as if he were expecting company. His cat was at his feet, meowing as if wanting to be picked up. The Spider bent over and lifted the cat to his chest, giving the cat what it wanted, affection from its owner. Lei placed the cat back down and continued cleaning.

Later, after a shower, Lei looked at himself in the mirror; no emotion was displayed. He inhaled deeply, then exhaled fully, and bowed his head to himself. Next, he took the few steps to the tiny kitchen, just off of the living room, and removed a bowl from the cupboard. A curtain on a rope served as a divider between the room and the contents beneath the kitchen sink. Without looking, his right hand found what it was reaching for, a bag of cat food. Lei filled the bowl on the counter and then placed it down onto the floor next to another bowl that was already overflowing with cat food.

Two bowls of food sat next to two, filled with water. Lei even took extra care to ensure the four were perfectly aligned with each other. Lei then removed from the floor; a few scattered pieces of cat food that had been knocked from the bowl while the cat buried its snout in the food. The black cat rubbed against his leg, purring heavily. Lei pet the cat for a moment before standing.

Turning toward his shanty abode, he took a long look around the room as if to take it all in, all of the memories that lived there and all of the ones that never would. His glance then went to the door and the small bag that lay next to it. Making his way, he was careful not to step on the cat's tail with his first step. He passed a chessboard that was always in a constant state of play. Lei looked over the board one final time. Pondering his next move, he pursed his lips. His final move was the black knight to F4. After completing the move, he smiled and nodded his head. Slowly, he reached for the white king, laying it on its side in a position of surrender, or defeat.

Now, at the front door, he turned to take-in one last look of the dark, musty apartment that he'd called home for the last five years. Picking up his bag, he stepped through the door and turned to close it. After doing so, he turned to leave, stopped halfway, and reached for the door handle. He opened the door to precisely four inches, nodded his head in affirmation, and then walked away.

Location: Wenchang, Hainan, China. Wenchang Spacecraft Launch Site – Seven Hours Later.

After a four-hour flight from Beijing to Wenchang, located in the Hainan province, Vadik Lei arrived at the Astronaut launch preparation compound. As he walked through the door, he was met by Minister Li Kenong and the Chinese Eclipse rocket ship's crew chief.

"Ah, welcome, Vadik Lei!" The minister walked up to Lei, squared himself, grasped both of Lei's shoulders, and kissed each of his cheeks in a ceremonious gesture. The Spider fought hard not to recoil in disgust. His hatred for his boss could not be disguised. Lei hated Kenong, and Kenong hated him.

"I see that you have not changed your mind or defected to the United States, as did your cowardly associate, Kai Chang," Kenong's rancor was thick.

"From what I saw on the news, it would appear my accomplice in your industrious affair did his job quite successfully," snickered Lei.

"Yes, and then he fled," Kenong rubbed it in. "But you, Spider-Boy, will have nowhere to flee to, will you?" the minister laughed out loud, looking to the crew chief, expecting that he would be laughing, too.

"I am here to serve my country, not you, Honorable Leader Kenong," Lei's words dripped with disdain.

"Yes, well then, Crew Chief Máo, please show Mr. Lei to his quarters."

Michael Cook

In less than 24 hours, Vadik Lei, explosives engineers, computer science experts, a medical doctor, and space aviators would embark on a journey that would take them to the strange and wonderous, once earthlike planet. Once there, they will endeavor to ravage its central nervous system and steal its wealth of medical science and space travel technology and then destroy it, preventing other countries on Earth from reaping its benefits.

Location: Wenchang Spacecraft Launch Tower.

T-minus three hours before launch, Vadik Lei and the other eight crew members boarded a shuttle bus, took the short ride to the massive launch tower and the CZ-2Z Class Chinese Eclipse rocket ship.

The sun came across the horizon, hitting the top of the rocket before anything else, resulting in a long shadow on the ground that pointed west. The shadow served as a symbol. It was an arrow pointing to everything the eastern cultures hated about the west. A giant middle-finger to the pompous western culture, and its people.

The Chinese people were proud, proud of their culture, proud of their nationalism, and proud of their manufacturing might. This was East versus West, again. But this time, the East would rule the world, and the gluttonous Americans would choke on their lack of discipline and anti-Chinese rhetoric. Anti-Americanism began in China in the early 19th century with the Boxer Rebellion and the 1905 Chinese boycott of American goods. After the Chinese Revolution, there would be an undeclared war between the two countries during the Korean War, beginning in June of 1950 and ending in July of 1953. The war resulted in 33,686 American deaths, while more than 180,000 Chinese soldiers died in the conflict. North and South Korea would lose an estimated 600,000 soldiers and civilians combined.

In more modern times, the trade wars between the U.S. and China had gone on for the better part of ten years. The 'Us' versus 'Them,' however, would finally be over. World War III would begin with the simple blast of a Chinese rocket and end when the mighty Chinese Eclipse returned with answers to questions the once-great Americans would never be able to answer.

"We have ignition," was heard in the comms of all onboard the Chinese Eclipse. Vadik Lei, for the first time in his life, felt like his destiny was not in his hands. As the rocket rumbled and shook violently, The Spider knew that he would never see Earth again. His destiny awaited him on a distant planet; his only wish would be to die an honorable death, one befitting an ancient Chinese warrior. He hoped for the opportunity to defend himself against a worthy adversary. He wished for a glorious death. And finally, Vadik 'The Spider' Lei wished he could be there when the man he hated with every fiber of his being, Minister Li Kenong, died a very unceremonious death.

Location: McClean, Virginia. Home of James Clapper – Sunday Evening – May 9, 2027 – 7:17 pm EST.

"Honey, the phone's for you," said Angie Clapper, the CIA director's wife.

"Take a message, Ang. I'm heading out for a walk with Rushton." Rushton was a Golden Retriever that the Clappers had had for ten years. Walks with his beloved dog seemed to be the only time the busy CIA Director could relax his mind and let the world somehow function without him.

"It's Matt Solstice. He says it's important," Angie yelled from the kitchen.

Clapper walked into the kitchen and shook his head at his wife. "You should've just told him I was already out the door."

"He can hear ya, you know?" she warned.

Clapper picked up the outdated landline phone and said, "What is it, Matt? You do know that it's Sunday night? Right?"

"Sir, rocket launch detected in the Hainan Province of China, this is it, sir!"

Angie Clapper saw her husband raise his chin. She only saw him do that when he was faced with a national security emergency.

"When?" asked Clapper.

"About twelve hours ago."

"What?!" Clapper's face went red. Angie hightailed it out of the kitchen. "How in the hell did that happen?" he was furious.

"Our satellites didn't catch it, sir. It was the Brits who informed us."

"But we've been watching that region for months!" said Clapper.

US intelligence had been monitoring the Chinese space program and its activities in the Hainan province since their rebuke of U.N. Resolution 2978.

"Our satellites were offline for several hours, so the Brits picked it up," Solstice tried to explain.

"Matt, get everybody to HQ now!" instructed Clapper. "I'll meet you there in an hour."

"Yes, sir!" Angie, now back in the kitchen, heard Matt's words through the phone.

"Oh, and Matt, see if Mars Johnston is still in town. We'll need him there, too."

Location: Home of Jordan Spear – Five minutes later.

Jordan's cell phone rang; he got up from the dining room table to take the call. Kinzi, and Jordan's parents, were not alarmed even though it was a Sunday and work was calling. Jordan always seemed to be on duty since rejoining the CIA early the previous year.

Jordan said, "It's Matt. I'll be right back. Go ahead and start without me."

Kinzi asked Jordan's mom to pass the bread.

"Hey Matt, what's up?" Jordan said as he walked out of the room.

"Jordan, they launched!"

"My God!" Jordan had a moment of panic as he had never told Kinzi that he'd officially committed to Clapper that he'd be on the Neptune One to Black Earth should the Chinese launch their Saturn Eclipse rocket. He secretly wished they never would.

"Matt, are you sure?"

"Jordan, it was a CZ-2Z. It launched from Hainan."

"Fuck!" Jordan said under his breath, but his parents and Kinzi heard him. "Okay, this is it then! I'll be there in an hour."

"I called Mars," said Solstice, "he'll be there, too!"

"Alright, buddy! I'll see you there." Jordan hung up and turned toward the dining room. When he did, he ran into Kinzi, who had gotten up to investigate what Jordan was doing.

"I'm not waiting to find out what that was all about." Kinzi was steadfast. "Before you walk out that door, you tell me what Matt said!" she demanded.

"Walk with me!" Jordan said as he grabbed his jacket and keys and headed for the door.

"It's the Chinese, isn't it?"

"Kinzi, they launched their CZ-2Z; they're going to Black Earth!"

Now standing in the driveway, Kinzi said, "My God! It's happening, isn't it?"

"Kinzi, listen..." said Jordan, before being sharply cut off by Kinzi.

She looked into his eyes and said, "I'm going, too. Call me later when you know more!" Kinzi knew what was happening; she'd overheard many conversations between Jordan and his father and had decided long ago that if Jordan was called to return to Black Earth, she wanted to go with him. She knew the Chinese were up to no good and that only the U.S. could stop them. This gave her renewed purpose in her life because Black Earth was no longer only in her past. Now, it was in her present and her future. She had a reason to go there again because she knew she could contribute to the cause of stopping the Chinese.

Jordan didn't know how to respond. He kissed her goodbye without another word and wasn't sure if she'd realized what she was agreeing to.

Location: Artesia, New Mexico. The Michaels Home – Sunday, Late afternoon.

"Lola!" Carrick yelled up the stairs. "I'm going for a run!"

Lola could barely hear Carrick over the sound of crying babies. "What?" she yelled down the stairs, now standing at the top of them with a crying baby Lilly in her arms. All she heard back was the sound of the front door closing.

Lola cried. Carrick was gone again, his heart, his mind, his soul: *he just wasn't there*, she thought. Not for her, and not for the twins. She stood there and wept, not because she needed his help with the babies, because she did, but rather because she needed love from the only man she'd ever loved. Lola wondered what he was running from.

Outside, Carrick was running, not just down the street, but toward something; he still didn't know what. Like his life before finding Zenith, he was searching for the unknown, but what was it? Black Earth cast a long shadow, and Carrick was still in it.

Chapter 27 – The Neptune One

Location: Langley, Virginia. George Bush Center for Intelligence, CIA Headquarters. First-floor conference room – May 9, 2027 – Sunday night, 11:00 pm EST.

More than an hour after the contentious meeting began, Clapper slammed his hand down on the table; those in attendance were taken aback by the CIA Director's rare show of emotion.

Mars, Jordan, and Matt Solstice immediately stopped arguing and sat at attention, hanging on Clapper's next words.

"As we sit here and argue the where's and the when's, the how's and the why's, the haves and the have nots," said Clapper, "the Chinese are now more than sixteen hours into their journey to Black Earth. We are not leaving this room until we have put together a plan that has us on the move to that black menace in less than sixteen days. Now, who wants to argue that?" Clapper challenged.

"Director Clapper, sir," Mars was respectful, "we don't even have a crew named yet."

"Mars, I told you on April 27 to have that ship ready to go! I told you that the minute the Chinese launched that we'd only have days before we would have to lift-off!" Clapper was un-nerved.

"Director Clapper," Mars was pragmatic. "Do you have any idea what it's like to recruit someone in your program to get onto a rocket, just days after they witnessed their friends get blown out of the sky? They're not lining up to get into the Neptune One!" Mars stood up for himself. "The ship is ready, and on the pad, it's the crew that I'm having trouble with."

"How about you tell me what we do have instead of what we do not?" Clapper tried to steer Mars in the right direction. "How about starting with that?"

"Okay," Mars shook off the stress of the moment and said, "Jack White is in for sure to navigate Neptune One. Sebastian Colt is also committed. From there, it gets dicey."

"I'm in!" said Jordan Spear. He then hesitated for a moment and said, "Kinzi's in too." He exhaled with the words, not sure what he was signing Kinzi up for.

Mars looked relieved with Jordan's words. "Okay, that's a pilot, a crew doctor, a biologist, and a trained killer." Mars immediately regretted his characterization of Jordan. He barely managed to look in Jordan's direction before Spear responded.

"Nice, Mars, not sure I've been called that by someone who actually knows me." Jordan was only mildly offended. "To be clear, I've only killed three people in my life and hope not to kill another."

"Sorry, Jordan," Mars looked extremely uncomfortable.

Clapper broke in, "So, who else do we need onboard the Neptune One?" asked Clapper.

"We still need a co-pilot, a cyber engineer, a chemist, a meteorologist, and an astrophysicist," said Mars, thinking out loud. He wondered which of the understudies from the original crew might consider it.

"How about Mike Swimmer, or Ollie Taylor?" Jordan was spit-balling.

"Mike's out. He was diagnosed with prostate cancer last year."

Jordan grimaced.

"Ollie might consider it, though. He's been working with the ESA for the last two years." Mars raised an optimistic brow.

Clapper said, "Now we're getting somewhere!"

"I think I might have a chemist in mind," said Jordan.

Mars and Clapper immediately chimed in with an emphatic "No!"

"Jordan, you forget you ever had that thought, son," Clapper spoke with clarity. "That boy is an international hero and likely the only living bloodline relative to Erik Erickson. Additionally, he and Lola just had twins. He will not be on that rocket!" Clapper was adamant.

"Jordan, if something were to happen up there, and he didn't return...," Mars pondered, "well, there'd be no coming back from that."

"He'll want to go. He knows The Triad better than anyone." Jordan was confident. "With what's at stake, he'll demand it."

Mars and Clapper didn't see it that way.

Location: Artesia, New Mexico. The Michaels Home – Later that night.

With the kids down for the night and dinner out of the way, Carrick and Lola finally settled down. Lola was finding it hard to approach Carrick regarding where his head was these days, so she opted to internalize it and wait for him to open up about his feelings.

Carrick grabbed the remote and turned on the television. When clicking through the channels, he spotted the red NCN Breaking News banner at the bottom of the screen. 'Chinese Launch Rocket,' the banner read. Carrick pulled himself to the edge of the couch while Lola focused more on her husband's body language than what was on T.V.

The NCN anchor reported that roughly eighteen hours earlier, the British detected a launch from China's Hainan province. Carrick, having once been there, knew it was the CZ-2Z rocket. He knew the Chinese were headed to Black Earth. Without words, he ran upstairs, grabbed Erik's journal, and returned to the living room.

Lola looked at him with some confusion and said, "Babe, what's going on?"

"I'm sleeping at Erik's house tonight. I'll see you in the morning." Carrick avoided making eye contact with Lola. He then slipped his shoes on and walked out the front door. Lola sat and wept.

Moments later, Lola picked up her phone and called Kinzi. Worried she might wake her because of the time change, she was relieved when Kinzi answered on the first ring.

"Hello," answered Kinzi.

"Kinzi, it's Lola."

"Hey Lola, it's late. Is everything okay?" Kinzi knew it wasn't but had no idea what, if anything, Lola already knew.

"Kinzi, what's going on? We just saw the news about China, and Carrick ran out of here to sleep at Erik's. He's never done that before. Something's wrong. I'm worried."

"Hmm," Kinzi paused. "Lola, I don't know exactly what's happening, but since the Saturn Six exploded, the government's been on high alert. Jordan's rarely ever home."

"Kinzi, I'm scared." Lola started to cry again. "I can't seem to reach Carrick. He seems lost. I'm terrified!"

"Hang in there, Lola! Things will work themselves out." Kinzi knew she wasn't being truthful.

"It's just..." Lola cried, "the babies, the Saturn Six, Erik's death. Everything is going to hell, and I don't know what to do. Can you please come out here to visit me? I need someone that I can lean on."

Kinzi bit her tongue, trying to avoid answering Lola.

"Carrick would love to see you, and I need a shoulder to cry on." Lola sniffled.

"I'm not sure. Let me get with Jordan, and I'll get back to you in a couple of days."

"Okay, I understand. I'll talk to you soon." Lola suspected that Kinzi was being insincere.

"Hold on to those babies, Lola."

The call disconnected abruptly, and Kinzi wondered if it was a dropped call or that perhaps Lola hung up on her.

Location: Outer Space. A half a million miles from Earth – May 10, 2027

While scientists aboard the Chinese Eclipse studied their dossiers, and the pilots monitored the crafts vitals, Vadik Lei was trying to acclimate to the weightlessness of outer space. After not eating for twelve hours, he knew that he would have to try. He knew he needed to be in peak condition once they landed on Black Earth.

Over the next two hours, The Spider would consume as much protein as possible and begin his scheduled exercise routine. He would do resistance training that would work his back, shoulders, arms, and legs. Lei was trained that after four months in zero gravity, the gravity on Black Earth would drain his energy within minutes of landing. He hoped that if the Americans pursued him and his countrymen to Black Earth, he would have a several day head start to adjust to the near-Earth gravity and the planet's hostile surroundings. He would look for any advantage he could get over whoever would try to stop him.

He knew that he would likely die on Black Earth, and if he did, the man who lived his entire life without honor would choose to die with it.

Location: Office of James Clapper – Tuesday, May 11, 2027 – 10:14 am.

"Director Clapper." Colleen's voice came over his desk phone.

Clapper turned toward his desk after staring out the window. "What is it, Colleen?"

"Mars Johnston on hold for you, sir. Line 3."

Mars was back in Florida now and had been working on the crew options.

"Thank you, Colleen. I'll take the call." Clapper sat back down at his desk, straightened a few items, then took a deep breath. "Mars, give me some good news."

"Jim, it's good news," Mars sounded elated. "Ollie Taylor is on a plane to Florida now, so we have our pilots. The ship can't fly without them." Clapper couldn't see the grin on Mars' face but detected that he was smiling.

"Who else is on board?" asked Clapper.

"You're gonna be happy," said Mars. "We now have Kinzi London, Jordan Spear, and Jin Ho Mae from Japan is back in, he was on the

Silver Comet. He originally backed out but reconsidered. I pulled a rabbit out of my hat for our meteorologist. Satoshi 'Sun' Kanai has also agreed to join the crew. He was on the New Horizon, our first mission to Black Earth."

"Well done, Mars!" Clapper was pleased. "Where does that leave us?"

"We still need a cyber engineer and a chemist."

"Isn't Carrick a Chemist?" asked Clapper.

"Now wait a second, Jim! We talked about this. It just can't happen." Mars again conveyed his disapproval. "It shouldn't happen."

"Mars, I need to inform you that as we speak, Jordan Spear is on a plane to New Mexico."

"Holy hell!" Mars' feelings were mixed. While he thought Carrick shouldn't go, he would selfishly love to have him on the crew.

"Jim, you made it clear, though. You told Jordan the answer was no. You were adamant."

"Listen, he'll likely say no. I mean, no way he would leave his wife and newborns," Clapper reasoned.

"Yeah, and what if he says yes? Then what?" challenged Mars.

"He'd have to make a compelling case for both of us to sign off on it. That's what!" countered Clapper.

Location: Artesia, New Mexico. Hilton Garden Inn, Downtown Artesia – The next morning – May 12, 2027.

Jordan prepared to leave for Carrick's house; he planned to show up completely unannounced. He'd figured that if Carrick had time to think about his visit, then it might complicate things. Jordan preferred to read people as they experienced the highest of highs or the lowest of lows. He knew that the truth revealed itself during the release of raw human emotion. First, he had to check in with James Clapper.

"No, he doesn't know I'm coming, sir," Jordan told his boss.

"You think that's the best way to approach him?" Clapper wasn't a fan of Jordan's tactics but knew that he got results.

"It'll be fine. Either he's in, or he's not. I don't plan on pressuring him." Jordan wasn't planning on interrogating his friend; he just wanted to talk. He'd figured that it was a long shot. Even if Carrick wanted to go, it would be his job, as a friend, to try to talk him out of it. If he couldn't do that, that would mean that Carrick truly wanted to make the journey.

"Okay, you call me the instant you leave his place. Got it?"

"Yes, sir, Director Clapper."

Thirty minutes later, Carrick was feeding the babies in the kitchen while Lola was straightening up the living room. The two were oblivious to the parked Uber out in front of their house.

Jordan, sitting in the back of the Uber, was on the phone with Kinzi, confirming the address. "You sure this is the right address?"

"Yes. 143 Lewis Road. That's the right place." Kinzi read back the address that she'd scribbled on a post-it note for him before his departure.

"Jesus! The place is huge! We need to bring back one of those diamonds from Black Earth," Jordan joked while in awe.

"Don't be silly, just get in there. Oh, and remember, Lola's in bad shape. Be sweet to her," Kinzi cautioned Jordan. She knew that Lola would be shocked to see him unannounced at her front door. She knew Lola would've expected to see her long before Jordan.

Jordan exited the Uber and took a deep breath. He wasn't sure how things were going to go. He was beginning to re-think his decision to show up unannounced.

Standing on the sidewalk in front of Carrick's massive house, he looked to his right and said to himself, "That must be Erik's old house." He took a moment to remember the old man fondly. He remembered the confession when Erik won him over. He missed him and missed the way things used to be.

Suddenly, a car honked its horn just down the street, snapping Jordan from his thoughts. He turned to see the Uber disappear around the corner. "Guess I have to go in now," he reasoned.

After making his way to the front porch, he hesitantly reached for the doorbell and then recoiled his hand. He was uncharacteristically nervous and stood there for another few seconds before pushing the button.

Inside, the doorbell rang. Carrick yelled from the kitchen, over the noise of the vacuum in the Living Room. "Babe, you got that?"

"Got it!" she yelled back.

Lola briskly walked to the door, wondering who it might be. She opened the door slightly, peeked out, and then threw the door open wide and jumped into Jordan's arms.

"Oh, my God! You guys came! I'm so happy!" Lola couldn't contain her excitement.

Jordan was delighted that his visit was so well received until he was again stricken with fear. He played back Lola's words in his head. She said, 'You guys.' Jordan thought that Lola was expecting to see Kinzi as well. "Oh-oh!" he thought aloud.

After Lola released Jordan, he gave her a nervous smile and said, "Lola, it's just me."

Looking around Jordan's left, then to his right, Lola said, "What do you mean? Where's Kinzi?" She was puzzled for a moment, and then a look of dread drenched her face.

"I'm here to see Carrick," again, Jordan smiled nervously.

Instantly, it dawned on Lola. The Chinese launch; their rebuke of the UN Resolution; the Saturn Six disaster. She knew that Jordan was there to recruit Carrick to go back to Black Earth. Without a word, her eyes welled up, and she began to cry. Resentment quickly overcame her, and she impulsively slapped Jordan across the face. Jordan stood frozen in shock.

In her moment of frustration, Lola believed Carrick had invited Jordan to New Mexico. She slammed the door, leaving Jordan standing on the front porch, then ran into the kitchen, snatched little Erik from Carrick's lap, picked up Lilly and went upstairs.

Carrick, confused as to what was happening, could only reason it was one of the Spencers at the door with bad news about Lilly. He got up and walked to the closed door. Opening it tentatively, as Lola did, he saw his friend rubbing a red handprint on his left cheek.

Carrick took a deep breath, knowing exactly why Jordan was there. Then, in the words of the immortal Erik Erickson, said to Jordan, "What took you so long?" Those words sprung from Erik's lips every time someone showed up at The Triad unannounced. His words were a welcome sign to Jordan.

He immediately interpreted Carrick's words as a resounding 'YES.' The two would be going back to Black Earth...together.

Later that evening, Carrick and Jordan sat in Erik's house, discussing the details of their journey.

"Are you sure you want to do this?" Jordan was pragmatic. Again, his job as a friend was to talk Carrick out of it.

"Jordan, listen..." Carrick was ready to be honest with someone and hadn't been able to approach Lola about his feelings, knowing that it would break her heart.

Jordan could tell that Carrick had bottled up whatever feelings he was about to share for a long time. Carrick looked like a man bursting at the seams to clear his mind. He was more than happy to listen.

"...long before Zenith, long before Black Earth was discovered, I was always looking for something. I never had a father figure in my life, so when I met Erik, we bonded instantly, long before I ever knew we were related. He helped to fill the black hole inside of me. After we returned to Earth, he was there, everywhere. I spent far more time with him than I did with Lola."

"Right around the time we stopped traveling the world, and we settled back here, I began to get restless, needing an outlet."

Jordan nodded. "I had such a great time traveling on a few of your stops around the world with you and Erik. It was awe-inspiring to tell the world the story of Zenith. It was amazing to hear Erik speak." Jordan understood completely and could empathize with his friend.

"Since he died, the hole inside of me has grown bigger, wider, deeper. It needs to be filled." Carrick looked defeated and incomplete.

"Carrick, is this about Lola?" Jordan thought that perhaps Lola wasn't the one for Carrick.

Carrick shook his head in frustration. "No! No! That's just it, Jordan, it's never been about Lola. I love her with everything I've got! She's the only woman I have ever loved and the only woman I WILL ever love. It's not her, though. It's about me."

For a moment, Jordan thought that Carrick's words were a sign of depression. When someone is unable to find happiness, no matter where they look or how hard they try, perhaps they need to talk to someone.

"Carrick, listen, I'm going to share something with you that you can't tell either Lola or Kinzi. Okay?" Jordan wasn't sure he should break someone's trust by sharing their story of pain and suffering. In this case, though, he thought it might help his friend.

"Kinzi sees a therapist because of her childhood and her relationship with her parents. She was never good enough in their eyes, and to this day, she still feels inadequate."

Carrick interrupted, "Jordan, let me stop you right there." He put up his hand in a 'stop' motion, as he wanted to make sure Jordan understood what his feelings were really all about.

"Jordan, I've seen therapists over the years, and that's not what this is about. I've been looking for space...and to find out who I am."

"You mean away from Lola?" Jordan wore a look that would suggest that he didn't understand his friend.

"You're not getting it, man!" Carrick raised his arms and shook his head in frustration. "No! I told you, this isn't about Lola. It's about me," repeating his earlier sentiment.

"I need to be up there." Carrick pointed skyward. "There is nothing I need more right now."

"Jordan, I don't just want to be on that ship to Zenith. I HAVE to be!" Carrick was passionate. "The Neptune One will not fly without me on it."

Jordan now realized that what Carrick needed was to fly, fly Into space, to get back to Zenith. Like an aging football player who can't bring himself to retire. Or, like a fighter pilot that flies into near-certain death, or a boxer that wants one more fight. Carrick needed this; he needed to get back to Black Earth.

"But...," Jordan paused, "the babies? Lola? Carrick, it's dangerous! My God, the Saturn Six was blown out of the sky. Hell, I'm scared, for Christ's sake!"

Jordan said what he had to say, as a friend, as a person, and as a human being, but his words were only half sincere. He was just checking the boxes that Kinzi, Lola, and Clapper would expect him to. Carrick was going to Black Earth, and selfishly, that brought Jordan a great deal of comfort.

"Jordan, I have to be on that ship! No matter the risk."

"Why do you 'have' to be on that ship?" Jordan detected that there was something else that Carrick wasn't telling him.

"Wait here for a moment." Carrick stood, held his index finger in the air, and said, "I have something I need to show you."

Carrick disappeared down the hall into Erik's old bedroom. He lifted the pillow on his old bed, adjacent to Erik's, and found the journal that Erik had left for him. Moments later, he returned to the Living Room, where the two had been talking, and tossed the journal onto the coffee table.

Jordan looked down to where the journal had landed, then back up at Carrick and said, "What's this?" He then reached for it.

"Open it," Carrick encouraged his friend.

Jordan flipped through the pages, not sure of what exactly Erik's words meant.

"What is this? Some sort of diary?" he asked Carrick.

Now seated across the table from Jordan, Carrick revealed, "It's a roadmap." His facial expression was meant to affirm why he 'had' to be on the Neptune One, which would fly in just a matter of days.

"A what?" Jordan was even more confused.

"Jordan, Erik wants me to go back to Zenith. He knows countries will go to war for its riches, its cures, its technologies. Lilly Spencer has cancer, Erik wants her, and every other little girl, boy, man, and woman, to be cured of it."

Jordan didn't completely understand. "What exactly are you saying?"

"Jordan, that journal explains everything I need to know to divert electricity and oxygen to any of the three sectors of The Triad. Just in case The Northwest Sector has gone dark, in the nearly three years since we left," he explained.

"There's still hope we could get there before it's too late," Carrick sounded optimistic.

"Carrick, there's something you don't know...," Jordan hesitated before sharing classified information.

"What is it?"

"Carrick, not only are the Chinese going to steal every secret The History Library holds..." he paused, "but then they're going to nuke it!"

Carrick's eyes went wide.

"They want it all and will ensure that when another country arrives there, The Triad will be in ruins."

"When do we launch?" Carrick was even more determined to get there.

"The ship's nearly ready," said Jordan. "Mars is finalizing the crew lineup, but he's having an issue finding a Cyber Security Engineer who is also an astronaut. Either way, we have to launch no later than the 26th." Jordan was nervous that that would be too soon for Carrick considering Lola and the twins.

"Okay, I'm in."

"Looks like we can check Chemist off of Mars' list." Jordan wore an expression of relief.

"Cyber Engineer, too!" Carrick shot Jordan a smile.

"How so?" he was perplexed.

Carrick grabbed the journal and stood up. "It's all in here! I know exactly how to extract and save information from The History Library's mainframe."

Jordan just stood there in amazement at Carrick's revelation. "Erik Erickson will never cease to be a hero! Living or dead."

Jordan then caught himself, "Wait, what's Lola going to say?" his expression turned to fear.

"Lola is the strongest woman that I've ever known. She'll understand," Carrick hoped. "Let's go talk to her."

"Whoa, I am not going back into that house!" Jordan shook his head from side to side. "It wouldn't be right that I'm there for that conversation. She'll feel outnumbered, and I don't want to get hit again."

"What's the plan then?" asked Carrick.

"I'll head back to Virginia, and you get ready. American Airlines, they'll be a one-way ticket to Houston waiting for you at the airport." Jordan added, "You need to leave in two days. Friday at 9:00 am, be on that plane, Carrick."

"I'll see you in Houston!"

"Kinzi too!" Jordan surprised Carrick.

Carrick's eyes flew open wide, and he said, "Oh my God! That's amazing!"

The two embraced, and Carrick left Jordan behind as he made his way back home. His heart was beating out of his chest. He knew the conversation that he was about to have with Lola would change both of their lives forever.

Jordan grabbed his phone to call James Clapper immediately.

"Talk to me, Jordan!" Clapper was curious to know how it went with Carrick. He, too, selfishly wanted Carrick on the rocket to Black Earth.

"Sir, he's in! Carrick's in!" Jordan was elated.

"Okay, so now we have our Chemist and local Black Earth resident, but we're still missing a cyber engineer who's also astronaut trained." Clapper was pragmatic.

"Sir, I found us a cyber engineer! It's Carrick." Jordan was stoked.

"Carrick?! What in the hell are you talking about, son?" Clapper had no idea what Jordan meant.

"Erik left us a roadmap, sir! He left Carrick a journal telling us how to extract the information from The History Library."

"Well, I'll be damned!" Clapper was amazed. "I need to call Mars immediately. Get back here to Virginia. Oh, and Jordan...," Clapper paused.

"Yes, sir?"

"Good job, son."

"I'll see you in Langley later today!"

Minutes later, Carrick found Lola in the nursery. From the doorway, he could see that her face was chaffed from her tears. He stood there thinking that he'd have to break her heart one last time. He loved her and those children, but Zenith was calling, and he needed to answer that call.

"Babe, how're the babies?"

"Sleeping." Lola's face was ravaged by heartache.

Lola knew Carrick would leave. She knew there'd be no discussion. Though she knew that he loved her and the children, Carrick was always searching for something else. Not love from another, but rather purpose. She was certain that he'd never find it and that he'd never stop searching for it.

"When do you leave?

"Friday morning," he was ridden with guilt.

"So, I have tonight and tomorrow with you," she paused, "then I'm alone again! Just me and the kids!"

Carrick began to cry, dropped to his knees, and put his face in Lola's lap.

"I'm so sorry! I'm so sorry, Lola!" he sobbed.

She combed the back of his head with her fingers. "We were meant to be this way, weren't we? It's the way that it's always been and always will be. You out there somewhere, and me here...," she sighed, "wondering if you're ever going to come home to me."

She lifted his head and cradled his face in her hands, and said, "You better come back to me!" now letting her tears flow.

The two cried for several minutes, and like clockwork, the twins woke up and joined them in their tears. Lola and Carrick laughed as they wiped their faces.

Carrick grabbed little Erik and said, "I'm always gonna be here for you, son." Kissing the little man on his forehead.

Lola grabbed little Lilly and whispered to herself, "You better be."

Chapter 28 – The Realm of Heaven

Location: Houston, Texas. Christopher C. Kraft Jr. Mission Control Center, Building 30 – May 14, 2027 – 6:00 pm CST.

In Conference Room B, on the third floor of the Kraft Building, sat NASA's Chief Administrator and the Neptune One crew. The team was working around the clock to ensure that everyone was prepared for the nearly four-month journey that would wreak havoc on both the body and the mind. While three crew members were on the Silver Comet: Navigator Jack White, Japanese Meteorologist Jin Ho Mae, and British Biologist Sebastian Colt, none of the remaining crew members had trained for the dangerous mission. However, Carrick, Kinzi, Jordan, and Ollie Taylor, had all made multiple journeys to Black Earth, with Satoshi Kanai making the inaugural trip to Black Earth. This meant that if they passed their physicals, they would be mentally prepared for the seven-and-a-half-month trip, there and back.

"Okay, folks, let's all have a seat." Mars gathered the group, who were all making each other's acquaintance.

"While we're still awaiting the results of everyone's physical exams, we have to move forward with our preparations as if all of you are going to pass," said Mars.

"I see that you've all met one another and had a chance to talk for a little while, but I'd like to make some formal announcements regarding this very experienced crew." Mars was visibly excited and speaking extremely fast. The team could feel his enthusiasm. "First, in case you've been living under a rock for the last ten years, I'd like to introduce you to Kinzi London. Kinzi is NASA royalty, as her mother traveled to space twice back in the 1980s, on the Space Shuttle. Kinzi, along with Ollie Taylor, made all three of the previous journeys to Black Earth. Kinzi will be the crew's medical doctor. Listen to what she has to say as she'll make sure your bodies can handle the strain of deep space."

Mars looked over his notes. "Making their third trips to Black Earth will be Carrick Michaels and Jordan Spear. Carrick will serve as our resident Chemist, but for this mission, he has a bigger part to play as well. Carrick and Jordan will be attempting to harvest the same data from The History Library that the Chinese will be attempting to steal."

"As I mentioned, Jack White is the ship's navigator, this being his first trip to Black Earth, as his first one was cut short. He'll have great support from Ollie Taylor, who as I mentioned prior, has been on all three of the previous missions," said Mars. "Ollie will guide the ship into Black Earth's orbit smoothly. Right, Ollie?" Mars smiled and winked in his direction.

Ollie Taylor modestly nodded his head and returned Mars' smile.

"Along with Jack, Jin Ho Mae and Sebastian Colt were all on the Silver Comet, and we're grateful that they've elected to get back in the saddle after their first ship was yanked away from them." Mars nodded with a heartfelt debt of gratitude for the three men.

"Oh, Carrick and Jordan, if you need a little muscle should things get sticky up there, Sebastian is a former Bellator MMA fighter and a damn good one. I followed his career before he joined the ESA."

The group all turned toward Colt and made eye contact, and nodded their heads in a show of respect.

Sebastian was slightly embarrassed, saying, "Long since retired, and a little out of shape."

Jordan looked over at Colt and studied his disfigured ears. Jordan used to tell people that, 'if you ever run into a guy with cauliflower ears, you better not cross him. Those ears are like that because that person's been in a lot of scraps.' Jordan thought it was good to have a back-up like that on Black Earth. The two made eye-contact, and Jordan nodded his approval to Colt's presence.

"The surface crew will be as follows: Carrick Michaels, Kinzi London, Jordan Spear, Sebastian Colt, and finally, Jin Ho Mae."

"Holding down the fort, at an altitude of 250 miles or so above the surface, will be our navigators: Commander Jack White; Co-Pilot Ollie Taylor; and Meteorologist Satoshi 'Sun' Kanai."

"Oh, and I almost forgot to mention, Commanding the surface team will be none other than...," Mars paused for effect. He hadn't forgotten anything. He was simply waiting to make the special announcement until the end of crew introductions.

The crew all thought that without question, it would be Carrick again.

Mars continued, "...the most decorated female astronaut of all-time, Dr. Kayley 'Kinzi' London. No one has ever made more landings on Black Earth than Kinzi." Mars was so happy to make the announcement. Kinzi London was as accomplished as any astronaut, man, or woman in human space flight history. "Congrats Kinzi! I can't think of a more qualified person than you to lead our team down onto the surface."

Everyone turned their eyes to Kinzi. Her look said it all, not quite crying, but close. The pride she felt, the pride that her family would hopefully feel, left her speechless in a moment when no words were needed. Carrick stood and began to clap for his friend. The rest of the team followed his lead.

Moments later, after everyone returned to their seats, Mars said, "Okay, so there you go, team!" Mars finished his introductions. "Now, let's talk about a few other items. One, I have personally come up with a name for the Neptune One."

The team was waiting with bated breath for what silly name Mars had come up with this time. They knew he took great pleasure in naming the rockets and the mission handles to Black Earth.

Mars paused for effect and said, "The ship's name is *The Leviathan*!" he looked immensely proud at that moment.

The team looked at each other and then back to Mars; they all wore a look of approval. "Damn Mars!" said Carrick. "That's an awesome name!"

Mars said, "Thank you, Carrick. I thought a rocket of that size, and being part of the 'Neptune Class,' deserved a name that was befitting an ocean-going vessel. Over the years, I have often referred to space as the Black Sea. Though Neptune is the Roman God of waters, he is also the brother of Jupiter and Pluto. The three brothers preside over the Realm of Heaven."

Mars struck a nerve for the group. They instantly felt more connected and part of something majestic, powerful, and significant. The name was perfect; everyone on the crew thought so.

"I also have another important announcement to make." Mars was both nervous and excited about his next disclosure. "For this particular mission only, Vance McDonald will not be serving as your Flight Director..."

There were several gasps from Jack White, Jin Ho Mae, and Sebastian Colt, while everyone else in the room looked at each other without words. The three men had all developed a great working relationship with McDonald. They suddenly became worried about whom Mars brought in for the job and how that might affect the crew's chemistry on the ship, as well as Mission Control back in Houston.

"I will be your Flight Director!" Mars pronounced with great joy. "I will be in Mission Control for your mission, and frankly, I can't think of a better person for the job," he smiled humbly.

Those who had traveled to space with Mars as their Flight Director could count on an empathetic, calming voice in their headset. Everyone on the team was especially happy with Mars' decision.

"Don't worry, Jack, Jin, and Sebastian, Vance will be right by my side for your entire journey, and whenever I need a bathroom break, Vance will be in your ear!" Mars loved cracking his silly jokes. It was at that moment that Mars opened a plastic Walmart bag he'd been hiding under the table; in it was a gift for The Leviathan Crew.

Mars pulled out baseball-sized stress balls from the bag, which looked like mini globes of the planet Earth. He then began tossing them around the table to each member of the crew. The team looked at one another and wondered what the hell was happening. It was just Mars being Mars; their look of surprise and big smiles said it all.

"Listen, these next ten days are going to be stressful," he said. "Be sure to take your stress out on these, and not each other. You guys know that I carry one of these around Mission Control when you guys go up there. If it works for me, then it'll work for you."

"Last bit of laundry to hang out there," Mars was nearly finished with the opening of the meeting. "While all of us review the flight plan and daily schedules for roughly 104 days each way, there will also be break-out sessions with the CIA. We're not just flying to space, guys; we're trying to head off the Chinese. Things could get dicey up there. We all need to be ready for that," Mars cautioned the team.

"Jordan, you should also know that you'll all be spending some time with good old Professor Conrad Schuyler in the coming days," Mars joked with Jordan.

Jordan sarcastically said, "Whoopie!" While he did not exactly have fond memories of sitting alone in Schuyler's class, he did have great respect for the man after being his only student for weeks.

Later, after the three-hour briefing with Mars and the crew, Carrick called Lola.

"Hello," Lola answered the phone. It was just after 8:00 pm in Artesia.

"Hey, Babe? How are you and the little ones?"

"We'd be better if you were here," Lola purposely tried to make Carrick feel guilty.

"I know, I know. It's just...," he paused, trying to compose his words, "this is something that I have to do. Lola, this is bigger than the next eight months of us being apart. It's about the safety of the world." Carrick continued his attempt to make Lola understand, just as he tried to the day before.

Lola was highly agitated. "Carrick, you know what? You'll have to pardon me if I'm feeling a little selfish right now, as I have two little babies lying next to me and a husband that chose to abandon his wife and family in their time of need. I can't exactly take on the role of caregiver to the world right now."

"Well, I guess that's my job, huh?" he poked back at her.

"Yep, Carrick saves the world!" she mocked him. "Let me know when you plan on saving our marriage."

"Lola, come on!" Carrick was shocked by her words. "That's not fair!"

Carrick heard nothing but silence for a few seconds before he noticed his phone's home screen come on, indicating that Lola had hung-up on him.

"Dammit!" he said aloud. "She'll come around," he fooled himself into believing.

Location: Kraft Building, Third Floor, Conference Room C – Thursday, May 20 – T-minus five days until launch.

James Clapper and Matt Solstice were waiting in the conference room when Carrick and Jordan walked in.

"Gentlemen," said Clapper, as he and Matt stood to greet them. "It's good to see you, fellas. How's it going so far?"

"So far, so good," said Jordan. "Tomorrow, the five of us not part of the Silver Comet crew, are going to complete Centrifuge Training," Jordan looked pale.

Clapper smiled. "In just five days, you're stepping onto the biggest rocket ever made, and you're worried about that darn simulator?" Clapper shook his head in mild disbelief.

"It's the going around in circles part that I don't like." Jordan swirled his hand and index finger in a circular motion.

"You'll be okay, son." Clapper seemed fatherlike in his empathy.

The four men sat down, and Clapper said, "Matt, whatta ya got?"

"Okay, good news!" Matt perked up. "The Chinese have hacked into the Interlink Communications Corridor...," he said before being cut off by Carrick.

"How in the hell is that 'good news'?" Carrick looked miffed.

"...They don't know that we know." smiled Solstice.

"Okay...and?" Carrick wasn't quite sure where Matt was going.

Jordan jumped in, "So, we get to hear what they're saying, and they get to hear what we want them to THINK we're saying?"

"What?" Carrick shook his head, still confused.

"Carrick," said Clapper, pulling a manual out of his bag. "Matt, and the team back in Langley, have come up with a new language. He tossed the two-inch thick, five-pound manual onto the table, making a slapping sound when it landed. "When we provide mission-related information to you, it may, in fact, purposely be misinformation. This manual will help Jordan decode the information we communicate through the corridor."

"Ahh," Carrick finally got it. "So, if you say to us that we're two days away from landing on Zenith, it might actually mean that we're only one day away? Does that sound about right?" Carrick nodded his head up and down.

"Now you're getting it, son!" Clapper smiled. "For the next two hours, Matt is going to review the terminology in the book. It'll seem like a lot, but you'll have plenty of downtime up there to figure it out."

"Okay, let's move on." Solstice opened another file folder and removed its contents. "We've been able to translate the voice and data communications coming from the Chinese Eclipse back to Beijing..."

Jordan interjected, "By the way, how do we know with certainty that they don't know that we can hear them? Perhaps they too are transmitting false or misleading information to fool us."

"I was getting to that part," Solstice would address Spear's concerns, "bear with me, first things first. So, what we know about their journey thus far is that they are currently on schedule to arrive on Zenith September 5. That will give them 24 hours on the surface before we could get there. Apparently, they're making better time than we thought. We were originally expecting them to arrive on the 6th."

"So, we won't be intercepting anyone or anything, will we?" shrugged Clapper.

"I'm afraid not, sir," responded Solstice.

"Why can't we just leave a day earlier?" added Clapper.

Carrick said, "We're already rushing it. We have one shot at this because there is no back-up rocket waiting on the sidelines for us."

"In an emergency, India will be there should something bad happen on Black Earth that prevents us from lifting off. It would be four months before they could get there, though." Carrick furrowed his brow and pursed his lips. "First things first, we need to get The Leviathan safely into orbit around Earth."

"Engineers are scrubbing the ship as we speak. Kyle Bradshaw, and NASA computer engineers, are running cybersecurity diagnostics on all of the ship's computer systems as we speak," revealed Jordan.

"Listen, we probably don't want to be landing right as they do anyway. The surface is too unstable to be duking it out in 800° temperatures." Carrick understood that if a showdown were to happen, it would be better if it happened inside of The Triad. That was familiar territory to him. "We'll have the upper-hand inside. I know that place like the back of my hand."

"What do we know about the types of weapons the Chinese will have with them?"

Solstice said, "No guns if that's what you're worried about." He gave Carrick and Jordan a reassuring nod. "The Serpent said what our NASA friends have been telling us for a while now. Ammunition is just too volatile in high radiation settings. Neither country would risk the safety of their ride home."

"Back to the stone ages, huh? Sticks and stones, I guess." Jordan shrugged his shoulders.

"And fists!" Carrick's eyes flew open. "Did you see the ears on that Colt guy?"

"Yeah. He'll come in handy for sure if we run into The Spider up there," said Jordan.

Internally, Jordan was consumed with his role on the crew. As Mars innocently revealed the week before, Jordan was a hired killer. He wasn't lying to Kai Chang during his interrogation of the SHA Militant. They did have something in common. They were both hired guns and expendable to their governments. Jordan knew that the crew would count on him to save the day if things went south on Black Earth.

Matt finished up. "Jordan, regarding your earlier question concerning whether the Chinese know we can hear their chatter on the Interlink Corridor. We believe that they have sent fake messages to see if we would react to them."

"For example?" Jordan raised his brow.

"One example," offered Solstice, "24-hours after they launched, they pinged every beacon along the Interlink Communications Corridor, all 150 of them. The message they sent was supposed to look like a sophisticated self-destruction code, instructing each beacon to shut down," Matt explained. "It was a bogus code, but they wanted to see if we would react by sending an over-write code that would counter the code they sent."

"How do you know it was a bogus transmission," asked Carrick.

"Two reasons," Clapper jumped in. "The Serpent let us know to expect such bogus transmission feeds. And the code could have been written by a grade school kid. Our cyber-security experts deemed it not credible within about five minutes."

"That's great!" said Jordan. "But why in the hell are we trusting The Serpent? That son of a bitch lied to us about the computer planted on the Saturn Six, saying it was a bomb."

"Jordan," said Clapper, "The Serpent is back in play, for now."

"Why?" Jordan was about to board a rocket after one just exploded in the sky. He wanted all precautions taken by U.S. Counter-Intelligence personnel.

"The Serpent thinks his government is on to him and gave him misinformation about the Saturn Six operation," offered Solstice. "It has a ring of truth as your boy, Kai Chang, said the very same thing. Only the brass knew it was a computer."

Jordan mouthed the words, "My boy?"

"Jordan," Clapper jumped back in, "he contacted us about the phony transmissions sixty minutes before they went out to the Corridor. He then followed up by providing other information about Chinese-North Korean relations and Chinese-Russian relations. Everything he said checked out."

"Listen, I don't like the man or woman, but I'm starting to believe whoever this person really is," revealed Clapper. "The info he provided will likely save hundreds of US lives in the Middle East and within our spy network around the world. I won't go into detail now, as you have another job to do. I promise to brief you in eight months, after a successful mission to Black Earth and back.

"Your goal is to stop the Chinese from hacking The History Library and getting that information back to China. My job is to avoid World War III back here on Earth." Clapper wanted to make sure Jordan stayed focused on his task at hand on Black Earth.

Clapper looked at Jordan and Solstice before sharing something with Carrick that only Mars Johnston, POTUS, the Joint Chiefs, and high-ranking members of the CIA knew. "Carrick, if we're successful, the Chinese surface lander will not make it back to Earth. In fact, they won't make it out of Zenith's atmosphere."

"I don't understand," Carrick looked away from Clapper, now observing the facial expressions of Jordan and Matt Solstice. "Okay, clearly, I'm the last to know. What's the plan, and how dangerous is it?"

"Carrick, stowed away on The Leviathan is a package that Jordan will deliver to the Chinese landing craft," explained Clapper. "In it, is The Chameleon. We're returning it to its rightful owners." Clapper was stone-faced.

"Holy shit!" Carrick finally realized how serious things were about to get up there. "So, to be clear, we're not taking a bomb with us on The Leviathan, correct?"

"That's correct, son," Clapper reassured him. "It's just a computer."

"Okay, how's it gonna work?" asked Carrick.

"I'll fill you in once we're on the way." smiled Jordan, as he clutched Carrick's left shoulder with his right hand.

Location: Cape Canaveral, Florida. Launch Complex 41 – T-minus 48 hours until launch – Sunday, May 23, 2027 – Late Morning.

The crew was now in Florida, and the hours were passing by very quickly, as hundreds of NASA, FBI, and CIA officials were ensuring both crew and ship were ready for the Tuesday launch.

No one on the crew felt even remotely confident or ready for their journey, but they did have great confidence in the engineers, scientists, and security experts, who all had their backs. They would fly alone, but the mission took hundreds of dedicated professionals to pull off.

Today was the final walk-through; the crew would be outfitted in their launch suits and helmets and file into the crew cabin, along with the close-out team. Officials behind the scenes, technicians on-site, and those at Mission Control back in Houston, were all in place for the mock countdown.

Before entering the launch tower elevators, Jordan looked over to Carrick and Kinzi and said, "Man, that's a beast!" All three of them were looking up at the rocket. "Mars was right on when he named that thing The Leviathan."

"It's biblical!" Carrick shook his head side to side as his eyes bulged.

Kinzi laughed. "Aren't you an atheist?"

"Not at the moment," said Carrick, unable to look away from the top of the rocket. "I wasn't last night, either, when I prayed to the man upstairs." He didn't actually pray to God, but he did talk to Erik though. He was trying to make sure that Erik actually wanted him to go back to Black Earth. He wanted to make sure that Erik, wherever he was, would be proud of his grandson.

"I bet Erik's proud of you, Carrick," Jordan said quietly.

"I bet he's proud of all of us," countered Carrick. "We're going there to save the integrity of Zenith."

"And for the cure to cancer," said the only Medical Doctor of the three standing there.

"That, too!" smiled Carrick.

Minutes later, the eight crew members, Mars Johnston, and two launch tower technicians, walked under the safety netting and into the cramped elevator. After three minutes and the three-hundred-and-fifty-foot climb, the crew exited the elevator onto the platform surrounding the crew compartment.

Jordan Spear, who was afraid of heights, made sure he didn't stand on the group's outside perimeter.

"Look at that view, huh?" said Mars Johnston, taking in the view of the Atlantic Ocean.

"It's something," said Carrick, taking in a deep breath of the cool ocean breeze at that altitude.

The elevator doors closed behind the team; it would return to the ground to fetch two close-out team members.

One by one, the crew, carrying their helmets, passed through the White Room, an environmentally controlled chamber that led to the spacious crew compartment. Inside, there were three rows of couches, staggered with three on the bottom/aft row, four in the middle row, and three in the top/forward row. Though the ship was designed to carry eight scientists and two navigators, this would not be a scientific mission. This was a mission to intercept and to stop the Chinese in their efforts to steal every secret The History Library held, then ransack The Triad by blowing it up.

Seating positions would have Jack White and Ollie Taylor, the ship's navigator's, occupy two of the top/forward couches. In the middle-row would be Kinzi London, Jordan Spear, Carrick Michaels, and Sebastian Colt. Finally, the back row would seat Jin Ho Mae and Sun Kanai. Once the team was situated in their couches, the close-out team would ensure that everyone was properly strapped in. From the Canaveral complex and Mission Control back in Houston, all comms were checked over and over.

After three hours, the walk-through was complete, and every member of The Leviathan crew, ground crew, and Cape and Mission Control teams were confident and ready for launch; now only forty-five hours away.

As the astronauts exited the elevator at ground level, Carrick would be the first to slip under the netting. After emerging from behind the net, he turned his eyes toward the shuttle bus and saw something that would bring both tears and joy. Lola was standing there with a double stroller. She and the twins made the trip to see their husband and father before he disappeared into the black void between the stars.

Carrick hugged his wife as his babies looked up at their father. The display of human emotion touched the crew and they quietly passed them by, allowing them their privacy. Mars trailed the group, and before getting onto the shuttle bus to wait for Carrick, he turned and looked back. Though Carrick faced The Leviathan, with the bus at his back, Lola could see Mars over Carrick's shoulder. A smile escaped her face through the tears and conveyed to Mars a debt of gratitude, as he had arranged for Lola to be there. Mars returned her smile and then boarded the shuttle.

Mars instructed the driver to proceed without Carrick. As the bus pulled away, a black car was revealed, sitting near the launch pad. Mars had arranged a car and driver to take the couple to a nearby corporate condominium that NASA maintained for International and VIP guests. Lola and Carrick would spend the next twelve hours together before Carrick would be required to enter into the 24-hour quarantine before the lift-off.

The evening was quiet, just Carrick, Lola, and the twins. Dinner would be delivered, and they'd watch a movie and turn in early.

Location: The Leviathan – Tuesday Morning, May 25, 2027 – T-Minus four hours before launch.

The crew met in the staging area at T-Minus three hours. They would discuss final onboarding procedures before entering the

'White Room,' two astronauts at a time. There, the seven-person Close-Out team would prepare the crew's air rescue packs and make sure their comms were working properly. Then, the Closeout team attached parachutes on each of the flight crew. Kinzi even had her hair braided so that it wouldn't get stuck in the suit collar.

Once the crew was secured in their couches, the Close-out team leader ordered the hatch to be sealed. After it was sealed, the Close-out team remained on stand-by for twenty minutes while crew cabin pressure was regulated and checked for leaks. After that, the team returned to the ground as the White Room retracted back into the launch tower. Once back on the ground, they would take the shuttle bus to the fallback area some three miles away. There, they would listen to the count-down and watch the rocket take off.

Inside the ship, the crew was comfortable despite wearing roughly fifty pounds of flight gear. In each astronaut's ears, comms were continuously checked, with the sound of Mars Johnston's voice coming through loud and clear.

Mars couldn't resist a corny space joke to lighten the mood for the anxious crew.

"Hey team, why did the astronaut leave his girlfriend?" Mars asked the crew.

The crew chorused, "Why, Mars?" while rolling their eyes.

"Because he needed some space!" Mars laughed heartily at his joke while everyone else said, "Ha-Ha-Ha!"

Carrick didn't laugh, though. The joke reflected exactly what he'd been feeling for many months. He was feeling melancholy at that moment.

"Wait, I got another one for ya..."

Mars was cut off by the crew, who implored him to stop at just the one. He begrudgingly honored their request.

"You guys got your stress balls?" asked Mars.

"I got mine," said Carrick.

"Yep, me too," said Sebastian Colt.

"We all have them, Chief!" said Jack White, through his comms.

Minutes later, another voice came over the comms. "Alright, team, we're at fifty minutes until lift-off. Stand-by as we complete diagnostics checks and lift the netting," said Assistant Flight Director Vance McDonald.

"Is that you, Vance?" asked Jack White.

"Roger that, Jack. Mars stepped away for a second."

"Great to hear your voice!" said White.

"Yours too, Jack!" McDonald wore a big smile.

Down the hall from the Mission Control room, Mars was in the bathroom vomiting into the sink. His nerves were shot. Looking in the mirror, rinsing his face with cold water, he said, "This launch has to be successful."

Mars was forever connected to those astronauts on board, not just through their connection to NASA, but by the connection to Black Earth. Carrick, Kinzi, and Jordan were all like his kids. He loved them and couldn't bear the thought of anything happening to them.

Later, Mars would say the familiar line that every astronaut anxiously waits for but also somewhat dreads. "Okay, team, we're at twenty seconds to lift-off. Now at 10 – 9, we have ignition, 6 – 5 – 4 – 3 – 2 – 1, we have lift-off." Mars could barely breathe. He'd stand frozen in place, clutched the mini Earth stress ball until the third stage had separated and The Leviathan was in orbit.

Carrick, again, was in his own head. As the rocket cleared the pad, five of the eight-person crew experienced a rumbling sound and vibration that they'd never felt before. While Sebastian Colt, Navigator Jack White, and Jin Ho Mae all figuratively crossed their fingers, hoping not to experience the same fate that took their colleague and friend from the Silver Comet crew, Cindy Nakamura.

For Carrick, because he'd lifted off on five other occasions, he'd try to align every nerve in his body to the vibrations of the launch. He'd search for any sign that something might be wrong so that he could react instantaneously to an emergency. Just like past launches, though, Carrick knew that the massive thrusters were in control and that he and the others were simply along for the ride. He did take solace, however, in the safety upgrades that NASA had made with the Saturn Six and Neptune One class of rockets, both having the ability to jettison the crew compartment in the event of catastrophic engine failure.

Next to Carrick, Jordan's and Kinzi's hands found each other and held on tight as The Leviathan rumbled toward the Realm of Heaven.

Chapter 29 – Greatest American Hero

Location: Dawodang Depression, Guizhou Province, Southern China – FAST Observatory – June 6, 2027 – 11:16 am, Local time.

Sitting in the newly built secret Black Diamond communications shed, just outside of the main campus building, were SHA Agent Zhang Hui, and Dewei Wan, a communications expert from the Ministry of State Security.

Hui was on his laptop, addressing encrypted messages from the Strategic Huyou Agency and the Ministry of State Security. Wan sat nearby, wearing headphones, trying to interpret data passing through the Interlink Communications Corridor.

Only three men had access to the communications shed. In addition to Zhang Hui and Dewei Wan, another communications expert, Dong Wei, also had 24-hour access. Wan and Wei worked twelve-hour shifts, and Hui worked two eight-hour shifts daily, with only four hours between each, and was on-call twenty-four hours a day.

At 11:27 am, the door to the shed flew open wide, and in walked Minister Li Kenong. Surprised, Dewei Wan jumped to his feet and stood at attention, his headphones landing on the console in front of him. While Wan recognized the significance of the un-announced visit from Kenong, Zhang Hui took his time when standing at attention, showing little respect for his superior.

"You may continue your work Agent Wan. I am here to see your associate Zhang Hui." Kenong walked into the cramped quarters and closed the door behind him, leaving his bodyguard just outside.

"Minister Kenong, what brings you all this way, sir?" Hui inquired.

"I am here for an update of the recorded audio dialogue from the American ship," inquired Kenong.

Hui was puzzled by the request. "Forgive me, Minister. There is no dialogue to report, sir." Surely his boss didn't travel all the way from Beijing on a Sunday to ask for such information, Hui thought.

"But how can that be?" asked Kenong. "The Americans are surely talking to their astronauts by now. It's been twelve days since they launched." Kenong looked at Hui as if he were incompetent.

Hui quickly realized his Minister was as stupid as he'd always thought he was. Turning and walking back to his desk, then turning to face Kenong again, he said, "Minister Kenong, you should have called to get your questions answered. We are monitoring chatter and data sent through the Interlink Communications Corridor..."

"Do you take me for a fool, Hui? I know what your job is!" Kenong was red-faced.

"Minister, please let me continue." Hui feigned respect. "The Americans will not utilize the first beacon in the corridor until they have reached it. The first beacon is 500,000 miles away, sir."

Kenong felt like a fool but did not outwardly show it. "Of course, I know this to be true."

"Well then, you also know that we will not hear voice transmissions until they employ the Interlink beacons along the route to Black Earth. At 25,000 mph, they should reach the first beacon by day twenty, sir." Hui tapped his heels and bowed his head; again, feigning respect.

"Well, I have business with the FAST Director, Toshi Keung, in the morning. Continue your work, Soldier Hui." Kenong lied in an effort to hide his ignorance.

"Of course you do, Minister." Hui tilted his head again.

Kenong turned to go when Hui stopped him. "Ah, Minister Kenong, did you receive the classified communication that I sent to you early this morning?"

"I have not received anything from you, Agent Hui," Kenong was dismissive.

"Sir, I will have our man Dewei Wan provide you with the details," said Hui. "Wan!" Hui yelled so that the comms expert could hear him though wearing headphones.

"Yes, Agent Hui?" Wan stood from his console.

"Minister Kenong, I understand that you were traveling at the time, sir, but you will find the classified information regarding the anomaly in your secure inbox, sir." Hui referenced his laptop. "The message will be time stamped 7:15 am, Local time."

"Dewei, please share with the honorable Minister Kenong the anomaly that we found earlier today," instructed Zhang Hui.

"Fine! Fine! What is the anomaly, Agent Wan?" Kenong was impatient, acting as if he was late for something.

"Sir, I'm sure that it is just an error, but the data bouncing off of the first beacon from the American rocket indicates to us that they are closer to the beacon than they should be."

Kenong looked confused by the revelation.

Hui continued, "Sir, our data shows that the American craft is going too fast."

"What does all of this mean?" Kenong looked back and forth between the two men. "Be direct with me!" Kenong wanted the simple version of the analysis. "I have no time for your Yúchǔn de huájī dòngzuò!" he shouted in Mandarin.

Wan spoke back up, "We are not playing foolish games with you, sir. We believe that the American ship is traveling faster than it should be."

"And?" Kenong hung on Wan's hypothesis.

"Sir, if our data is correct...,"

"Yes?" Kenong was frustrated. "Just spit it out, you fool!"

"The Americans will intercept The Chinese Eclipse on or around the time we land our surface module on Black Earth, sir," explained Wan, tapping his heels, and bowing to the Minister.

When Kenong realized what Wan was saying, his face went white. He was having trouble comprehending what such a revelation meant for the potential of the mission's success. The Chinese never considered the fact that the newer class of American rockets might be faster than their predecessors.

Location: Deep Space. The Leviathan – June 10, 2027 – T-plus 16 days since launch.

At a table situated between the galley and the sleeping pods, in the back portion of the now expanded crew cabin, sat Jordan Spear and Carrick Michaels. The two were discussing the CIA manual given to them by Clapper and Solstice.

The ship was now approaching the first Interlink beacon, and the Chinese would soon be able to listen to the dialogue between The Leviathan and Houston. The crew would have to ensure they never revealed their true proximity to Black Earth. They knew that the element of surprise was on their side, as long as the Chinese believed that they were farther away from Zenith than they actually were.

"Okay, the reason we shut down our audio transmission communication to the Interlink beacon is that the Chinese have been listening," said Carrick. "However, we needed to keep data communications going so Houston could constantly monitor the health of the craft. The minute our readings didn't match theirs, it would mean a systems failure. If that happened, we would have to open up dialogue."

"I think I get it but lay it out for me anyway." Jordan wanted to make sure he and the others were all on the same page.

"The beacon that we're closest to will pick up our signal and relay it back to every beacon between Houston and us, and Mission Control will then be able to hear us in near 'real-time.' In this instance, our signal will go out into space, find the nearest beacon, and relay our chatter back to Houston. If we don't use the beacon, our voice and data feed will take longer to get back to Earth. No big deal for the first several million miles, as the data will travel back to Earth at light speed," explained Carrick.

"Apparently, the Chinese think that we need to pass the first beacon before it will relay the ship's audio," explained Carrick.

"Why do they think that?" asked Kinzi.

Carrick said, "They're still learning how it all works. By the time they figure that out, it won't matter because we'll be long past the first beacon and talking in code."

"Got it." Jordan nodded his head.

"We have to stay radio silent until Plus 20, so they don't know how fast we're traveling. If they figure that out, they'll be lying in wait for us." Carrick furrowed his brow. "So much for the element of surprise."

Location: The Chinese Eclipse - June 6, 2027 - T plus 16 days since the American launch – Minutes later.

Vadik Lei was making no friends on the Eclipse. The crew members all had human emotions and could possibly change their minds regarding completing their mission. If they did, Vadik Lei was given explicit instructions to kill anyone who found contempt with their orders. Lei chose not to become friends with anyone he might have to kill. No one on board suspected that he carried such orders, only thinking he was there in case they needed protection from an American surface crew once on Black Earth. Though the ship's navigators wondered why there were three of them, as protocol suggested, only two pilots were needed. Lei knew why, though.

He'd continue his workout regimen and continue to nod his head to his fellow shipmates as they passed him by, but he had a job to do, and there'd be plenty of time to talk when he met his foe, Captain America.

The Spider knew that the Americans would send their very best and that Jordan Spear would be part of the mission to intercept them. The greatest of all American heroes would attempt to stop Lei and his countrymen from completing their mission. He looked forward to seeing the CIA Officer again, and he looked forward to killing him, too.

Location: The Leviathan – July 5, 2027 – Aft Section of the Crew Quarters.

Carrick Michaels sat alone while the others finished lunch in the ship's galley. Carrick had no appetite on this day. The craft and crew would be at the half-way point of their journey back to Black Earth in a matter of weeks, and Carrick felt Zenith's gravity as it tugged on his soul. He was going Home, and he couldn't escape the feeling that the black, burnt, desolate menace was somehow his actual home. He stared out the portal into the blackness that was space; he stared out into his past, his present, and his future.

From the short distance from where the crew sat laughing and carrying on, Kinzi noticed Carrick in his familiar spot, just staring at nothing, at everything. Kinzi was reminded of the journey back to Earth; after Carrick refused to come with them on the initial journey to Zenith, it haunted her still. She, too, stared out that window. She knew exactly where he was, and knew he was lost, caught somewhere between here and there, near and far, somewhere between his beginning and his end. Kinzi knew that feeling herself, and she felt the need to go to him.

"Hey," Kinzi said as she floated up behind him. "Whatcha doing Rock." She started the conversation on a light note, calling him by a nickname that no one had called him in several years. To the world, he was Carrick Michaels, grandson of Erik Erickson, son of Lt. Mike Michaels. But who was he really? She knew. He was a man that echoed in her heart whenever she found herself trapped in the corner of loneliness. She loved him. Not like she loved Jordan, though. It was different with Carrick; the two were connected by Black Earth, The Triad, and Erik's meeting. She loved him as a friend and a soulmate. He shone light in the dark corner of sadness in the back of her heart. She loved him dearly, and she always would.

"Hey, Kinz," Carrick only half-smiled. "What's up?"

"Where'd you go?" she asked with a whisper.

"I wasn't very hungry."

"No, I mean, when you were looking out the window. Where'd you go?"

"Just thinking about Zenith," he turned back toward the window.

"Yeah, Jordan says it could be dangerous for all of us if we end up confronting the Chinese." Kinzi looked slightly terrified.

"It's funny. Danger is not what I feel when I think of Zenith. Such a hostile place to be, but I always felt safe there." Carrick shook his head side to side and pursed his lips. "Feels like I'm going home."

Jordan yelled from the galley, "Hey guys, let's go! Meeting time!" His words pierced through their conversation. The landing crew would walk through the details of individual responsibilities once on the surface.

Carrick and Kinzi pushed off the back wall and grabbed the ceiling straps, pulling their way back up to the galley. There, sitting, standing, and floating around the table, were the other landing crew members. Kinzi and Carrick joined Jordan, Sebastian Colt, and Jin Ho Mae. Sun Kanai excused himself.

"Okay, let's discuss how things are going to go down there once we land." Jordan reviewed some crude notes he'd taken.

"First of all, we're going to land about a mile from where the Chinese land. It'll be a little further out from our previous landing spots, we'll end up passing by the old lander bases and rovers," explained Jordan.

"Jin, you're responsible for staying with the landing module. You'll monitor the lander from outside the craft in four hour increments, returning to the lander for oxygen replenishment and to cool your suit down. Four hours outside and two hours inside. You'll repeat that cycle for as long as we're gone. Understood?" asked Jordan.

Jin nervously nodded in affirmation.

"The Chinese Taikonaut staying with their landing craft will undoubtedly see our thrusters on the way down. We're going to light up that black sky. It's a sure bet that he or she will then radio the rest of their team, who'll either be on the surface or in The Triad." Jordan started to sound like a battlefield technician, reveling in the strategy aspect behind the plan.

"We have a plan in place that will distract them and cause some confusion, though..." said Jordan as Jin Ho cut him off.

"So, what if someone approaches the lander?" tentatively asked Jin. "What then? What if they try to hurt me or the craft?"

"Jin, listen, their ship is full of scientists and computer geeks. They'll avoid us more than we hope to avoid them," Jordan spoke in a voice meant to calm and reassure Jin.

"There's one man on that ship that means to do us harm, but he'll be with the geek squad inside of The Triad." Jordan knew it would be The Spider. "Because they think we're arriving days later, they won't be able to react quickly enough." Jordan had an air of confidence. "We won't land on the surface until it's the middle of their day when nearly all of their crew will be inside The Triad working. Plus, we have a little surprise for them." Jordan smiled.

"What's that?" asked Jin Ho.

"They won't know where we landed, and it's dark! But we'll know where THEY landed."

"How's that?" asked Sebastian Colt with a look of intrigue.

Jordan smiled. "We hacked into their HACK of the Interlink Comms Corridor! We also have GPS on their craft." Jordan wore a sinister smile.

"Damn!" Colt was impressed.

Carrick finally entered the conversation. Smiling, as Jordan looked over at him, he said, "Our guys back in Houston have been feeding them a whole bunch of bullshit! They think we're going to land on the old launchpad in the center of The Triad. They'll look for us there first."

"But our thrusters?" Jin looked a little confused as he held the handle strap on the ceiling.

"Jin, first of all, please sit down. You're making me seasick! You're everywhere over there." Carrick looked perturbed.

Jin Ho grabbed the table with his left hand, pulling himself down to the bench on the side of the table that Kinzi and Jordan were seated on. He placed his feet in the foot straps under the table and said, "Is this better?"

"Yes! Much!" said Carrick. "Now, where was I?" he paused. "So, this craft has two rovers on it and a new feature on the landing module that the Horizon Class landers didn't have. We can jettison the rovers to lighten our load during our descent."

"That's cool, but how does that help us with the Chinese?" asked Sebastian Colt.

"With your permission Kinzi," Carrick looked her in the eyes, "as you're the crew Commander for the landing team," Carrick showed respect. "I'm gonna steer the lander over the middle of The Triad, and at about 50,000 feet, drop one of the rovers right onto the middle of the launchpad."

Kinzi looked curious. "Where was I when you got that simulator training back in Houston?" Kinzi wondered why she was left out of that particular training session.

"It wasn't in Houston!" Carrick smiled, "It was at the Cape, two days before we launched. I only got four hours of training," he shook his head. I was supposed to get four more hours the night before, but Lola showed up with the kids." Carrick's eyes went wide as he shook his head, half-smiling.

"The nerve of her!" joked Kinzi.

"I know, right?" Carrick laughed.

"Don't worry, I got the other four hours of training," said Jordan. "Sorry, Kinz!" Jordan had an 'oh well' look on his face as he shrugged his shoulders and threw up his hands.

"You bastards have been holding out on me for the last 41 days," she said as she punched Jordan in the chest and shot Carrick an evil eye.

Jin Ho jumped back in, still looking confused. "So, what does all of that mean?"

"The rover package that we'll drop deploys massive chutes," explained Carrick, "but it also has massive spotlights on the bottom of it. Anyone outside will see the lights slowly descending to the surface, landing within The Triad's massive open area between the three Sectors."

"They'll also have bogus intel that we fed them, telling them that that's where we'll be landing," offered Jordan.

"But they'll see our descent thrusters, too?" said Kinzi, as Jin Ho looked on, nodding in agreement.

All eyes went back to Carrick. "Only if they're outside or looking out the window of their lander," said Carrick. "If by chance they do spot us, they'll have a choice to make, won't they?" he smiled.

"Which location do they go to first?" Jordan chimed in.

"Exactly!" said Carrick. "Their muscle will be on the inside of The Triad, which means it would make more sense to investigate the launch pad. That confusion will buy us precious time," he added.

"We understand from their communication back to China that they suspect we're closing the distance with them, but they're still uncertain of exactly when we'll arrive. As you know, Jordan's been feeding Jack and Ollie inaccurate info to radio back to Houston. So, the element of surprise is still on our side," said Carrick.

Jordan added, "We also know that the SHA militant will always be with the computer hackers inside. His job after they get what they need is to blow up The History Library. The Serpent has told us that they plan to blow up The Southeast and Southwest Sectors, too. They fear the other History Libraries hold the same information as the one in The Northwest Sector. They're carrying mini-nukes with them."

"Jesus Christ!" exclaimed Jin Ho Mae.

"Okay, so let's discuss what everyone else will be doing," said Jordan.

"Since our comms have been upgraded, we should be able to communicate with each other from inside of The Triad, both inside and outside of the structure," explained Carrick.

"Jin, that means you'll know what's going on inside at all times," said Jordan. "And you'll be able to report to us what's happening back at the lander."

"Not if we're in the sub-levels." Carrick reminded the team, "Don't forget the platinum walls and dense floors!"

"That's where we have the advantage," explained Carrick. "Do you guys remember how to get to Barrack 5?" Carrick knew all the levels very well, and the Chinese will likely not venture below the surface levels as there was nothing of value down there.

"Sure do," said Kinzi.

"Roger that!" said Jordan.

"That's our fallback if things go south. The Chinese will never know how to find it," said Carrick.

"They're only interested in The History Library anyway," Jordan said out loud. "And maybe a diamond light fixture or two," he added, winking at Kinzi.

Colt spoke back up, "So, I'm not really here for my qualifications as a Biologist, am I?" Sebastian Colt didn't exactly know how to feel about the realization that his MMA background was NASA's motivation for having him on the crew.

Carrick started to address Colt when Jordan cut him off.

"Sebastian, listen, you earned your stripes as both an astronaut and a biologist. That's why you were selected to be on The Silver Comet. Then, after it was blown out of the sky, you and Jack were the first two to volunteer to be on The Leviathan." Jordan was trying to be as delicate as possible. "The fact is..., your MMA background was a plus. You knew that we were coming here to intercept the Chinese. You knew the risks."

Sebastian smiled, "I'm just busting your chops. I just thought that I would never fight professionally again." Sebastian's smile was an instant relief to everyone at the table. "And besides, I owe those assholes! They almost made my wife a widow and my kids fatherless."

Jin Ho weighed in, "Looks like I'm here because of my astronaut training and not because I'm a physicist, huh?"

"Jin, we needed bodies, and you had the courage to step up after the Saturn Six was blown out of the sky," Carrick wanted to ensure that Jin Ho felt valued.

For the next two hours, the group laid out details of the plan they'd execute immediately after landing on Zenith. Jin Ho Mae would stay with the lander and radio the team if he ran into trouble. Kinzi, Carrick, Jordan, and Sebastian, would make their way to The Triad, but first, make a stop along the way.

Once on the surface, the four would drive the rover to within one hundred yards of the Chinese lander, and then, Jordan would quietly approach the craft and deliver The Chameleon to its backside. The Chameleon would silently, and without detection, commandeer the craft's computer systems and overwrite the launch code. It would instruct the craft to disengage all thrusters once it achieved an altitude of 1500 feet during its ascent, then gravity would do the rest. Among the fallen craft remains would likely be the stolen computer files the Chinese stole from The History Library.

The team would then approach The Triad and enter through the front entrance of The Northwest Sector. They would shed their EVUs and then hide them in a storage closet near the Grand Hall. They would also be armed with titanium retractable stick batons for personal protection. With a release of a button on the side, the batons would expand to four feet long.

After that, they'd make their way to The History Library on Surface-Level 3 and confront the Chinese. They'd hope to catch the Chinese in the act and get there before any explosives were detonated. If they were too late, they'd go to Carrick's Plan B, get to The History Library in The Triad's Southwest Sector. They all hoped the Chinese hadn't brought guns with them.

For the next sixty-five days, the NASA crew would review their plan and work through contingencies for every possible scenario they'd face. The only thing they didn't have a plan for was if The Triad had lost all power before either they or the Chinese made it there. Erik Erickson had always said that The Triad would go dark soon after he died, and Erik had now been dead for nearly a year.

Location: The Eclipse 2 – Two Hundred Miles above the surface of Black Earth – September 6, 2027.

Vadik Lei refused to close his eyes during the 8G descent through the thin atmosphere of Black Earth. Jarring maneuvers sent the Eclipse Lander spinning and tumbling as its heat shield jettisoned, and the first of the drogue parachutes deployed. Lei studied the Lander pilot and watched as he struggled to get the ship under control as it fell to the surface. His eyes remained fixed on the pilot until the ship righted itself. Only after he saw relief come across the face of the terrified man would he look away. The eight-minute descent was punctuated as the ship's thrusters activated, pushing back on the near-Earth gravity that was now in control of the lander.

Location: The Leviathan – September 6, 2027 – Minutes after the Chinese Eclipse landed on Zenith's surface.

Ollie Taylor and Jack White successfully navigated The Leviathan through the Orbit Insertion process; a technique where the ship would shed excess velocity via a rocket firing known as an Orbit Insertion Burn. During the maneuver, Ollie fired the spacecraft's engine in their direction of travel to slow its velocity relative to the target, enabling The Leviathan to enter into Black Earth's orbit.

"Holy Shit!" exclaimed Jack White, as he got his first look at the black mass. "It's huge! It's as big as Earth!"

Ollie Taylor smiled and said, "It's like a black pearl. I didn't think I'd ever see it again. Man, there's no place I'd rather be right now."

In the aft crew compartment, the team rested in their pods until their schedule was aligned to that of the Chinese. They needed to make sure that all but one of the Taikonauts were in The Triad before they landed.

Eight hours later, Sun Kanai assisted the crew with suiting up. The process of donning their EMUs and loading them into the lander would take several hours. Afterward, Jack White would remotely engage and separate the landing craft from The Leviathan. Once separation was complete, Carrick would take control of the craft.

After the Lander was fully prepped, Sun Kanai informed White and Taylor, who then relayed a phony intel back to Houston, stating that they were seven days away from Zenith and preparing their braking techniques now.

"Houston, we show five-million miles to go, can you confirm? Over." Jack White said into his comms.

"Roger that, Leviathan!" said Mars Johnston, who clicked off his mic and looked at Vance McDonald.

"Vance, that means that they're preparing the lander to disembark." Mars was nervously excited.

"Okay, Jack," said Mars, "let's plan to check in again in 24 hours."

"Roger that, Houston!" confirmed White. "All systems are a go! We look forward to the 24-hour check-in. Over and out!"

In 24 hours, the fate of the world would likely be determined. The Leviathan landing crew's success was critical to ensuring the Chinese didn't hack and then destroy the information housed in The History Library.

Location: Dawodang Depression, Guizhou Province, Southern China. Black Diamond Communications Shed – September 6, 2027 – 6:46 am, Local time.

As SHA Militant Zhang Hui was getting ready to leave for his four-hour break, Dewei Wan monitored all transmissions between the Chinese Eclipse and the Eclipse 2 landing craft. Simultaneously, Dong Wei monitored The Leviathan and all data and radio transmission through the Interlink Corridor.

As Hui was walking out the door, Dong Wei shouted, "Agent Hui!"

"Yes, what is it?" said Hui.

"Sir, something isn't making sense!" Wei seemed concerned as Wan looked over.

"What is it, Dong?" Hui was exhausted and just wanted to leave.

"Sir, The Leviathan navigators just radioed Houston saying that they were five million miles away from Black Earth...." Wei was quickly cut off by Zhang Hui.

"What does that mean, Dong? Just tell me!"

"Sir, our data suggests that they were five million miles away seven days ago. I think they are close to Black Earth. I think they might actually be there." Wei seemed confident.

"On the surface!" Hui exploded with concern.

"No, sir, the voice data being transmitted from The Leviathan to Houston doesn't seem to indicate that. But..."

"But what?!" yelled Hui.

"Listen to this, sir." Wei removed his headset and put the audio speakers on so that Zhang Hui and Dewei Wan could hear playback on the last voice transmission coming from The Leviathan.

Hui and Wan leaned in, as Dong Wei played back the recording.

The three heard, "Roger that, Houston! All systems are a go! We look forward to the 24-hour check-in. Over and out!"

Hui said, "I'm confused! What's abnormal about their transmission?"

"Listen again, sir!" said Wei, as he played the recording again.

"Roger that, Houston!" confirmed the commander of The Leviathan. "All systems are a go! We look forward to the 24-hour check-in. Over and out!"

"That means nothing! You're just as tired as I am!" the SHA Militant barked at the communications expert. "I'm going to sleep now. Call me at once if you get anything of actual concern.

"But sir, he said, 'GO'!" Wei pleaded his case as Hui walked out the door.

"Dong, what did you detect in the voice data?" asked Dewei Wan.

Wei was frustrated and concerned. "Dewei, the pilot, said to his bosses in Houston that 'All systems are a go.'"

"So what! What does that mean?" Wan looked slightly confused by his associate's concern, as did Zhang Hui.

"He should have said, 'All systems are GOOD,' not 'All systems are A Go.'"

"Okay, you are tired, as Hui said! You need to get some sleep like that crazy SHA bastard." Dewei Wan encouraged his associate to take a short break.

Some sixty minutes later, with Comms to Houston shut down, Carrick's voice came over the comms, "5 – 4 – 3 – 2 – 1!" After a short pause, Carrick added, "We have separation of the Neptune Landing Module from the mothercraft The Leviathan!"

The Neptune landing module began to float freely away from The Leviathan. The mood surrounding the astronauts was one of relief.

"Okay, guys, now the real work begins," said Surface Commander Kinzi London.

Location: Two hundred miles above the surface of Black Earth – Sixty Minutes Later.

At sixty-minutes before touchdown, Kinzi radioed Jack White to report the Neptune landing module was ready to initiate its de-orbit burn.

The craft would fire its engines in the opposite direction of the surface, which would allow it to penetrate Black Earth's atmosphere. All on the crew had experienced this before, with the exception of Sebastian Colt, who looked a little nervous. Carrick Michaels looked over at him, winked, and smiled.

After penetrating Zenith's atmosphere, the lander was in a freefall. While the crew admired the fiery orange glow that engulfed the lander just outside the craft's windows, Carrick was working through the planned steps to jettison one of the rovers onto The Triad's launchpad. After that, he would search for a smooth spot to land the craft roughly a mile away from the Chinese lander.

"I see it, guys!" Carrick's nervous excitement rang out as he studied the radar.

Kinzi was quietly thankful that it was Carrick landing the craft in place of her.

Carrick could now see The Triad on his screen. "God, it's beautiful." Only now did he fully realize how much he missed it. His breath was taken away for a moment until he realized that Erik wouldn't be waiting for him inside. No matter, Carrick was at peace, he was home.

Fourteen minutes after the Neptune's drogue parachutes had deployed, Carrick released the first rover, high above The Triad.

"We have deployed Rover One above The Triad," calmly said Carrick into his Comms.

"Roger that, Carrick!" responded Jack White.

"It looks like a good release, Carrick!" said Ollie Taylor.

"Carrick gave an emphatic thumbs-up to the cameras around the interior of the landing craft and his crew-mates. Internally he hoped for a successful landing of the rover inside The Triad's triangular open-area between the three outer sectors.

Back on The Leviathan, Jack White, Ollie Taylor, and Sun Kanai could see the very radar that Carrick was using for the Neptune's descent and landing. They also had multiple visual feeds coming from inside of the Neptune Lander.

Back in Houston, Mars Johnston, Vance McDonald, and dozens of others held their breath while remaining radio silent with the craft. Mars' stress ball was noticeably missing some chunks from its side.

After another twenty minutes, Carrick sporadically used the lander's thrusters to slow the craft while it searched for a landing spot. Then, with a heavy jolt and booming thud, the Neptune landed on the black surface after a one hour and nine-minute descent.

"Okay, team! We did it! Nice work, Carrick!" Kinzi's relief was evident by the tone in her voice.

"You guys be careful down there," Jack White's voice came over the comms.

"Roger that!" said Kinzi.

The celebration for this successful surface landing was more subdued than previous ones. The team on the ground would face a hostile foreign foe, along with an atmosphere that would attempt to take the lives of everyone onboard every single second they were there. Lives would be at stake. Everyone knew it, but no one voiced their concerns out loud.

Chapter 30 – Home

Location: The Triad – Four hours earlier

After spending the previous day trying to locate The History Library, it was day two for the Chinese, and they were headed back to The Triad to continue their work that they'd only just begun the day before. The Chinese cyber techs and computer engineers were able to locate The History Library's mainframe; they did it using a device they'd developed after stealing Intellectual Property from an American Firm in Silicon Valley back in 2024.

The device, known as Wǎngluò fànwéi, English translation, *Cyber Scope*, could detect the central nervous system of any computer. The Chinese weren't sure it would work on Black Earth, but it did, perfectly. The device was also used to help overwrite the door code for The Northwest Sector's main entrance and Temperature Regulation Chamber, allowing the Chinese to enter the structure without explosives.

While computer engineers began stripping the mainframe of The History Library's computers, found behind the twenty-foot wide, liquid-glass monitor on the back wall of The History Library, Vadik Lei unpacked two C4 explosive canisters and attempted to place them on the mainframe.

"You cannot place explosives yet!" said Bai Tsong, the lead computer engineer. "We are working here."

"You have your job, and I have mine," said The Spider to the three technicians, trying to intimidate them.

"We cannot do our jobs if there are explosives attached to the mainframe. What if there was an accident and the data was destroyed before we could download it?" said another of the technicians.

"Please, let us work, we need six hours. Come back then," requested Tsong.

"Very well then, I will return in six hours. Be ready for me." Lei sounded threatening to the computer engineers.

The three men bowed their heads, not wanting to upset The Spider.

The Spider's job included not only blowing up the mainframe of the computer, but then traveling to The Southeast and Southwest sectors, where he'd plant mini nuclear devices at the base of the exterior walls, closest to where it was determined The History Library would be. The goal was to destroy all historical data and records of Zenith's past, medical cures, and space travel propulsion systems, in an effort to prevent other countries from possessing the information.

With the six hours he now had, he would exit The Northwest Sector and travel to the other two sectors first and plant the explosive devices.

After suiting up, Lei drove the Eclipse rover to The Southwest Sector first before making the trek to The Southeast Sector. Blowing up The Southeast Sector would likely haunt Lei as it once housed his Asian ancestors. He planned to do it last just in case he changed his mind. The Spider was melancholy as he approached middle age and would question himself regularly in instances he never questioned before.

Two hours later, while programing the nuclear device on The Southwest Sector's western wall, Vadik Lei saw a bright light falling slowly from the northern sky. He studied it for a moment, smiled, and said, "The Americans have arrived!" He again smiled at the thought of killing Captain America. After all, that's the only reason he agreed to be part of Operation Black Diamond.

Lei determined that the approaching object appeared on a trajectory to land just northeast of his current position; or in the center of The Triad's three-sided structure. *The landing pad*, he thought to himself.

Vadik Lei set the timer on the device to detonate in 24 hours and then jumped back into the rover, heading back to The Northwest Sector. He hoped to find his way to the sector's interior entrance that led to the giant launch pad in the middle of the megaplex.

Minutes later, as Lei traversed the rugged terrain and the two-plus miles back, he again saw something in the black sky that caught his attention, thrusters from a landing craft. *Two crafts?* he thought. "Hmm, one must be a decoy," he surmised aloud. The Spider had already determined that hand to hand combat on the black surface would not be wise regardless of the number of men he might have to face due to his restricted movement while wearing an EMU. That meant that if a confrontation occurred, it would have to be inside the Triad where his space suit wouldn't be required and his skills could be better utilized, particularly when it came to using his throwing stars. But regardless of any possible confrontation, he knew that his priority was to protect his fellow countrymen, and ensure the destruction of The History Library.

The Spider did not radio any of his associates in fear the Americans were listening. Instead, he would lie in wait along the path to The History Library. Planting the second explosive device on the southeast side of The Southeast Sector would have to wait, as he needed to get word to the engineers working inside.

Location: The Neptune Lander – Four hours later.

The Neptune had been on the black surface for two hours, and the crew was ready to disembark.

Forty minutes later, Jordan, Kinzi, Carrick, and Sebastian Colt, were on the surface and working to release the second rover; Jin Ho Mae would join them later. After the thirty-minute process was complete, the four loaded onto the rover and headed in the Chinese lander's general direction. Jin Ho Mae would stay put and position himself 100 feet from the Neptune lander and ensure that no Taikonauts approached in an effort to sabotage the lander, as they did the Saturn Six. Mae was instructed to remain vigilant and incognito, with only his HUD illuminated inside of his helmet.

Within minutes, the Chinese Eclipse 2 was in sight. It appeared that no Taikonauts were guarding the perimeter. The rover stopped roughly 100 yards away, and Jordan dismounted with the package, a silver tantalum briefcase that contained The Chameleon.

Jordan stealthily approached the lander as the other three looked on. Colt dismounted the rover, wanting to be ready in the event

Jordan was discovered. Spear would be easy to spot as the lander had its exterior lights on, and though Jordan was in an orange EMU, instead of the white ones worn on previous missions, it easily reflected the light due to the Vanta black surface.

Jordan approached the side of the craft with no windows and gently planted the device on the aft section of the Eclipse 2, just below the Chinese flag, payback for the Saturn Six.

When attaching The Chameleon, it made a loud clicking sound when the magnets adhered to the metal skin. This alarmed the Taikonaut inside the craft, who began to investigate by looking out of the craft's three portals.

Inside the Eclipse 2, a scientist named Chung Lee radioed to the group that he'd heard a disturbance outside and would egress the craft to investigate. Those listening from the Chinese Eclipse orbiting overhead, the Ministry of State Security in Beijing, the Hainan Space Center, and Zhang Hui, and the other two in the Black Diamond Communications Shed at FAST, all knew what that meant. The Americans were there. "Proceed with caution," said the Chinese Eclipse commander, Captain Liú Qian, who was orbiting overhead at an altitude of some 200 miles.

"Don't exit that lander," warned Vadik Lei in a very calm voice, talking low. "The Americans are here."

"Where...?," said Zhang Hui, back at FAST, "on the surface?"

"The surface! They're here! Now everyone go radio silent until you hear from me," directed The Spider. "Our chatter is no doubt being heard by the Americans, so now they know their cover is blown. The element of surprise is gone for both sides. Rest assured," he paused, "I will kill them all. Radio silence starts now!"

Location: FAST Observatory – Real-Time.

In the Communications Shed, the phone rang out loudly. Hui answered and said, "Zhang Hui here!" He knew that it would be Kenong.

"What have you fools done?!" Minister Li Kenong shouted into the phone. "You have failed. You will suffer greatly for your incompetence!"

Zhang Hui hung up on Kenong in mid-sentence, grabbed his jacket and backpack, and then immediately exited the building, disappearing into the dark forest.

The phone rang again moments later, and Dewei Wan answered. "Put the SHA idiot back on the phone," shouted Kenong.

"I'm sorry, sir, he left in a hurry," said Wan.

"Do not let him escape!" Kenong was incensed.

"Yes, Minister Kenong, I will attempt to stop him, sir!" Wan ended the call, put his feet up on the console and his hands behind his head, interlocked his fingers, and began whistling. The last thing he was going to do was attempt to apprehend and detain a SHA Militant, in the forest, in the dark.

Location: Houston, Texas – Mission Control.

"Leviathan, this is Houston. Do you copy?" Mars Johnston's voice came through the Comms unexpectedly.

Orbiting 250 miles above Black Earth, Jack White, Ollie Taylor, and Sun Kanai, who were all listening on voice chatter from the surface team, nearly jumped out of their boots with the incoming word from Mars. They knew it was bad news.

"Houston, we copy," said White.

"Hey Jack, our Meteorologists detect a storm is moving in on the surface, heading straight for The Triad. Have the surface team stand down and return to the lander at once. Have them remain there until further notice. Over," said Mars.

"Roger that, Houston! We're on it!" copied Jack White.

Mars' words were code in case the Chinese could hear their voice transmissions.

While a "storm" was code for trouble, anyone who knew Zenith's composition would know that no active weather systems had altered its surface for thousands of years. If the Chinese were listening, they would likely know that Mars was speaking in code.

"Surface Team, did you copy that?" asked White.

"London here, we copy you," said Kinzi. Since she was the surface commander, only she would communicate with The Leviathan unless incapacitated.

"Kinzi, you have a storm headed your way. Houston advises you to take shelter in the Neptune Lander." White passed along the code for 'proceed with your mission but use caution. The Chinese now know you're there.'

Kinzi looked at Carrick and Sebastian with eyes wide opened. The green glow of her Heads-Up-Display revealed her fear.

"Roger that, Leviathan, we're heading back now."

The five surface crew all heard White's words and the warning hidden in them. They would continue with their plan but would be on high alert.

After successfully planting The Chameleon on the Eclipse II, Jordan returned to the rover and witnessed Kinzi making hand gestures. She hand signaled the numbers 0-1-3-0 to Carrick, Jordan, and Sebastian, meaning to change their radio frequency to 0130.

"Leviathan, this is London. We show outside temperatures rising, be advised," Kinzi spoke in code.

"Roger that, Kinzi. Sun Kanai will monitor from here," said Jack White.

Kinzi's transmission told Jin Ho Mae and The Leviathan to change their radiofrequency to the Emergency back-up channel, 0130. Once they did, they could speak freely to each other on the surface and with The Leviathan overhead. However, Houston would hear nothing other than what The Leviathan communicated directly to them through the Interlink Corridor. The Chinese, if listening, would no longer be able to hear them.

The stress ball that Mars was gripping was now in tatters; he needed a replacement. He dipped into his stash in a drawer of a nearby podium in the front of the Mission Control room. When the drawer opened, more than a half-dozen mini globes were revealed rolling around inside.

Now on channel 0130, Kinzi spoke freely. "Okay, guys, our cover's blown!" she said. "Get your batons out and ready to extend."

"Leviathan, this is Jordan, the package has been delivered, and we're en route to The Triad."

"Roger that! Proceed with caution and leave your Comms on at all times so that we can listen in," said White.

"10-4!" said Kinzi. "Stay quiet up there as any distractions in our ear could get one of us killed."

A few minutes later, Sebastian Colt said to Jordan, "The craft blowing up on lift-off...that's a bad way to go!" he reflected on his experience being on the Saturn Six the month before. After thinking more about it, he was torn by the CIA's decision to bring down the Chinese lander.

Jin Ho panicked and raced back to the Neptune lander and boarded, fearing he would be harmed if he remained outside.

Within twenty minutes, the team passed by the previous landing site of the first mission. As they passed, at only two mph, Carrick took notice of something.

The wool flags, planted by Carrick and the international crew members of the first mission to Black Earth, were still in place with the exception of one. The flag that Neil Armstrong had presented to him and his mother when he was only ten years old was long since gone. The nylon, polyester blend stood no chance against the 800° surface temperatures on Zenith.

Seeing the charred remains of his childhood, dangling from the now almost empty flagpole surrounded by the others, was symbolic. Carrick saw his childhood in much the same way; it was now gone. Carrick's youth was no longer a burden that he had to carry with him; he had officially passed that on to his newborn children.

Kinzi, sitting in the back row of the rover with Carrick, observed what he was looking at. She knew that the charred flag would weigh heavily on him. Kinzi remembered what Carrick said and the tears he shed as he became the first astronaut to plant his feet into the black surface. A moment in history that would link Carrick to his past, present, and future.

Jordan and Sebastian, sitting in the front row, paid little attention to the original landing site. They instead focused their attention on the danger that lie ahead. They couldn't know what Kinzi, and Carrick were feeling at that instant, two friends connected by history. They were a part of Black Earth's first and final chapters. A story of both human triumph and societal failure. Kinzi looked forward, thinking that the final act still needed to be written. Carrick, on the other hand, just stared into the void.

Jordan spoke up, "There it is! I see it! 12 o'clock high," Jordan spotted The Triad in the distance and snapped Carrick and Kinzi out of their emotional trance.

"It's huge!" said Colt.

The others were just as amazed as they were the first time they saw The Triad. No words were needed.

Colt, Kinzi, and Jordan saw a massive black behemoth, but what Carrick saw was Home.

Chapter 31 – Boom!

Location: The History Library – September 7, 2027 – Minutes Later.

"How much longer will it take?" Vadik Lei was agitated at the time it was taking the engineers to complete their task. "The Americans are likely approaching the building now!"

Two hours earlier, after witnessing the descent of the American Lander, it took Vadik Lei nearly an hour to get back to The Triad's main entrance. From there, he quickly shed his EMU, then raced to The History Library to see how much longer the engineers needed to complete the data upload.

"It will take another hour, maybe more," said Bai Tsong.

"You're not hearing me very well! The Americans are closing in! Leave your equipment and take only the data!" ordered Lei.

"We cannot leave until the upload is complete. We'll all be executed if we return without the data."

"If you don't hurry," Lei got close to Tsong's face, "I will execute you right here!"

The two other technicians heard what was said and began working faster, avoiding eye contact with The Spider.

"Sir, can you buy us a little more time?"

"Hurry up!" shouted Lei. "They are coming!" He then turned to open his satchel, removing the C4 explosives.

"Sir, remember what I said about the explosives? We must not be distracted by you planting bombs where we are working," said Tsong.

Without warning, The Spider lunged at Tsong, grabbed him, and slammed him up against the wall, his forearm pressed against the engineer's throat.

Tsong tried to speak but was unable. A look of terror filled his eyes as he was now at the mercy of the Strategic Huyou Agency's most deadly assassin.

Lei pressed his nose against Tsong's and said, "Shut up and do your job!" Removing his forearm from Tsong's throat, he added, "And I will do mine!"

Bai Tsong, now weeping, said nothing. He slid down the wall as his backside came to rest on the floor. With wide eyes and holding his throat, he motioned to Vadik Lei to do what he wanted.

Lei grabbed the explosives and went to work alongside the other technicians. After 10 minutes, he finished attaching the two explosive devices to opposite sides of the mainframe. Before turning to leave, he pressed red buttons on both of the bomb's detonators, activating their timers.

Lei looked at the three men and said, "You have sixty minutes to finish. Be done," he paused, "or be dead! Your choice." With the stealth of a cat, Lei ran to the front of The History Library and disappeared through the double doors.

The two technicians working on the upload looked at the red numbered timers, then back at each other. 59:22 and counting showed on each device. They swallowed hard, stricken with fear, then looked at their supervisor. Tsong was still sitting on the floor, his face ravaged by fear.

Moments later, Bai Tsong rose to his feet and yelled, "Hurry, the Americans are approaching! We must finish at once!" Tsong now shared The Spider's concerns and took on his demeanor.

Location: Main Entrance of The Triad's Northwest Sector.

As Jordan, Sebastian, Carrick, and Kinzi approached the Temperature Regulation Chamber; they could see the Chinese rover parked haphazardly in front of the door.

"Shit's about to get real!" said Jordan. Kinzi looked at her baton and thought to herself, *I don't even know how to use this thing.*

Carrick had regained his focus and said, "Kinzi, stay close in there!" His eyes were wide, conveying his caution with a nod.

Instead of stopping, Jordan drove past the entrance to a small alcove on the side of the building, just southwest of the entrance.

"Jordan, where are we going?" asked a confused Sebastian.

"I'm hiding our ride back to the lander. I don't want those pricks to disable it like I'm about to disable theirs."

The four disembarked the rover, and Carrick said, "Good thinking, man!"

"Damn right! There will be no quick getaways for those guys!" added Jordan.

As the four walked the hundred or so feet to the entrance, Kinzi tossed her Survival Pack to Jordan and her backpack to Sebastian and said, "Carry these." Kinzi then radioed The Leviathan.

The Survival Pack contained medical supplies, surgical instruments, protein-rich drinks, and antibiotics. Kinzi's backpack, however, was more of a medical first-aid kit.

"Surface Crew to The Leviathan, do you read?"

"Copy that, Kinzi!" the three orbiting overhead were on edge. Hearing everything play out from 250 miles was nerve-racking. "You guys be safe in there! Keep us posted."

"Copy that," said Kinzi.

Another few steps closer, Kinzi said, "Do any of us really know how in the hell this is supposed to go down in there? I mean, we don't actually expect them to surrender and give us a giant jump drive, do we?"

"That would be a mighty big jump drive!" said Carrick, jokingly. "About fifty-thousand-years-worth of information."

"Maybe we can beat them over the head with it," Sebastian got in on the jokes.

"Get your game faces on, people!" Jordan ended the fun. "They could be right around the corner."

"We gotta get out of these suits as fast as we can!" said Sebastian.

"He's right. If these get damaged, we only have two back-ups on the Neptune." Carrick reminded everyone.

"Yeah, and we've got no mobility!" said Jordan. "They've got the upper-hand until we shed these. As soon as we're inside," he paused, "we lose these EMUs."

Jin Ho Mae, back at the lander, was listening to the team and said, "I'll have the suits on standby, but I won't be able to carry both of them the whole way."

"Jin, you stay on the outside of that lander until told otherwise!" said Carrick. "If they sabotage our ride, then none of us are going home!"

"I understand, Carrick. I am outside the lander keeping an eye on it," said Jin, from inside the lander.

"Reminder to everybody, we look for footprints around the lander before lift-off. Any prints that don't match ours is a problem," said Jordan. "Stay on high alert, Jin!"

"Got it!"

As the team approached the entrance, Carrick walked to the right side of the door to activate the touchpad.

"This rover's pretty nice!" said Colt, admiring the Chinese technology.

"Sebastian, stay focused, man!" said Jordan. "When that door opens, there may be a surprise waiting for us."

"You think they rigged it to explode?" responded Colt.

"I wasn't thinking that at all, actually," exclaimed Jordan, "but thanks a lot for planting the seed in my head. Everybody stand back up against the wall while Carrick enters the code."

Carrick shook his head and smiled. "Don't worry about me over here," he said, busting Jordan's chops, "I'll take one for the team if it blows."

Carrick wiped away the screen so that it could read his thoughts when suddenly it began to open without a code. "Damn! Those guys are smart! They rigged it so that no code is needed." Carrick looked impressed.

Before entering the Temperature Regulation Chamber, Jordan took his baton and smashed in the console on the Eclipse Rover's dashboard. After smashing the faceplate, he reached in and pulled out a wire harness, then removed it from its housing.

"Let's see those bastards jump start this thing now!" Jordan was celebratory. "Ain't gonna happen! They're gonna have to hoof it!"

The Temperature Regulation Chamber door began to open, making the sound of escaping air. It was a sound that was familiar to Carrick. He closed his eyes for a moment and flashed back to the last time he was here when he and Erik left The Triad for Earth. He took a deep breath and then opened his eyes.

"It's clear, let's go!" Carrick called up the other three.

The team filed into the chamber, with the door closing behind them, they would have to wait for the temperature regulation process to cool their suits down. Sebastian Colt was happy to be standing on a surface that he could actually see.

"Now, this is better. Felt like we were walking on black gravity out there," Sebastian looked relieved. "Vertigo was kicking in a little."

Kinzi said, "Yeah, you never really get used to it."

As the team waited for the regulation process to finish, Sebastian asked, "What's taking so long?"

"This chamber evens the temperature from the outside of The Triad to the inside of the structure," said Carrick. "Whether you're coming or going, the chamber has to slowly cool or heat your EMU, or equipment, so that the materials aren't thrust into 800° temperatures, coming out of only 80°, and vice-versa."

"Makes sense," Sebastian nodded.

Jordan quickly changed the subject. "Okay, stay alert, guys! There might be someone on the other side of that door," said Jordan.

"Carrick and Sebastian, get up against that wall," Jordan pointed to the wall opposite of where he and Kinzi were standing. "Kinz, get over here with me!" Jordan was worried there could be projectiles thrown at them as the door opened.

Three minutes later, the inner door began to open, but no one was there. Each of the four exhaled in relief.

"Okay, let's drop our suits here!" said Carrick. "I know where we can stash them." Carrick remembered a storage facility behind a false wall in a room just twenty feet down the main hall on the left.

"Leviathan, do you copy?" Kinzi radioed the others.

"Copy that, Kinzi! How's it going down there?" said Jack White, orbiting overhead.

"We're dropping our EMUs and Comms. I'll have the walkie-talkie with me, but I'm turning it off for now. We'll reach out with updates along the way," she said.

"Roger that! Be safe!" said White.

"Jin Ho! Did you copy that?" asked Kinzi.

"Roger that, Kinzi. I copy you." Jin was uneasy with the radio silence.

Following that transmission, Jack White's attention went to the monitors that displayed the Neptune lander's crew cabin. He could see that Jin Ho was inside of the lander when not scheduled to be.

"Jin! Get your ass outside of that lander ASAP!" yelled White through the comms.

"Roger that, Jack!" responded a frightened Jin Ho Mae. "I was changing out my oxygen supply and cooling down my suit. I'll head back out shortly."

Back at The Triad, the crew were now out of their EMUs and worked quickly to gather the multi-layers of their suits, PLSS back-packs, and the Survival Pack.

"Come on! Come on! Follow me!" Carrick started down the hall ahead of the others.

Jordan made sure to keep his eyes focused down the long hallway with doors staggered along each side.

The four of them walked into a large room, thirty feet by thirty feet, that was originally used as one of four Welcome Centers. After its construction, arriving lottery winners first entering The Triad would be processed prior to being housed in the megaplex.

Carrick remembered back to his time on Zenith when Erik educated him about *The Chance*.

A lottery, called *The Chance,* was enacted only after each of the three remaining nations on Zenith was allowed to pre-select no more than 30,000 individuals who were masters in their field of study. These people, the brightest and the best, along with their immediate families, were automatically granted access to The Triad. After that, everyone else went into the lottery; Carrick remembered Erik saying.

The Allied Assembly issued bar-coded numbers to each family in the three nations. Then, random numbers were drawn, and those families whose numbers came up were granted an invitation to live in The Triad. They could decline if they chose, but none did.

In the four thousand years since then, the room had been used for everything from a housing unit to medical facilities, a pharmacy, a laboratory, and now a storage unit. The room had broken furniture, metal cartons, metal racks, and other miscellaneous items scattered around. If Erik had never pointed out the concealed room to Carrick, no one would've ever known that it was there.

Now inside the room, Sabastian looked around in awe and asked, "What is this place?" He was amazed at how modern The Triad looked, even though it was ancient.

"Now you know what four-thousand-year-old platinum looks like!" Carrick said as he tossed components of his EMU into the wall unit. "It looks a lot like platinum!"

After securing their EMUs and cooling suits, the team was ready to move out. Outfitted in only their Under Armour designed spandex bodysuit, they'd have to leave their comms behind. Kinzi wore a backpack with medical supplies in case anyone got hurt. Her primary reason for being there was for medical support; she was no fighter.

"Are we sure about leaving our comms?" asked a concerned Colt.

"Can't fight with headsets on!" said Jordan. "Don't worry, Kinzi has the walkie."

Walking toward the door, Jordan asked the team, "Everyone got their batons?"

Each of the other three showed Jordan their only weapon.

"Okay, let's stick to the plan, there's strength in numbers. Separate only if we need to," said Jordan.

"Sebastian, where's the fallback if everything goes to hell?" Carrick quizzed him before exiting the room.

"Barrack 5, Sub-Level 7!" Colt knew where to go.

"You got the map?" asked Carrick.

"Right here!" he patted his pocket to make sure it was there.

"Carrick, you got the journal?" asked Jordan, referring to the journal Erik left for him. It would be the team's blueprint if the Chinese destroyed The History Library and if the place lost power.

"Got it! Now let's go!" Carrick was both anxious and nervous. But most of all, he was pissed. He felt like the Chinese had invaded his actual home and was feeling territorial. This was personal for him, it was Erik's home, and Lilly's, too. He wanted them out, and now.

Just then, the lights went out for a few seconds and then came back on. Everybody looked around, wondering what was happening.

"What the hell was that?" Kinzi looked nervous.

"It's the ECS!" Carrick didn't look surprised.

"What's that?" asked Colt.

"The Energy Conservation System. It's about to shut this place down. It could go dark at any time," said Carrick. "It should've gone dark years ago."

"Great! And we've only got the one flashlight." Sebastian Colt was more and more skeptical of the plan.

They would only have one walkie-talkie and one flashlight by leaving their gear behind, both carried by Kinzi in her backpack. If the ECS shut down power throughout the structure, Carrick knew where to go, the Survival Storage Unit on Sub-Level 7. It was where he and Erik went to suit up for the tour of The Triad's sub-sub levels. There, they would find oxygen, headlamps, heat resistant suits, and the Black Widow.

Carrick knew The Northwest Sector so well he could get there in the dark. That's where he'd take the team if the ECS shut everything down.

"Okay, The History Library is on Surface-Level 3. We have to go through the Grand Hall to get there," said Carrick.

"Let's move," chimed Jordan.

The team made their way down the hundred-foot hallway that led away from the main entrance and toward the Grand Hall.

The Grand Hall was a circular atrium, fifteen stories tall, with elevators wrapping around it on every level. It was the gateway to every area of The Northwest Sector, including the monorails that led to The Southwest and Southeast Sectors of The Triad.

The long hallway was dimly lit, with many rooms on both sides; all of them had to be cleared. They couldn't take the chance that the Chinese might be hiding in one of them, waiting for them to pass, and enabling them to escape The Triad unopposed.

After checking each room, Sebastian asked, "Can they get out the main entrance without coming down this hallway?"

"No, this is it," said Carrick.

"Hmm, should one of us stay behind in one of these rooms?" he asked the group. "I mean, at least we'd know if they got out or not."

Jordan again chimed in, "If they get out and make it to the lander, they'll have a rude awakening at about 1500 feet!"

Sebastian Colt again wrestled with his feelings of Jordan planting the device on the Chinese lander, as he was just blown out of the sky five months prior. He reasoned that the fate of the world rested on the Chinese not getting the data from The Triad back to Earth. "A few Chinese lives today versus a world war later," the British Biologist reasoned.

The team made it to the Grand Hall, and things seemed quiet. "We need to take the stairs," said Carrick, "the elevators are all out." It was evident to all as the lights on the door panels were dark.

"That actually works better for us. They won't be able to slip past us if they need to take the same stairwell," said Jordan.

The team's goal would be to spread out with roughly twenty feet between each of the four and then make their way around the circular atrium to the stairwell that led to the third surface level. The ECS had shut down the elevator banks since Carrick was there last to rescue Erik, more than three years prior.

Carrick was out in front, with Jordan following behind him, followed by Kinzi, then Sebastian. The skilled fighters bookended the team's medical doctor.

Just as Carrick rounded the turn, he was struck in the left shoulder by a metal projectile. He made a wincing sound and then went down to the ground. Before Jordan signaled the others to get down, he saw a shadowy figure dip into the very stairwell the team was headed for.

After going prone, the team rallied to Carrick's aid; they could see a metal object protruding from his shoulder as they got closer to him.

"Dammit!" said Jordan, as Carrick quietly moaned. "It's a Chinese Throwing Star! Fuck!" he said under his breath.

Carrick squeezed his shoulder while Kinzi pulled gauze from her backpack. "It's okay Carrick, it got the meat of your shoulder and didn't reach the bone. You'll be good once I wrap it." Kinzi tried to mask her terror. The star struck Carrick just inches from his jugular vein.

Jordan's eyes met with Kinzi's. He, too, realized her fear.

"Okay, what do I need to know about this guy!" Sebastian said, looking more worried now. He wanted to better understand his potential opponent's skill-level, in case he ended up face-to-face with The Spider.

"He's fucking Bruce Lee, and apparently, he's got a pocket full of Chinese fucking throwing stars!" Jordan was simmering, though trying to be restrained.

Carrick said, "Let's go kill that fucker!" He rose to his feet and rotated his wrapped shoulder. "Just a flesh wound!" as he worked his axilla.

"Okay, here's the plan," said Jordan. "Kinzi, gimmie your backpack. I'll lead the way holding the backpack in front of me. We stay in single file until we get to The History Library."

"The stairs won't be a problem. It'll be tough to get any velocity throwing down a stairwell," said Carrick. "It's the hundred-foot long hallway leading to the library that'll be the problem."

"Let's do this!" Sebastian was fired up, and his adrenaline was in full effect.

The group headed for the stairwell, with Jordan leading the way. Making their way up the three floors, they ran into no resistance from The Spider.

Now at the top of the stairs, Sebastian said, "Damn, my quads are on fire!" He finally felt the effects of Zenith's near-Earth gravity after experiencing none in the last four months.

"Gravity's a bitch!" said Jordan.

"Carrick, remind me when we go out the door, do we go left or right?" asked Jordan.

"We go left, but unfortunately, we have to go back around the atrium."

"We're sitting ducks!" Jordan collected his thoughts and said, "Okay, here's the plan."

He explained to the team that he would run out of the stairwell and go prone behind one of the pillars. Four pillars wrapped around the glass railing that overlooked the open atrium. The atrium looked up to the two floors above it and down to the twelve floors below. He thought to himself how much he would love to launch The Spider over the railing and watch him fall into the black abyss below.

After making it to the pillar, he'd take cover and toss the backpack back to Sebastian, who would come out next. Kinzi would then follow Colt, and then Carrick would come out last.

As Jordan opened the stairwell door on Surface-Level 3, he held the backpack up to shield himself from the next incoming star. When doing so, the team heard a muffled thud. When Jordan recoiled the backpack, the team saw a hole in it. The backpack caught the incoming star.

Jordan shook his head and said, "Damn, this guy's good! That's where my head was supposed to be."

Jordan held the door open a few inches and yelled out to The Spider, "Now we have two of your stars, Motherfucker! See how you like it when they come flying back at you!" Jordan was pissed.

Just as he said that another star came through the six-inch opening of the door. The star rattled around in the stairwell, narrowly missing the others before coming to a rest at Kinzi's feet.

"Now we have three, you son of a bitch! You're not going home, Spider!" Jordan yelled out the door.

"This guy's good!" said Carrick, with a nervous smile.

"I should have killed him in London years ago!" said Jordan.

The four heard distant laughing. "You die tonight, Captain America!" came the words from The Spider, echoing around the atrium.

Kinzi shook her head. "Captain America?" she said. "Was that meant for you?"

"Yep! Apparently, all SHA assassins want to kill me."

"When were you planning on telling me that?" asked Kinzi.

A second later, Colt smiled and said, "Captain America, huh? I could see that!"

"Don't encourage him," said Kinzi, shaking her head.

Carrick weighed in, "You guys almost finished?" he said, shaking his head. "There's an assassin out there trying to kill us."

The group refocused and got serious for a moment.

"Could any of you make out which direction his voice was coming from?" asked Jordan.

"It's a circular atrium," said Carrick, "there's no telling."

Jordan said, "Okay, let's all just run out there in different directions. He can't hit us all!"

At that instant, another metal star came flying through the narrow opening.

"That's four now!" yelled Jordan out the door. "Fucking guy!" said Jordan to the others.

"You sure about running out there, all willy-nilly Captain America? He seems pretty accurate to me." Colt kept it light but didn't agree with Jordan's idea of a free for all.

"Has he missed yet?" wondered Carrick. "I didn't hear anything hit the wall out there."

Jordan racked his brain, trying to come up with something.

"Okay, I got it!" Jordan looked focused.

Kinzi saw the look in Jordan's eyes and said, "Don't even think about it!" shaking her head from side to side.

Jordan raised his brow and smiled, then, without a word, flew out the door, the backpack leading the way.

Kinzi screamed, "Jordan, no!"

"What the hell just happened?" Sebastian was startled.

"Captain America, that's what! He's nuts!" Carrick said as he slid over to the spot where Jordan was holding the door.

The three huddled close to each other in the stairwell, could hear metal stars rattling off the walls and glass, and Jordan counting each one out loud.

Jordan had run out to the right and not left, knowing The Spider would expect him to go to the left side of the atrium. With his head low and covered by the backpack, he sprinted to the four-foot-high glass railing and slid feet first up against the glass. When he did, he could see The Spider duck into the hallway leading to The History Library.

"I guess he's got to run out of these soon, right?" said Sebastian, holding four metal stars in his hand.

After an unsettling several minutes of silence, Jordan came back to the stairwell and yelled under his breath, "Let's go! Follow me!"

The team quickly rose to their feet and followed closely behind Jordan.

"He ran around the atrium toward The History Library!" Jordan was high on adrenaline but talking low.

"I heard him talking to somebody. There's at least three of them." Jordan wasn't sure if he heard three or four men talking.

"What were they saying?" asked Carrick, still favoring his shoulder. The gauze was bloody, but the bleeding appeared to be under control.

"They were speaking in Mandarin. All I could make out was, 'It's done!'. I guess they got what they came for!" said Jordan.

"So, now what?" asked Sebastian, who was still amped up on adrenaline.

"They're trapped!" said Carrick. "This hallway is the only way out."

The four huddled closely at the mouth of the hundred-foot-long hallway that connected The History Library to The Grand Hall.

"Okay, but there are lots of rooms on each side of the hallway. They could be in any one of them," Kinzi looked frazzled.

"I saw which one they ran into." Jordan looked ready to pounce.

"Well, we can't just bust down the door. There's more than one of them, and they've got stars!" said Carrick. "We could wait them out."

"Wait them out?" Sebastian was perplexed. "That doesn't make any bloody sense. We could be here forever."

"No, we have to approach and draw them out," said Jordan, looking for a fight.

"Let's go, Spider! You're trapped!" Jordan yelled down the hall.

From the dimly lit hallway came a voice speaking in Mandarin that said, "Lái zhǎo wǒmen!"

"What the hell did he say?" Kinzi asked Jordan.

"He said, 'Come find us.' Man, I hate this guy!" Jordan shook his head. He just wanted the situation to play itself out, no matter the outcome.

"You speak Chinese?" Colt asked Jordan, wearing a look of surprise.

Spear ignored the question and said, "We're going in! Extend your batons!"

"Wait, what?!" asked Carrick.

"Let's go to the door and open it a crack and see how many there are in there." Jordan was antsy.

The other three had to psych themselves up. They all stood. Sebastian stretched, bending at the waist, and touching his toes. When he stood fully erect, he flicked his baton open. Kinzi, Jordan, and Carrick followed suit.

"Okay, they're in the third door down on the left. Sebastian, follow me down the right side of the hall, stay close to the wall. Kinzi, you follow behind Carrick, six feet apart," directed Jordan.

"Then what?" asked Carrick.

"If someone rushes out of that door, they'll see Sebastian and me first and engage. If that happens, Carrick, you knock the fucker into next week with that baton," said Jordan. "Kinzi, you have his back."

"Then?" asked Kinzi, looking skeptical.

"Then it's survival of the fittest," said Jordan.

"You've got to be kidding me!" Kinzi was beside herself. "That's not a plan!" she whispered loudly.

"Kinzi," said Carrick. "They don't have a plan either. They thought we were a week away. All but one of them is pissing their pants right now." Carrick tried to be reassuring.

"Then why'd they bring the Spider guy along with them?" she asked.

"In case his guys changed their mind," said Jordan. "His job is to kill anyone on his crew that doesn't follow orders."

"Jesus Christ!" whispered Kinzi.

"Let's just do it!" said Carrick.

Kinzi shook her head in agreement; she was now ready.

"When we get to the door, I'll pull it wide-open and get out of the way. They'll throw their stars if they have any left, thinking we're going to rush in," said Jordan.

"If they rush the door, the Spider will come out first. I'll handle him. You guys will then rush in and subdue the cyber guys," said Jordan, talking low.

"How do you know the men in that room with the Spider are just technicians?" asked Kinzi. "Maybe there's another killer in there with them."

"The Serpent told us who would be on that rocket," said Jordan. "Besides, we brought this killer with us!" Jordan looked toward Colt.

"Did we ever find out who the Serpent is?" asked Sebastian.

Jordan shook his head, "No."

"Man, this feels like a set-up! That's the same guy who gave you wrong intel about the bomb on the Comet." Sebastian Colt was leery, but like the others, he too was ready to go. He cracked his neck and wiggled his arms to loosen his shoulders. "Okay, I'm good. Let's go!"

"Okay, let's do this!" said Jordan under his breath.

The three Americans and one Brit made their way down the hall, two on the left and two on the right. Only baseboard lights lit the hallway, and the air was thick. Batons were drawn and extended; the four closed the fifty-foot distance slowly. Getting closer, Jordan made the 'Shhhh' gesture, putting his finger to his mouth.

As he crossed the hall and stood ready to grab the door handle, the four heard a faint beeping sound. They all stopped in their tracks to listen more closely.

"Do you hear that?" whispered Kinzi.

They all looked at each other with dread on their faces just before Carrick said, "Oh shit!"

Without further warning, a massive explosion rocked The History Library, blowing its massive double doors off of their hinges, launching them down the hallway toward the team. Along with the doors, mortar, platinum shards from the blown-out walls, and other stone materials from the exploding floor, came at the team with high velocity, striking each of them with enough force to knock them unconscious.

As the team lay on the floor, the door that shielded the Chinese opened partially, obstructed by debris. The Spider pushed it open fully, allowing the three engineers to egress the room. Dust and debris filled the air, and visibility was low, as many of the baseboard lights were covered with soot and powder. Stepping over the bodies and debris, the engineers, with their equipment, were able to escape down the hall en route to the Eclipse lander.

The Spider, however, remained. Standing over his prey, he smiled.

Chapter 32 – Checkmate

Location: Zenith. The Northwest Sector of The Triad. Amongst the rubble of The History Library – September 7, 2027 – 11:44 pm CST Earth time.

As the smoke cleared, The Spider stood at the hallway entrance leading to the now destroyed History Library. Lights flickered and surged throughout the structure, as any electricity that once flowed to The History Library was now redirected, by The Triad's Energy Conservation System, to other areas of The Northwest Sector. The ECS was working through internal computing conflicts, unable to reconcile why The History Library was not utilizing the energy directed to its cause.

While The Spider stood contemplating, he could hear the electricity being restored to the multiple elevator banks in The Grand Hall. Looking over his left, then right shoulder, multiple times.

Colonel Vadik Lei was not contemplating whether to leave or stay, but rather which of the four casualties, if not already dead, would be the first to die. He brushed the dust and debris off his black body glove undergarments, worn by all Taikonauts, then began down the hall. Lei came upon Kinzi first, still not moving, blood dripping from her right ear and mouth. Using his foot, he pushed her mid-section, looking for signs of life; he saw none.

Next, he saw Carrick, unsure whether it was Captain America or not, as he was covered in soot and debris. Moving a large piece of metal sheeting from the top of Carrick, he determined it to be the grandson of Erik Erickson. Based on his size and stature, he knew that Jordan Spear was a much larger man. He again used his foot, looking for signs of life, giving Carrick a shove. He didn't move. Lei's eyes then went to a bulge in Carrick's back waistband. Inspecting further, he found a black journal. Thinking that it might be important, he secured it in his back waistband.

As Lei's attention went toward the other men, he knew which one was CIA Officer Jordan Spear, as the other casualty in the heap of stone and metal appeared to be a black male. Before moving on to

Spear, The Spider noticed something about the black male. Bending over to inspect Colt's head more closely, he spotted the former MMA fighter's disfigured ears. Vadik Lei pursed his lips and tilted his head, nodding in respect. He knew that the man that lay dead or unconscious before him was a warrior. One who likely experienced many battles in his lifetime.

At that very instant, movement came from the direction of his mortal enemy and sometimes muse, Jordan Spear.

Spear moaned and groaned, spewing blood and soot from his mouth. Ragged, weary, and now coughing, Jordan shook his head in an effort to shake the dirt from his hair and face. Now on all fours, Jordan attempted to get to his feet when The Spider leaned in with his foot and pushed Jordan back to the ground.

"The mighty Captain America," he said in a monotone voice. The Spider was calm and calculated and very much looked forward to stretching out the final moments of Jordan Spear's life. He would take great pleasure in the process of killing the American.

Jordan, again on all fours, tried to stand. The Spider would help him up, grabbing a hand full of Jordan's hair and pulling him toward The Grand Hall.

Jordan, still incoherent and unsteady on his feet, wasn't exactly sure what was happening. Was it his friend Carrick Michaels pulling him from the rubble? After a few more steps, Jordan was now conscious of who was leading him by his hair; it was The Spider.

Jordan immediately tried to free himself, using both hands to wrestle Vadik Lei's hand from his head. Lei realized Jordan was now fully aware and, by his hair, tossed him several feet out into The Grand Hall. Jordan went spinning, not fully in control of his senses as his equilibrium was off due to a shattered eardrum. When landing on the stone-tiled floor, The Spider could see dust and soot particles flying off of Jordan's body.

The Grand Hall was dark, with only elevator bank lights, the stairwell door light, and baseboard lights illuminating the perimeter flooring of the massive Grand Hall.

Jordan coughed again and made his way to his feet. Spitting blood and wiping bloody snot and saliva from his chin, Jordan was fully aware that he and The Spider were about to fight to the death. Jordan could feel that several of his ribs were broken and that the ringing in his ear was likely due to a ruptured eardrum. When surveying the rest of his body, he determined that no other bones were likely broken, and though he was concussed and off-balance, he had a good chance of warding off a pending attack from the much smaller foe standing before him, some ten feet away.

"So, the mighty Captain America, huh? You look much bigger on television," said Vadik Lei, now tossing his remaining supply of metal stars and two knives to the ground, landing some fifteen feet away.

Jordan watched as the razor-sharp killing instruments landed. He would try to ensure that he remained between The Spider and the weapons as the fight progressed.

Lei then reached over his right shoulder, and with his right hand, drew his battle stick. It, too, was tossed to the side.

"So, why not just use your stars or knives to kill me quickly?" asked Jordan.

"No-no, my friend," Lei said while waving his finger in the air. "You are already injured, and I was hoping to fight you at full strength."

"Well, even at half strength, I can still kick your ass!" said Jordan, not believing his own words.

"So, the mighty Americans sent their very best, and look at all of you now. Dead, or about to be," said Lei with a wicked laugh.

"The mighty Captain America will die right here, in my arms, tonight," Lei smiled again, now stretching and flexing like a caged warrior would, just before facing off with his opponent.

Jordan shook out his arms, then palmed the back of his head with his left hand, cupping his chin with his right, and gave his neck an adjustment. The familiar sound of bursting fluid sacks could be heard, much like the sound of bubble wrap being popped.

"So, I'm Captain America, huh?" asked Jordan, now slowly circling to his opponent's right, forgetting the advice of SHA Militant, Kai

Chang. Chang had used sign language before his death to advise Jordan to attack The Spider from his left side.

"I guess that makes you Spiderman then, huh?"

Vadik Lei smiled and shook his head. "Funny man, superhero!" he waved his finger in the air again. "No, I've never been called that before." Lei had entered the circular dance with Jordan Spear, also circling to Spear's right.

"You know, our paths crossed years ago in London," said Vadik Lei.

"Ahh yes, I remember that night. You didn't stay long, though. I'm guessing you wanted nothing to do with me?" said Spear, keeping his eyes locked onto The Spider.

"You guessed wrong, Captain America," laughed Lei. "I had more important people to kill that day. I knew I would kill you eventually, though."

The two men continued to circle each other.

"The first time I saw you, I wanted to kill you," Lei paused, "movie star-looking American." The Spider hocked up some phlegm and spat it to the side, showing great disdain for both Jordan and his Western culture.

"You sure do talk a lot for a ruthless killer. Do you always exhibit your fear through words before killing someone?" Jordan taunted The Spider.

"No, actually, I say nothing, but killing you is different."

"How's that?" asked Jordan.

"It's like my final game of chess. I want to breathe it all in and savor my victory before I actually achieve it." Lei was enjoying the foreplay with his foe, much like a cat jabs at an alley rat before pouncing on it.

"Chess, huh?" said Jordan, remembering the confession of Erik Erickson just down the hall in The History Library.

"Yes, except all of your pawns are laying in the debris down that hall," Lei motioned with his head to Jordan's left.

Jordan glanced out of the corner of his eye, looking for signs of life down the blown-out hallway; he saw none.

"It would seem your King and Queen are both exposed, and your black Knight can't save you either."

"I see what you did there," said Jordan, "the whole Chess analogy. That's cute."

Jordan again remembered the conversation he'd had with his good friend Erik Erickson in The History Library. Erik told him about his good friend, named Kim Moiseyevich Weinstein. 'Weinstein,' Erik told him, 'spoke with both conviction and with great confidence. He was so convincing; most of the people he spoke to believed his every word and rarely questioned what he said. They were so taken with his confidence; they became convinced that what he was saying must be true. Many times, when at the end of a game of chess,' Erik said, 'he would pronounce checkmate, though he hadn't actually mated his opponent yet. He said it with such confidence that his opponent would almost always lay down their King in defeat and walk away. He would sometimes say it to me when we played, and many times my next move would checkmate him. The look on his face would be that of someone who was outsmarted and couldn't believe that I didn't concede.' Jordan recounted Erik's words and began to think that maybe The Spider wasn't as confident as he appeared to be.

Jordan then began to smile, "So, are you calling 'checkmate' before you actually have me mated?" asked Jordan, feeling more confident now.

"Much like you dying tonight, Officer Spear, the outcome of this match is not in question," said Lei. "Chess is a game that I enjoy very much. And the conclusion of this one, right here, right now, is 'yes,' you will be mated." Vadik Lei looked puzzled. "I'm not sure why it is that you wear that smile."

Jordan stopped his motion to Lei's right and instead began to circle to his left. Lei also reversed course and began to move to Jordan's left. He was confused as to why Jordan had changed his course; Jordan noticed the look in his eye.

"That look on your face right now, Spider," said Jordan. "I've seen it before. It's why I'm smiling now. Not because I'm enjoying the charade that you're putting on, but rather because I'm putting an end to it," said Jordan, borrowing the words of the greatest man he'd ever known, Dr. Erik Erickson.

At that instant, The Spider lunged and threw a right leg kick to Jordan's left rib cage. Jordan saw it coming, though, grabbed his leg, and threw a straight right hand catching Lei on the chin, dropping him. Jordan, feeling lucky, quickly back-peddled away from the always dangerous Spider.

"How you feeling, Spider? Is that blood I see?" taunted Jordan, without smiling.

Lei quickly snapped back up to his feet. His mouth now bleeding, he said, "The fight hasn't begun until I taste my own blood. Your blood, I will taste next!"

With cat-like quickness, The Spider ran and jumped off of the pillar near where Jordan was standing, vaulting himself airborne, while throwing a flying right kick that landed flush on the left-side of Jordan's head, knocking him to the ground.

Jordan collapsed in a heap to the ground. Still conscious, he rolled around in pain for a moment. Vadik Lei, admiring his work, backed off and let Jordan get back to his feet.

Jordan wiped his nose, which was now dripping profusely with blood. Though unsteady on his feet, he began circling to The Spider's left again.

Suddenly, Vadik Lei feinted a right-handed punch and instead used his left leg to sweep Jordan's right leg out from under him. Jordan's stance widened, dropping the level of his head down to that of Lei's. Lei seeing the opening, delivered a short right hand to Jordan's jaw, dropping him again.

Lei dropped back again, dancing left and right. He knew the fight would soon be over but enjoyed the pain he was inflicting on Captain America.

Jordan again rose to his feet and waved on the tenacious Spider, though he was clearly hurting, as his face was covered in blood. Vadik Lei obliged him by running straight at him and delivering a flying knee that connected with Jordan's sternum. Jordan absorbed the blow and bear-hugged The Spider, then body-slammed him onto the hard floor. The Spider moaned as he rose to his feet. Jordan fell back to a safe distance.

After both men regained their composure, both slowly closed the distance. Now standing just feet away, Jordan remembered what Kai Chang told him, 'attack The Spider's left side.' Jordan stepped forward and leaned into The Spider's left side, delivering a crippling body blow that crumpled Vadik Lei.

Lei staggered backward and was pissed, holding his side momentarily. Jordan then came in for another body-blow attempt but was intercepted by Lei, who completed a spinning back fist that knocked the badly wounded Spear to his knees.

Jordan, badly hurt, slowly rose to his feet and lunged with a right hook that missed wildly, exposing his back to The Spider as his torso spun. Seeing Jordan's back exposed, The Spider latched onto the much bigger man and performed a rear-naked choke.

Jordan, still standing, flailed wildly, trying to reach back and peel The Spider off of him; it was to no avail. The spider had Spear in a guillotine, with both legs wrapped tightly around Jordan's waist. With his breathing now cut off, Jordan dropped to his knees, searching for his release. Lei rolled himself onto his back, positioning Jordan on top of him, and continued to choke out the bigger man.

Just before Jordan lost consciousness, The Spider let go suddenly. Jordan, gasping to get air into his lungs, wasn't sure what had happened. As he rolled around on the floor, looking to avoid The Spider's next assault, he saw two men rolling around on the ground through the darkness.

It was Sebastian Colt, the black knight, who was bouncing The Spider off of the stone floor like a ragdoll. Jordan's eyes cleared, and he could see Colt entering into a rear-naked choke on Vadik Lei. Colt now had a full-body triangle on The Spider, who was now being choked out himself.

The Spider lost consciousness within seconds, and Colt rolled his limp body off of him onto the hard floor.

Sebastian Colt knelt by Jordan's side to render aid. Jordan was alive but beat up pretty badly.

"You okay, man?" Sebastian asked of Jordan.

"I'm okay. Thanks!" Jordan looked into Sebastian's eyes. "Kinzi? Carrick?" Jordan wondered aloud if the others were okay.

"They're alive!" said Colt.

Jordan looked relieved as Colt helped him to his feet. "Where is he?" Colt motioned to Vadik Lei's position, some twenty feet away.

Jordan looked over in Lei's direction and saw him moving around on the ground, beginning to regain consciousness. Relying on pure adrenaline, he ran over to Lei, who was now on one knee, grabbed him by the collar, and raised him into the air. Jordan steadied himself and mustered what final strength he had left, raised The Spider over his head, and began running toward the railing, just fifteen feet away.

"Jordan! No!" screamed Sebastian Colt, running toward the two men.

Before Colt could stop Jordan, Spear launched The Spider over the railing, into the black abyss, twelve stories below. As The Spider fell, Jordan could be heard saying, "That's Checkmate Mother-fucker!"

The Spider made no sound as he plunged to his death, but Jordan watched him fall into the blackness, and just seconds later, both he and Colt heard the terrible splat of human flesh striking the ground at terminal velocity.

Colt got to the railing just as the sound of certain death echoed around The Great Hall's fifteen stories.

Colt looked nauseous, while Jordan turned and fell onto his backside, with his back up against the four-foot glass railing, searching for air to breathe.

Colt joined him against the railing and said, "What was all that about? That 'Checkmate' thing?"

Jordan looked over to him and said, "From now on," he paused, "you're the Black Knight."

Sebastian shook his head, thinking Jordan was concussed from the explosion and fight with The Spider and didn't know what he was saying.

Colt then rose to his feet and said, "Come on, man!" He extended his right hand to Jordan, who obliged him. Sebastian pulled him up, and the two men walked toward the blown-out hallway. Turning the corner, they witnessed Kinzi rendering aid to Carrick.

Kinzi saw the men walking toward her; Jordan's arm was over Colt's shoulder as Sebastian helped his friend. Kinzi smiled though she could see Jordan was hurt. She was relieved that all of them survived the blast, and The Spider.

Chapter 33 – Barrack 5

Location: The Triad, Surface-Level 1 – Thirty Minutes Later

Nervously looking over their shoulders, the Chinese engineers finished suiting up and made their way to the Temperature Regulation Chamber. They feared the Americans would intercept them before they could escape to the Eclipse II landing module.

Location: Surface-Level 3. The blown-out hallway.

In a side office down the long hall leading to what was left of The History Library, Kinzi administered aid to her friends.

With Jordan lying on a nearby table, recuperating from his injuries, Kinzi treated Carrick, who suffered from multiple head, neck, and shoulder injuries.

"Carrick, you saved my life," said Kinzi. "You were between me and the blast. I'm not sure that I would've survived."

"I survived. You would have, too," Carrick said, as Kinzi wrapped his head in gauze.

"What's left of The History Library?" Worry blanketed Carrick's face.

"Nobody's been down there yet, but I'm sure it's completely destroyed." Kinzi knew how important The History Library was to Carrick, and how it helped to forge the relationship between him and Erik.

"The Spider's dead, I guess?" asked Carrick.

Kinzi nodded, "Yes, Jordan killed him, but he took an awful beating." They both looked over in his direction.

"Is he gonna be okay?" Carrick looked back at Kinzi.

"Yes, mostly facial lacerations and a few broken ribs. He looks worse than he feels. He'll be okay, but he's going to be sore for weeks," said Kinzi.

"Oh shit, the engineers?" Carrick sat up too quickly, showing concern for the whereabouts of the stolen data. When sitting up, he winced in pain, clutching his side.

"Carrick, you're going to pull out the stitches that I just gave you," Kinzi wore a look of concern. "Sebastian's out looking for them now."

"Kinz, if they escape...!" Carrick said before being cut off.

"Carrick, Jordan planted The Chameleon, remember?"

"Oh, yeah." Carrick was also concussed and not thinking straight.

Fifteen minutes later, Sebastian Colt walked through the door. "They're gone!" he announced.

"Dammit!" said Jordan, now sitting up.

"Listen, we need to get to the outer observatory!" Carrick sat up.

"Why?" asked Kinzi.

"We need to make sure the Chinese don't escape," Carrick was determined. "Help me up!"

Jordan and Sebastian rallied to Carrick's side and helped him to his feet.

"Kinzi, where's the walkie?" asked Jordan.

"It got damaged in the blast," she said. "It doesn't work."

"Oh shit!" Carrick patted his back pockets. "Erik's journal? Where is it?"

"It's got to be in the rubble. We'll find it!" said Sebastian.

They all agreed. Exiting the room, they did a cursory search in the rubble on their way to the outer observatory deck. The Outer Observatory was on Surface-Level 5 and faced the Northeastern sky. From there, the team would be able to see the Eclipse Lander jettison skyward.

After several minutes of searching for the journal, Carrick said, "We'll come back for it later. Right now, though, we need to get upstairs."

Now in The Grand Hall, Carrick noticed the green elevator lights illuminated on each elevator door panel, circling the entire atrium. Carrick found that odd, as many of the elevators no longer worked.

Moments after Kinzi had pushed the 'Up' button on the elevator nearest to the team, the door opened, and the team stepped forward to enter the elevator.

"Stop!" Carrick yelled, holding his arm out to block the others from entering. The other three didn't understand why. They looked at each other with confusion.

At that instant, the lights inside the elevator and around the perimeter of The Grand Hall flickered, startling the team.

"What's going on?" asked Sebastian with a quizzical look on his face.

"The ECS is acting up. It's confused," said Carrick.

A second later, the lights went off, and the elevator banks powered down. The team just stood there in the dark.

"Jesus Christ! What just happened?" asked Jordan, barely unable to make out the faces of his friends.

Click. Kinzi turned on the flashlight. A second later, the stairwell lights and outer door sign lights re-illuminated to the team's relief.

Kinzi handed Carrick the flashlight, and he said, "You know, if we'd gotten on that elevator thirty seconds earlier, we'd all be stuck there with nuclear bombs getting ready to detonate at the other two sectors," said Carrick.

The team shook their heads at the thought of it. They would've likely all died in there.

"Okay, let's move!" said Carrick.

With Carrick leading the way, the team moved as fast as their injuries would allow. They entered the stairwell and headed up. As their tired legs scaled the stairs, the lights overhead flickered, evoking fear and consternation in those following Carrick, but not him. Carrick was home, and he knew every stair as if they were words in the story of his life.

Seconds later, they pushed through the door on Surface-Level 5, the top level of The Triad. Back in The Grand Hall, the team bent over at the waist, clutching their knees in exhaustion. They were tired and hurt and needed to rest, but Carrick pressed on. Ahead of the group now, he rounded the corner and faced another one-hundred-foot hallway that led to the observatory.

Kinzi asked Jordan if he was okay, and he nodded in the affirmative, "I'm good!"

Sebastian wrapped his right arm around Jordan's waist and pulled Jordan's left arm up over his shoulder. "Let's go, big man," said Sebastian, helping Jordan down the hall.

As they turned the corner, they could barely make out Carrick entering a door at the end of the hall. The tiny lights running along the baseboard, the length of the hallway, were flickering, enabling the team to see their pathway.

"That's it!" said Kinzi, having been there once with Carrick when Jordan was interrogating Erik in The History Library more than four years earlier.

Moments later, the three entered the Outer Observatory, joining Carrick. They opened the door and witnessed their friend just staring out of the massive, heat-shielded, triple-paned glass façade.

Jordan and Sebastian joined Carrick near the window.

"God, it's hot as hell in here!" proclaimed Sebastian. All four in the group were covered in sweat and dried blood.

Jordan, feeling weary, took a seat in the over-sized command chair. Behind the men, Kinzi surveyed the master console on the back wall of the observatory. Though it was dark, she saw empty foil pill-packets opened and empty. She wondered what they were doing there. She didn't remember seeing them there from her first and only other visit to the observatory. Sliding her finger through the white powder residue on the console, she licked the tip of her finger and determined it to be a pain-killing narcotic, similar to Oxycodone on Earth.

Her attention went to Zenith's black sky when Carrick's words rang out, "Look! Do you guys see that?" Carrick pointed out the massive window to their left, or due North.

Jordan shot out of his chair, wincing when doing so, while Sebastian and Kinzi pressed their faces against the glass next to Carrick. The group was able to make out the exterior lights of the Chinese Eclipse landing module.

Staring for a moment, Jordan said, "Well, they're not gone yet!"

"Son of a bitch," said Sebastian. "They weren't that far ahead of me."

"They're performing pre-launch activities right now," guessed Kinzi.

"Yep," said Jordan.

Carrick was quiet. The fate of the world was in the hands of The Chameleon, magnetically attached to the aft portion of the craft.

"I wonder if they found the device?" said Kinzi. "The footprints?" she said as she looked over at Jordan.

"It won't matter," responded Jordan. "The Chameleon would've hacked their computer by now."

"But they won't lift off if they see your footprints!" thought Kinzi aloud.

"They will if they think we're right behind them," said Sebastian.

Seconds later, the speculation ended. The four in the observatory could see the orange and blue glow of the lander's rocket boosters. The surface was so black and non-reflective, the glow from the lander was almost blinding to the group, like staring at a nearby star.

The group watched with mixed feelings; Sebastian knew the horror that would soon befall the Chinese Taikonauts, as his experience of the Saturn Six explosion was still fresh in his memory. Kinzi, being a medical doctor, knew precisely what physiological reaction the Chinese crew would experience when falling at terminal velocity back to the surface of Zenith, impacting it at nearly 300 mph. She shuddered her eyes for a moment and contemplated the terror the Chinese crew would experience.

Suddenly, the Chinese craft jettisoned skyward, its light was brilliant, but the team couldn't look away. They squinted while holding their breath, counting down the seconds until they'd have to squint no more.

After only eight seconds, the flames went out, and the team could no longer see the Chinese craft.

"Where is it!" Kinzi was frantic. Tears began to well up in her eyes.

No one answered her. They all now understood that their actions would kill at least four Taikonauts. With the team desperately searching the sky for the doomed craft, a massive explosion occurred just miles from where they watched in horror. There were no celebrations, no high fives, and no words.

Sebastian and Kinzi had tears in their eyes, while Carrick's were filled with determination. Without saying anything, Carrick walked out the door with Jordan in tow. Kinzi and Sebastian collected themselves and followed the two men. After Sebastian walked out the door, Kinzi stopped and took one last look at the ball of fire raging on the bottomless black pit that was the surface of Black Earth. She wiped her last tear for the Chinese and then raced to join the men.

"Where to?" asked Jordan.

"We need to find that Journal, and fast!" said Carrick. "My guess is that we have less than twenty hours to lift off, or none of us are going home."

Kinzi and Sebastian caught up, and Colt asked, "What's the plan?"

"We need to find the journal and get to The Southwest Sector as fast as we can," urged Carrick.

Carrick walked faster than he should have been able to, considering his injuries. Kinzi kept her eye on him, making sure he didn't pass out from blood loss and exhaustion.

Back in the bombed-out hallway, the four sifted through the debris.

"It's not here!" yelled Carrick.

"It's got to be!" said Kinzi, as she frantically sifted through the rubble.

After ten more minutes of searching, they'd all concluded that the journal wasn't where it should be, somewhere between where Carrick had been standing and back toward The Grand Hall.

"It's simple physics! It has to be in this area," offered Sebastian.

Jordan spoke up, "I think I know where it is." In a monotone voice he added, "Follow me."

He walked the group out into The Grand Hall and over to the four-foot glass railing that wrapped around the circular atrium.

"Where! Where is it?" Carrick yelled, directing his emotions toward Jordan.

"Kinzi, give me the flashlight."

She handed it to Jordan. Jordan grabbed the flashlight and pointed it down into the black abyss that was the twelve-story drop into the hole that The Spider was thrown into.

They all looked over the railing in confusion until Sebastian realized what Jordan was trying to communicate to the group.

"The Spider's down there," said Sebastian. "Jordan put him there, and he has the journal."

"Sorry guys, he had to die," Jordan paused, "and so he did."

"Okay, okay! Here's the plan." Carrick was pragmatic. "I'm going down there, and I'll find the journal." Carrick quickly removed emotion from the equation. He was a problem-solver, and he'd solve this one.

Kinzi shook her head, no. "Carrick, you might make it down there with the help of gravity, but it's that very gravity that will certainly prevent you from making it back up. That's thirteen levels down and ten back up again! You'll never make it!"

"He will if I go with him," Sebastian Colt spoke up. "Listen, I'm uninjured and feeling good."

"You just said your quads were on fire two hours ago!" said Kinzi.

"It doesn't matter, Carrick and I are going, and we're going now." Sebastian was resolute.

Carrick interjected, "The clock is ticking, and if you thought The History Library explosion was big..." Carrick gestured with his eyes, opening them wide and nodding his head.

"Let's go!" said Sebastian.

"Let's all go down to Surface-Level 1. I have a plan!" said Carrick.

Minutes later, on Surface-Level 1, the crew walked out into The Grand Hall.

"Okay," said Carrick, "this is it! Kinzi, you, and Jordan will go to the storage closet, just down the hall where we left our EMUs. Once there, you'll suit up and restore Comms to the Neptune, The Leviathan, and Houston," instructed Carrick.

"Houston? What about Interlink..., the Chinese?" Kinzi cautioned Carrick.

"It doesn't matter! The Chinese can do nothing now!" said Jordan.

"That's right!" agreed Carrick. "Tell them what's going on!" he looked her straight in the eye.

"Okay, go!" encouraged Jordan. "If you're not back here in an hour, I'm coming for you."

"Got It! Let's go, Colt!" Carrick ran off.

The two men descended the stairs, making good time. However, when they got to Sub-Level 7, Carrick inexplicably walked out the stairwell door into The Grand Hall. Sebastian looked perplexed.

Following Carrick, he said, "Where are you going?! He's at the bottom!"

"I have to do something first. Stay here in the dark or follow me, your choice!"

Sebastian threw his hands up and just followed Carrick. After five minutes of walking, with Carrick saying nothing, the two men came upon a door with a sign hanging above it.

"Barrack 5," said Sebastian. "I'll be damned!" he shook his head and smiled.

"I need you to wait out here," said Carrick.

"Ah, okay..." Sebastian seemed a little nervous.

"I'll just be a minute."

"Roger that!" said Sebastian.

Carrick walked through the door into the hallowed ground. The barrack where he and Erik had their late-night talks. It was as if he'd never left. Time had suddenly frozen for him, and he was glad it did.

He remembered kicking Erik's bunk once, waking the old man, and Erik sleepily saying, "Mind your foot, young man, unless you want to lose it." Carrick laughed out loud.

Then, he remembered Erik barging through the door with a birthday present. He laughed again. The diamond light fixture had provided financial stability for him and Lola, and now his twins.

He marveled at Erik's subtle genius, the way he taught people about life and themselves. The humble teacher of truth, of life, of love, and of sacrifice.

At that moment, Carrick dropped to his knees at the side of Erik's old bunk and just cried into the pillow where Erik once laid his head. He cried, and he screamed into that pillow. He cried for his past, his present, and his now certain future.

Moments later, he rose to his feet, then made his way into the shower area. There, he walked over to the sink where Erik would wash his face in the morning. Looking in the mirror, he splashed some water onto his face in an effort to wipe the blood away. With only the light from the flashlight, he could see that his face was ravaged. Ravaged by his fatherless childhood, by time, by distance, and now by devastation. He saw the cuts on his face, cuts so deep it was as if each mile back to Zenith was a razor that put them there. It was time to go. It was time to save humanity...again.

Back in the dark hall, Carrick emerged from Barrack 5. "Let's go!" he kicked Sebastian Colt, who was resting on the ground.

"Yes, sir!" Colt shot to his feet.

Walking back toward the stairwell, Sebastian asked Carrick, "How are you feeling?"

"Never better!" said Carrick.

Sebastian was surprised by the 'get up' in Carrick's step.

"Carrick, is it getting hotter in here, or is it just me?" Sebastian wiped the sweat from his forehead.

Carrick didn't answer. He just kept on walking, a little faster now.

Now at the stairwell, Carrick passed it up. Colt got nervous again, wondering what in the hell was going on, thinking that Carrick was losing his mind.

"Carrick, where are...?" he said before Carrick cut him off.

"Just follow me, Colt!"

After another two minutes, hallways, and turns, the two arrived at the Sub-Level 7 Survival Storage Unit.

Walking in, Carrick went to flip on the light switch, forgetting that the lights hadn't worked in years.

Carrick knew exactly what to look for and where. Shining his light toward the back of the unit, he navigated the dark narrow room.

"What is this place?" asked Sebastian.

"This is where you go...," Carrick paused for a moment before finishing, "when it's time to die."

"What in the hell does that mean?" Sebastian looked nervous.

"It means we're dying and need to get a few things if we plan on getting back up to Surface-Level 1."

Sebastian Colt shook his head, he thought Carrick's concussion affected his train of thought, but he trusted him strangely.

Carrick opened a trunk, and in it was an assortment of items: uniforms, helmets, safety suits, equipment, and oxygen tanks.

"This is our life support system when everything in The Triad just stops. The Triad is only meant to live for so long. For years, the ECS has systematically been shutting down The Triad in preparation for the end of its usefulness." Carrick looked at Sebastian and said, "That end is now upon us, my friend. The Triad is going dark, and it's getting hot! The Neptune lander needs to lift-off in less than 16 hours, or everyone dies." Carrick guessed the time left by approximating how long ago the Chinese began their day and how much time since the team witnessed the Chinese lander parked in front of The Triad. Time was ticking, and Carrick didn't want his friends to die on Black Earth.

Sebastian Colt swallowed hard.

"Here, put this on." Carrick handed him what looked like to Colt, to be flimsy silver overalls.

"Heat suit?" asked Sebastian.

Carrick asked, "Do you know what heat does to the human body?"

"Yes, I do, actually. I'm a biologist," Sebastian shook his head.

"Yes, of course, you are!" smiled Carrick. His grandfather was a biologist, too.

"Here. Put this on and then follow me." He handed Sebastian a helmet and a small oxygen tank.

"Follow me!" Sebastian noticed Carrick grab some extra headlamps and a small metal case on the way out of the narrow room. He chose not to ask what was inside the box.

The two were now outfitted in suits that would shield them from the rising heat and provide them with much-needed oxygen. If they were to climb the ten stories back to the surface, their muscles would need the pure oxygen to do so.

Now at Sub-Level 10, the two exited the stairwell and saw a horrific sight. The Spider was laying in the center of the Atrium, and blood was splattered everywhere. Vadik Lei's head was crushed from the force of impact, and he was almost unrecognizable.

Sabastian ripped off his facemask and vomited onto the floor at his feet. However, Carrick took a deep breath, walked up to the dead SHA Militant, lifted his black body glove shirt, and revealed the black Journal that Erik had left for him. It was tucked into the waistband of The Spider's spandex pants.

With Journal now in hand, Carrick breezed by Sebastian Colt on his way to the stairwell.

Sebastian quickly pulled himself together, donned his mask, and quickly followed Carrick into the stairwell.

Carrick stopped, turned, and said, "We slowly walk up these stairs, taking deep breaths even if we don't need to. Get as much oxygen into your bloodstream as possible and don't exert any extra energy. We walk, not run. Do you understand?"

"Yes, I got it."

Location: The Triad. Surface Level 1.

Kinzi and Jordan were now suited up with their Comms restored.

"Surface crew to Houston, do you copy?!" Kinzi was out of breath.

Those in Houston, The Leviathan, and the Neptune Lander were relieved to hear Kinzi's voice after nearly four hours of no contact. Everyone worried about the four inside The Triad.

"Kinzi, it's Mars! We read you loud and clear! What is the condition of you and the others?"

"We're banged up, but we're okay." Kinzi exhaled heavily.

"Kinzi, what happened in there?" asked Mars. "The Walker Trace satellite laser's detected a tremor around The Northwest Sector some two hours ago."

"The Spider's dead. Carrick and Jordan are hurt, with multiple contusions and fractures, but they'll be okay."

"The Chinese lander, it crashed. They're all dead! The data was likely destroyed," reported Kinzi.

"I know, Jin Ho informed us," said Mars. "The fireball could be seen from space by The Leviathan after Jin reported it to them. We're all sick about it, Kinzi." Mars had great empathy for her and the Chinese crew. Both Kinzi and Mars mentioned nothing about The Chameleon during their transmissions. They were careful, just in case the Chinese were monitoring their chatter.

The Chinese knew nothing of the device being planted on the Chinese Eclipse II, nor would they ever. They would only suspect that their craft simply failed to escape Black Earth's gravity.

The Chinese Eclipse spaceship was now headed back to Earth. They would return with four fewer Taikonauts and one less Spider.

"Kinzi, what's the plan?" asked Mars.

Talking in code, Kinzi said. "We have to head south and collect our gear, then get back to the Neptune Lander."

"Roger that!" said Mars.

"Jin, get back to the lander and wait for our signal. When I tell you to, begin the pre-launch checklist," ordered Kinzi.

"Roger Kinzi. I'm already here. After the explosion, I took shelter from the falling debris."

'Gear' was code for the data upload from The History Library, and 'South' was code for The Southwest Sector. This told Mars, the orbiting team, and Jin Ho back at the lander, that The History Library in The Northwest Sector was destroyed, and the team would have to make the perilous trek to The Southwest Sector.

Chapter 34 – The Sacrifice

Location: Outskirts of Beijing, China. Special Operations Command Center, Sector 3, Room 223 – September 8, 2027 – 2:14 pm, Beijing local time – 2:14 am CST, Houston local time.

"Sir, they said they're heading south," said a Special Ops Communications Specialist for the Ministry of State Security.

"What does that mean?" asked Minister Li Kenong.

"That's likely code for one of the two southern sectors."

"So, that means The Northwest Sector is history? Hmm." Kenong nodded his head. "The Spider did his job after all! And died doing it apparently," said Kenong. "Imbecile! I never liked him."

Those around Kenong nodded in agreement. They understood the feeling as they all loathed their superior, the Minister of State Security.

"So, our landing craft wasn't up to the test. Our boys escaped with the upload, just to die on that black desert! What a waste!" Li Kenong was dismissive. "There is incompetence at CNSA!"

While Li Kenong portrayed a man in control, blaming others for his own failures, he knew very well that he would likely be killed for this miscarriage. Success for China meant world domination. Failure meant sanctions at the very best, a war with the United States, at worst. After all, they did bring down an American rocket with an international crew on board.

His nervous smile said it all. Kenong was certain that his government would make his death look like a suicide. His wife and children would be awarded his retirement benefits and a small, one-time cash award from the Ministry of State Security. Kenong, however, didn't plan on dying like the insects from the Strategic Huyou Agency. He would escape the country immediately. Using his connections abroad, he would execute his master plan in the coming days.

Location: Black Earth – One hour later.

Now at Surface Level 1, Carrick and Sebastian exited the stairwell and collapsed onto the floor from exhaustion. Jordan and Kinzi were nearby and rushed to their aid, offering protein water and cold packs from Kinzi's medical Survival Pack.

The Triad was completely dark now, and the temperature was rising fast. On Jordan's EMU, the armband computer showed a temperature of 101° and climbing three degrees since he last checked thirty minutes prior.

Jordan and Kinzi assisted Sebastian and Carrick in putting on their EMUs. The cooling undergarments would immediately relieve Colt and Michaels, helping lower their body temperature in quick fashion. Now, with access to more supplies, Kinzi injected the two men with an antibiotic and gave them painkillers to ingest orally. After each man consumed a liter of water, Kinzi administered vitamin C onto each of their tongues using a plastic syringe.

Now ready to move, Carrick walked everyone through the plan. Since Comms were restored, the team orbiting overhead, and Jin Ho Mae back at the Neptune Lander, were able to listen in. Comms were again cut off to Houston so that the team could speak freely.

"Okay, we're going to walk out the back of The Triad and utilize the Neptune Rover that we dropped onto the launchpad during our descent," Carrick explained. "We'll drive to the interior entrance of The Southwest Sector and make our way to The History Library."

Carrick looked over the Journal and said, "From there, it seems pretty straightforward. Erik wrote that The Tabrikon can be removed without tools or power."

"What's a Tabrikon?" Kinzi looked puzzled, as did the others.

"It must be the hard-drive, I'm guessing," reasoned Carrick.

"How big and how heavy it is, is what matters?" said Jordan. "Carrick, what's the plan if that thing is six foot long and weighs 200 lbs.?"

"First things first, I guess," Carrick shrugged. "Let's just find it first, then we'll figure it out."

The group was now suited up in their EMUs, which included 50% more oxygen than the EMUs from previous missions to Black Earth. That meant twelve hours of breathable air, minus the hour-plus already spent on the surface. Though exhausted, they trudged on.

Following Carrick, they made their way to the interior side Temperature Regulation Chamber of The Northwest Sector. Carrick recited the familiar code into the touchpad without keys. 12121965, and the panel said, "Code Accepted, Carrick."

"Well, that was awesome!" Sebastian Colt was impressed. "How did it know your name?" he asked Carrick.

"It read my mind," smiled Carrick, giving Sebastian a wink.

Inside of his helmet, Colt's jaw dropped in amazement.

After several minutes of temperature regulation, the team exited the southwest side of the sector and was now staring at the interior area of the triangular megaplex, an area 4.5 square miles in size.

"Activate your HUD, everyone!" instructed Kinzi.

As the team walked, everyone, except for Carrick, was taken by the vastness of the area. They were also surprised by their ability to see the launchpad and the three sectors' interior walls, and the two-mile-long connecting walls that housed the monorail system.

"Jesus! It's huge! I can see the launchpad without my HUD on!" Sebastian was amazed.

"If you guys kill your HUD and look closely, you can not only see the launchpad but looking a little further, you can make out the inner portions of The Southwest and Southeast Sectors." Carrick was now giving a tour of The Triad, just as Erik gave him years earlier.

"My God, you're right. I can see both corners," said Kinzi. "The launchpad is massive! How is it possible that I'm able to see anything out there with all of that black carbon covering everything?" Under her helmet, Kinzi wore a look of astonishment.

Carrick explained, "The inner and outer observatories of all sectors, along with the launchpad, needed to remain clean of the black particles. So they have an electromagnetic shield that repels the ferromagnetic elements in the carbon soot. The reaction keeps those surfaces clear of the black material. It won't be long before it all goes black, though. The ECS is shutting down power to the shield as we speak."

"Okay, enough history! We need to get to work and find the rover!" Carrick began walking toward the launchpad.

"Do you guys see the drogue chutes anywhere?" asked Kinzi, who was unable to see the chutes or their rope lines.

"I can't see them!" said Jordan, walking in the opposite direction as Kinzi.

The team was now on The Northwest Sector side of the massive launchpad and still couldn't see where the rover had landed. Carrick was surprised because he was confident that he nailed the landing.

"Shit!" said Carrick. "Look over there!" He was looking in the general direction of the western wall, connecting The Northwest and Southwest Sectors.

"Where?" chorused the others as they all looked at Carrick and then toward the direction he was facing.

"I don't see anything," said Kinzi. "Where are you looking?" she asked Carrick.

The others were looking at ground level when Carrick said, "Look up."

Carrick witnessed their helmets move up to look toward the top of the western wall connecting sectors. The wall was nearly one-hundred feet tall.

"Look at the rope line dangling from the wall," he said while pointing.

The rover had crashed on top of the western wall, between The Northwest and Southwest Sectors.

"Dammit!" exclaimed Jordan. "Now what?"

"We walk it!" said Sebastian.

"No, we don't!" Carrick had hope. "Activate your HUD and look to the left of where we exited."

The team spotted a familiar shape but wasn't exactly sure what it was.

"Is that what I think it is?" Jordan sounded excited.

"It's The Northwest Sector's shuttle rover!" Carrick smiled as his memories took him back to Erik and their visit to the launchpad. He missed his grandfather, and he missed his friend.

As the team got closer, the shape was unmistakable. It was the rover.

"That's gonna save us a lot of energy and oxygen, guys!" As the only doctor in the group, Kinzi understood how important that was. The group members were injured and exhausted. While adrenaline might get them across the two-plus mile, 800° black expanse, they would have had to walk back the same way. Kinzi knew they would never make it. Now, she hoped the rover still worked.

Now at the rover, the four of them began to brush the thin black layer of soot off the seats and dashboard control.

"You think it still works?" asked Kinzi.

"I have no doubt," said Carrick, happy to be sitting in the rover once again.

Carrick took a moment to jog his memory, then reached for a black screen that illuminated with his touch.

"It's ready! Get in," Carrick directed the team.

Jordan and Kinzi stepped up on the rover and positioned themselves in the second of three rows, while Sebastian joined Carrick in the front.

"This thing is huge compared to ours," said Jordan, as he turned to inspect the third row.

The black screen illuminated in several colors, with the battery power meter lit up in brilliant green. The battery life was at around fifty percent, and Carrick was confident it would carry the four of them the four-plus mile roundtrip.

Carrick remembered that the accelerator was on the steering wheel's back right, while the brake was on the back left.

Gripping the wheel at 9 and 3, Carrick squeezed with his right hand, and off they went. The rover was three times faster than the NASA-made vehicle, traveling at a robust 12mph.

At twelve miles per hour, the one-way trip would take ten minutes to complete.

Now at The Southwest Sector's interior entrance, Carrick referenced his journal and confirmed what he already knew. The code to get in was 02272007. Carrick dismounted the rover, walked over to where he'd suspected the screen was, and wiped away the fine black powder.

"There you are!" Carrick celebrated under his breath as the remainder of the team dismounted the rover, too.

Carrick tapped the right side of his helmet, turning off the HUD, stared directly into the screen, and recited the code. *02272007,* he thought to himself.

After completing the mental command, he heard the panel's computer say, "Code Accepted, Carrick." He turned back to look at the others, eyebrows raised, smiled, and said, "We're in!"

Colt said, "Man, that shit never gets old! It's amazing!"

"I love you, Erik," Kinzi whispered under her breath, thinking what a hero he was, not only in life but in death, too.

The four walked into the chamber, and the outer door closed. The Temperature Regulation Chamber was faintly lit up by red lights that graced the base of the walls, where they met both the ceiling and the floors. The red glow was an eerie sight for the exhausted team that had experienced so much dread in just the last ten hours. They were tired, but the end of their journey seemed to be close at hand.

After only seconds, the inner door opened to the surprise of all. The temperature regulation process usually took several minutes. Once the door was opened, the team noticed that the place was completely dark. Each member of the team was caught off guard, and apprehension quickly filled the air.

Carrick took the first step forward, but the others all hesitated. After stepping into the corridor, Carrick checked his Honeywell armband computer, looking for air quality readouts. His readings suggested only minute traces of oxygen, with overwhelming traces of carbon dioxide and methane. Temperature readings indicated that The Southwest Sector was a staggering 680°. Everyone now understood why the temperature regulation process took only seconds.

Carrick turned and said, "Looks like we're keeping our helmets on." Adding, "Are you guys planning on coming in, or not?"

The others stepped forward with Kinzi, saying, "Lead the way."

"You guys be careful in there," said Mission Commander Jack White.

"Roger that," replied Kinzi.

The group moved slowly down the hallway, nervous with Carrick's pace, helmet lamps lighting their paths.

While Carrick seemed to know exactly where he was going, The Southwest Sector was completely dark and terrifyingly absent of life. The sector had been abandoned more than one hundred years ago, and no one had stepped foot in it since.

To Kinzi, it felt like she was a sub-mariner on a sub that had lost all power and was sinking to the bottom of the ocean, fast. The deeper they went into the dormant structure, the closer they were to smashing into the ocean's black bottom.

Nerves were fragile for Sebastian, too. He was reminded of when he was five years old and accidentally locked himself inside the trunk of the family car on a hot day. He and his mother had just unloaded groceries, and Sebastian was asked to close the trunk. Too small to reach the raised trunk, he climbed in and pulled it down while still inside. It took nearly thirty minutes for his family to realize what had happened. After the incident, Sebastian was paralyzed by fear. He suffered from claustrophobia for years until he finally conquered it in his late teens. Now though, Sebastian Colt was starting to feel claustrophobic again.

For Jordan Spear, he looked the part of a warrior, showing no fear as he walked just over Carrick's left shoulder. While under his protective suit, however, he was relieving himself into his NASA-issued diaper.

Now in The Grand Hall, Carrick turned left, leading the team to a stairwell door. The group climbed the stairs to Surface-Level 3 and exited back into The Grand Hall.

"God, this looks familiar," said Sebastian. "I mean, it's the exact same floorplan."

Carrick spoke up, "All three sectors have identical floorplans. You guys don't need to worry about me getting us lost in here.

Now walking down the one-hundred-foot-long hallway, approaching its doors at the end, Carrick started to feel the effects of PTSD, almost seeing the exploding double doors of The History Library coming his way. He fought the urge to duck the oncoming debris, not wanting the others to know what terror he was experiencing.

Now in The History Library, Carrick was melancholy, remembering the thousands of hours he'd spent with his best friend and grandfather.

Sebastian spoke up and said, "Where're all the books?"

Carrick laughed and said, "No books, my friend!" repeating Erik's words to him when he'd asked the same silly question.

Sebastian looked all around him. It was a sea of computer stations and monitors, everywhere the eye could see, or at least as far as the helmet lamps could illuminate.

"So, how many....? Sebastian began to ask a question when he was quickly cut off by Carrick.

"Seven hundred and ninety-eight."

"Wow!" mouthed Sebastian, shaking his head inside of his helmet.

Jordan looked over to a table they'd passed and was reminded of Erik Erickson's confession.

Now, at the back of the massive library, Kinzi stepped up onto the 4D holographic image island. It was ten feet in diameter and one foot high, just like the one in The Northwest Sector's History Library. She remembered standing on the circular hologram platform, dodging traffic on a futuristic street back in April of 2023. She wanted nothing more than for it to light up again and reveal happy people going about their day. She was saddened for a moment, thinking about the once utopian society that was Zenith, being reduced to blackness, heat, and desolation.

Carrick examined the back wall of The History Library. "Okay, let's get to work. My guess is that we have less than ten hours to get the Neptune lander off of the surface."

The team gathered around Carrick, offering him the light from their helmets. Carrick flipped through the journal and found the page he was looking for.

"Okay, we need to relocate this screen before we can start," said Carrick.

"That thing?!" Sebastian pointed to the twenty-foot wide, liquid glass monitor. "It's too big!"

"It's going to be a challenge in our EMUs, but it says here that it's not that heavy." Carrick went to the right side and looked behind it.

"Jordan, you, and Kinzi take that side. Sebastian, you're with me," Carrick motioned.

Twenty minutes later, the screen was removed and laid flat onto the image island.

Carrick referenced Erik's journal for a moment, then removed a four-foot panel that clicked into place. Behind it was a touchscreen that normally would require a code, but the journal provided details for how to remove The Tabrikon without one.

After several more steps, Carrick removed another panel, which revealed a circular tube with a handle on its top. It appeared to be eight inches in diameter, but its length remained undetermined, as the tube appeared to be inserted directly into the computer's mainframe like a battery fits into the back of a long flashlight.

"Look at that!" said Carrick. The team squeezed in closer for a better look.

"You'd never know it was there unless given instructions." Carrick imagined the Chinese engineers never found The Tabrikon and likely used other methods of removing the data from the mainframe.

"Here goes!" Carrick grabbed the handle and pulled as the team backed away, fearing that something bad might happen.

Carrick groaned, trying to pull it out. He was unsuccessful. "Jordan, give it a try."

Jordan, too, was unsuccessful, then Kinzi failed in her attempt. The team was tired and fatigued.

"Damn, that thing's in there pretty good," Carrick again thought about how much time was left before the nuclear devices detonated, killing them all.

"Let me give it a go!" said Sebastian in his heavy British accent.

Sebastian stepped up and grabbed the circular handle. Turning it firmly to the left, he heard a click. The tube released and sprung out several inches, indicating that it was ready for extraction.

"You do it, Carrick," said Sebastian, wanting Carrick to feel the release of The Tabrikon.

Sebastian yielded to his American brother and fellow scientist. Carrick nodded humbly and accepted his offer.

Stepping in and reaching for the data capsule, Carrick used his good hand, gripped firmly, and pulled. Out came a three-foot-long cylinder that glowed a pinkish hue. The vibrant color caught the four off guard, and they gasped.

"What in the hell is that?" Jordan was amazed.

"The information in here is going to save millions of people from deadly diseases around the world, from this moment forward," said Carrick. "Now, let's get the hell out of here, fast!"

"Is it heavy?" asked Kinzi.

"No," said Carrick, bobbing it up in down in his hands to get a sense of its weight. "I'd say about fifteen pounds."

"But Carrick, you're injured," Kinzi was worried for her friend.

"You want me to carry it?" Jordan offered.

"Nope, I'll be fine." Carrick wanted to ensure its safety. At least for the time being. He knew he'd have to trust the others at some point.

Within ten minutes, the team was back at the exit to the interior portion of The Southwest Sector. Attempting to open the Temperature Regulation Chamber from the touchpad failed. Carrick was perplexed.

"What's going on?" asked Kinzi, who looked fearful.

"It's not working!" said Carrick.

Jordan and Sebastian looked at one another and wondered what this meant for their escape.

"Kinzi, try it!" Jordan stepped aside. "Just think 02272007 into the screen!" Carrick looked scared.

Kinzi looked square into the middle of the touchpad. "Nothing! It's not working."

Jordan, then Sebastian's attempts failed, too. Carrick flipped through the journal and thought the team might have to walk the two-plus miles back through the monorail tube.

Each sector had two monorail tubes, each leading to one of the other two sectors.

"Looks like we're walking, guys." Carrick was resigned to their fate. Whether the team liked it or not, they couldn't sit around and debate it. The clock was ticking, and they all knew it.

"Follow me!" Carrick led the way. "I've never been inside one of the tubes, but Erik said that he once rode on the monorail for an educational function when he was in his twenties."

Thirty minutes later, the four stood on the passenger platform and were in awe. It was a modern-day train station with two separate rails, one coming and one going.

"This is amazing!" said Sebastian. "It's a modern-day Tube!"

"You're not in London anymore, Dorothy!" Jordan made a *Wizard of Oz* joke. Colt had no idea what he meant and didn't bother to ask.

"Okay, luckily, the rail cars are open. We need to walk to the far end of this one," Carrick pointed to the left car, "and then hope we can get out the other end and then down onto the actual rail."

Like earlier, the team looked nervous. It was dark, and they were going someplace Carrick had never been. They had no idea what awaited them.

"Let's move!" Carrick refused to lose time standing around.

Carrying The Tabrikon, Carrick led the way to the end of the rail car, and the team was easily able to exit out onto the rails.

Now onto the tracks, Carrick said, "Jordan, will you carry this for me?" Carrick didn't want to share the responsibility, but his body was breaking down, and he was unable to bear the extra load.

Jordan smiled at his friend and said, "I thought you'd never ask." He knew Carrick was badly hurt and was happy to take responsibility for The Tabrikon.

"What am I, chopped liver?" said Sebastian, with subdued laughter.

Now free of The Tabrikon, Carrick shook out his arms to loosen them up and restore circulation. He looked at his armband computer and said, Jesus, it's 850° in here. We have to get back to The Northwest Sector, fast.

The four walked for roughly a mile and needed to stop as Carrick was feeling weak. Kinzi injected eight ounces of protein water into a valve on the front of Carrick's EMU. Carrick was then able to drink it through a mouthpiece in his helmet. Kinzi repeated the process for herself and the others before they continued. Jordan asked Carrick if it was okay to pass The Tabrikon to Colt, and he affirmed his request with a nod.

After a full hour of walking, the team climbed up into the rail car at The Northwest Sector. Skimming through the car, brushing the rows of seating with their EMUs, they finally exited out onto the platform.

After leaving the monorail station, the team threw up their visors and exhaled. Sebastian, in particular, was relieved to breathe the air in The Northwest Sector. Even though it was warmer than before they left, his claustrophobia was still lingering. He looked forward to being back on the Lander where he could shed his EMU completely.

After a short rest, the team made its way through the dark halls and finally made it to the hallway leading to the Temperature Regulation Chamber. The finish line was in sight, and they were all relieved.

Now at the very place they'd entered The Triad just twenty hours before, they were walking casualties. They hadn't slept at all in the last twenty-four hours, and each of them bore some type of injury that included loss of blood.

Carrick knew what the others had forgotten. The touchpad would likely not work as the ECS sent The Northwest Sector into darkness, just as it had in The Southwest Sector.

Knowing the result, he attempted to open the chamber door, but it failed. The team was locked in. He turned to them with a look of resignation.

"What's going on?" Kinzi looked frantic. She, too, realized they were trapped.

"My God," Sebastian Colt shuddered with the revelation. "We're trapped.

"No way!" said Jordan. "There's got to be a way out!"

"There might be," said Carrick. "I may hold the answer here in my hand." Carrick held up Erik's journal.

The other's hopes were buoyed. They waited for his next words.

"I have an idea," Carrick looked resolute. He would save his friends, and then he would save Little Lilly.

"Wait here!" he said.

Carrick could be seen by the others walking halfway down the one-hundred-foot corridor toward The Great Hall. The three watched as he took a left into the storage closet where they'd stowed their EMUs earlier.

Minutes had passed, and Carrick finally re-emerged from the room. The team was puzzled to see him wearing the heat resistant suit that he and Sebastian wore up from the lower levels. Under his right arm was his NASA issued EMU helmet.

As Carrick walked toward them, they each looked at each other in confusion. They had to get back to the Lander, and Carrick would need his EMU to get there. What was Carrick up to? They wondered.

Jack White, orbiting overhead, chimed in, and said, "Guys, what's the holdup?"

"Give me a minute, Jack," said Kinzi as her attention was fixed on Carrick.

"Carrick, what are you doing?" Kinzi felt sick to her stomach. Her mind raced back to the time when Carrick, standing next to Erik, told her that he wasn't returning to Earth with her or the others.

"Where's your suit, Carrick?!" she demanded.

"Kinzi, Jordan, Sebastian, turn off your comms for a minute."

"Why?!" Kinzi yelled.

"What's going on down there?" demanded Jack White through their comms.

Carrick nodded reassuringly. He then mouthed the words, 'Just do it," followed by a smile.

Kinzi looked at the other two and signaled her approval of shutting off their comms.

Carrick looked at the stunned faces inside of the three helmets and began to speak.

"Listen, I have to go back down to the Sub-Sub-Levels, to The Black Diamond Reactor."

"No, no, no!" Kinzi was shaking her head frantically.

"Carrick, you'll never make it back up!" said Sebastian, who knew how difficult it was to ascend the stairs after he and Carrick fetched the journal from The Spider.

"Carrick, what are you doing, Brother?" Jordan was calm.

Carrick waved the journal and said, "I can funnel whatever energy is remaining to this chamber. I can do it! I'm sure of it."

"Carrick, even if you make it," Kinzi struggled to get the words out, "you'll never make it back up here!" she was now frantic.

Then came the three words that would be frozen in the minds of Carrick's three friends forever, and they were not ready for them. The three words Kinzi feared the most.

"Don't you dare say it, Carrick!" Kinzi started to cry as Jordan and Sebastian looked on.

"I'm not leaving." Carrick smiled. There was a look of calm and peace on his face. He no longer looked ragged and weary, as he had for the last twenty hours. The three others saw no fear in his eyes.

"Carrick! No!" Kinzi lunged forward and grabbed his chest with both of her gloved hands. Jordan and Sebastian were in shock.

Kinzi then repeated the words she said on that fateful day back on March 24, 2022, at exactly 11:30 am. "Get your fucking suit on, NOW!" she wailed.

Carrick squinted his eyes slightly, tilted his head to the left, and said, "I'm not going with you," his exact words then and now.

Jordan stepped forward and said, "Carrick, get your suit on now, Brother." His look was serious but full of dread.

"Jordan, we're all about to die," Carrick reasoned. "Either I die, or we all die. It's simple math, my friend. The three of you need to get The Tabrikon back to Earth."

"Carrick, what about Lola and the twins?" Jordan questioned Carrick. He couldn't understand how he could sacrifice himself, knowing he would leave behind a widow and two fatherless children.

"Lola is the love of my life. She always has been and always will be. The twins will be alright. They'll always have each other. They'll also always have Uncle Jordan and Aunt Kinzi."

Kinzi sobbed. She was inconsolable. Jordan searched deep to find another solution, but he couldn't. There were no words.

"Kinzi, do you remember the code?" asked Carrick.

"12121965," she said.

Carrick nodded in the affirmative. "When these lights come back on, you guys get the hell out of here!"

Carrick turned to Jordan, his helmet now raised in his hands, his name etched just above the visor, handed it to him and said, "Will you please give this to my son?" Carrick finally let out a tear; it ran down his left cheek and across his smile.

Jordan could no longer contain his heartbreak, and both of his eyes released his emotions. "I will, Carrick. I will make sure that little Erik gets it. I will," promised Jordan.

"Kinzi, you're my best friend, and I love you!"

"I love you, Carrick! I love you!" Kinzi fell into his arms and held him tight. She never wanted to let go.

Seconds later, Carrick turned, asked Sebastian if he could have a moment with his two friends.

Sebastian, still holding The Tabrikon, said, "Of course."

Carrick led Kinzi and Jordan some fifteen feet away. They raised their visors, and he whispered something to them. Sebastian could see that the moment was emotional as he again witnessed Kinzi embracing her friend, still inconsolable.

Carrick then walked up to Sebastian and said, "Take good care of that," pointing to The Tabrikon. "There's a little girl back on Earth counting on its safe return."

"I sure will, Carrick. I sure will," smiled Sebastian.

"And please make sure that those two make it safely back to the lander, would you?" added Carrick.

"I'll do my very best," said Sebastian.

Carrick went to walk away when Sebastian grabbed him by the arm. Carrick turned back toward Sebastian and waited for his words.

"Carrick, it has been my honor to know you." Sebastian offered his hand to shake. "I will tell my children, and one day my grandchildren, all about you."

"Will you tell my children and grandchildren, too?" Carrick's expression was one of peace.

Sebastian, let go of a single tear and said, "I promise you, I will." He then released Carrick's hand and hugged his friend.

"When you get back to England, have a spot of tea and think of me, would you?" Carrick said, smiling.

"Only if I can call you my best mate?"

"Bloody right, you can!" Carrick looked at him in the eye and said, "Take care." Then he turned to walk away.

He walked back over to Kinzi and Jordan, who were embracing. He shook Jordan's hand and then hugged him. Letting go, he turned toward Kinzi and hugged her, too.

As he turned to walk away, Kinzi called to him. She then ran to him and gave him a space kiss on the side of his helmet.

Carrick took Kinzi's hand, put it over his heart, and said, "Stay close, would you, Kinzi?"

Through her tears, she said, "Friends always do." She paused and said, "Goodbye, Carrick. Jordan and I will keep our promise." She struggled to speak, "We'll keep our promise."

"I love you." Carrick lowered his visor and disappeared into the darkness. At the end of the hall, the beam from his flashlight went dark.

Ninety minutes later, the sound of power being restored to the regulation chamber could be heard as the overhead lights powered up in the hallway. The three could now see a green glow illuminating the chamber door's facial recognition screen.

Kinzi cried again as she thought the code into the touchscreen. It didn't work. Her emotions confused the computer that opened the chamber door. Jordan then stepped in front of the screen and thought, *12121965*, then suddenly the regulation chamber door opened.

Chapter 35 – A Message

Location: The Leviathan – Three Hours later.

The landing pod had been docked for thirty minutes, and the crew had begun to change out of their surface gear and get themselves cleaned up. Kinzi hadn't uttered a word since exiting The Northwest Sector.

Jordan was on the flight deck, trying his best to explain the events that led to leaving one of their own on Black Earth. Mars was part of the conversation and was livid.

"Mars, the situation was fluid. Either Carrick died, or we all died. It was that simple."

"Nothing is that simple!" Mars screamed through the console speakers. "Carrick can't die!"

At that moment, a massive blast was detected on the surface of Zenith. The vibration could be felt on The Leviathan.

Kinzi released a raw moan, and screamed, "No!"

Jordan turned to look toward the aft section of the ship.

"Jack, we need to get out of here!" said Ollie Taylor.

"You're right!" said White. "The second blast could be worse. Zenith's atmosphere is much thinner than Earth's. It's possible small debris could make it all the way up here!"

"Jordan, get back there and buckle up, and get the others situated, too," said White.

Location: The Outer Observatory Deck – Ten minutes earlier.

Carrick sat in the oversized command chair, almost three hours after seeing his friends lift off the surface.

Carrick stared out into space, not regretting his decision, but rather celebrating it. Like his grandfather, Carrick sacrificed his life so that the others could live. He would miss his true love, Lola, and he would miss the children that he never got the chance to know. What he did know, though, is that the information contained in The Tabrikon would hold the key to solving mankind's greatest medical mysteries. Little Lilly Spencer would live free from cancer.

The data stored in The Tabrikon would also provide humans with the ability to travel deeper into space than they had previously thought. It would also provide them with the history of their ancestors that they deserved to know. History books would be re-written. Humankind might finally learn from their past mistakes and embrace the 'blink of an eye' existence that we all have to live. To love each other and keep our eyes opened wide through both the good and the bad times.

As Carrick stood staring at the little white dot in the sky, that was Earth, a massive explosion lit up the sky, and The Northwest Sector shook violently. After the initial shock, Carrick could see large and small debris falling from the orange sky. Then, a large object struck the glass canopy above his head, causing it to crack. Carrick quickly shot to his feet, startled by the crash and subsequent damage. He took in a deep breath and turned toward the master console, just ten feet behind where he'd been standing.

Now at the console, he laid down Erik's journal to the left of a metal cup full of red fruit. To the right of the cup were several foil pill packs he'd gotten from the infirmary. Just to the right of the pill packs was a metal box. When Carrick opened it, it revealed the Black Widow, a metal syringe nestled in a close-fitting housing, with a CO_2 cartridge attached to it. The first time he saw it, he was with Erik in the Sub-Level 7 Survival Storage Unit. He remembered saying to him, "That looks like the kiss of death." Erik smiled half-heartedly and said, "Pure death in a syringe. We call it *The Black Widow.*"

Carrick sat there and pondered how and when he would die. He looked at his choices and thought that all of them were better than the heat outside that was desperate to get in.

Location: Beijing, China. Chaoyang Park – Beijing's Wealthiest Residential District, Home of The Serpent – Four months later – January 15, 2028, 8:47 pm, GMT +8.

The Serpent arrived home and called out to his wife and children. Near the door, bags were packed for their trip. At the base of the stairs of the 4000 square foot, luxurious townhome, The Serpent yelled out again to his wife and 11 and 8-year-old children. He saw the family's four passports and four one-way airline tickets sitting on the counter in the kitchen. The family had a scheduled trip to the States; they would leave at midnight.

The Serpent became worried at how quiet the house was. Was the wife in the shower and the kids napping before their long trip? he'd wondered. Making his way up the stairs, he yelled, "Yenay! Jia, Liang!" The Serpent climbed the stairs, and with each step, his apprehension grew.

Now at the top of the stairs, he turned right and headed for the master bedroom. Walking through the door, he could see his wife's travel dress laid out on the bed, ready to be worn. In the bathroom, he heard running water. "Yenay, I've been calling for you!" he said as he opened the bathroom door. To his surprise, the shower was on, but his wife was not in it. He checked the master closet, nothing.

Now worried, he walked quickly toward the children's rooms. "Liang!" he yelled to his son as he burst through the right bedroom door at the end of the hall. The room was dark, and no one was there. Now in full panic, he raced to his daughter's room. "Jia!" he screamed. After opening the door, he saw his family in the far corner, bound and gagged on the floor, crying for their father and husband.

As he approached them to remove their gags and ropes, a dark figure emerged from his daughter's bathroom; it was SHA Militant Zhang Hui.

"I wouldn't do that, Minister Kenong! Or, shall I call you...," he paused, "The Serpent?" Hui smiled.

The last time Zhang Hui spoke to the Minister of State Security was from the FAST Observatory four months prior. Making his escape into the woods before authorities could apprehend him, Hui had been on the run until he could clear his name.

Li Kenong's heart sunk. While he didn't immediately recognize the disguised mercenary, he did recognize that he and his family were about to die.

"What is the meaning of this?!" said Kenong, trying to be brave for his wife and children, who sobbed in terror just feet away.

"I have a message for you, Serpent," smiled Hui. "A message from the grave. My brothers, Kai Chang and Vadik Lei wanted me to deliver it personally."

Kenong fell to his knees, sobbing uncontrollably. He now recognized Hui and realized his fate. Groveling at the feet of the SHA Militant, Li Kenong begged for his life.

Zhang Hui grabbed Kenong by the hair and led him away. Fifteen minutes later, Hui returned. When he'd entered the room again, the children sobbed at the sight of him while Kenong's wife wailed in agony. They all wondered what had happened to their father and husband.

Hui untied the children first and instructed them to go into the bathroom and wait for their mother. As he released the rope around Liang's wrists, the eleven-year-old boy lashed out at the militant, striking him several times before again being ordered to the bathroom. Once in the bathroom, the two children cowered in the bathtub, crying in each other's arms, while they awaited their fates.

Now Hui turned to Yenay, Kenong's wife of twenty years. As he approached, she moaned under her gag, pleading for her life with her eyes. He spoke to her before removing her gag.

"Mrs. Kenong," Hui was calm and non-threatening, "Your husband betrayed his country and will die tonight...."

She groaned in agony.

Hui placed his right index finger to his mouth and said, "Shhhh." He looked around to make sure the children hadn't left the bathroom. "You will be on that midnight flight to the United States. Once there, you will be met by a Chinese diplomatic official." He grasped her shoulders as she cried. "You and your children will not be harmed. However, if you miss that flight or contact the local authorities, you will all die," he paused, "tonight!" His look told her that he was serious.

She nodded in the affirmative and exhaled some of her fear with his words.

"I'm going to remove your gag and restraints now. If you scream and try to run, the children die. Do you understand?"

Her gag, now pulled down, she cried, "Yes, I understand."

"That's good," said Hui calmly.

"What will become of us?" said Yenay.

"You will spend the rest of your life in the U.S. You have family in Ohio, no?"

"Yes, yes," she cried.

"You will be reunited with them and receive a monthly allowance from the Ministry of State Security for the rest of your life, and then your children will receive an allowance after you die of old age, I hope," said a compassionate Zhang Hui.

"I hated him!" Yenay whispered to Hui. "I hated Li!"

"Yes, we all did. He had many enemies."

"How will he die?" asked Yenay.

"Suicide," said Hui. "Now take your children and go! You and your family are no longer safe in this part of the world. Many in our government would like to see all of you dead. Go to them now!" he looked at her and nodded.

After their tearful reunion in the bathroom, Yenay Kenong and her children apprehensively exited the bathroom to find Zhang Hui gone.

Location: Suwanee Georgia, Level Creek Cemetery – Wednesday morning, January 19, 2028.

The southern Bermuda grass was brown, the wind was blowing, and the air was cold. Standing in front of four graves, two of them empty, were Carrick's wife, Lola, with the twins and her mother

Laura, and Carrick's mother, Maggie. Just days before, they'd all attended a massive service at New York City's St. Patrick's Cathedral, where Pope Francis eulogized Carrick Michaels.

At the cemetery, Lola was joined by Mars Johnston, Jordan Spear, Kinzi London, and the Spencer family. Little Lilly, suffering from Leukemia, couldn't fathom that she had outlived both Erik and now Carrick; her little heart was broken. The group gave Lola, Laura, Maggie, and the twins, not even a year old, their time alone with Carrick. Maggie stood to the side with the empty graves, marked with her husband and son's names. In her arms was baby Erik.

After a few minutes, Laura took baby Lilly from Lola's arms and walked away. Maggie Michaels handed baby Erik to Lola, and then she walked away. Lola bent down and let baby Erik crawl over the grave. He managed to crawl over to the headstone and pull himself up. Unbeknownst to the ten-month-old, he slapped at the tombstone, touching the engraved letters that spelled his father's name. After Lola scooped up the little guy, she too, walked away to join her mother and mother-in-law.

Jordan nodded at Mars as if to say, "Go ahead," to the person who first served as a father-figure to Carrick after he'd joined NASA at the age of twenty-six.

Now standing over Carrick's empty grave, Mars said, "Hey Carrick, Mars here. Gosh, so much to say, Buddy. I'm gonna miss you. The world's going to miss you," Mars' brow went up. "I promise you this, young man, I plan on telling your kids all about their dad. I will check in on Lola every single week until the day I die. You're my hero, son." Mars broke down and cried. Sobbing now, he said, Carrick, I love you like a son. Thank you for joining NASA when you did. You always made my job easier." Then, instead of looking down at the grave, Mars looked up to Black Earth and said, "Take care, young man."

Mars walked away, giving a nod to Jordan and Kinzi.

"You go," said Kinzi to Jordan. She wanted to be the last to say goodbye to Carrick, and she wanted to do it without anyone by her side.

Jordan walked over to Carrick's grave and immediately began to cry. It was hard for everyone to see such a big strong man like Jordan break down and cry even from a distance. He was strong while speaking to the thousands in attendance in New York, didn't shed a tear, but standing over the grave of his friend made it impossible.

Jordan wiped his tears and began to speak. "Carrick, I am at a loss for words. What can you say about the greatest man born on this planet? You and your grandfather were the most inspirational men I ever knew," he wiped his tears again. "I will keep the promise that Kinzi and I made to you. We will stay by Lola's side until she no longer needs us. Little Lilly Spencer will get the care she needs. Cancer will not define her. When I have children someday, I'll want them to grow up next to your children. They'll be better people in the presence of your bloodline." Before he walked away, he looked up and said, "Goodbye isn't forever, it's just for now," then he pointed to the sky and walked away.

Jordan walked back to where Kinzi was standing, and the two embraced. "Take your time, Kinzi."

She nodded and walked toward her best friend's grave. Seconds later, she stood over his grave and began to speak. "I love you, man!" she laughed and cried. "It just doesn't seem real, feels like your still here, like you're gonna walk through the door or something." She exhaled and took a deep breath, and continued, "Jordan and I kept our promise; we moved in with Lola. Carrick, we're going to help raise your babies and make sure that we talk about you every single day." Kinzi tried hard to maintain her composure, but it wasn't working. After a moment, she took a deep breath and continued. "Your helmet is in little Erik's room. I think he likes it. We put it down on the floor so he can play with it. He beats it like a drum and says 'Da-Da,'" Kinzi cried.

"Man, I wish you were here," she paused, "because I have some news. I'm pregnant. Jordan doesn't know yet, though," she laughed again through her tears. "I was kinda hoping you would tell him for me. It's a boy! And he's going to grow up with little Erik and little Lilly. They'll all be best friends." As she turned away to break the news to Jordan, she looked up to the sky and smiled. She then looked down, rubbed her belly, and said, "Come on, Little Carrick, let's go Home."

Epilogue:

Location: Houston, Texas. NASA Campus. The Parking Garage across from The Johnson Building and The Astronaut Cantina – September 8, 2057 – 8:14 pm CST.

"Today is the thirtieth anniversary since I lost my best friend, Carrick 'Rock' Michaels, the greatest man I ever knew. He was my rock, and God, I miss him more than ever! Every day I miss him, but I miss him even more on the anniversary of his death. A lot of people never knew how he got his nickname, 'Rock.' He explained it to me once on Black Earth, the night before we met Erik for the first time. The name Carrick is Irish. It's Gaelic, meaning 'Rock.'"

"Jordan and I have been married now for more than twenty-nine years, and we're still very much in love. Little Carrick Michael Spear isn't so little anymore. He hasn't been since he was twelve. He's twenty-nine now and plays football in the NFL for, you guessed it, the Pittsburgh Steelers. He's a bruiser, 240 lbs. of twisted blue steel, just like his dad used to be. I laugh because Jordan has a little belly."

"Jordan and I live here in Houston now. We're both retired. We eventually left Lola's place after all three of the kids went off to college. We kept our promise to Carrick, though. We stayed with her until she didn't need us anymore. For twenty years, we all lived together, one big happy family. Jordan served as a father-figure to Erik and Lilly, and the kids grew up with two moms."

"Every year, the three of us who survived The Triad that day back in 2027 get together for dinner and drinks. Mars would come along, too. He never missed it. We always meet at the restaurant on the NASA campus, in the Johnson Building. Jordan's already in there getting our table. It's packed because Carrick's anniversary fell on a Saturday this year. No matter, they always know to expect us, and we never have to wait for a table."

"Every few years, they change the name of the place, but I kinda like this one, 'The Astronaut Cantina.' It has a nice ring to it. The last name was, 'The Star Gazer Café.' Pretty lame, huh?"

"The building it's in sits just across the street from the 'Carrick Michaels Memorial Training Center.' Upon completion of their training, for the last twenty-five years now, every astronaut receives a rock, yes, an actual rock. It's a five-pound rock, and it has their name etched into it. It's called 'The Dr. Carrick Michaels Award.' It's really cool! I want one, but they won't give it to me. Every year, when I attend the graduation, I keep waiting for them to call me up onto the stage, but they never do. Oh well, maybe next year!"

"Like his mentor, Gene Thomas, Mars went on to become Deputy Director at the Kennedy Space Center in Florida. He served for five years and then retired to Houston."

"The anniversary will be different this year without him, though. You see, Mars died this past Christmas. He was ninety. He always brought his special spirit to the dinner, and we always laughed at his silly jokes. None of us are looking forward to seeing his empty chair at the table. I brought the stress ball with me this year, you know, the one Mars gave to each of us pre-launch back in 2027, the one that looks like Earth. I'm going to sit it on his place setting at the table. I'm pretty sure I'll cry when I do, I'm such a baby."

"Good old James Clapper retired shortly after we returned from Zenith. He was ready. I think because Jordan left the agency when we got back, he also felt it was time. He passed away five years later, just months after he lost his Angie. He was a good guy. Hard as a rock, but he definitely had a soft spot."

"As far as Little Lilly Spencer, well, she finally opened up her own medical practice. For the last seven years, she'd been a pediatrician working at Artesia General Hospital, in the Pediatrics Department, the department that Lola used to run. In his will, Erik Erickson made sure her college education was completely taken care of. I bet you're wondering if she lives in Erik's old house? Yep, she even sleeps in the same bedroom that she did as a child, the back right one, opposite of Erik's room. The back left bedroom is still the way it was when Erik died there. Last time I heard, anyway."

"I know, I know..., you're wondering whatever became of Carrick's twins. Lilly and Erik both live back in Artesia, near their mom. They moved back after College. Lilly followed in her mother's footsteps and also became a doctor. She worked with me in my private

practice and then took it over for me when I finally retired six years ago. As for Erik, he's a chemist, just like his father was. Both have had multiple opportunities to move away, but they'd never leave their mom the way Carrick would always leave Lola. She means everything to those two, and they, to her. No more astronauts in either of our families. I'd say we gave enough to humanity, wouldn't you?"

"As far as Lola goes, she finally remarried last Fall, only after years of me and Jordan begging her to. She didn't change her last name, though. She never will. I'm sure of it. Her new husband's name is Ryan, he's a retired dentist, never leaves town to go anywhere, definitely not to outer-space. She seems happy now, genuinely happy. Jordan and I never wanted her to be like Carrick's mother, Maggie, or grandmother, Lillian Michaels. Neither remarried after losing their one true love. Carrick never had a father-figure as a child. That might have been part of his heartache. Though Lilly and Erik are adults now, they'll have Ryan to bounce things off of. No one should be without a father."

"Lola never dared dating anyone until the kids finished college. It was all about them until they got on with their lives and moved out. After that, she was at home alone, with her memories of her lost love, Carrick. She recently joked that the house went from being too big to too small, back to too big again. I agree, but she'll never leave that house, though. Ryan seems fine with all of it. He's a good guy."

"Just sitting here alone in this car, before going in, I think about Carrick and his sacrifice. He gave his life so that Sebastian, Jordan, and me, could continue living ours. That guy is, and will always be, my hero."

"Oh, I bet you're wondering about The Tabrikon, too? We just call it 'The Brick' these days. Anyway, It took three years for MIT level engineers to access the data inside of it. It did, in fact, hold the cure for cancer. Little Lilly was finally cured at the age of fourteen, along with tens of millions around the world each year since they retrieved that data. Oh, and the mystery of propulsion systems that don't need fuel? I forget what it's called, but the European Space Agency just used the technology to send an unmanned craft to

Pluto. It only took five years to get there instead of ten. I heard it's cold there.... burr!"

"To date, historians have found that many U.S. Presidents were either from Zenith or first-generation Zenithians here on Earth. The list is up to seven last I read. George Washington? From Zenith? Crazy stuff!"

"The Migration Shuttle, you ask? Well, believe it or not, they never went back to salvage it. Too dangerous at those depths. They did mark it, though. There is a buoy floating in the ocean, 36,013 feet above its final resting place. I'm glad they never went back. To me, it's a graveyard of memories, and it deserves to be left alone. Same for Zenith, they never went back, I hope they never do!"

"As far as China goes, the world never knew that they were responsible for bringing down the Saturn Six or that we brought down their lander on Zenith. In fact, it was as if it never happened as far as the world was concerned. Business as usual when it comes to geopolitical affairs, I guess."

"You know, over the years, I tried my darndest to solve the mystery of why Carrick didn't try harder to help all of us escape The Triad that night. I mean, with a wife and two babies at home....it just didn't make sense to me. I scrambled my brains for years until I finally figured it out. It was on his birthday of last year, December 12, he would've turned 68. 68?! Crazy, we're all getting old. I'm 69 now. I still look pretty good, though. Jordan thinks so, anyway."

"So, anyway, I was driving down the road, and it hit me like a meteor. See what I did there? You see, Carrick was always lost, always looking for something. On the outside, it was easy for me and others to dismiss his depression on the fact that he never knew his father. But Carrick was far more complex than that, though. I think I know what it was, and after I figured it out, it all made perfect sense to me. You see, the black hole in Carrick's heart wasn't a hole after all. It was a sphere, a black sphere."

"Carrick was now Home. He was whole when he was on Zenith. That was his real Home. When he was there, he cried no more for his past. Leaving Lola behind, he always did that. It wasn't because he didn't love her, because he did. Rather, it was because he was

always searching, trying to be whole. It was Zenith that made him whole. That was supposed to be the place where he lived, and the place where he died."

"So, you're wondering how he could have left his twins alone in the world like his dad left him? I believe that Carrick knew in his heart that they'd be okay. Unlike him, being an only child, his twins would never be alone. They'd go through life together. They'd always be two halves that made a whole. They'd always have each other."

"Finally, for us, the three survivors of The Triad: Sebastian, Jordan, and me, Carrick Michaels had become our Erik Erickson. We're all here today because of his sacrifice. We're eternally grateful for our time with him, thankful for his knowledge, his wisdom, but mostly, his sacrifice. I know it sounds crazy, but it still feels like he's out there, somewhere. Like he's going to walk through the door at any moment. Who knows, maybe tonight as we sit down to celebrate his life, he'll finally come walking through that door. Maybe, just maybe. Hey, a girl's allowed to dream, right?"

"Okay, I see Sebastian walking out of the parking garage. I guess I better get in there now. Let me see if I can catch him."

"It's a little chilly tonight, windy, too. Sebastian! Hmm, he didn't hear me. Oh well."

"Though it's cold tonight, my heart is warm, as I stand here waiting to go in to celebrate the life of my best friend. I can see the guys hugging it out at the table through the glass windows of the restaurant. Tonight's thirty years. I wonder if they did the math?"

"Wow! The sky is so clear. I wish that I could see Zenith! Earth was so visible from Black Earth. I bet if Carrick were alive, he could see me standing here looking up at him right now. If you can, Rock, I want you to read my lips right now. I-LOVE-YOU!"

"Okay, Kinzi, wipe that tear and get in there and celebrate the life of the man who gave you yours."

Kinzi London joined the two men inside of the restaurant, and together they laughed and cried. Sitting there for hours, they shared their memories of Carrick, and they shared their regrets. They talked about Mars, too, he and his little Earth stress balls, and his silly jokes. He was like a father to all of them, to everyone in the program.

And of course, they talked about what might've been? What could've been? Could they have done something different that night to alter the course of their four lives? The three agreed that there was nothing they could do, but secretly, they would each continue to live with the guilt, to be haunted by it.

The three marveled at the legacy Carrick left behind; Little Erik and Little Lilly, who look just like their father, are wonderful human beings. Little Carrick is a part of his legacy, too, not just in namesake, though. You see, he would never have been conceived if Kinzi and Jordan died that night in The Triad, along with their friend, Carrick 'Rock' Michaels.

The End – almost...

Location: Zenith. The Southeast Sector of The Triad. September 8, 2057 – Two hours earlier, Houston local time.

Carrick awoke alone for the ten-thousand, nine-hundred and fifty-seventh day. Looking in the mirror, he was again thankful. Thankful for another year of knowledge and another year of knowing that his love Lola, his children Erik and Lilly, and Little Lilly Spencer, all lived on a safer, healthier planet. He surmised that *The Tabrikon* must have held all of the secrets that they'd hoped it would. He'd figured that the reason humankind on Earth never returned to Zenith was because they never had to.

You see, thirty years ago, Carrick looked over his choices for both how and when he'd die. As he stared at the cup of Red Fruit in front of him, narcotics at its base, then looked to its right, seeing the Black Widow, his eyes went to the left. There, he saw Erik's journal and wondered, 'What if?'. Carrick guessed that maybe The Spider never made it to The Southeast Sector, maybe the crew's early arrival prevented him from planting the device. Maybe he couldn't bring himself to destroy the very complex that housed his ancestors for thousands of years. Either way, he never did plant the nuclear device; if he did, it never detonated.

Carrick read through Erik's journal as the heat crept into The Northwest Sector, then made his way back to the storage unit on Surface-Level 1, the place where the others had made their final escape. There, attempting to put on his NASA EMU, he laughed after realizing he'd given his helmet to Jordan to take back to Earth for his son. From there, he worked quickly to locate the Zenithian EMUs. After donning a spacesuit, he walked to the Neptune Lander's launch site and retrieved the NASA rover. From there, he drove the roughly three miles to the main entrance of The Southeast Sector. There, he recited the code in his head. The one Erik had provided in his journal; 09152008. It worked!

After a short rest, Carrick made his way to the Black Diamond Reactor, which still had enough power to provide life-supporting resources for only two levels of the Sector. Carrick chose to funnel electricity to Sub-Level 7, where he'd sleep at night in Barrack 5. He'd eat breakfast every morning in The Culina, it didn't have Red Fruit, but he found a new favorite, Black Ice. He also chose to provide electricity to Surface-Level 3, of course. There, he'd spend his days studying the past forty-thousand years of Zenith's history, but mainly the Erickson bloodline. Carrick learned that the Erickson's had always given themselves to humankind's greater cause: doctors, scientists, civil servants, and politicians. An Erickson even sat on *The Allied Assembly*, the leadership council that helped form *The Alliance Accord*, the very pact that guaranteed the survival of the human race.

His life on Zenith was now at its end; today would be his last. The Triad's Energy Conservation System finally shut down the life-sustaining resources Carrick would need to continue on living. He hadn't been to The History Library in months; without that, there was no reason to continue living.

Carrick wouldn't let the heat take him, though. Today, he fixed himself two cups of Black Ice. After donning his heat suit, he visited The History Library for one last time. Though it was dark and hot, he was able to get one last look at his favorite place in The Southeast Sector. A short while later, he visited the 800° Outer Observatory on Surface-Level 5. Staring up at Earth, the brightest light in the night sky, he mouthed the words, 'I-MISS-YOU,' as a single tear ran from his eye.

Finally, now back in Barrack 5, he ingested his cocktail, closed his eyes, and went to sleep, this time deciding to lay in the bunk opposite of his. Before he died, though, Carrick dreamt of Lola, Erik, Kinzi, Jordan, Little Lilly, Mars, his mom, and dad, and of course, his twins. Carrick died exactly thirty years after he saved his friend's lives, but did so without regret. If they ever do find him, they'll find him wearing a smile. Carrick 'Rock' Michaels was Home, and he always would be.

The End

Follow Me On
Twitter

@BlackEarthHWGH

@AuthorMichaelC

@MichaelwCook

and on Goodreads

and on Medium

@AuthorMichaelCook

**Back to Black Earth and Black Earth –
How We Got Here are also available on:**

www.BlackEarthSaga.com

In Loving Memory of:

Dianna Mae Cook

1944-2020

Never Forgotten!

Made in the USA
Middletown, DE
18 June 2022

67019087R00265